An Eye For A Deadly Eye

A Kenny Carson Novel

by

John A. Wooden

Published by
JBOW Productions
14108 Grand Avenue NE
Albuquerque, NM 87123

ISBN 10: 0-9767404-1-9
ISBN 13: 978-0-9767404-1-4

Dedication

To retired Chief Master Sergeant Elliot Lucas. Thanks for your mentorship, support and inspiration. You will be missed. Rest in peace!

Your boy,
Petey

An Eye For
A Deadly Eye

Intro For The Living

Chicago, Illinois

HIS ROUTINE HAD BEEN the same Monday through Friday for the past five years. He took two final drags from his cigarette, stomped it into the ground before entering the pool hall and traveled down the six stairs to the main entrance. He had become a creature of habit, and that made him laugh inside. As a special agent for the FBI, he had no routine. *Never take the same route to work or home, never shop at the same supermarket, never hang out at the same pub.* Unlike local police, who adopted a neighborhood pub as their official hangout . . . always a no-no for federal agents.

During his first two years of retirement, he kept telling himself he needed to make time to find two or three other pool halls to frequent. Though he had plenty of time, he never made time for that. He didn't know if it was good or bad on his part.

He placed his case on his favorite pool table, the third table in a row of five, and flipped the first latch of the two-latch case before looking up. He was surprised to see a new bartender. In his five years frequenting Harry's Billiards and Grill, Harry had always informed him when another employee would open the hall. Harry hadn't called. He had checked his voicemail prior to leaving home; Harry also had his cell phone number. *He definitely hadn't called.*

He reached inside his jacket for his Beretta, but before he could pull it out, he felt the first shot enter the left side of his lower back. Before he could swing around, another bullet pierced the back of his right shoulder. He stood as tall as he possibly could to face his assailants. He smiled at the leader of the band of killers.

"We n-n-n-never th-th-th-thought . . . e-ven imagined," Scott Rooker stuttered, with blood flowing from his mouth. A tear formed in his left eye and he hoped it did not roll down his face. In many ways, however, it was a fitting end to a case that was never solved.

"How could you imagine? Remember, I was an invisible person. Always have been, always will be." These were the last words former FBI special agent Scott Rooker ever heard. The shot rung loud and he fell back onto his favorite table, the third table in the pool hall, with a hole in the middle of his forehead.

Houston, Texas

Special Agents Bonner McGill, Harold Corners and Lawrence Kirkman had been on their stakeout for the past seventy-two hours — around-the-clock surveillance of a Cuban drug ring. They had leased a room in a seedy hotel across the street from the Cubans' main hangout, another equally seedy hotel.

The agents had alternated eight-hour shifts for the past three days, ensuring at least two agents were awake and on-duty at all times. Special Agent-in-Charge McGill, the senior of the three, lay on the only bed in the small hotel room. Though he had been on his share of stakeouts in his twenty-five years as an agent, he still had trouble sleeping.

His mind could not find a relaxing comfort zone to call home. A place to rest. A place of peace. Peace that could be so hard to find for some and indeed, was hard for SAC McGill.

It had been twelve years and he still hoped he would find that place. He closed his eyes and his mind traveled to a place he called sleep: a turbulent and troubled unconsciousness.

Before his mind could venture to dreamland, a loud bang echoed through the small room. The lead agent's eyes popped open immediately and within a split second, he had surveyed the room like an experienced agent.

He looked at his fellow agent, Corners, and immediately saw the bullet that rang loudly through the door had found a home in Agent Corners' back. McGill swung his head around to the door and reached for his FBI-issued nine-millimeter automatic handgun. But before he reached it, he saw a barrage of bullets rip through the torso of his other partner, Agent Kirkman.

Before he could get off his first shot, a bullet penetrated his right bicep. He instinctively dropped his weapon and grabbed his arm with his left hand. He looked again at the door and saw his four aggressors.

"How do, Bonner?" the friendly voice asked as he bent down and picked up McGill's gun.

"You! How could you? Why?" the bewildered agent asked his aggressor.

"Why not?" was the answer to his question, as a single shot from his own weapon entered his head, right between his eyes.

Columbia, South Carolina

For the past two years, Doris Northwood had maintained the same routine as president of the First Bank of South Carolina. Everyday, she came out of her second floor office at one-thirty and looked down at the bank operation. She liked doing it after the lunch rush, when the turmoil of serving the bank's mass of patrons had died down. To her, it was the best benefit of being president of the oldest bank in South Carolina, located in the downtown area of the state's capital.

Her focus was on the head teller, a position she once held. As an employee with the bank for over fifteen years, she always considered the head teller's position as her most rewarding. She looked forward to the employee from the Treasury Department arriving exactly five minutes before the bank's vault automatically opened.

The vault took precisely five minutes to completely open. When the system completed its opening cycle, one of the bank's security guards would post outside the door. By the time it was opened, the Treasury Department's courier would have delivered an unspecified amount of treasury bonds and cash, and departed the bank like any other customer conducting banking business. The bonds and cash would then be stored in a safe inside of the vault by the head teller. Only two people had the combination to the safe: the bank president and the head teller. Two hours later, an armored truck from the Federal Reserve Bank would pick up the bonds and cash.

As bank president, now Doris just oversaw the monthly operation from the second floor. She would ensure her head teller put the packages in the vault before the ten-minute time limit expired. At the end of the ten-minute limit, the vault door would automatically close. The door only took two minutes to completely close.

Prior to her head teller storing the packages, she did her usual ritual. She closed her eyes and sucked in her breath, appreciating her good fortune as the first female and African-American president of the downtown branch. Unfortunately, this time she didn't fully exhale and she never would.

The bullet hit her in the middle of her chest. It was the only shot fired and it got the attention of everyone in the bank. The five bank robbers were dressed in suits and were methodical in their movements, approaching and disarming the security guards first. One of the robbers jumped on top of the bank tellers' counter, primarily for effect, and wielded his two Glock 30 semi-automatic pistols and told everyone to calm down and be cooperative.

The authoritative voice told everyone if all went well, Miss Northwood would be the only one dying that day. He continued to bark out orders, and the tellers and bank patrons cooperated. One robber went directly to the head teller, gave her a large duffel bag and demanded she put the money from her cash drawer in the bag. *She complied.* When the robber saw the six thick packages, wrapped in regular brown nondescript paper, he demanded the teller to also put the packages in the duffel bag. *She complied.*

Another bank robber entered the bank's vault with another large duffel bag, and returned within a minute.

The whole operation lasted less than three minutes. When the Columbia Police Department arrived on scene and questioned the employees and customers who witnessed the robbery of the First Bank of South Carolina, the only description they received was the robbers wore masks resembling Abraham Lincoln, Frederick Douglass, Poncho Villa, Susan B. Anthony and Robert E. Lee.

Intro For The Dead

THE DREAMS WERE WHAT haunted her nightmares. Dreams of happiness, a loving marriage and a terrific family. Dreams she could not get away from. Dreams that became nightmares twelve years ago, when the man she loved never came home again. He was more than her husband; he was also her best friend and the best father two sons and a daughter could have. A man who understood her and let her be her own person.

She kicked and punched the heavy bag that hung from the basement ceiling. Once in her lifetime, she had had it all. She was considered one of the best agents in the Bureau. She was a member of the elite "Hot Squad," a group of handpicked agents who handled cases with a high probability of killing and a higher probability of death. Her family life was her balance. He was her balance. *Dreams and nightmares.*

She had released a lot of frustration, pain, grief and sadness on the heavy bag. She remembered when he bought the bag—about six months before his death. She had had one of her screaming fits with their daughter, Janessa, and he decided she needed something to release the stress of job and motherhood. Inside, she smiled at her reference of motherhood. He was always father and mother to Janessa and their two sons, Jarrod and Jerald. So many times, he used to joke that her job was the nine-month pregnancy and his job was everything after delivery. In so many ways, he was right. But that was his nature. Mr. Everything: from husband to father to brother to one of the best investigative agents in the Federal Bureau of Investigation, Steve Carson was the man.

The past twelve years had been tough on her as a person and parent. She wasn't built for parenthood. Her life had always been about her. Steve allowed her to continue to be her wild, rambunctious self. But when the bottom fell out, it fell hard. The bottle became her friend. Janessa, her daughter, became the mother, the parent. Her brother-in-law, Kenny, made sure the bills were paid.

When she went to rehabilitation for alcohol abuse, she thought her life was over. Then came an old friend. He told her, "Enough of the shit" and encouraged her to get back in the saddle. There was a job for her — a special job. She ensured her rehab went well and went fast. Her motivation and spirit returned. She was reborn.

She threw one last hard punch and looked at the picture on the black entertainment center. She continued to smile inside. She and her man standing body to body; he occupied the left side, she the right. They were half hugging each other; his left arm was around her waist while his Bureau-issued handgun occupied his right hand. Her right hand was around his waist while she held her sawed-off shotgun in her left hand. He was topless, no shirt, while she wore a bulletproof vest. They were both smiling. Now, she only smiled inside at what once was. Outwardly, she hadn't smiled in twelve years, not since the day Steve Carson was shot investigating the case from nightmare hell.

Part I

Death becomes death, the spirits of living souls of life. It's the deaths that boil at my insides. The deaths that chill my heart, awake my sleeping thoughts. It's a life of love; it's a life of death. It's a death of dreams, stolen hearts, childhood memories. Yep, it's death that becomes me. The death that eats at my soul. The death becomes me.

Chapter
1

IT WAS A LOVELY day — sunny blue skies and a slight breeze created a mood for a romantic walk on the beach or sea shore. But romantic walks were far from our thoughts. The breeze from the Atlantic Ocean felt good when it blew. I looked at my wife, the former Julia McEntyre, and I knew she had looked better. Like the day several months ago when she walked down the aisle and said, *"I do"* — the best day of my life, a day long overdue. It was a day that reminded me of how good life could be, how good life was. She was beautiful that day, and she was beautiful this day . . . just another version of beautiful.

She stood a tall five feet nine with long legs and a beautiful smile; a smile that usually graced her radiant face. But not today. Today, her milk chocolate complexion was hidden by the black chalk under her eyes mixed with the dirt and grime on her face. She was sweet as the day was long, but everyone knew, she was not the woman to cross. Her tall and slender frame made her intimidating; her quiet and deceiving personality made her dangerous. I had heard the stories of her exploits but never from her. She didn't share her complete Bureau life with me. When I first met her, she was an executive assistant for the regional chief in the Baltimore area. This regional chief happened to be her uncle and had later become the Deputy Director of the FBI, Elliot Lucas.

As she walked towards me, I took in every step. It was as though she was walking in slow motion like the scenes from a movie or sports highlight film when the camera would slow the walk of the athlete or actor. I didn't think Hollywood could ever overdo the slow walk. But my lovely wife quickly pulled me back into the moment. She slammed the ball down after her 20 yard quarterback scramble. She gave me a high five and we both gathered in the huddle with our other teammates.

"Damn it, we have one minute left and the score is 12-12. Enough of this junk, I wanna score and I wanna score now. Ya'll feel me!" came from the mouth of my lady love. We all responded in the positive.

We invited over forty family members and friends to our beach house in Virginia Beach that sat on the Atlantic for our annual flag football game. The game included some of our closest friends and associates including males, females and even children. That is, if their parents allowed them to play, like we allowed our son, Steve, to play. Our backyard consisted of two-and-a-half acres of crayon green grass that we converted into an eighty-yard football field once a year, with chalk and yard markers but minus the goal posts.

As a former professional football player in the National Football League, before my days as an agent with the FBI, I worked out at least four or five times a week. In the past, I had a reason to stay in shape. Now, it was about staying healthy and being ready for our annual game. Since I left the Bureau last year, I had lost at least ten pounds. At 180 pounds, I was the lightest I had been in five years. My six foot frame looked and felt the best it had in a long time.

"Melvin, you quarterback. Me and Charlie will be split left. Gloria has been a thorn in my side all day, but enough is enough, this is my play." I looked at my wife and continued to smile at her intensity. She wore a black Oakland Raiders bandana on her head and the black chalk and gruff on her face made her look like she was a pro football player playing on Sunday afternoon. Needless to say, Julia took her football very seriously — and that was probably an understatement.

"Charlie, you split wide. I will be in the flank. KC, you flank right and go in motion. Charlie, you do a down and in. I'm doing a down, out and up. We need to make sure we intersect each other at the right time. KC, you do a deep post and take Quentin with you. We cool."

"We cool," Melvin Clayton, my homeboy and friend responded. "On three, listen, on three, ready, break."

Clay was the second member of our three-man team. We actually grew up in the same neighborhood, Binghampton, in Memphis, Tennessee. At five ten, he was the shortest of the three of us. Clay had the gruff look, too. He wore his hair damn near bald, and his slender frame made him look like a rougher version of Louis Gossett. He was a forensics expert and homicide detective with the D.C. Police Department.

The third of our three amigos was right in front of me. His name was Quentin Morales; Q to those who knew him best. Q was half-Hispanic, half-Black and all crazy. We were around the same height, roughly six feet tall. But Q outweighed me by at least fifteen or twenty pounds. He was a fanatic about everything he did. From being the best at the Bureau to weightlifting to stroking his own ego, he usually overdid everything. His mixed nationality and his short, wavy curly afro made him a looker for many women. He was married but not happily. He had the most investigative experience of the three of us. He had spent time with the CIA and the State Department before landing at the Bureau.

We had an unwritten policy. The three of us could not be on the same team. Since Q and I were considered probably the best athletes, we usually ended up opposite each other. As much as we loved each other as boys, we also loved competing against each other. However, regardless of the competition, I always knew Q had my back — and that worked both ways.

We were about thirty-five yards away from a touchdown. Though I felt we could run four or five plays within the last minute, I was not the coach of our team. Julia was, and she made the decisions. When it came to football, I couldn't say I disagreed with her. We had won the last two games the past two years based on her coaching and I was not about to question her now.

We chose different teams every year and my NFL experience should have made me the most coveted player.

But in fact, Julia was the main attraction. She had been on the winning team every year of our annual game. I was fortunate. This was my third year in a row being on her team.

Clay called the cadence and one of the opposing players jumped offside and put us five yards closer to our destination — the end zone. We re-huddled to find out the new count. Once again, Clay called the cadence and the action began. I went in motion and patted Clay on the side as I passed him. He took the snap. I saw the play develop as I ran my deep post pattern, with Quentin dead on my tracks. Charlie and Julia ran good patterns that threw off their defenders, Rick and Gloria. I faked and made my break and Quentin fell for the fake. I looked back and Clay was scrambling to the right, trying to get away from the rush.

He stopped and threw a beautiful spiral pass to the left side of the field. Julia was usually our quarterback, but she and Clay alternated as she saw fit. I looked as the ball traveled through the air. On the receiving end of the pass, I saw Julia with an outstretched left arm, Gloria dead on her butt, not giving her an inch to maneuver. But somehow, Julia got a fingertip or two on the ball and managed to haul the pass in, as both women of the gridiron fell to the ground and tumbled over each other.

Julia jumped up immediately and held the ball high to let us know she caught it. Then she spiked it hard in front of Gloria. I held my hands up as our fellow teammates ran and congratulated the star wide receiver. We celebrated as if this were the last play of the game.

When I saw the helicopter hovering overhead, looking for a safe place to land, I knew it was the last play of the game.

I saw three familiar faces; faces that any other time, and separately, I would have loved to see. But the three faces together meant trouble. The first to deplane was Deputy Director of the FBI, Elliot Lucas, followed by Special Agent Dr. Beth Storm, and my sister-in-law and former special agent, Denise Anders-Carson.

Chapter
2

THE PILOT PARKED THE helicopter in the center of the field. My first thought was *what a butthole*. As big as the field was, he could have found another place to park. But I knew Elliot Lucas and I knew he gave the order to park in the center of the field. Obviously, everyone was wondering what was going on. Julia looked at me and I could see the concern in her eyes. Her thoughts were my thoughts. The only thing these three people had in common was FBI business. Asides from that, they would never be seen together.

My mind immediately went in reflective mode. *Why?* I had only seen Elliot twice since I quit the Bureau last year and I hadn't seen Beth at all since that time. Additionally, I hadn't seen Denise in the past three years. She was my older brother, Steve's wife. During their marriage, we never truly got along. However, she and Steve was a match made in heaven. Unfortunately, I thought he could have done better for himself than to marry another FBI agent. I was wrong.

Steve and Denise had three kids together. I spoke with my two nephews, Jarrod and Jerald, on a weekly basis. My niece, Janessa, the oldest of the three kids, was a graduate of Howard University and she worked for me. We talked to each other at least a couple of times a week.

Still, seeing Deputy Director Lucas, Beth and Denise together sent chills up and down my spine. I didn't like the smell of this.

His presence was still powerful. His demeanor still demanded respect. Elliot walked up and greeted us. He was a big man with big hands. He stood at least six feet five and probably weighed in at a good 260 pounds. But he was not a man with a lot of fat on his body. He took his appearance seriously. He believed in representing. He hugged his niece and former secretary: my wife, Julia. When he shook my hand, I tentatively returned the gesture. We looked at each other for a brief moment.

Before I could ask why he and his company were invading our annual game, he had directed us to the house for a sit-down discussion. Everyone followed the orders immediately except for Denise, Julia and me; we simply stood where we were for a few minutes. Julia was by my side. Denise stood in front of us a few feet away. She slowly walked toward me and gave me a hug. I felt strange, but I returned the love. She whispered, "Nice seeing you again." She then hugged Julia and the three of us walked toward the house. I expected my sister-in-law to clue me in on what was going on, but instead she said nothing. *Sometimes, it's the knots in our stomachs that tell a story.* A story too often we fail to listen to. The knots sing a tune in our heads, a tune we should run from sometimes. That same tune was telling me to prepare to run.

We walked through the patio door of the study of our six bedroom beachfront house. Elliot was sitting at my desk, like he was sitting at his own desk in his office in the J. Edgar Hoover Building, in the nation's capital. My study resembled a meeting of FBI agents. My friends and associates from the Bureau, Special Agents Quentin Morales, Rick Peoples, Charlie McClary and Damon Blake were sitting around with Dr. Beth Storm and DC Homicide Detective Dr. Melvin Clayton, waiting on the unofficial meeting to begin.

"You three find a seat and we can get this thing started," I heard from the mouth of the self-proclaimed leader of this congregation.

"Sir," I interjected. "This is our beach house, not the headquarters of the Bureau. And I do not appreciate you coming into our house and making it a damn FBI conference room."

I looked at Julia and I was surprised at the indifferent look on her face. Everyone was looking at me as if I was a leper. Denise had already found a seat. I looked at Clay and he looked as though he did not have a choice about staying or going.

I was starting to feel the knots more and more in the deep crevices of my guts. Julia pulled my hand as she and I walked toward two chairs that Charlie and Clay had placed for us.

"Sit down, KC, and stop complaining. Hear me out, then you can kick me out."

I sat, still brewing in my own apprehension. I wanted to be angry but I knew Elliot. He wouldn't have been there if it weren't important. Any other time that might be fine, but the way the knots in my stomach were playing ping-pong with each other made me think I was about to hear something I definitely did not want to be a part of.

Elliot asked Julia to take notes, which also rubbed me the wrong way. She was no longer his secretary. She was my wife and the chief executive officer of our corporation and other business ventures. I felt like I was losing control of the situation. I guess I never had control of it in the first place.

The Director began his briefing. "What I am about to say is confidential; not only confidential but also vital to the well being of the Bureau and national security. KC, this briefing is for you, Julia and Dr. Clayton. I want to solicit the help of each of you for a case that is personal to all of the present and former agents of the Bureau. Actually, recruit may be a better word. Before I start the briefing, this is your opportunity to leave."

None of us stood up; I looked at Clay and his attention was completely directed at Elliot. I didn't know what to think. I loved Elliot Lucas like he was my big brother or uncle. Through marriage, he *was* my uncle. But having him in my study, sitting tall at my desk, made me feel like Muhammad Ali was using my insides as his punching bag. Still, I listened intently.

"Ok. Let me begin. Three days ago in Chicago, a former agent with the Bureau, Scott Rooker, was gunned down in a local pool hall he had frequented everyday for the past five years. It was a habit he started when he left the Bureau."

My attention had just been piqued. Scott was one of Steve's former partners. He was one of four other agents Steve always worked cases with. He also took me under his wing and showed me the ropes when I first became an agent. Scott was good at chastising me for becoming an agent and not continuing my football career. But I was so intent on catching Steve's killers that I lost my desire and focus for football. Scott's discontent for my judgment did not deter him from teaching me everything he knew about being a great agent. He drilled me, kicked my ass and made sure everything sunk in. Now he was dead.

"Two days ago, not far from here, Agents Bonner McGill, Harold Corners and Larry Kirkman were also shot down while on a stakeout in Norfolk."

Elliot stopped and looked around the room. He knew he had everyone's attention. This was not coincidental. I looked at Denise and she was already staring at me. Did I know the significance of what he had just briefed?

Bonner McGill was also a partner of Steve's. I answered my own question. Yes, I knew what was going on. The reason I had joined the Bureau in the first place was the reason my former boss and mentor, Elliot Lucas, was in my study trying to recruit me back and solicit the services of Julia and Clay. In many ways, this was family business. This was personal, which automatically made it dangerous.

Chapter
3

IT WAS THE HISTORY that got me sometimes — the various historical events that told a story about life, people, places, organizations and much more. All academy students at Quantico were given a case, a cold case, to investigate as part of their curriculum. These cases ranged from the minor to the major. Every student wanted something simple. During my time as a student, I wanted only one case — the case that included my brother's murder.

Yep, it was the history that got me sometimes. It was the history Elliot was disseminating to us. It was a history that included my brother, Steve, and his team of fellow agents; a team that reminded me so much of my last band of merry men and one woman. My team included Quentin, Beth, Patrick Conroy and Clayton. Yep, my band of merry men, comrades or renegades; whatever name we were called, we responded.

I listened attentively as Elliot broke down the history of FBI folklore that never made national or local news. This folklore pre-dated CNN, MSNBC and Fox News, and included the murders of agents trying to do their jobs. This history also included the story of Steve Carson and his team's last case.

"For years, since the creation of the Bureau, agents have sometimes been victims themselves of random crimes or murder sprees. Every so often, we at the Bureau have come to expect that we will be the victims of someone's random acts of hatred and discord. And even though we may expect it, reality always hits us by surprise. But we deal with it."

I noticed the deliberation in Elliot's voice. His even tone was never emotional. I realized with every spoken word that this was personal; personal for a man who didn't believe in making cases personal. For the second time within a year, the Bureau was working a case that was personal to its deputy director.

My last case with the Bureau involved the murder of potential presidential candidate, Senator Bobby Cowens of Alabama. The senator's throat was slit from ear to ear in a hotel in Crystal City, right outside the nation's capital. Attached to his right ear was a photograph of fifteen white teenagers and a lynched black man. My team was tasked to find the murderer of the senator as well as prevent the murders of the remaining members of the lynching party. Ironically, the lynched black man was Elliot's best friend, Marcus Murray. He was a former FBI operative who was with the Bureau before blacks were called agents.

"Yeah, we deal with it." Elliot stopped and looked around the room. His eyes stopped at me.

"Deep in the piles of unsolved FBI crimes is a case that many of us wish we could be the ones to solve it. In a case that began in 1982, a total of twenty-one agents were murdered. Agents were killed on stakeouts, in their cars, at stores, jogging and yes, at home. Though we committed unlimited resources to the case, we never found out who was responsible. No person or group took credit for the crimes. As fast as it began, the murder spree stopped. It lasted three months."

Elliot had our undivided attention, especially mine. Every class of new potential agents was briefed on the infamous 1982 murder spree. But I had actually studied the case a hundred times over. It used to be an obsession of mine. At every opportunity, I visited and re-visited the Bureau's case library to study the case. Elliot knew that. He had piqued my interest and my anticipation level was higher than it had ever been. Elliot was still looking at me as he began part two of his history lesson, a lesson some of us were already intimately familiar with. It was part two of the case file from hell.

"In 1993, similar crimes against former and present agents began. The first murder was a former Chief of the Criminal Investigation Division. That murder was followed three days later by two teams on stakeouts in Berkeley, California and Richmond, Virginia, being gunned down like members of the mob. After that, we started receiving letters and messages from different groups and individuals, taking credit for the crimes, unlike the 1982 crime spree. Another interesting thing was several of the letters were on point with a lot of the details of the murders.

"And no, we didn't play the media game. This was our case — personal, family business. This didn't concern the public. Additionally, this was right after Desert Storm, our first war with Iraq. And that was another thought. Was this payback or Iraqi sympathizers getting revenge? We considered everything.

"We studied every piece of correspondence that came in. If it was a phone call, we checked the voice properties a thousand and one times. We tracked e-mails which was a fairly new entity back then, had handwriting experts check out all hand-written correspondence and broke down every inch of typed communiqué. We could tell you if it came from a typewriter or computer, as well as what kind of typewriter, computer and printer."

I must have been losing my sense of observation. Elliot took a drink of water and I hadn't noticed the water pitcher on the desk. He took more than a swallow. He almost completely finished his glass before continuing with his history lesson. His eyes bored into me as he began.

"Over two months had passed since the killings in Richmond and Berkeley. By this time, we had infiltrators in many of the hate and militant groups. Then one day, we got our lucky break. While one of the forensics technicians was checking out one of the letters with infrared light, he noticed a very small skull in the bottom right corner. Above the head of the skull was the word "just." On the bottom of the skull was the word "cause." *Just Cause.* None of us had ever heard of a hate or militant group called *Just Cause.*

"We put together a dedicated team of forensics technicians to go back and check out all the correspondence we had received. The more we checked, the more letters we found."

Elliot finally took his eyes off of me. He surveyed the room, where every eye was glued to him. Several of his attentive audience's eyes were glassy with anticipation. Elliot had what all of us wanted at one point or another: a captive audience.

"As soon as we thought we had something, the murders started again. Two former agents who were now politicians were killed two days apart from each other. Within a week, four of our agents investigating the case were murdered outside a restaurant after having a late dinner. We couldn't catch a break. Then the same technician who initially found the skull letter informed us of more bad news. The letters his technicians had found were from different groups. Not only that, but the letters were very detailed about the murders and murder scenes. And the final nail in the coffin for us; the letters were not just detailing the 1993 murder spree, but the 1982 spree as well. The same group or groups were making a statement.

"That cliché — *being up shit's creek without a paddle* — that was us. And let me tell you all now, you don't know how it feels to truly be up the creek until you face a case like this. We didn't have any information on *Just Cause.* Additionally, we had agents who had infiltrated the groups that we had received letters from. And yes, we told our agents to try and find out about *Just Cause* and what it took to become a member. Within days, several of the agents who asked questions came up dead.

"Now for the good stuff. The letters were from the Pure Angels, a Neo-Nazi group; the Black Mavericks; the Deadly Skinheads; and the Red Death of Mercy, an Asian group. We had hate groups working together to kill agents of the FBI."

Chapter
4

ELLIOT WENT ON TO explain that over the next three months, another fifteen agents had died at the hands of the group called *Just Cause*. Fifteen more good men and women. Age, gender, nationality or sexual preference did not make a difference. *Just Cause* was an equal opportunity hate group. And though my former boss was detailing the case, I was already familiar with it. It was Steve's last case.

We used to talk to each other at least once or twice a week, except when he was on a major case. During those times, we barely talked. Sometimes we didn't talk at all until his case was over. But this case was his albatross. We talked every other day and I knew something was wrong.

Steve often told me about his cases. It was his highlight reel to me. We were never in competition: he raised me. Big brother or not, he was more my father than our own dad, Howard Carson. He saw my NFL highlight reel as much as possible on ESPN's Sportscenter. And I liked listening to him talk about his cases. He fascinated me with his investigative stories, so much so that I wanted to be him or at least, be like him.

But his albatross was wearing him down. He let me know he had solved the case, but he wouldn't divulge the killers to me. The next day, his albatross got the best of him.

"After four months, we finally had three of our agents penetrate *Just Cause*," Elliot Lucas continued with his folklore. "We found out *Just Cause* consisted of 32 members, which included our three agents. The membership was divided into groups of eight members. Initially, we thought there was no one leader of the group. The leadership consisted of four members, the Disciple Board, a board of directors, if you will. And of course, the Board was made up of the leader of each group. Each leader chose the remaining seven for their group. Unfortunately, our agents could never figure out the criteria for picking a member of the group. From all accounts, there were no particular prerequisites, requirements, qualifications, et cetera. The members of the Board probably saw a certain something in a member of their group and recruited that person.

"Another thing, the overall 32 members and eight members per group were not set numbers. Each group started out with three members and grew to eight. Additionally, they were located throughout the country. And they only met once a month and always in different locations. We were fortunate though. We had three damn good agents as infiltrators. Only two of the three knew each other. We had Steve Carson in the Black Mavericks, Adrian McCarthy in the Deadly Skinheads and Gerry Ho in the Red Death of Mercy. Carson and McCarthy had worked together before. But neither man knew Gerry Ho."

Surprisingly, Q interrupted Elliot. "Two questions, sir. First, how did our agents penetrate the *Just Cause*? In other words, what made these guys attractive to their respective group's leader?"

"Like I stated earlier, Morales, there was no set requirement. However, still a good question. Our guys did give a little insight. In Carson's case, he relayed that he was quiet and reserved, but his attentiveness to his surroundings was what caught the attention of the leader of the Mavericks. In McCarthy's case, it was his gung-ho attitude, his 'let's kill all of these motherfuckers' attitude' that brought him to the attention of the Skinheads' leader. As for Gerry Ho, we never knew."

Q wasted no time asking his second question. "Why didn't the agents know each other? What made Gerry Ho so special?"

"Because Gerry was special," was the surprised response from Denise. "Gerry was a soloist. He went at it alone. And he worked great alone. It was a two-way street; they didn't know Gerry and Gerry didn't know them."

I looked at my sister-in-law. No particular look, just a look. Her speaking just brought back so many memories. She lived the case, just like Steve, but in a different capacity. Denise had always been very professional. But as an agent, she was also wild, rambunctious and sometimes uncontrollable. And like Special Agent Gerry Ho, Denise was a soloist, too. But in the truest meaning of the word, they did not work alone. They worked together. Denise was Gerry Ho's contact. He fed her information and she, in turn, relayed that information back to the Bureau. Initially, the system worked well. None of the three agents had anything to worry about. At least, not until everything went awry and the hate group known as *Just Cause* knew every single move of the FBI.

The more I thought about it, the more I knew what I wanted: the guy who provided *Just Cause* with the information on the agents who penetrated their group.

"Unfortunately, something went wrong and all three agents ended up dead," Elliot said in a soft-spoken but imposing voice. Everyone looked in my direction, including Denise. They all knew Steve and I were brothers. They all knew this was his last case.

"Sir, I can't do this." The words escaped my mouth, but I couldn't believe I said them.

I wanted to be a part of this so bad, but I had an obligation. That obligation began and ended with Julia and the boys. Chasing the bad guys was not my gig anymore. I had lost my edge and didn't know if I could get it back. Actually, just the thought made me afraid.

Calmly and coolly, Elliot responded to my statement. "Ok, Carson, not a problem. I know why you joined the Bureau; just wanted to see if you still wanted a piece of the action."

"Thank you, sir, but no thank you. I have a family now. I like the life I'm living." I didn't make eye contact with anyone. I was looking in the direction of Elliot, but his face was a blurry vision to me. I could feel the eyes of both Julia and Denise on me, and probably everyone else in the room too. Both women had a stake in my decision. One was my wife, the love of my life, and the other was my sister-in-law, who unequivocally loved my brother until death parted them.

Elliot got up to leave, walked in my direction and shook my hand. He leaned in and whispered in my ear, "I understand, KC. Probably a very good decision, but watch your back. You're still a former agent. Be careful, son, and take care of my family."

A few minutes later, I watched as Elliot, Denise and Dr. Beth Storm entered the helicopter and took off. Denise didn't say anything to me when she departed. Steve stayed on my mind.

I thought about what Elliot said, *Take care of my family*. That was my intention.

But more importantly, Elliot was right. I was still a former agent.

Chapter
5

"SO HOW YOU THINK you guys will do this year," Steve had asked me. It was the same question he asked the beginning of every football season. Since the helicopter departed with Elliot, Denise and Beth on it, my mind had stayed on my brother. I remember us growing up and he being what he was, my big brother. He took up for me, but it didn't take much. His reputation as a hothead was solid. No one messed with Steve Carson, unless he didn't like his life.

He was my hero in more ways than one. He took up for my mom, Kathy, and me when my father or dope-head older siblings, Gerald and Beverly, got out of hand. Steve was no-nonsense and physical. His six feet three, well sculptured body made him an intimidator to many. But those who truly knew him and the destruction he could deliver knew his reputation was deserved. He was my big brother and my protector. He taught me how to be responsible and accountable — how to be a man.

Even though I missed him, I was throwing away my opportunity to capture the folks responsible for his death. I really didn't know if I was doing the right thing or not. But I had to think about my family — Steve's family too. After all, I was Jarrod, Jerald and Janessa's uncle, and unfortunately, since Steve's death, Denise was having a hard time of it. They needed me — and I had tried my best to be there for them.

Death was a real possibility to me. I thought about it often. It was an alternative I didn't believe in. But death was a part of my life, my history. My mother died at a young age. My sister, Alyse, died a year ago. I didn't know the status of Gerald and Beverly. Dope-heads or not, they were still my brother and sister, and I honestly did not know if they were dead or alive. And Steve was dead.

Q, Clay and I were sitting on the huge balcony of my beachfront house. The smell from Q's Cuban cigar permeated the air. I was standing at the rail looking out at the darkness of the water. Water I could barely see but I knew it was there, like the feelings in my heart. I couldn't see them but I knew they were there.

I should have been concerned about the lack of lights in our huge backyard, but my mind was elsewhere. I was thinking about a brother long lost and the opportunity I gave up.

Q was sitting on a lounge chair — cigar in one hand and a beer in the other. I could feel his eyes burning a hole in the back of my head. I knew he had thoughts on his mind, but I hoped he respected my decision. He just thought it was the wrong decision.

Clay was sitting on the loveseat on the balcony, with his feet resting on a coffee table. He also had a beer in hand.

Still looking at the darkness, I asked my friends a loaded question, one I already knew their answer. "Do you guys think I made a bad decision?"

Q was the first to speak up. "Not bad, just rash. Way too quick, especially considering why you joined the Bureau in the first place." He stopped talking long enough to take another puff from his cigar. "You have a responsibility and you are shucking it. Call it what you want but your first responsibility is to yourself."

"No, Q. Where in the hell did you get some shit like that from?" I replied.

"From me," came a surprising comment from Clay. Clay's brother, Julian, and I played sports and graduated together. Both brothers went into law enforcement; Julian was now the Chief of Homicide Detectives in our hometown of Memphis, Tennessee, and Clay was the best damn homicide detective and forensics expert in the nation's capital.

"I don't shuck responsibility, both of you know that. It's an insult to even think that about me." In a way, my feelings were hurt. These were my two best friends and they knew me. Then again, that might have been the problem: they knew me.

"KC, we don't know what you are going through," Clay began. "But we are boys and we have gone through a lot together. We may not know firsthand but we know you. You joined the Bureau for one reason and one reason only. But you became good. No, take that back, you became great at what you do. But your edge was always knowing that one day, you would have the case you desired. Now you have it. Presented to you on a golden platter, gift wrapped, just waiting, and instead of entertaining the thought, you shoot it down before Alicia Keys even started singing."

"Alicia Keys?"

"Yep, tired of the whole fat lady singing," Clay responded. I smiled; Clay played it off, while Q laughed it up.

"I have a family now, fellas, you guys know that. I am not the KC of old. I don't have that edge anymore. Steve would have wanted me to live my life and take care of my family."

"Fuck you, KC." A surprised response from Q. "Steve wanted your black ass to finish up your football career, but did you give a damn about what he wanted then? No! Actually, hell no!"

I looked hard at Q. What in the hell did he know? He was sitting forward in the lounge chair with his cigar in his right hand. I was pissed. Q was on the border of disrespecting me. He didn't know Steve. How in the hell did he know what Steve wanted?

"What, you want to flex up to me now, KC? Why? Because we're telling you shit you don't want to hear. Get your ass out of your head and clear the fucking cobwebs, man, because your ass is living vicariously through your wife. Have been ever since our last case."

I lurched toward Q. He had crossed the border and then some. Before I could reach him, Clay was already in the middle, stopping me. I was even more pissed Q did not move an inch. Clay told me to chill out and take it easy, two things I did not want to do.

"Q, you're out of line. You don't know shit about my brother and what he wanted *from* me."

"You mean, for you, right?" I guess Clay was correcting me, but on what?

I turned to Clay and confusion joined my anger. "What?"

"You said, 'from me,' but I'm sure you meant, 'for me'."

I turned back around looking at the dark ocean, listening to the tides roll in. We didn't speak for several minutes. My mind was cloudy, full of thoughts beating each other up for equal time. I was mostly pissed at myself, because I knew Q was right. Hell, both he and Clay knew he was right. I think that ate at me more.

If Steve wanted anything *for* me, it was to finish my football career on top, winning a Super Bowl and receiving most valuable player honors in my last Pro Bowl. He would not have approved of me becoming an agent with the Bureau. I joined because of him. I wanted to find his killer, avenge his death. I used what influence I had to become an agent. I worked hard and studied long hours going over case file after case file. I talked to every damn agent I knew, many of them Steve's former colleagues, about investigating skills, instincts and approaches. Guys like Scott Rooker, Bonner McGill and Steve's best friend, Jay Joiner, took me under their wings and schooled me on the *A to Z* of being an agent and investigating a case. There was not a stone left unturned; they taught me all and they taught me well.

Yes, they were there for me. Yet, they still let me know Steve would have been disappointed in me for becoming an agent. But my heart told me he wanted me to live my life and take care of my family.

"Hey, Super Jock, you can apologize whenever you ready," Q whined.

I turned around and a smile was on all of our faces. If anyone knew how to work your damn nerves one minute and have you smiling the next, it was Quentin Morales. He threw his cigar butt at me and I refused to catch it. I bent down to pick it up, when a shot intended for me broke the patio door. Simultaneously, I heard Julia frantically call out my name. Inside, I thanked Q for throwing his cigar butt. He may have saved my life.

We stayed low as we raced downstairs to protect our loved ones.

Chapter
6

THE PROBLEM WITH BIG houses is the primary reason we buy them — too spacious. The staircase from the master bedroom was about fifty feet down the hallway. The three of us raced through my bedroom, down the hallway and hit the staircase. I was the first one running down the staircase when I noticed two bodies already down at the front door, which sat forty feet from the bottom of the staircase.

When we were halfway down the long staircase, at least five or six assailants came rushing through the door in black jackets and pants with black masks on and armed with Uzis. I jumped over the balcony in the nick of time, as the assailants started shooting as soon as they hit the door. I saw Julia lying on the floor on her back with two semi-automatic pistols blazing the front door with gunfire. She was picking them off as they came through, but unfortunately several of the assailants got shots off before she took them down.

I was dumbfounded. We had an elaborate and sensitive alarm system. It was a foolproof system that could not be bypassed. One of the top five security system experts in the world hooked it up. The only way to disable the system was in the basement, where the alarm panel was located. It was a thought that stayed with me for mere seconds. I immediately realized there were more pressing matters at hand.

Underneath the staircase was a small armory. Julia had already opened the door. Like me, Q had jumped over the side of the staircase and we were grabbing weapons. I called out to Julia and asked where Gloria and the kids, Steve and

Devin, were. She told me she sent them down to the basement. I asked Q where Clay was and he relayed Clay had been hit. Though that news affected me, it was time to take care of business quick, fast and in a hurry. I didn't want to know if Clay was dead or not. It was a distraction we didn't need just then.

Julia told us she had the door and she did. There were at least five bodies piled up at the front door and the number was increasing each time someone attempted to enter the house. Q and I worked our way to the back of the house in separate directions. I met no resistance. I heard shots in the living and dining room areas. Q called out that three were down. I reached the kitchen and the door was opened, but I saw no bodies. I called out to Q to check the basement.

I cautiously but quickly made my way to the back door and I saw three men running to motor bikes. I wanted to catch them before they hit total darkness. I had never shot anyone in my years with the Bureau. I believed in deadly force, but most of the cases could be closed out without a shot being fired. But this was different. These assholes threatened my family. Actually they tried to kill me and my family.

I dropped to one knee and aimed my .45 automatic Colt pistol. Two shots later, two men in black were down for the count. I got up and took off running again. I called out to the escaping assailant to stop or I would shoot. He ignored me and kept running. Though the lighting was not the greatest, I had my eye on him. He was just another bastard trying to kill my family.

I was cognizant that someone hiding in the darkness could have easily taken me out. I called out again, "Stop or I'll shoot!"

The assailant jumped on his motor bike and tried to shoot at me, but I dropped to the ground, fired my weapon several times and took him out. I ran over to him and he was still breathing, but barely. I asked him repeatedly, "Who are you? Who sent you? Why me?" He didn't answer me. I had shot him twice in the chest, the heart to be exact. But he was trying to hold on. I noticed he was losing a lot of blood. I pulled my tank top off and tried to stop the bleeding. I asked again, "Who sent you?"

He answered, "M-M-M-M-McKale's Army." With that, he faded away, dead.

Before sprinting back to the house, I checked the other two bodies. I had shot one in the back of his head and the other assailant in the back of his neck. Both were dead. They died trying to kill my family. For now, I had no remorse. Maybe it would come later.

With four bullets, I had killed three people without remorse. It seemed incredible to me — a former agent who'd never fired his weapon and now three were down.

I asked myself, "Who in the fuck is McKale's Army?"

Chapter
7

WHEN I ARRIVED BACK at the house, Clay was shot, seriously injured and unconscious. Gloria was crying over her man. They had rekindled their love and relationship since our last case. She had moved back to the D.C. area, after spending several years in a small town called Brew Spring, Alabama, the location where my career as an agent ended. Or so I thought.

Julia was busy applying pressure to Clay's wound. He had been shot in the right shoulder, but the way he was bleeding told me the bullet probably hit a major vessel or artery.

The Virginia Beach Police Department and an ambulance from Virginia Beach General Hospital arrived only ten to fifteen minutes later. They were transporting Clay to the local hospital and Gloria was riding in the ambulance with him, while the boys in blue cleaned up the mess we had made by necessity. They controlled the media, actually shutting them down from even entering our street. I was appreciative and indebted to the boys in blue. I had always made it a point to contribute to the police association ever since I moved down here, and had gotten to know several of the guys. I knew my next contribution would be a lot higher.

Julia had also called Elliot and the regional chief in this area. A team of agents would be here soon to do their own investigation.

The final body count was seventeen. Julia amazingly killed eleven at the door and Q killed another three in the living and dining room areas. The three bodies outside in our humongous backyard, near the beach, were my handiwork. Julia said she could take care of herself and I guessed she could.

My mind, once again, was in a state of flux. I looked at the carnage around me and I could feel myself getting upset and pissed off. Clay was hospital bound with an upset Gloria by his side for support. My boys, Steve and Devin, had seen people killed and could have been killed themselves. Q was like me, pissed off to no end that all of this had happened.

Then there was Julia. The one I was the most concerned about.

She was just chilling, watching everything transpire. I was somewhat shocked at her attitude. After Q finished talking to the police, he waited for the other agents to arrive. Steve and Devin were downstairs, playing video games. I preferred for them to do that than try to sleep and have nightmares about dead bodies. I was still pissed they were put in this position.

I could have stayed mad at myself, but it was not my handiwork. I didn't put myself or my family in that position. Someone wanted me, or wanted *us,* dead. Q and I were FBI, active and former. Looking at Julia, I sometimes forgot that she, too, was former Bureau. Evidently, all of the stories I had heard about her were true. I never really gave the rumors much thought, but after viewing the carnage littering my property, I knew.

I walked over to my ladylove, who was sitting on the staircase, watching Virginia Beach's finest do their thing. She looked at me and the glare in her eyes told a story. Whether I wanted to be in or not, I was in. *I knew it and she knew it.*

"I guess they got what they wanted," she stated matter-of-factly.

"Yeah, I guess so."

She cracked a smile and I felt good. I could see the genuineness on her face. Her smile spoke to me. Yep, some people were in trouble. *I knew it and she knew it.* We didn't have to say much. We knew what we knew. She was sitting on the sixth step from the bottom. Sometime during all of the madness, she was able to put on sweats and one of my oversized tee shirts. Though she was still concerned, those serious eyes had mellowed. They were now inviting. I stepped up and gave her a kiss. Our tongues met and my hardened heart calmed down a notch or two.

She rose and hugged me tight. Though she was a warrior, I was her support just as she was mine. We had and we would always be there for each other. In my mind, she had always been there more for me than I for her. She adopted my son, Steve, on the day he was born. She was the only mother he knew. My nephew, Devin, was the son of my sister, Alyse, who committed suicide and homicide in a jealous rage. Julia had cared for Devin ever since. Easily, she had been there more for me than I had for her.

"I love you," she whispered in my ear.

"I know, baby, but not as much as I love you. You are my world and don't you forget it."

We were silent for mere moments, relishing the thought of how fortunate we had been. Clay being hurt was a shock and hurt me immensely, but I knew my world would have been turned upside down if something happened to my love or the kids.

"When the bullet missed me upstairs and I heard you calling, I thought you guys were gone. Everything flashed in my mind. I could see the deaths of my mom, brother and sister."

I pulled back to look at Julia. She had tears in her eyes and though I had a trace of sadness in my heart, I had more rage — a controlled rage.

"I promise you, baby, they fucked with the wrong somebody this time. I'm back. The old KC is back. They threatened my family. The same motherfuckers who killed my brother. This is personal. They wanted me in, I'm in."

"I'm in, too."

We looked at each other. Hell, what could I say? By all accounts, she was a better agent than me. For now, she had me speechless.

"Don't worry," she told me. "I know what I'm doing and I can take care of myself. Anyway, I called Denise, and Jarrod and Jerald will be coming down here to stay. As always, Janessa is just like you and her daddy, hardheaded and has a mind of her own. She refused to come down, so I assigned a couple of guards to be by her side at all times. I also called Howard and he will be here tomorrow to watch the kids."

My happy disposition had just changed. Howard was my father. For me, he was only a father in name, not in the true spirit of the word. He was not much of a husband to my mother or father to me or my siblings. He was a man devoid of feelings. After my mother's death, he became a father to his youngest child, Alyse. He spoiled her as much as he could before Steve and I moved her in with us when I went to college in Nashville and Steve was an agent stationed there. Alyse loved Howard. I didn't. Everyone has a sperm donor — Howard was mine.

"You know someone betrayed us," Julia said, bringing me back to the bigger issue at hand. For the moment, I forgot about Howard.

"What was that, baby?" I replied.

"Someone betrayed us," she repeated. "If I didn't hear the beeping downstairs, I never would have checked the security system. Someone intentionally turned the alarm off, someone who knew how to manipulate the system. That's why I unlocked the armory and sent Gloria and the kids downstairs. Someone betrayed us."

She was right. Someone we knew and had broken bread with us, betrayed us. I felt my blood boiling. But the time would come when that problem would be handled.

I hugged and held Julia. The song, *Me and You* by Tony Toni Tone' played in my heart. *"Just me and you, just us two, don't worry about a damn thang."*

Problem was, I *was* worried.

Chapter
8

THE TWO MEN FIRST met in a boxing ring more than 30 years ago. Back then, the young, tall, lanky Caucasian was new to the Bureau, a graduate of Harvard Law, looking to make a name for himself. He was ambitious and energetic, waiting to set the world on fire. John Tellis was his name and from day one, his aim was the chair of the Director.

His opponent in the ring was a slender but muscular Afro-American. Several years earlier, he was referred to as an FBI operative but had become a bona fide agent.

John Tellis gave up a couple of inches and at least 20 pounds to his Afro-American opponent. At six feet three, he hadn't fought many agents his height. His long jab usually kept the bigger guys at a distance. As soon as the bell rung, he rushed to the middle of the ring and led with a couple of jabs and a left/right combination. The first round went fast and was uneventful. John Tellis was cocky and over-confident. When he came out for round two, he was surprised when his opponent came out throwing his own left/right combination, followed by two punches to Tellis's stomach.

John Tellis was not a humble man back then. His father was a cop and the coach of the youth boxing team on the North side of Chicago. John was his star pupil. He won over 30 matches with the youth league. At Harvard, he boxed for the fun of it. His fun resulted in over 70 wins during his time in college and law school. He didn't believe there was an upside to losing. Neither did his opponent, Elliot Lucas.

After the punches to his stomach, Elliot connected with a left hook to the head of John Tellis and threw a straight right that landed on his chin. The tall, lanky agent hit the canvas. After his mandatory eight-count, John Tellis got back up. When the match was over, he had been knocked down six times. Each time, he got back up.

At the end of the match, the men shook hands. As they both returned to their respective positions, they talked and that one conversation led to a lifetime friendship. They never fought again, but Elliot did teach Tellis a thing or two in the ring. That was over 30 years ago. The then Director, J. Edgar Hoover, was on his last leg but no one would even attempt to tell him so.

In spite of Hoover's cruelty, lack of fairness and dictatorship mentality, he was a smart man. That's what those who served under him appreciated — his intelligence. Many sat back and learned from the unofficial dictator of America. John Tellis was one of the many.

After the September 11, 2001 attack on the Twin Towers, there was only one choice for the Director position of the FBI. That man was the quiet warrior. If anyone asked him to describe himself, he would probably say he was as smart, ambitious and shrewd as the legendary J. Edgar Hoover himself, but with a stronger sense of fairness.

From day one, his intelligence and sense of fairness served him well. He remembered stating to another agent that one day this would be his Bureau. His fellow agent laughed and shook his head. But Tellis had the drive and determination to reach his goal. He took on some of the Bureau's toughest jobs and toughest cases. Everyone who knew him knew his day would come. He was the quiet warrior. He was still as cocky and over-confident as he was more than 30 years ago, but he was also more level-headed. He had become the Director of the FBI. He had his dream job.

The tall, lanky leader looked at the target of his next shot. The artificial green of his putt putt course had been a form of comfort for him in his four years as director. His second in command, Deputy Director Elliot Lucas, had been the other comfort in his demanding position. The men had formed a bond in the long time they had known each other, built on mutual trust and understanding. Trust and understanding they needed back then as both were assigned to spy on the people who made up their generation. People classified as enemies of the state, whose only crime was voicing their disagreement with their government.

"I hate this, Elliot," Director Tellis stated as he prepared to hit his ball. "This is the third time we are going through this shit — burying fellow agents, enduring the killing of our comrades in arms. And this time is different." He looked up to see the aggravating expression of the equally tall, but thicker, deputy director. He cherished this moment, seeing the man devoid of expressions actually displaying a look of frustration.

Elliot sat in a comfortable leather chair in his customary position: right elbow resting on the arm of the chair and his chin in the palm of his hand. Some would call his facial expression stoic, but he was a man who knew the importance of being calm and collected.

"I remember the presidential campaign and Senator Browning asking Cabot did he ever work with the Bureau," Elliot began. "You remember what he said?"

"He said he never worked for the FBI and in theory that was the truth." The director looked at his next in command with a lighted-hearted smirk on his face. "Come on, Elliot, he told the truth. Officially, on paper, he worked at the State Department."

Elliot Lucas's stoic expression was replaced with a smile. "Touché." Both men continued to smile.

"President Cabot asked me if we needed assistance before offering me help," Tellis stated, as he finally hit his golf ball. "He is understandably shaken since his lead Secret Service agent was killed in his home. Damn, I liked Cody Richards, too. I remember when he first came on at the Bureau." The director looked at Elliot and shook his head in disgust.

As leaders of the nation's lead investigative bureau, both men knew their charge — to keep America safe. They had seen their share of death, their share of betrayal. This was their third time as agents dealing with attacks on fellow agents.

"Yeah, Cody worked for me when I was the regional chief in Baltimore and Dallas. He was definitely one of the good ones. One of the best damn agents I ever worked with. I still can't believe someone snuck in his place and shot him in the head."

John Tellis set his putter to the side and picked up his golf ball. He lightly tossed the ball in the air with his right hand as he walked to a chair several feet from where Elliot was sitting. A small table sat between the two men.

"Elliot, before we talk brass tacks, let's talk politics. President Cabot wants me to be his Secretary of State. As you know, Ian Bradley has been diagnosed with lung cancer and will be stepping down soon. I told Cabot I would take the position only if he made you the first *African-American* Director of the Federal Bureau of Investigation."

Elliot's expression did not change. His mind recalled his earlier days at the Bureau and the struggles he and other agents of color had to endure over the years. They all wanted to be a part of the team, to make a difference in the safety and security of their country. But it was a fight, and for years it seemed like it would be a fight that would never end. All of a sudden, he was on the brink of history and he had no expression. However, he had feelings of jubilation and triumph — feelings he chose to keep to himself.

"So what you think? Think you want the job?"

"I definitely want the job. The question is, what did the President have to say?"

"It's your job if you want it. We agreed to make an announcement on both positions after this case is solved. In other words, let's get this off our plates because we both need to get ready for confirmation hearings."

Elliot slowly nodded his head in the affirmative. Two men, whose journeys had been different yet similar, enjoyed a moment and shook hands as a congratulatory sign. Before a true celebration could be enjoyed, there was still business at hand.

"Let's get down to business," Director Tellis changed focus. "How are we going to catch these maniacs? You know these are sticky times. So much junk is happening in the world, in our country. But my saving grace has been what we have been able to do here at the Bureau. President Cabot and his staff know we are the healthiest we have ever been. But for a hundred and one positive and great things we have accomplished, it only takes one negative to bring the walls of Jericho crumbling down. And the walls directly affect us — you and me, old friend."

"Don't worry, I guarantee the walls will not crumble on our watch. It pisses me off that we have buried so many of our fellow agents on two previous occasions and now, a third. But this time, John, I promise you . . ."

Elliot placed his arms on the small table and leaned closer to Director Tellis. His calm and collected demeanor was in tact, but his eyes were fiery and his blood pressure was up. He was a man who meant what he said.

". . . no, I promise the agents who have died at the hands of these fucks that I will bring these assholes to justice."

Director Tellis walked over to his desk and picked up a sheet of paper. He gave it to Elliot, who perused its contents. He stood and both men looked at each other.

"What do you think?"

"Interesting, but I will check it out. Remember, we are the Federal Bureau of Investigation."

Both men smiled. Elliot turned to leave and before he opened the door, Tellis called out.

"Elliot, I and all of the agents who have perished, know you will make it right. You always do."

Chapter
9

HIS POWERFUL PRESENCE WAS felt as he walked through the door. Those in attendance were in awe of the tall, muscular, older man. He went by the handle Boss, a handle he did not impose on himself. Some leaders wield authority loudly, while others' pure presence quietly announced their leadership.

Every step he took was pronounced. His six foot five inch frame was covered with a black lightweight trench coat. A black Kangol hat covered his head and dark Rayban shades hid his eyes. His thick mustache connected to the well-groomed facial hair on his chin. He was a man dressed from head to toe in black, further adding to his intimidation.

"I am not happy!" his husky, bass-filled thick Northeastern accent blasted. "And when I am not happy, people die." He looked around the table at his following of ten. Leaders from the hate groups that now made up the leadership or Disciple Board, as he liked to call them, of the group called *Just Cause*.

He reached in his inside coat pocket and several of the members jumped. A smile came over his face, displaying his pearly white teeth, and the scared members calmed down. "Don't worry, you will all know when I plan on harming any of you." He pulled out a plastic bag with balled up paper towels inside and threw the bag in the middle of the table.

"Harassment, open the bag and pull out the contents," he ordered one of the group leaders.

The Mexican leader of the hate group called Los Banditos did as ordered. He unwrapped the paper towels and jumped back as did several other members at the table as a bluish purple finger with a thick gold wedding band fell out of the paper towels.

The man called the "Boss" leaned forward in his seat at the head of the table. "This is what happens when you make decisions without my approval. I did not authorize the attack on Agent Carson's residence." He straightened up in his chair and pushed the chair back. He got up and stood tall. "But who am I?" he asked facetiously. "Who am I to stand in the way of any of you making the decisions for the group?"

He looked around at each and every member at the table. The makeup of the group had changed over the years. In his mind, he missed the old days. The new groups were much dumber and more combative than the old groups. In the past, though the groups did not like each other, they worked together as a team. Today, these so-called hate groups were more gang-related than hate groups; many didn't know the true meaning of hate. And they all wanted to be the leader. Although he didn't show it, he was disappointed at the so-called hate groups of today. They truly represented today's generation of "me first" and "you can't tell me anything." He knew who he would kill first and wondered how many more of these *fools* he would have to kill before his mission was complete.

And for the Boss, it was both a mission and a game. He served his time with the Bureau, waiting on a break that never came, waiting on his advancement that always went to someone else. He was the best but he was never recognized. He never played the race card, never wanted to make it an issue. But it was an issue — and he knew it always would be. If it wasn't the good ole boy network, it was correcting past wrongs. For him, it all added up to one thing . . . his opportunity given to someone else. They brought this upon themselves. They created his mission — to prove his worth; and the game – to seek out and kill those perceived to be the best. But over the years, both the mission and the game changed, didn't it? Both had become about public embarrassment for the country's top investigative organization. Public embarrassment he was responsible for.

"Special Agent Rick Peoples of the FBI found out how I feel about mavericks. Yes, that's his finger. His little act of bravado, his game of *I want to be the leader* just knocked us off track. My plans were foolproof. Now we have to deal with his stupidity. I told each and every one of you that how all of you felt about each other before you became a member of *Just Cause* was old news. I also told you that how you feel about each other after our mission is complete is your business also. But as the Boss of *Just Cause*, I call the fucking shots!"

The Boss slammed his fist on the table for effect. Inside he was torn. It was a sign of respect that several members jumped, but he was equally disappointed because of the fear of the members. Fear was not a luxury he could afford to deal with.

The Boss walked around the table looking at each and every member across from where he walked. His blood was boiling. He was a man out to make a point. Rick Peoples represented the agents of today who were unhappy with the present leadership of the FBI. He thought he was the future of *Just Cause* as well as the future of the Bureau. But he was anxious, too anxious. He wanted his moment in the sun today, not tomorrow.

When the Boss found out about his act of defiance, he acted fast. As Rick Peoples was exiting his car in the garage of his Alexandria, Virginia three bedroom townhouse, the Boss surprised him with a hard hit to the head. When Agent Peoples awakened, he was in a field in Northern Virginia. He had been there before with the Boss. He had helped dig the graves of others who went against the orders of the Boss. He looked around to survey the environment. What he saw did not make him happy. There were three other members of *Just Cause*. The grave had been dug. When he looked at the Boss to beg for mercy and reassure him he would never cross the line again, the Boss didn't give him the opportunity. The shot was between his eyes. One shot.

"I always get amused when dealing with the super bad," the Boss continued his oration as he stopped in his tracks and focused his eyes on the leader of the white Aryan group, Hitler's Nazis. "Remember when I first approached you, Maxi? You told me to fuck off. When I told you all of the benefits of being a member of *Just Cause* and the carnage and message we could send to America, you still weren't fazed. Then I mentioned the money and your eyes lit up like a kid staring at a hundred gifts under his first Christmas tree. But do you recall what I told you, Junior Hitler?"

The bald-headed man in his mid-twenties with a swastika tattooed on the top of his head had fear in his eyes. He looked at his defacto leader. A man he never thought of as a leader, especially his leader. From day one, he liked the Boss's ideas but knew he was not the man who should wear the title of Boss. He was the man and he just needed the right person in the group to help him take the Boss down. Special Agent Rick Peoples was that man. But Agent Peoples was impatient and wouldn't listen. He wanted to take over immediately and not wait on the perfect moment. They thought it would be a quick takeover, but the bluish purple finger proved Agent Peoples time ran out. Now his time was also up.

"Nothing to say, Maxi?" the Boss asked. Before entering the conference room, every member had been searched for weapons. The Boss's policy was a weapons-free meeting. That applied to everyone except the Boss. Maxi knew there would be trouble when the emergency meeting was called.

Maxi made an attempt to get up and at least run for his life. The members around him moved to get out of the line of whatever would happen next. Out of nowhere and with a quickness none of the members had seen before, the Boss pulled out two .357 magnum handguns and fired each gun once. Both shots found their intended target. The man named Maxwell Joyce fell hard against the wall with two bullets in his chest in the location where his frozen heart resided. The hole was huge. The other members looked in disbelief as they all re-took their seats.

The man called the Boss walked back to his seat and resumed his meeting.

Chapter 10

AN ANGRY PATRICK CONROY sat anxiously in the office of the deputy director, with numerous questions on why he was pulled away from his assignment. Bank-robbers had robbed five banks over the past two months, wearing various masks of famous people: politicians, movie stars and entertainers. It wasn't his typical case but they also weren't typical circumstances.

He remembered getting the phone call from his mom almost two months ago, telling him his older brother, Ryan, had been shot and killed at work. Ryan was the president of the Second American Bank of Arizona. The police report stated five masked men came into the bank together. As soon as Ryan stepped out of his office, the bank robber wearing the Clark Gable look-a-like mask shot him. The report further stated the robbery lasted three minutes at the most. Clark Gable and the other robbers wearing masks resembling Paul Robeson, Mae West, Spencer Tracy and Dorothy Dandridge, exited the bank killing only one person, Ryan Conroy.

Patrick was assigned to the case and given information from similar past cases. To his surprise, there actually were many similar cases. Elliot gave him files from both 1982 and 1993. In 1982, ten banks were robbed in a similar manner by bank robbers wearing masks, during a time when the FBI was too preoccupied to assign many agents to the case. During that time, former and present agents of the Bureau were being killed in droves. Eleven years later, the bank robberies started back and coincidently, so did the killing of former and present agents of the FBI. This time the Bureau realized the bank robberies and the agent killings were connected.

"I would say a penny for your thoughts, but it'd probably be money wasted," the big man quipped as he walked around his big oak desk to the leather chair that sat behind it. Patrick Conroy was surprised. He was so off into his own thoughts, he failed to hear the deputy director enter the room. Elliot reached over the desk to shake the hand of his agent. It was the greeting of men on a mission. Though they had the same goal, it was the strategy that differed.

"Why pull me off the case, sir?" Patrick questioned. "I was making progress. I know I can break this case."

"Patrick, your case is part of a bigger case. We knew it was only a matter of time and that time is upon us. I explained all of this to you before you went to Phoenix to investigate your brother's death and the bank robbery. That was the second of the mask-wearing bank robberies. Now we are up to five robberies and you are no closer to solving the crime. This is going to take a team effort, one we have to kill two birds with one stone."

"How?" the agent asked angrily. He leaned forward in his chair; his normally pale white complexion had turned two shades redder. "Sir, no disrespect, but these motherfuckers have been on killing sprees twice in the past and were not caught. Now miraculously, you think we can catch the *uncatchable*."

"Yes!" Elliot Lucas empathically retorted. He too leaned forward in his seat. "You damn right I think we can catch the so-called *uncatchable*. If I didn't believe it, son, I wouldn't be in this chair, I wouldn't be a part of this organization. And if you think we as a Bureau, as an organization cannot catch these vigilantes, then you are probably in the wrong organization."

Patrick eased back in his chair. He didn't expect that from his second in command. He had always respected and been the biggest supporter of Elliot. Some looked at him as a *kiss ass* and he knew that. But he never wavered in his support of the African-American leader. Regardless of the color of his skin, Elliot was easily the best at what he did. To *many*, he was probably the best ever — Patrick put himself in that *many*.

"No, sir, I do not doubt we can . . . I mean, we will catch these guys. I guess I am just frustrated. I thought I had some good leads but then their strategies changed from the previous times they did this. They are changing all of the game rules from the last two times. It's like they know what we are going to do or where we are going to be."

"Yeah, Patrick, I know the feeling. I told you before you took the case that these guys are good. I told you they have a pattern but we haven't figured it out yet. I told you they are good at frustrating the best of agents. I told you patience is the key. Patience, Patrick. It goes a long way. But trust me, you are not the first to lose the game of patience."

"So what's the answer? What now?"

"Now, son, we work together as a team. Like the sports cliché, *there is no "I" in team.* You and your team made some strides but I know you were working solo. You blew your team off, Patrick. You made this your case and your case only. Though you were working with some of the best agents we have who have worked numerous bank robberies, you chose to blow off their input. Now it's time to reel you in and put you with your own element, your own kind."

"Who is my own kind, sir?"

Chapter
11

I SAT PERCHED AT the top of a hill overlooking the waves smoothly crashing into the beach. I was on the outskirts of our property line, on the edge of our backyard and the beginning of the beach in Virginia Beach. I was packing a steel blue Glock 37 GAP, short for Glock Automatic Pistol, and a small photo album of my family. The GAP was a birthday gift from Julia. It was my prize weapon of choice now.

My head was on throbbing headache number 150 — as in 150 proof powerful. It was about as powerful as the 150 proof corn whiskey the old men in my neighborhood used to drink when I was growing up in Memphis. I was sure it was from the unlimited thoughts vying for time in my head. Every thought seemed like a crisis — my brain was on overload and I was trying my best to maintain my cool. But how could I maintain my cool when someone tried to kill my family?

My mind finally rested on a memory from years ago when I was in the eleventh grade and playing football for the East High Mustangs. We were playing Douglass High, our arch rivals, for the district championship and an opportunity to advance to the regional. We had beaten Douglass earlier in the year by the score 35-8 and this was a revenge game for them. Unfortunately, we were a team plagued by injuries to several of our star players. But we put up a good fight. I was frustrated the whole game and penalized three times for unnecessary roughness before Coach Etheridge pulled me from the game and sat me on the bench.

We were losing 18-8 when the coach benched me to cool down. He kept telling me to get my head in the game and even today I can remember what I was thinking. *Get your head in the game! What in the hell does that mean?* When he put me back in, I picked up another fifteen yard penalty and stalled our drive. He pulled me out again with five minutes left in the game and I never saw action again. We lost 26 to 8 and I was dejected. Coach Etheridge didn't say anything to me that night. He just looked at me with that *where in the hell is your head* look or that *what in the hell are you thinking* look. I had great respect for Coach Etheridge and I knew I had let him down. But what was done was done.

I stood in the shower for about fifteen minutes when one of the guys told me my brother, Steve, was waiting on me. As Steve drove me home, it was quiet in the car and my mind replayed certain plays of the game. When we made it home, Steve parked in front of the house and we both just sat in the car. Then he told me something that would shape my life forever. He stated, "The only way you can make a difference in a game or in life is when you are on the field in both mind and body." I just looked at Steve.

He continued to tell me that the mark of excellence was maintaining your perspective on life and the issues or challenges at hand. I lost it throughout the game. I was the star player but I let the team down — both mentally and physically. Douglass High frustrated me and took me out of the game. My physical presence on the field was an advantage for them and a detriment to my team. What athletic prowess I had was negated by my stupidity or hotheadedness on the field. I vowed to never let my cool or lack thereof ever affect me again.

Years later, when I was a defensive back with the Raiders, we were losing 23 to 6 to the Denver Broncos at the beginning of the fourth quarter in chilling cold and wet Mile High Stadium in Denver. For whatever reason, Steve's comment played back in my head. To make a difference, I had to be on the field. At the beginning of the quarter, the

Broncos punted to me and I returned the punt over seventy yards for a touchdown. On their next series, I intercepted a pass and set up a field goal for us. We were still struggling with less than three minutes left in the game when I picked up a fumble caused by one of our linebackers and ran the ball back thirty-five yards for a touchdown. The score was tied 23-23. The Broncos were driving down for the winning field goal or touchdown when a pass was thrown over the middle and was deflected into my arms. I scampered back over fifty yards for what ended up being the winning touchdown. I was on the field; I made a difference.

Holding my small photo album, I looked at one of the pictures of my mom, Miss Kathy, and Steve, Alyse and I. Looking at the picture, one would think Miss Kathy was a single parent and we were her three brats. As sad as it sounded, I wished that was the truth. But missing from the picture was our father, Howard Carson, and dope addict older sister and brother, Beverly and Gerald. Howard and Kathy were Alyse's and my parents, while Steve, Beverly and Gerald were Howard's children by two previous wives. Beverly and Gerald's mom was also a dope addict who killed herself overdosing on heroin. Steve's mom had died from lung cancer when he was a child. It was the bond that held Steve, Alyse and I together — having mothers who had died much too young. Having mothers who loved a man who was not worth the love bestowed on him.

I remember the day we took the picture. It was a sunny spring day in Memphis and we climbed into our 1967 Buick Wildcat Convertible. We went downtown and took pictures at Goldsmith's Department Store. Alyse was only 5, I was 15 and Steve was 25. My mom was in her early forties but had lived a hard life and looked well over 50. But this day, she looked younger than her forty-something years. We all sported smiles and we looked like a happy family. Steve was in his police uniform and stood tall. Boy, how I wished for those days back. A year later, my mom died. Steve stepped up to the plate and took care of Alyse and me.

Somewhere during the memories and missing those I grew up with, a quick thought entered my mind on Gerald and Beverly. Both were the biggest druggies east of the Mississippi. I wondered if they were still alive and well. Something told me if they were alive, they probably weren't well.

I continued to flip through my photo album and stopped on a picture of Steve sitting in a chair with baby Janessa on his lap. He was reading her a book and the image of father and daughter started the bells to ring in my head. Steve used to keep journals on all of his cases as well as daily or weekly journals on his personal life. The more I studied the picture, the more I realized only one person could have the journals — Janessa, Steve's precious angel.

Chapter
12

IT HAD BEEN TWO days since the attack at our getaway home. Actually, it had been less than 36 hours and a lot had happened since then. Thanks to Julia we had a full house of people: my teenage twin nephews, Jerald and Jarrod; our own two brats, Steve and Devin; my father, Howard; and a contingent of eight security protection specialists who worked for our company.

"How long are you and Mama gonna be gone?" Steve asked as we were playing one of their many video games.

They decided to play Centipede since the old games like pinball, Ms. Pac-Man, Galaga, Millipede and Centipede were the only ones I knew how to play. We were all in the basement with the exception of Julia. She was giving the security specialists instructions and the ten cent tour of the house and grounds. The basement was our family room. Besides the kids' X-Box, Game Cube, Play Station 2 and whatever other games they had that connected to the TV, we had a pool table, ping pong table and entertainment center in the basement. The sofa we were sitting on also let out into a queen size bed to go along with the king-size bed we had down there. It was a great place for family bonding.

"I don't know, big guy. We'll be back when we get back," I said jokingly in response to Steve's question. I looked at him while we were playing our game. Looking at him, I realized he, Devin and Julia were my life. He was so intense, so into the game, trying to beat me with his tongue sticking out like he was the Michael Jordan of Nintendo or

whatever game station we were playing. Little Devin was
next to me rooting for Steve as he swung on my arm. We
must had had a good game going because Jarrod and Jerald
had made their way over from their ping pong game to check
us out.

I felt good. I looked at Steve and thanked God for his
birth, for his life. I'm not embarrassed he was not born out of
an act of love. I'm embarrassed it was not an act of love with
the woman I loved at the time and the woman I will always
love. Gloria had just lost her father and needed someone to
lean on. Julia was out of town, and Gloria and I had always
been the best of friends. Unfortunately, our friendship went a
step too far that particular night and resulted in Gloria's
pregnancy. Julia was upset and disappointed at our act of
betrayal, regardless of the circumstances. However, Gloria
asked the only person she could trust to raise her child, our
child. That person was Julia.

It was tremendously hard for her, but she forgave us
both. As I marveled at Steve, with his tongue sticking out
and his fingers working at an enormous speed, I felt good to
be with my family. I looked down at Little Devin and I
kissed the top of his head. He squeezed my arm tighter and I
was glad he was with me. I missed his mother, my sister,
Alyse. Her death was a tragedy but that was my life when it
came to my family — tragic.

My mother died at a young age and Steve was also killed
at a young age. My father was a recovering drunk and
someone I never had a good relationship with. He was no
kind of father to his five children and I thought we as a
group would always pay for the sins of our father. Maybe
Gerald and Beverly had paid for his sins. But I was sure all
of us had paid in some shape, fashion or form. My only
saving grace was hopefully his grandchildren would never
have to pay for the sins of their grandfather.

I was surrounded by the kids in my life except my niece,
Janessa. She was the oldest of my father's grandchildren and
Steve's oldest child. She was also probably one of the
youngest vice presidents of a major corporation. At age 26,
she was the VP of Operations at CarsonOne Corporation, our

safety and security firm. Janessa and I usually had lunch or dinner once a week. Over the past year or so, since the death of Alyse, it had cut down to probably once a month. But we still talked on the phone several times per week. Since the attack on our beach house, Julia assigned two permanent bodyguards to be with her, to stay by her side at all times.

She was fourteen when her father was killed. She survived the trying times and grieving from Denise and her twin brothers. In many ways, she became the mother, the nurturer. She raised Jarrod and Jerald, made sure they went to school, got good grades and participated in school activities. Denise had resigned from her position at the Bureau and went through a three year state of depression after Steve's death. Janessa stepped up and became the daughter and woman her dad always wanted her to be. She was the cornerstone of their family. Though I helped when she asked, she was the one who carried the reigns.

Sometimes it was hard for me to look at Jarrod and Jerald. They were both the splitting image of their dad. When I looked at them, I often thought of Steve when he was younger. He always had an edge to him. I think he was born an agent and just had to wait until he was old enough to pursue his calling. Looking at the boys, I wondered if they really had a clue what they wanted to be. Both had the athletic prowess of future superstars and I wondered if they would later pursue a career in sports or become a professional in another field.

This was my family. Along with Julia, these were the most important people in my life. Hell, they were my life. I had seen enough death of family members in my lifetime and this was the end. I couldn't take another death and the more I thought about it, the more I realized this was not just about killing FBI agents. It was about killing my family.

Someone wanted me on this case. I just wondered if they were truly ready for what was to come.

Chapter 13

MY MIND TRAVELED BACK to my high school days and a beacon of light named Selena King. There was something special about Selena, something I could never put my finger on. She was a chocolate complexioned cutie who defined beauty both inside and out. Unknowingly, she always put a smile on my face and a gleam in my eye. Whenever I saw her, the shyest version of me came out. Maybe she was my intimidator; the one I thought was too good for me.

But that was the magic of Selena; she was people, good people. She was down-to-earth and the purest form of goodness. The smile she put on my face, I knew she put on a thousand and one other guys. But we had a bond. Though we would never date, there was an attraction. It was an attraction I never took advantage of and Selena was an old-fashioned girl — she didn't believe in the girl making the first move. Since I was too afraid to make that move, we became friends and remained friends until we marched across the stage to pick up our diplomas.

A thought never too far from my mind was how when my mother died, Selena would sit with me at lunch, flashing that million dollar golden smile with her sparkling brown eyes. She never said she was sorry for my mother's death. Instead, the day she saw me after the funeral, she hugged me for several minutes. It seemed like an eternity, but no words were necessary. I held Selena tighter than I had ever held anyone before. After that day, I made it a routine of sitting alone in the school cafeteria but Selena would always make it a point to occupy my space with her presence. And for that moment in time, my world would be livable. I was too distraught to talk but she would hold the conversation for the both of us and the remainder of my day would be better. That was the power of Selena King.

Occasionally, I wondered how life ended up for her. Clay told me once she was married with several children but was in the middle of a divorce. When I heard the news, I wondered how any man could let such a beacon of life get away.

I looked at Julia and knew she was my Selena King — my beacon of life. I never thought I would ever meet another woman like Selena. I told myself if I did, I wouldn't be afraid to ask her out and pursue that forever beacon for myself. What Selena did for me so effortlessly years ago, Julia did for me today. The only exception was, Selena was a great friend; Julia was a great friend and more and could kill 11 people with 12 bullets. I doubted very seriously if Selena could do that.

Julia wanted to drive back to D.C. I much preferred to fly back but we were not in a hurry, plus we wanted to stop by the hospital to check on Clay. The doctor said he was as well as could be expected and for the life of me, I could never understand those damn words. He was still in a coma. His operation was successful but the bullet had traveled somewhere close to his heart. They were able to get it out, but the long surgery had left Clay weak.

Gloria was still by his side and she wanted to be the first person he saw when he opened his eyes. Julia made sure he had plenty of protection outside his room 24 hours a day.

As we drove to D.C., I could tell Julia had a lot on her mind. I was sure she finally wanted to disclose her role at the Bureau. A long time ago, we made an agreement not to discuss what we did professionally. However, that rarely stopped me from sharing about my cases. First of all, she was my sounding board. Secondly, I knew in her capacity as Elliot's executive assistant, she was also an analyst. She and Elliot frequently discussed cases, primarily for him to get her input. Many Bureau personnel, including Q, had told me about her prowess as an agent. Q also disclosed an important rule of thumb: once an agent, always an agent. I was never sure Julia McEntyre ever stopped being an agent before she became Julia Carson.

"How you feel?" She asked me from her seat on the passenger side.

I smiled. "I'm doing great, how about you?"

"Doing good, just wondering about you. You know this was your first time shooting anyone and I just wanted to make sure you're okay."

I reached my right hand over and grabbed her hand. I pulled it to my mouth and kissed the back of it. "Promise you, baby, I'm doing great. They wanted me in, they got me, I'm in." I looked over quickly and smiled. Driving on Interstate 95 North to D.C., it could only be a quick glance. From Richmond to D.C., most times of the day, it was lane to lane, bumper to bumper traffic of folks driving 80 miles per hour or faster. And those were just the slow lanes.

"I guess my question to you should be; how are you really doing?" I asked. "I can see it on your face that you have a lot on your mind. You wanna share?"

She looked at me and I was still holding her hand. She pulled my hand to her mouth and gently laid a kiss on the back of my hand.

"KC, I know we said we would never talk about what we did with the Bureau, but you need to know. You have always been an open book and we made that agreement because of me. I know Q, Melvin, Gloria and probably others have told you a little about my past, but you need to hear it from me. And I do appreciate that you never felt the need to ask."

I looked over and I saw the concern and worry in her eyes. Like anyone else, I was curious to hear her story. Primarily for me, it was because she was my wife and her life in so many ways had been an enigma to me. In one sense, it was funny — that's what I had been called by many, an enigma. In another sense, there was no humor; she was my wife and was my lover for ten years before that and I truly didn't know everything about her life as an agent. It was the life of a special agent — an *incognito* special agent. I learned that from Steve and Denise.

"When I became an agent, it was the happiest and proudest day of my life. I wished my mom and dad were still alive to see it. But like all of my accomplishments in life, Uncle Elliot and Aunt Portia were there as well as my brother, Mark, and my sister, Sharon, and their families. I will never forget that day, Kenny. I really felt like this was the best day of my life."

I could feel her grip tighten on my hand and in turn, I squeezed tighter. I knew what she wanted to tell me was hard. I couldn't imagine what all Julia had bottled up inside of her. Over the years, she hadn't spoken much about her life as an agent or as a child. She told me her mother, Elliot's sister, died from lung cancer when she was only two and her father, Ray McEntyre, raised her and her siblings. A cop in Dallas, he was killed when she was only thirteen. Both Mark and Sharon were attending college at the time, so Elliot and Portia Lucas decided to take her in.

"The Bureau thought I would be a good undercover agent. I was assigned to the New Orleans region. On my first case, a drug case, I shot two men. We were making an exchange in the back of a retail clothing store in Baton Rouge and they had already made my partner to be an agent. Out of no where, bullets started flying. My partner was shot in the chest but fortunately, he lived. But during the gunfight, I shot two of the four assailants. I was recognized by the Bureau for a job well done, but the Bureau's psychiatrist had a problem with me not showing any remorse. She said it was abnormal. If I had been a man, no problem. But being a woman, she thought I had a happy trigger finger."

"You would think that analysis came from a man versus a woman," I interrupted.

"No shit," she flashed a smile. I think my interruption put her more at ease, which was what I wanted to do. I wanted her to know that I was there for her and that sometimes, it didn't make a difference what you said, but how you said it.

"I was pissed, KC, but like it was when I was growing up, Uncle Elliot came to my rescue. He relocated me to Raleigh, North Carolina, where he was a regional chief and mentored me. I thought it would be awkward working for him, but he didn't treat me any different than the other agents. He wanted me to learn and the only way I could was to be in the fire. I didn't have a life. The job was my lover and my husband. And Elliot was terrific at teaching you how to investigate a case inside out. He taught me how to turn over every rock and question a suspect. Hell, he even taught me how to deal with the media, if need be, or squeeze blood from a turnip."

I laughed at the comment and I could see she had become really comfortable.

"Things were great until John Tellis asked me to investigate a case in the New York area with the CIA. The case had international espionage written all over it. Uncle Elliot was not too happy but he let me since I wanted to so badly. The case was a piece of cake but it introduced me to another part of the Bureau which intrigued me. I got a chance to work with a clandestine branch of the Bureau called Section H."

She looked at me when she said that and my facial expression didn't change. I knew about Section H. Knew it well. I had always had my doubts but in actuality, never really wanted to know. My sister-in-law, Denise, was a member of Section H before Steve died, and she resigned from service. Section H was often referred to as the *Hot Squad* and the rumors were that everyone connected to Section H was a killer, through and through. I could see Denise being cold and ruthless when it came to killing. It was hard as hell for me to see my sweet, lovable Julia being a hard, cold-blooded killer.

"No comment?" she asked. I shook my head no. "Kenny, I know Q mentioned it to you. I know because I asked him to drop a dime on me."

She was right, Q had mentioned it a couple of times in passing and I blew him off every time. I remembered him once stating that Julia was one of the three baddest women he had ever known. I laughed him off but the thought always stayed with me.

My lack of a reply didn't deter her from continuing. "Since that case, Kenny, I have been Elliot's executive assistant and analyst. It's my cover as a member of Section H. When I used to go away for a week or a month or longer, I was on a case. I haven't actively participated in a case in the past four years, since I told you I wanted to be a full time mom to Steve and now, Devin."

"Why are you telling me this now?" They say never ask a question you don't want to know the answer to. I didn't want to know the answer but I had to know. My curiosity had beaten me down.

"I am on this case because they threatened my family, just like you, baby. Because I remember the last time this happened; you know I was a member of the Bureau then. Because you are about to deal with something you have never dealt with before and I want you to be prepared for it."

"What is that?"

"Agents betraying other agents," she stated matter-of-factly.

Chapter
14

THE MAN CALLED THE boss sat alone in the airport terminal awaiting his flight. He answered his phone on the second ring. No greeting was necessary, he was expecting the call.

"I think we fucked up royally by rushing into this."

"No, not at all, the Bureau is up in arms. They didn't expect it or see it coming. As always, we have the upper hand and the top nigger and his cronies are trying to play catch up."

"Why are you disrespecting Elliot?" the Boss asked with irritation in his voice. "You know he is smart as hell and we were very fortunate he was not *The Man* back then. He is today."

"Maybe you give him too much credit, you ever thought about that? Sometimes we go about life only assuming what we see or what society or others want us to see. Elliot Lucas is just a good nigger who has stuck it out, been around forever. The good white agents taught him everything he knows and because of loyalty, he is reaping the benefits of being a good nigger with the patience of Job."

"Maybe you should put yourself in that category of good *white* agents who taught the nigger how to rise above the bullshit," the Boss laughed at his comment. However, internally he was in knots. He never liked the derogatory racial epithets that plagued America. He did his time in the trenches called the FBI and was surprised at the language thrown around the organization. It was the seventies and eighties, and the world was changing. But the nation's top investigative arm of the government was reluctant to change with it. In those days, he thought it was a sad state, especially when seventy percent of the agents had law degrees.

"So you think that's funny?" the angry voice snapped back.

"Yes, I think it's funny and you best remember who you are talking to. I put up with your shit most times, but remember, this is a partnership. I am not doing your bidding for the hell of it."

"Calm down, we have both benefited well from our arrangement over the years. Hell, since you left the Bureau, you have been on Easy Street and so have I. Do you think I want that to change? Hell no! You have nothing to worry about — like the past, we will succeed. *Just Cause* will once again rule the day."

"Don't worry, I'm calm. It's just so damn hard dealing with these kids today who call themselves hate groups. You and I both know these are just snotty nose, suburban kids playing dress up to get a rise out of mom and dad. Hate groups! Ha! I laugh at the thought. Suburban gangs, that's what they are. But I must remember, we are in America and to be classified as a gang, you must come from a social status of very low to extremely low income." The Boss shook his head in disgust. "A good number of these pricks in these groups actually come from some well-to-do homes. And the ones who don't probably don't know why they are listening to these pricks that do."

"It's called progress, Boss." The man lightheartedly laughed at his choice of words as well as the moniker bestowed his partner.

"Why do I get a nervous feeling when you call me that?" the Boss tried to make light of his partner's humor, but deep inside he had never liked the man. Some people are to be tolerated for what they can do for you. It's not always about not burning bridges but hoping to avoid the burning bridge. But with age also comes patience — or sometimes, a lack thereof. The Boss's patience was on thin ice.

"Ok, we need to get on the same page. We have already crossed the line. It's too late to turn back. We must press ahead and finish what we started. Agreed?"

"Agreed."

"Columbus is next and then Oklahoma City, plus let's hit the operations we agreed on. Instead of spacing them apart, let's go back to back."

The Boss didn't say anything but his partner knew something was wrong. He waited impatiently for the voice of displeasure. It never came.

"I actually think that is a great idea. It's the same thing I was going to recommend."

"This way it keeps them off-balance and keeps them thinking."

"Agreed."

"Also, I like how quick you acted on Rick Peoples but you know Damon Blake may be a problem. They were like brothers and I don't know if he can keep it together. You know Rick was the rock in that friendship."

"Don't worry, execution is my department," the Boss replied as he hit the end button on his cell phone.

Chapter
15

WHEN WE ARRIVED IN D.C. and I dropped Julia off at the FBI headquarters building, I went to our D.C. home and got myself together mentally. Instead of relaxing at home and getting my wardrobe together, like I promised myself, I occupied my mind with the remnants of the group called *Just Cause*. My thoughts also led me to strategizing on possible investigative angles.

Julia implied there were agents betraying other agents and that's why the Bureau was unsuccessful in solving the previous cases. I didn't know what to think. I had virgin ears when it came to betrayal of this magnitude. I couldn't fathom the thought of another agent selling me down the river for a couple of dollars or worse, because of ill-feelings or conflicting personalities. But this was life and in the game of life, sometimes there are no rules.

I didn't know how long I dozed off but when I awakened, I once again had thoughts of Selena King. The last time I saw Selena was when I went home to Memphis after my sophomore year in college. We ran into each other at a mall and decided to have lunch. Our luncheon turned into a four hour conversation reminiscing and catching up on each other's lives. At the time, I was dating a nice sistah named Shannon, who years later would play a major part in what supposed to be my last case with the FBI.

Selena and I talked about a variety of subjects and somehow got on the topic of sex versus lovemaking. Selena did what she always did — schooled me on the ways of life.

Though I was a jock and considered to be a superstar athlete in many eyes, I did not have the sexual prowess or reputation of my fellow athletes. At that time in my life, I was still shy and probably standoffish when it came to people. After my mother's death in high school, for several years I stayed in a self-imposed cocoon. Selena and Shannon were only two of a very few people I truly let in my world. Probably my biggest breakthrough was on the football field.

I ended up telling Selena I wasn't confident I was pleasing Shannon physically in the bedroom. I let my friend know that was my biggest fear. In turn, she told me something I would never forget. Selena was engaged at the time and I recall her smiling at me and putting her hand on my hand. She told me the key to making a woman feel like a woman was making her feel special. It wasn't the act of having sex but the act of truly making love to that woman to where she felt it in her heart. She clued me in that women are emotional, and if a man could get in their heads and their hearts, and make the act of having sex feel like an act of making love, then 75 percent of the job was done. She further informed me that sex was easy and definitely all about the physical, but knowing a woman's body and knowing what turned her on physically and mentally was worth a pot of gold and sent a message. She shared that knowing what stimulated a woman mentally was the true foreplay. I could remember being mesmerized with every word that came out of Selena's mouth. She was my relationship education teacher without the degree.

She left me with this, "Women can love hard but the only thing they truly want from men are love, friendship, partnership, support, loyalty, dedication and someone who will always cherish and make them feel special." When she got up to leave, we hugged and she gave me a peck on the lips. It wasn't a true kiss but I think we both felt sparks. We hugged again and Selena whispered in my ear, "The most important thing in relationships is showing love through action and not expecting your loved one to guess or assume you love her." As she walked away, I felt encouraged and enlightened, and I knew I would never see my beacon of light again. But I also knew she had left me empowered and with the knowledge of love and ingredients to one day find my own beacon of light.

Julia came in around ten that night. She drove Elliot's car home. I had grilled some stuffed pork chops and sweet corn on the cob, and cooked green peas, rice and dinner rolls. I was happy to see her. Thinking about Selena made me miss the woman who became my forever and always — Julia. As soon as she walked in the door, I met her and gave her a kiss. It started out light but progressed to something more. Our tongues met and we knew we were in trouble. Between kisses, I managed to tell her I had made dinner and kept it warm for her. I didn't think she heard me.

I couldn't explain it, but whenever I had a case or Julia went out of town on her trips, we always made love like we would never see each other again. For me, I knew I had dormant thoughts in the back of my mind of losing everyone important to me and I wanted this woman to know how much I loved and appreciated her in case something did happen to me. Sometimes I thought Julia lived with those same thoughts, too. After all, she had lost her father and mother at an early age.

We continued kissing and pulling our clothes off as I led her to the sofa in the living room. By the time we had fallen on the sofa, my clothes and Julia's top and bra were off. Though we were in a rush, I instinctively slowed my roll. I wanted this to last. In the back of my mind, latent thoughts of the things Selena told me were speaking to me, like, "know what pleases your lady."

I kissed Julia's forehead and let my lips travel down to her eyebrows and eyes. I laid soft kisses at every stop and continued to let my lips travel to each cheek and her nose. I could hear Julia softly moaning, "Shit, shit . . . ah damn." Additionally, she was playing with and licking my nipples with the tip of her tongue, a weakness for me. For us, this was our challenge sometimes, to see who could drive whom the craziest. Next, I laid a soft kiss on her chin before quickly kissing her lovely lips. I could feel her hips gyrating and the warmth of her body.

I slid down, kissed her neck and ran my mouth across her shoulders and arms. My tongue was smoothly making love to her body and her soft profanity-laced moans kept me going and excited. I was beyond stimulated as my mind was doing what it did at times — traveling from thought to thought, thinking about almost losing my true and only love two nights ago to another case dripping with vengeance, and then to thoughts of Selena telling me how to show a woman I love her.

My mouth found Julia's firm breasts and her long nipples were hard from anticipation. I didn't disappoint. My mouth was sucking like a suction pump but I made sure I was gentle, not sucking too hard. I occasionally flicked my tongue over each nipple and laid soft kisses on both breasts. They still stood upright like they did eleven years ago when we first met. After several minutes of paying homage to her breasts, her hands pushed my head down. My tongue slid further down her body, past her stomach. In one jerk, I had pulled off her slacks and panties.

As soon as my mouth found her wetness, she let out a scream. Her hips gyrated and lifted up. I put my hands on her buttocks and raised her butt. Her legs were draped over my shoulders and one of her hands was on the back of my head, pushing my face deeper in her wetness. This was our moment. We always had a very healthy sex life but that night I think we were both possessed. I wanted her to know I loved her and she was my life.

I started kissing her thighs and continued kissing down until I reached her toes. I put her toes in my mouth and sucked them one at a time, before raising her legs. When I finally penetrated her wetness, I immediately enjoyed the blissfulness of the moment. She was wet and hot. I could not remember the last time we were this turned on. With every thrust or slow grind, we could both feel the love. We kissed while we were making love and tried our best not to fall off the sofa. It was the heat and passion that kept us going. Occasionally, we had our quick and dirty sex, our afternoon delights. But most times when we made love, we were in it for the long run, another one of our many marathon sessions. As we climaxed together, we fell asleep on the sofa, with Julia's head resting on my chest. Before falling asleep, I silently thanked the Almighty for blessing me with a good woman.

Chapter
16

THROUGHOUT THE NIGHT, VARIOUS thoughts kept popping in and out of my head. I woke up in the middle of the night and picked up my baby and took her to the bedroom. I couldn't say it was a bad idea, but we did make love again. This time Julia was in the mood. We both have always made it a point not to turn the other one down.

Afterward, she was wrapped up in my arms with her head on my chest. Looking at her, I knew how fortunate I was as I kissed the top of her head. I absolutely loved Julia and I was happy we were working together. A part of me wanted to ask her to sit back and let me do this. But I knew her and she was a woman who needed to capture the world. The more I thought about it, the more I realized we were probably too much alike except for one thing: she had killed more people than me.

I recalled asking Steve how he felt about killing someone in the line of duty. He looked at me and his eyes spoke volumes of the grief, disheartening and indifferent effects of taking a life. He told me everyone reacts differently. Additionally, many times it depended on who you killed. He explained to me how some assailants deserved to die. Some criminals lived to die like the villain in a movie; always hoping someone would make them a martyr after their death. Others couldn't control their destinies. They lived by the gun and died by the gun.

Steve told me the first person he killed was a drug dealer who had intentionally killed over twenty people, including several children, by lacing his drugs with poison. The assailant made a play and Steve shot him three times in the chest. He relayed the killing didn't affect him and he actually thought something was wrong with him. Shortly thereafter, Janessa was born and he realized he had done the right thing by taking the drug dealer out. He was a killer of children and in Steve's mind, the worst criminals were those who harmed kids.

I didn't feel anything after killing the three attackers at our beach house; probably because they tried to kill my family, my friends and me. Killing affects everyone differently, whether the kill is justified or not. Being in law enforcement, I had heard and read the reports of agents, cops and even military warriors who couldn't handle the justified death of another. I always thought killing someone would affect me differently, but it didn't. I was all right.

Something told me before this case was over, my kill count would be higher. Someone wanted to kill me and those I loved. I was buzzing. I was back. My mind was in an investigative mode. Someone wanted to kill my fellow agents. *Agents.* It finally hit me. I wasn't the only agent at the house. Maybe they were after me but Q was there as well as Julia. Both were top notch agents. Additionally, this was about agents and Julia had briefed me on agents betraying agents. Hell, other agents may or may not have known her history as an agent. From listening to her, many, if not all, of the older agents knew her.

Motivation can come in many forms. I had motivation — the death of my brother. The assault in Virginia Beach gave me extra motivation. Elliot gave me an invitation because I initially joined the Bureau to avenge my brother's death. My reasons were already dripping with motivation and I probably didn't need any more. But the more I thought about it, the more sense it made. Julia was not only an analyst, she was Elliot's analyst. Damn, we were all potential targets.

I needed to get back to sleep but my mind was moving. What about Elliot? Though he had been in the position for four years now, he was still the first African-American Deputy Director of the Bureau.

Elliot ran the day-to-day operations of the Bureau. Director Tellis was the politician. The Director never worried about the daily operations of the Bureau, since he had his friend who had his back. His friend was the cornerstone of the Bureau.

I was missing something. What, I didn't know. It had to be a connection between all of the agents. But what? What did all of the murdered agents have in common? Research, research, research . . . that was my only thought. My first five years at the Bureau, I devoted many hours in the archive file section trying to find out what all of the victims had in common besides just being agents or ex-agents of the FBI.

I was racking my brain thinking about this case when I should have been sleeping. In a short span of time, a lot had happened. In my mind, I was trying to organize it all. Enough was enough; I had to get some shuteye. One more thought popped into my head though and I had to think it through. Before we departed Virginia Beach, Howard Carson approached me when I was in the kitchen. He wanted to talk before I left for D.C. I told him I didn't have time for a long, drawn out conversation. His words were still engraved in my mind.

"I understand, son. I just wanted to say, I love you," Howard surprised me. "I also wanted to thank you for the house and letting me be a part of the family."

I looked at him and I saw the glint in his eyes. I knew he was holding back the tears. I responded, "No problem, Pop." But he couldn't let it go at that.

"No, Kenny, it is a problem. I wasn't much of a father to you or your brothers and sisters. Hell, Steve raised you and Alyse. If I was half a damn father to any of you, maybe your brothers and sisters would still be alive. I look at my grandchildren downstairs, and I realize, to them, you represent the Carson family. Not me, their grandfather."

I felt bad for Howard. But he was right about everything he said. I didn't know how to respond. He was my father, but in my eyes he would always be the man who provided my mother the seed. I didn't hate him, but I didn't love him, either. If not for my sister, Alyse, or my wife, Julia, he wouldn't be a part of my life.

"Pop, your grandchildren love you and they know where the name Carson comes from. The past is the past and you shouldn't let the past affect your relationship with your grandchildren. Whatever you are feeling, get over it and just be there for your grandkids."

"I guess that's what I wanted to say. Thanks for letting me be a part of their lives. I know you bought my house because of Alyse and I'm in the kids' lives probably because of Julia. But you could have told both of them no. You are a bigger man than me, a better man than me. I just wanted you to know I am proud of you. In spite of your father, you made something out of yourself."

He hugged me and I hesitated before hugging him back. When I did, I felt the tears falling down his face. He was my father and for the first time in my life, we embraced. Looking over his shoulder, I saw Julia and she had a smile on her face and tears in her eyes. I refused to cry, but something told me my father wanted me to avenge his son's death. I was already on board; I didn't need any pushing.

My thoughts had overwhelmed me. The more I thought, the heavier my eyes got. I had had enough rest but Julia and I had made love twice — two powerful lovemaking sessions. I deserved to be tired and deserved to be asleep. I let my mind rest, kissed the top of Julia's head one more time, whispered "I love you" to my sleeping beauty and let the burdens and thoughts of the world slide off my shoulders for the next couple of hours.

Chapter 17

JULIA WENT TO THE office early. She drove Elliot's car. Though he was a man who did not abuse the privilege of being the FBI's Deputy Director, he and Director Tellis were being chauffeured around per orders of the White House. To my understanding, the orders came directly from President Cabot himself.

Though we had an eight o'clock meeting, Julia went in at six. When I entered the Hoover Building, it dawned on me that I no longer had a badge or Federal ID. Though I recognized several of the door guards, I knew proper protocol and knew I needed to call Elliot's office. But I was pleasantly surprised when Joe Crossley, the head security guard, walked up to me and gave me my old badge and ID card. He told me it was a gift from the deputy director. Joe and I shook hands and hugged. It was nice seeing him again. Occasionally, we used to shoot the breeze whenever we both had time.

As I walked in Julia's old office, she was standing at the door of Elliot's office. I assumed waiting on me. "Damn, you look good," she told me. I smiled and winked my eye at her. She pinched my butt as I walked pass her.

"Hot, isn't it?" I joked. "Watch it, don't burn yourself." Julia laughed, shook her head and this time, smacked my butt.

Our meeting was in an adjoining conference room next to Elliot's office. There were no windows and the room was dimly lit. I recognized the small collection of agents, including my boy, Q, my sister-in-law, Denise, Dr. Elizabeth Storm and several other agents. I also recognized Horace Schmidt from the Secret Service and Paul McGinley from the CIA. The last person I spotted was my former partner, Patrick Conroy.

"How do, Patrick?" I asked as I shook his hand and we embraced. "I am sorry to hear about Ryan."

"Thanks. Believe it or not, I'm glad you are back. I want these motherfuckers dead, KC. You understand what I am saying."

Patrick surprised me with his sentiments but we embraced again and I whispered in his ear that I was on board. He looked at me and I knew he saw the sincerity in my eyes. I knew his pain. He knew my past pain. Patrick and I were partners for most of my ten years with the Bureau. Often we butted heads but his job was always to keep me on track and provide support. Additionally, if I was the best or one of the best agents the Bureau had, most of the credit went to Patrick for always having my back. We worked and succeeded as a team, and during that time, we developed a friendship. Though many considered him Elliot's henchman, I considered him a good man to have on my side

I shook as many hands as possible before Elliot walked in and called the meeting to order. Next to him was the Senior Executive Assistant to the Director of the FBI, Jim Hudlin, the director's right hand man.

"Ok, let's get this meeting started. No sense in introductions, I think most of us, if not all, know each other. If not, you will by the time this whole ordeal is over." Elliot was strictly business, which was nothing I was not used to, but he was terse, straight to the point. His voice had a certain edge to it. An edge that was bad for those we were about to pursue.

"Those of you who were in the mass briefing yesterday, forget what you heard." I looked around the room and everyone was looking at each other. The agents who were there were evidently stunned by Elliot's statement. I looked at Julia, who was sitting close to the head of the table and she was not surprised. Regardless of how it was said, I perceived Elliot had just declared war on the group called *Just Cause*.

His demeanor was always a topic at the Bureau. Many didn't understand how he could always be so cool and calm when it seemed the world was falling apart. Words like distraught, upset, discouraged and many other negative descriptive terms were not used to portray him, ever. He regurgitated the history of the case, going back to 1982 and then rehashing the events of 1993. His briefing was succinct and concise. No fact was left unstated, no point was left unmade and no rock was left unturned. Elliot was on his game.

"Now brace yourselves. The 1993 case revealed the celebrity masked bank robberies were a part of the *Just Cause* plan. Prior to the 1982 case, they had robbed five banks over a six month period before killing their first agent. During the ensuing murder investigation, they robbed four more banks. In 1993, they had robbed seven banks over a six month period prior to killing their first agent and robbed another six banks during *our* investigation. And no, we never caught the robbers in the act or solved the case. But we were pretty convinced it was *Just Cause*.

"This time around, something is astray. Thus far, four banks were robbed in a two-week period before the first murder of an agent. Since we started our investigation, they have robbed one more bank in Columbia, South Carolina. On the prior crime sprees, everything was organized and calculated. This time, I think they are rushed, which I hope eventually will lead to sloppiness. If not, it means *Just Cause* is much better organized than we realize. Special Agent Pittman will brief you on the progress of her bank robbery detail."

Brenda Pittman was as tough as they came and she was also very headstrong. She was an average looking woman with short raven black hair. Her thick build made her look taller than her five foot six inches. It was interesting she and Patrick were working together, considering they used to see each other romantically. As thick as she was, it was hard to believe Brenda was a health nut. Patrick used to always complain about the meatless meals he had to endure.

She started her briefing by putting a slide on the overhead projector. The slide was a map of the forty-eight continental United States. Like a map of the states during an election year, some states were shaded in red while others were shaded in blue and the remaining states were in white. In one hand, Brenda had a pointer and in the other, a remote for the slide projector.

"Yesterday, Agents Patrick Conroy, Julia Carson and I spent hours going over the video tapes of all of the bank robberies from 1982, 1993 and the recent robberies. Though Conroy and I have already gone through these same tapes numerous times before, we thought it would be good to go through them one more time with fresh eyes."

I wasn't sure but it seemed Brenda was attacking Julia. If so, bad strategy. Elliot made Julia his analyst for a reason. He taught her but he knew from day one she had an analytical mind. She could take the smallest clue and make a case out of it. The more I thought about it, the more I realized she made many of my cases for me.

"Thus far, even with the additional help, we still haven't come up with anything tangible." I looked at Julia and I could see her patience wearing thin, and so did Elliot and Patrick.

"The red represents the states and cities from the 1982 robberies." Patrick abruptly stood up and took over the briefing. Brenda was pissed but before she could say anything, Elliot took a step and Brenda knew not to defy his authority. She had already pushed the envelope.

"The blue represents the robberies from 1993." Patrick took the remote from Brenda and clicked one time. Five states came up in blue: Wyoming, South Dakota, Washington, Arizona and South Carolina. Each state also had a star representing the capital city and the location of a robbery.

"What you see up here is the location of each robbery in the capital city of the state. The significance of the capital cities we do not know yet. But what we do know, every bank that has been hit has the name First, Second or Third in the name of the bank as well as the state name. The banks that have been hit thus far in the order they have been robbed are the Third Federal Bank of South Dakota in Pierre, the Second American Bank of Arizona in Phoenix, the Second Olympia Bank of Washington in Olympia, the First Wyoming Bank in Cheyenne and lastly, the First Bank of South Carolina. In every case, only one shot fired to get the attention of the bank employees and patrons. Unfortunately, that shot also killed the president of the bank in every robbery."

Patrick took a swallow of water and we all knew the pain he was in. The death of a loved one was never easy, especially when the loved one was murdered unnecessarily.

"The only pattern we have been able to figure out so far is an alphabetical connection by city and not by state. Dating back to the 1982 robberies, the first three robberies were in Albany, Annapolis and Atlanta. Then the group hit Trenton and Topeka — the other end of the alphabet. By the time the Bureau got involved, we did not have a good feel for their strategy. The final result: five banks in the beginning of the alphabet and five on the end.

"In 1993, the first bank hit was the Third Utah National Bank in Salt Lake City. The First Oregon Bank in Salem was next. Looking at the MO, this was our cue to get involved. We still had agents who had worked the 1982 case. The bank robberies picked up the alphabet where it had ended on the end of the alphabet. However, we did not foresee the murder of our fellow agents. By the time we learned about *Just Cause* and tied them to the bank robberies, it was too late. We were so focused on one part of the investigation, we failed to capture or stop any of the bank robberies. The final result: 13 total robberies, seven at the beginning of the alphabet and six at the end.

"This time around, the same strategy, starting alphabetically where they left off at the end of the alphabet: hitting Pierre, Phoenix and Olympia. The next two were Cheyenne and Columbia. Logically and I guess, alphabetically, the next bank should be in Columbus, Ohio or Oklahoma City. We only have one challenge ahead of us in both cities: there are several banks with First, Second or Third in their name in each city. We just need to figure out our next move."

"No need to, we have already figured out the next move," was the surprised and arrogantly echoed comment from Brenda Pittman. "We notified the banks and police officials in both cities and our regional offices. Both cities are boosting security personnel. Local police and our local field agents will be staking out the banks as well. This time, we are ready."

"I disagree," Julia spoke up. She stood to make her point. "For one, looking at the tapes and going through the customer data, we could never pinpoint one customer in any of these situations that may have aided *Just Cause*. We know they have been staking out the banks but from the outside security camera tapes from the banks, we never saw cars or vans staking out the banks. Maybe they were staking out the banks from nearby buildings. But I'm convinced this is an inside job. Everything we have just done has not only alerted *Just Cause* we are on to them, but if they decide to proceed with their plans, we may be in for a bloodbath — a shootout that could probably lead to the death of more innocent lives."

Chapter
18

WE WERE SHOCKED BY Julia's assessment. I was even more floored by the apparent catfight between her and Brenda. However, Julia was probably right. Though Brenda made the decision in her capacity as Chief of Violent Crimes/Bank Robbery Section, I think we all were thinking the same thing — she didn't consider everything. Maybe the need to flex her muscles or prove she was the better woman led to her zealous decision.

Elliot didn't let us think about it too long. He proceeded with his briefing; giving us the direction to take and the ins and outs of the group called *Just Cause*. He didn't know the rush of this crime spree nor was he willing to speculate. But he let us know that it was the FBI's case *and* we would have help. I knew Paul McGinley was there from the CIA because his director and deputy director were both former FBI agents. Horace Schmidt was representing the Secret Service because the President's top Secret Service agent, Cody Richards, was killed. Cody was also a former Bureau agent.

The bad thing about outside help on a case was agents never knew who they might be dealing with. The person or agency may have an agenda that would conflict with the Bureau's. But in a case or situation like this, we knew we were all on the same page. That was, until our boss sprung a surprise on us.

"Let me introduce you all to retired Lieutenant Colonel Bobby Small, Jr. He will be a consultant on this case. Colonel Small is a retired Special Forces commander, and the founder and CEO of the Southern House of Hatred WatchGroup."

I have never heard a legend described accurately. The Scot, William Wallace, of Braveheart fame was thought to be over seven feet tall; when in fact he was six six or six seven. Close enough, I guess. Bobby Small, Jr. was thought to be six five but he barely stood five eleven. He did look taller than that, though. His bearing and reputation were impeccable. His resume was even more impressive.

He was one of the many heroes of the first war with Iraq, Operation Desert Storm, but he stood out from the others. He was the media's darling. Gloria described him in an article as the man with the look and charisma that America had been lacking. He was the quiet warrior with the bravery and patriotism of GI Joe. The media considered him the real deal. Rumors had it the Iraqi soldiers immediately surrendered when they heard Lieutenant Colonel Bobby Small, Jr. and his Special Forces unit were headed their way. There were leaks that the Colonel could have taken Saddam Hussein out on several occasions if the White House had given the word.

Rumors alone made him a media superstar, but his action and leadership created the legacy. He didn't have disciplinary issues with his soldiers. They were marveled by his actions on the battlefield and off. They spread the word. I remembered seeing him doing interviews after Desert Storm and his confidence stood out. Though his presence reeked of self-assurance, I could see the danger in his eyes. He was a man not to be crossed.

Unfortunately, many probably did not see the danger in his eyes as I had. Several years after Desert Storm, his wife and two sons were visiting family in their native Alabama when they were attacked and killed by a hate group called the New Knights of Anger. Colonel Small was once again the media's focus. This time, he was not the hero but the grieving husband and father. I remember looking at the television and feeling bad for The New Knights. Colonel Small's eyes redefined the meaning of trouble. I saw a man who was destined to get his revenge. I saw a man who was destined to kill.

After turning down the rank of full bird Colonel, it took Bobby Small, Jr. almost two years to be released from the Army. Within two months, the 23 members of the New Knights of Anger were found dead. They were killed in various methods — from drowning to slit throats to shots in the head to finally, the last eleven being blown up in their clubhouse in Alabama. Of course, speculation focused on retired Lieutenant Colonel Small, but an arrest warrant didn't accompany speculation.

Soon after, Bobby Small, Jr. created the Southern House of Hatred WatchGroup. His group's purpose was to track the status of hate groups throughout the United States. It was also rumored their mission was to destroy them as well. When it came to information on hate groups, Bobby Small's website was the most informative in cyberspace or anywhere else.

"There are thousands of hate groups in America and all are dangerous," Colonel Small began his briefing. "We have been working on this case for the past four years and thus far, we have identified six groups involved with the group called *Just Cause*."

"What you mean four years?" was the question posed by Horace Schmidt of the Secret Service, but a question I was sure was on the minds of everyone in the room except one — Elliot Lucas.

Before Colonel Small could answer, Elliot took the floor. "We were expecting another attack from *Just Cause* but didn't know when. Director Tellis and I employed Colonel Small four years ago to identify, track and prevent a future attack on the Bureau. Unfortunately, we were not sanctioned to take action against anyone possibly connected to *Just Cause* unless they committed a crime."

Many eyes focused on Elliot but he did not flinch. Issue closed. Colonel Small was a patient and affable man. I got the feeling he was the real deal — a true leader. He picked up where Elliot left off with a slight smile on his face and a glint of hope in his eyes.

"Two of the groups identified as being members of *Just Cause* have been members since 1982: the Black Mavericks and Red Death of Mercy. The other groups are the Hitler's Nazis, the American Soldiers of Aryan and the National Aryans; needless to say, all White Aryan groups. The last group is the Ladies of Troy, a group of women of all nationalities who hate men in general. Rumors have it they are straight lesbians, and when they have sex with men, the men are usually killed after the act.

"I suspect there are at least two to four or more groups that may be a part of *Just Cause*. McKale's Army, the group that attacked the Carson household in Virginia Beach, is the seventh and probably most interesting group. They have been around for at least 10 to 15 years and only appear once or twice a year. I have been tracking them ever since I started the Southern House. Some of you may know the work of McKale's Army. Their resume includes attacks on civil rights organizations or events including the murder of the entire Chicago chapter of the Society of Help organization last year."

I think most of us in the room were surprised. The Bureau investigated the case but came up with nothing. Eight people were brutally killed in the downtown office of the civil rights group. Hate graffiti was spray painted over the walls and worse, spray painted on the victims. The President himself condemned the death of the eight victims. The outrage was heard throughout the nation. Now we had a name for those responsible. I wondered if the three attackers I killed had anything to do with the death of the eight civil rights members in Chicago.

"Every time we had a lead on McKale's Army or any meeting of the Disciple Board, something went awry. It was as if they were always a step ahead of us. I have put together booklets for all of you to study carefully. Consider it your homework. It consists of information on all of the groups I just relayed to you including what information we have on McKale's Army and the bank robberies. The robberies in my opinion have been accomplished by a combination of the different groups working together. Also, one thing I think has been overlooked in the bank robberies is the customer base. Most of the banks that have been hit cater to minority groups.

"The one thing I haven't been able to figure out is why. Why hit these particular banks? Is it because of the customer base and neighborhoods, or is it some other variable we haven't put our fingers on, yet?"

Chapter 19

OUR MEETING WAS ADJOURNING when Theresa Guyton, Elliot's executive assistant, rushed in and told Elliot we had to take this call. She was sporting a nice dark blue pantsuit and her usually curly Shirley Temple blonde locks were straight today. Actually, I think the curls had fallen out. Theresa was tall, standing at least five feet eleven and had a model's body. She didn't have the responsibilities that Julia, Elliot's last executive assistant, had. Being an executive assistant was her only responsibility. Julia told me she was very good at what she did. If her actions were an indication of her efficiency, then she was indeed good at what she did.

She crawled underneath the table and plugged the phone back into its socket, while explaining to Elliot what was going on. The Bureau's switchboard had received a call for Director Tellis. The voice on the other end of the phone demanded to talk to him immediately, stating it was a matter of imminent life and death for agents in the field. The call was transferred to the director's office, but the director's executive assistant told the caller the director was not in. The voice once again stated his purpose and this time demanded to be transferred to the deputy director. The last things Theresa briefed before connecting the call was the caller knew Elliot was in a meeting with some of his agents, the caller was using an automated voice machine and the call had been traced to Elliot's own office phone.

"This is Deputy Director Lucas."

"Elliot, nice to hear your voice," the automated voice responded. "First, let me congratulate you on being the first nigger to make it this far in the Federal Bureau of Investigation. Amazing what time and perseverance can do for you." The voice laughed.

Even the automated machine could not distort the heinousness and nastiness of the caller's laugh. I looked around the room and I think we all were wondering what in the hell was going on. Agents betraying their fellow agents played back in my mind. We were dealing with someone who knew us, knew our methodologies, knew our technologies and probably even knew our mindset.

"Secondly, let me congratulate your IT personnel on their best effort to trace the call. I know they are disappointed that after all of that hard work and scrambling through my twenty relays, the trail ends in your office."

Once again the heinous laugh. Elliot was sitting at the head of the table, expressionless and stoic. The automated voice had our complete and undivided attention. He had what we all wanted — a captive audience.

"You stated you had information on my agents in the field. Could you please elaborate?" Elliot asked in his even tone. He was leaning forward with his elbows on the conference room table and his hands clasped together. I could see his mind working overtime trying to figure out who was on the other end of the phone.

"Elliot, my poor Elliot. Or maybe I should call you Mr. HNIC. For you idiots who are dumbfounded as to what that means, it means *head nigger in charge*. Elliot used to be infamous, or should I say notorious for using that acronym when he took over a job as regional or division chief. Now don't any of you take me the wrong way, we all know the head nigger is not a racist, but I personally think at times the HNIC is a little confused. I actually think the HNIC thinks he is one of us; that his skin is white and his blood is American red."

"Are you going to talk to us about something concrete or insult me? Thus far, this is categorized as a crank call. You have sixty seconds to state the reason you are calling or this call is terminated." Elliot was maintaining his cool, but his posture was uneasy. I think this case had finally struck his chord. And his chord was the love and respect he had for his fellow agents.

"Testy, testy, my dear Elliot," the automated voice teasingly bantered. "Ok, Mr. HNIC, Mr. FBI Deputy Director, this is what I have for you. For me to call off my attack dogs, I want a hundred million transferred to an offshore account. I think that is only fair since the last Mega Million and Powerball lotteries combined winnings came up to ninety million. In return, we will cease killing your agents and robbing banks. I think that is a fair trade. What do you think, my nigger?"

"I personally think you are full of shit," was the surprising comment from Elliot. "But as you know, I am only the second man in command. I have a boss, who in turn, also has a boss. So I will shoot this up my chain of command and as an ex or current agent yourself, you are probably familiar with the protocols we have here at the Bureau. So please tell me the time criteria we have to meet your demands and I will get right on it."

"Why are you fucking with me, Elliot?" Though we were listening to an automated voice machine, we could tell the caller's demeanor had changed. He was no longer the teasing, jovial voice behind the machine. His tone was serious and cold. I was sure Elliot had returned the gesture and struck his own chord with our automated voice caller.

"You have four days, exactly ninety-six hours from now. And since you want to be flippant and a total asshole about this, expect a group of your agents to die today. And know this, Elliot. These deaths will be on you. Now you and your elite team just need to figure out what city and what bank. Also, know this, Deputy Director Elliot Lucas: after our demands are met, there will be one more death. Your death. And I will be the one pulling the trigger."

The phone went dead. Elliot wasted no time standing up and looking at Julia, Brenda and Patrick. "Ten minutes, you guys have ten minutes to tell me what bank may be hit," he stated as he started walking to his office.

"Ten minutes?" Brenda voiced excitedly. "Sir, be realistic. We can't tell you anything in ten minutes!"

Elliot stopped in his tracks and the look he gave Brenda could have frozen time. His eyes were steely and cold. He wasn't accepting no or any negative comments. He wanted action, he wanted results. I didn't want to be in Brenda Pittman's shoes at that particular moment.

"Agent Pittman," Elliot began, "your fellow agents are in grave danger and even before you try, you are going to give up?" Elliot's tone was still even but condescending. He was upset and trying to maintain a cool demeanor. "You are the fucking head of the Bank Robbery Section and I have to allocate resources to get you off your ass to do your job." He started walking towards Brenda and I think all of the color just abandoned her. Her face was pale white and you could see the fear in her eyes.

Before he reached her, Julia stepped in and stated, "Sir, we will have our best guesstimation to you in ten minutes for both Columbus and Oklahoma City."

Theresa Guyton grabbed Elliot's arm and told him Director Tellis was on the phone.

Chapter
20

Columbus, Ohio

THE THIRD INTRASTATE BANK of Ohio had never been this well guarded. Security was usually provided by two uniformed armed guards. Today, four uniformed armed guards were joined by a dozen plain clothes FBI agents and Columbus Police Department detectives. The bank was just one of sixteen banks in the Columbus area with the same type of security.

The security force was conspicuously a part of the bank's daily staff and customers. Two agents and two detectives were outside of the bank building in unmarked cars. One car was parked in the parking lot and the other was on the street. The three-story building sat on the outskirts of the Ohio State University campus. Most of its patrons were African-Americans and Hispanic-Americans.

The bank was unusually busy this morning. It opened at nine o'clock and its doors had been opened for fifteen minutes. The two tellers had already worked up a sweat. The head teller had just accomplished her monthly transaction with the employee from the Treasury Department. She had several nondescript packages wrapped in brown paper that she needed to put into the safe inside the bank's vault.

The staff was not briefed on the security force or the addition of two armed guards and several new staff members; only the President and Vice-President of the bank. The President chose not to come in that day; instead, the

Vice-President was in charge. Permanent staff of the bank was suspicious of the new staff members and the additional security. Their suspicions didn't last long.

Before the head teller could complete her monthly task, the unmarked cars outside the bank building suddenly blew up. Everyone inside the bank was caught completely by surprise. Before anyone could react, two shots rang out loud and two of the uniform guards went down. Two assailants pretending to be customers in the bank began to randomly shoot personnel, when a black van jumped the curve and drove through the front door of the bank. Four robbers dressed in black suits and donning masks resembling the latest version of Michael Jackson, the actor Robert Blake, O.J. Simpson and Ronald Reagan jumped out the van and joined their comrades in the continued assault on the bank.

"How do we plan on doing this people?" the Ronald Reagan impersonator asked, as he jumped on the bank counter and handed two knapsack type bags to the two tellers. Two more assailants came in the bank donning masks resembling Henry Kissinger and Jane Fonda.

"Cops and plain clothes FBI agents, identify yourselves!" Ronald Reagan continued. "Identify yourselves and no one else will be killed. However, if you don't all show yourselves, then we will kill everyone in the bank. In the meanwhile, start filling up my money bags. Time?"

"A minute, fifteen," the Robert Blake impersonator answered.

"Ok, no one wants to come forward, then . . ."

One of the agents wearing a brown suit and a tan tie stepped forward. Before he could open his mouth to speak, he was shot in the head by the Henry Kissinger impersonator. The other agents and detectives immediately reacted and reached for their weapons. Before anyone could fire a shot, the assailants opened fire and killed the remaining security force.

Before departing, the robbers ensured they completed their task at hand — robbing the bank.

Oklahoma City, Oklahoma

The security force at the First Oklahoma Bank at the Interstates 40 and 35 interchange had just received word about the bank robbery and blood fest in Columbus, Ohio. The leader of the security force, Special Agent Walt Matters, was distraught but duty called. He gathered the bank president and his team with the exception of two armed uniform guards in the office of the president to tell them the news. News he would never be able to deliver.

As the last agent walked in the office on the first floor, the window of the door shattered and blood from the agent's head splattered across the room. Before the remainder of the special force team could respond, a barrage of bullets from the Uzis and assault rifles of five armed assailants ripped the office and its inhabitants to shreds. When the staff of the bank was questioned, they stated five armed criminals donning masks of Charlton Heston, Teddy Roosevelt, Madonna, Jack Johnson and an unidentified/unknown female mask killed everyone in the office of the bank president, while another assailant wearing a Marilyn Monroe mask robbed the bank.

Chapter
21

I DON'T KNOW HOW others define a bad day, but I and many others at the Bureau defined a bad day as two bank robberies, 28 agents, policemen and guards dead and one bank president dead. It wasn't noon yet and 29 families were without loved ones. *Just Cause* had the upper hand in a big way. We had agents, local cops and detectives positioned at over thirty banks and the one thing we never counted on happened — two banks hit in one day.

Unfortunately, the second team that got hit in Oklahoma City thought as we all did that the Columbus, Ohio job was the only one. This was against their *modus operandi* and protocol. The guys let their guard down. I would have done the same thing.

Elliot was shaken when he heard the news but he was a professional. I didn't know if I could remain as calm and collected as him. The information he wanted in ten minutes was a moot point, especially since the first bank robbery occurred within five minutes of the automated voice caller hanging up the phone. As soon as the second bank robbery occurred in Oklahoma City, the automated voice called back just to say the clock was ticking. Before Elliot could say a word, the phone disconnected. Needless to say, the man I had a lot of respect for was visibly upset.

Elliot ordered Julia, Brenda and Patrick to continue analyzing all of the bank robberies, past and present, including the video feeds from that day's robberies. Agents who responded to the scene were able to transfer the security camera tapes to a computer media device and provide a video feed via the Bureau's classified Internet line.

Damon Blake and Q were dispersed to Columbus to investigate what happened. Todd Rivers and Franklin Long were dispersed to Oklahoma City for the same reason. Elliot was in a meeting with Director Tellis, and the Secret Service and CIA representatives. I was whisked away by Dr. Beth Storm, the Bureau's leading psychologist and a member of the Behavioral Science Unit.

Beth and I were friends — though we truly had a love/hate relationship. When I was an agent, she frequently disapproved of my methods. But it never prevented her from being a part of our team. She, Q, Patrick and I worked over twenty high profile cases together. We had a 100 percent success rate. I actually think it was Beth's job to keep me honest and on my toes. Our combativeness was a part of our chemistry.

As soon as we walked in her office, Beth surprised me.

"Come here, asshole, and give me a hug before we get started."

I was surprised. We had talked several times over the phone since I had left last year and made promises to meet for lunch or dinner, but lunch or dinner never came around. When I saw her get off the helicopter in Virginia Beach, I was happy to see her. We hugged for a long minute. It felt good. This was the calm before the storm.

"Let me take a step back and take a look at you," I chided. "Damn, look at you. All changed and stuff." She smiled. I smiled. Beth was around five foot seven, slender build. Her usual brunette hair was dyed blonde but still chopped short. Her complexion was smooth and she had a serious Florida tan.

"So I guess you like, Mr. Carson. Or should I call you Agent Carson?"

This was a different Beth. A more calm and relaxed Beth. I was glad she was taking life easy but strangely enough, I missed my combative partner.

"Beth, what happened to my Dr. Storm, the serious one?" I joked.

"I missed you, KC," she stated as she signaled for me to have a seat. "We had some pretty good battles but we had a great working relationship and I know your heart."

We were both smiling and I liked this Beth — the new and improved Dr. Beth Storm. She seemed to be more grounded. In the past, she was your typical psychologist; high strung, worried, with the weight of the world on her shoulders. Often times, she seemed to be more uptight and tense than those she was evaluating. At times, she even seemed as though she hated life. Now, she looked as though she was really enjoying life.

"So, where do we begin, Doc?" I asked.

"Depends, Agent Carson, I still have a job to do," her smile slowly disappearing.

"Honestly, Beth, I'm cool. Just ready to get back in the groove of things and hopefully make a difference."

"Understand. But let's talk about the attack at the house. How do you feel about killing three people? In the line of duty, you have never shot anyone and now, there are three people dead. Any remorse?"

"No!" I quickly responded. "They wanted to kill me and my family, Beth. You know me. Some things I deal with or put up with. Violence towards my family is not one of those things."

She didn't say anything. We were sitting not less than five feet from each other. She was in a comfortable looking office chair with a thick cushion. I was sitting on the small sofa. It was a small but quaint and comfortable office. Her desk was small and covered with several stacks of papers and folders. Three pictures of a waterfall, wild horses galloping and eagles flying adorned the walls. She also had two four feet five-drawer wooden cabinets, which somehow didn't fit with the decorum.

"How do you feel about Julia killing attackers? I know you had never seen her in action. Seeing someone you know to be sweet turn into a killing machine can be a little too much for most people."

"It doesn't faze me, Beth. She did what she had to do." I stopped and I really thought about it for a second. I looked at

Beth and before she could reply, I continued. "Damn, you know what? I was very proud of her. I had heard the rumors, but damn, seeing her in action was a sight. I really didn't have time to think about it. But, man, she had it going on."

Beth smiled and I realized I was smiling. She, my Julia, really was a hell of a woman.

"Ok, that's all I have," Beth surprised me.

I was stunned. "You shitting me, right?" I responded.

She continued smiling. She leaned forward in her chair and I did the same thing on the sofa. "I never truly realized your worth, KC. You have a way about you. I'm not necessarily sure Elliot needs you on this case. But I do know he wants you on the case. You bring something he likes to the table. You have great knowledge and investigative skills, but you also possess a certain edge. I miss your edge. I even miss our antagonism. But more importantly, I think Elliot really misses that edge.

Chapter 22

LIEUTENANT COLONEL BOBBY SMALL, Jr. was busy on his laptop computer when I returned to Elliot's office. I sat at the small conference room table and started reviewing the booklet on hate groups I had received at the briefing from Colonel Small. I studied the material and we sat in silence.

After several minutes, Colonel Small asked me, "Any questions on the material, Agent Carson?"

"No, not at all. Pretty interesting, definitely makes for good reading. By the way, call me KC."

"Cool, call me Bobby."

I smiled at the Colonel. *Cool.* And that's exactly what he was — cool. For a man trained in the art of killing, his eyes were polite. I thought back to the times I had seen him on television and his eyes always caught my attention. They were small and set back in his head. Since his hair was cut short, almost bald, his eyes stood out. They spoke of his mood. He was in a good mood at the moment and that confused me.

"Why are you smiling, Colonel? We lost thirty people today, you forgot about that?" My tone was inquisitive, not threatening or accusatory.

"Hey, don't take it the wrong way," the Colonel responded. "I am not in a good mood, just letting my mind think about something else. This is serious business and trust me, I know about death and the pain of death."

"Yeah, I know that, that's why I don't understand. Sorry if I read you the wrong way, sir."

"You didn't and nothing to be sorry about, KC. We are both men here and men communicate. Maybe if we had more communicating, the world wouldn't be so jacked up."

We looked at each other and I nodded.

"*Bobby*, KC, please call me Bobby. Colonel and Sir died when I took the uniform off."

"Once a soldier, always a soldier, Bobby. Once an officer, always an officer. Respect is earned. You have earned it and then some."

Bobby and I talked. It was a good talk. We were two men alike and that struck me as peculiar. I wondered if I could have killed a hate group if they had killed Julia and the boys. Considering what had happened at the beach house, I knew I would have probably done the same thing. Additionally, I had beaten and scared a man named Alphonso Enwright for his involvement with my sister's death. I broke in his house, tied him up and scared him into giving Devin, his and Alyse's son, a trust fund. Though Alphonso did not directly kill Alyse, I still wanted to kill him.

"Can I ask you a question?"

Bobby smiled and I knew he had probably been asked the same stupid question I wanted to ask.

"Maybe I shouldn't ask." He smiled and slightly laughed. Yeah, I felt stupid and shook my head at my stupidity.

"No problem," he stated with a smile still plastered on his face. "I usually don't answer, so no big deal."

I smiled and I understood. "I'm sorry, Bobby. I guess we as people can be so silly and inconsiderate sometimes. I'm truly sorry."

"No, don't be. But to answer your question, yes, I killed the members of the New Knights of Anger and yes, I'm glad I did. They killed my family and I had a choice, kill them or kill their families. I chose to kill them."

I listened to the man and I understood. On so many levels, he was a hero and we as a nation were fortunate to have him. How fortunate, I didn't think any of us in America really knew. He looked at me and I could see comfort in his eyes. Something told me his killing of the New Knights of Anger lifted a heavy burden off his shoulders and probably eased the tension behind his eyes.

He later told me it was the first time he ever talked about what he did. I had an instant respect for the military man. In a short period of time, he had already made an impact on me.

We talked a little bit about his booklet and the different aspects of hate groups. Discussing the information he had gathered and conversing the way we were, brought a lot of questions to mind, but one question just kept beating me up.

"Bobby, what do all of the victims have in common besides being members of the Bureau?" The question in many ways was as generic as could be. So something wasn't right. It had to be more than just them being members of the Bureau. My gut kept telling me that.

"I've been pondering that same question, KC. I actually wanted to talk to Julia about it. She's damn good at analyzing data."

"Actually, I'm just really realizing how great she is," I smiled as I made the statement. "Funny, even as long as we have known each other, I am learning more and more about her other life, like it was a secret." The words came out of my mouth and I didn't understand why or even how. I didn't know Bobby Small, Jr., but I was comfortable with him. He was a leader and motivator of men, and something inside of me told me he understood.

"KC, I have worked with Julia before and I have known about you for a long time. She has always loved you. I could tell by the way she used to talk about you. My advice to you would be to let her be who she is. You know her better than anyone else. You may not believe that right now, but trust me, you do. I have a feeling you have always known. Even the stuff you didn't want to know or the stuff you are just learning, in the back of your head, you probably knew."

I half-heartedly smiled but I realized he was right. I did know. I have always known.

"Plus, Mr. Carson, you love her, she loves you, you guys have a family and take it from someone who knows, you can never take that for granted."

Bobby Small, Jr. had a working mind and I was amazed at how his thoughts easily flowed from his mouth. From mind to mouth, his words flowed and the more he talked, the more I learned. When our conversation ended, I was educated. More importantly, I was ready to slay the dragon called *Just Cause*.

Chapter
23

JULIA CARSON, BRENDA PITTMAN and Patrick Conroy had been watching security camera videos for the past six hours. Elliot had given them a mandate of ten minutes to find the next bank to be hit. Sadly, Julia had selected the banks she thought would be robbed within the ten minutes but it was too late. They didn't have ten minutes.

After the news about the attacks in Columbus and Oklahoma City, Elliot sent them back to the media room to continue watching, diagnosing and analyzing every video from the multiple robberies. Brenda, as head of the Bank Robbery Section, thought it best to bring in five of her best analysts to review the robberies. With eight people now, Brenda recommended they break up in teams of two.

The reviewing of videos could be tedious at best. Every scene prior to and after the robbery had to be analyzed. Every person present in the bank before the robbery was a suspect. Additionally, an analyst must decide how much time prior to the robbery was relevant to the robbery itself. Many questions must be asked and answered before a valid lead could be followed or a recommendation could be made.

It took Julia and Agent Eric Whiteman four hours to come forth with something concrete to present to the remainder of the group.

Julia had gathered everyone in front of the big screen in the media room. The thin and studious looking Agent Whiteman had set up the projector and the sequence of videos to be reviewed. At Julia's insistence, he started the video.

"Ok," Julia began. "I know we all are tired, but I think we have something. Eric and I are going to walk you through what we have found."

The first sequence consisted of the security guards of the ten different robberies over the three decades. In every scene from 1982 to 1993 to present day, four guards kept appearing in the tapes. From city to city, state to state, the same four guards kept reappearing. In most cases, a combination of two of the four was working together. In other cases, only one of the four was present at the robbery.

"I'll be damned," Patrick stated. "That's pretty damn smooth. Twenty-three damn years and they have been using the same damn guards. I can't fucking believe this."

"How could we miss this, Brenda?" one of her analysts asked.

"Not Brenda's fault, Linda. Brenda didn't work the '82 or '93 cases. Plus, who would have ever thought anyone would be using the same guards they used in 1982. Very original thought. But look at how they have aged."

Julia kept rewinding the various scenes. In each scene, she pointed out how the men had not really aged much. The weigh fluctuation, along with the little mustache or facial hair here or there and the various hairdos over the years made a huge difference; unless one knew what to look for.

"What made you look that hard at the security guards, Julia?" Patrick asked.

Julia focused in on one scene from a robbery in 1993. "Look at how the security guards are lying on the floor. The bank robbers are not paying any attention to them." Julia pulled out a laser pointer and put the red laser light on each of the six robbers. Lastly, she settled the laser on the two security guards lying on the floor.

"Now watch this," Julia said as she kept the red light on the guards. They looked at each other and one looked at his watch, then the two men smiled.

Julia and Agent Whiteman continued to identify the numerous clues from the various videos. During the briefing,

Patrick took notes on areas of concern. He tried patiently to wait until the briefing was over before he asked his question. Since the death of his brother, his patience had deserted him.

"Who are the men?" he blurted out. Patrick and Julia looked at each other. He knew Julia. He knew she already had the information. She was meticulous like that.

"You can start with the guard from the Phoenix robbery," Patrick added.

"Linus "Demon Dog" Cummings," Julia immediately responded. "He has a record dating back to when he was a teenager and his early twenties, but believe it or not, over the past 25 years, he hasn't even had a driving ticket. He has moved around a lot, but we have several known addresses for him. We have some things in the work that will get us a better idea of his location."

"What things?" Patrick asked.

"Ok, let's take fifteen."

As the small group dispersed, Patrick and Brenda hung around to talk to Julia.

"Brenda, it's best if you grabbed a sofa or take a restroom break," Julia said.

Special Agent Pittman was not happy. As the lead person in charge of the section, she felt she had a right to be included on all discussions involving recent events. She knew Julia represented the deputy director, but protocol was protocol.

"No, I think I need to stay and hear what's going on." Her statement was in the form of a demand. A demand her new superior, Julia Carson, did not take lightly.

"I'm sorry, Brenda, this discussion doesn't concern you."

"Well, I think you're wrong. Before you came along, this was my—"

"That was then," Julia interrupted. "This part of the investigation is my responsibility. This is the second time you have been a pain in my ass. Make this the last time."

The women looked at each other. Before Julia could say another word, Brenda walked off.

"I want to talk about Linus Cummings, aka Demon Dog," Patrick began, "but there was something else in the videos I noticed you intentionally disregarded. Why?"

"Because it's privileged, tightly held information," Julia answered. "That was good of you to pick up on the drop of the money and the involvement of the head teller in every case, but this is something for Elliot to handle — not us. Additionally, everything you have thought of, I am already on it. I guarantee you, by the end of the day we will know where Demon Dog is hiding."

Chapter 24

"I . . . I . . . I CAN'T TELL YOU anything," came out of the mouth of Sarah McHartner. She was the head teller at the First Oklahoma Bank in Oklahoma City, when the bank was robbed. She didn't expect any more questions after she was quizzed by FBI agents and local detectives earlier that morning. Her boyfriend of the past three months, Lyle Hanscom, told her it would be simple. The bank would be robbed, a couple of folks might have gotten hurt but nothing serious and she would walk away with $50,000 dollars. What a scam. How could she have been so stupid?

"Earth to Sarah, earth to Sarah," the African-American agent with the nice, shiny, wavy black hair called out. Sarah was so into her thoughts, she had tuned out the world. She had a tendency to do that when she was nervous and scared. Today just might have been the worst day of her life.

"I'm sorry, sir. I mean, Agent . . ." Sarah was trying her best to stay calm and cool. But it was hard. The first set of questions by the other agents and detectives only concentrated on what actually happened at the bank. This was different.

"I'm sorry, Agent, I forgot your name that fast," she smiled.

"Morales, Quentin Morales, ma'am," Q stated with a slight smile on his face. He knew he had the woman. Nervousness and guilt were written all over her face. One side of his brain wanted to grab her by her thick neck and scare the hell out of her. He knew the answers would come quick and fast. The other side told him to be patient and he would get everything he wanted. Everything just included one thing for Q – Lyle Hanscom.

"That's a nice name," Sarah replied.

"Well, thanks, Ms. McHartner. I will make sure I tell my mother that." He smiled again, putting the teller more at ease. He knew she would never be totally at ease. How could she?

"Lyle Hanscom. You going to tell me about your relationship, Ms. McHartner?"

"Please call me Sarah, Agent Morales. And Lyle . . . I mean, Mr. Hanscom and I did not have a relationship. He works at the bank as a security guard and I'm a teller, and we see each other at work. He speaks everyday. He's a pleasant man."

Q shook his head up and down. He kept the half-smile on his face. He had her just where he wanted her. He turned around to his partner, Agent Damon Blake, and retrieved three photos from Damon.

"Ms. McHartner." Q leaned in closer to Sarah, making eye contact. His eyes had turned cold, his nostrils flared, his voice was deeper and his pleasant smile had disappeared. He had become a man who meant business. "Sarah, please look at the photos of you and Lyle Hanscom taken today. Two of the photos were taken inside of the bank. Notice the times. *Notice the times.*"

Sarah's hands were sweaty and shaking when she took the photos from Q. She didn't like his tone or his new demeanor. She wondered what happened to his sweet and easy persona. She suddenly felt weak in the knees. She was happy she was sitting down.

"The first photo was taken ten minutes before the robbery. Please notice how you and Mr. Hanscom are looking at each other with a nice, friendly, goo-goo eye smile. The next photo was taken about five minutes after the robbery. I can understand how you are scared and needed someone to hug and hold you after such an ordeal. But to my understanding, Mr. Hanscom has only been at the bank maybe three months max, and you have others who have been at the bank much, much longer and are your friends. All of the photos I have seen, you didn't check on any of your workmates. Only Mr. Hanscom.

"Sarah, look at the photo after the robbery. His hand is on the back of your neck. That's what people call a *hug of affection*. Whenever the hand is placed on the back of the neck, it means something. It means two people have a strong affection for each other. Family members stroke each other's necks like that. Husbands and wives, boyfriends and girlfriends, secret lovers — all stroke each other that way."

Q stopped talking and just stared at Sarah. He didn't know if the hand on the back of the neck really meant anything. He had heard it somewhere or seen it on the internet, and decided to use it. That was his job to use whatever was at his disposal and he was good at it. Using bullshit stored in the deep crevices of his brain was a lot better than using his hands and smacking the junk out of Sarah McHartner, which was what he really wanted to do. Half the smacks would be for being stupid for a bum like Lyle Hanscom and the other half would be for being indirectly responsible for the deaths of agents, cops and co-workers.

He continued to stare at her, without blinking, without changing his facial expression. She could not make eye contact. She just kept looking at the photo, trying to hold back the tears. She did feel terrible. She never thought that many people would get hurt. No, they didn't get hurt, they died. And she was responsible. But she didn't want to go to jail. She couldn't handle jail.

"Sarah," Q said. "Look at the last photo. That's you and Hanscom at your car. I like the way he affectionately kissed you on the cheek. That's sweet."

She finally raised her head to look at Agent Morales. The last photo was too much. The memory of Lyle's friends gunning down the agents and detectives in cold blood was too much. She loved Lyle. But just then, everything was too much.

All of her neighbors could see the FBI and police cars outside of her nice townhouse. Her phone had been ringing off the hook. She knew it was her family. She was sure some of them were outside right now but probably unable to get to her. Why? Lyle said this would be so easy.

"What do you want, Agent Morales?" she whispered, with tears falling from her eyes.

Q leaned in closer. "You know what I want," he whispered back. "Tell me which room he is in. I don't want to hurt him or you. Yes, I know some of the people who died today but I want to question Lyle. Plus, I'm sure you were innocent in all of this. Let me help you. Trust me, you want to help me. I don't completely know your part in all of this, but believe me, I know you were duped and sold a bill of goods. I'm your best bet."

"Can you really help me?" she whispered.

"Yes I can and I will," he continued to whisper. "But you better tell me what I want now, before the search warrant gets here."

"In the laundry closet. There is another closet with no shelves or anything next to the dryer. He's in there. There is no way out. But it's very inconspicuous and people usually don't see it."

She smiled again. As he rose up, Sarah grabbed his arm. "Please don't hurt him," she said.

Quentin Morales was an experienced agent. Many say he was born an agent. Though he liked that theory, he always gave credit to his years of experience. From the CIA to the FBI, he had strived to improve his craft year in and year out. Like a Michael Jordan or Magic Johnson ensured they worked on their game every summer, he tried to improve on his game every day. That was why Elliot Lucas loved him as an agent – he was the best at what he did.

Against the wishes of his partner, Damon Blake, he had Damon cuff Sarah and escort her outside. He wanted to deal with Lyle Hanscom himself. The heat was still too hot. Tensions were still high. His fellow agents from the Oklahoma City office and the local police department all wanted Lyle Hanscom. Too many of those outside the townhouse wanted him dead. But Q knew they needed him alive. Lyle Hanscom was truly a very small fish in a very big pond.

When he received the call from Julia, she told him everything he needed to know. Sarah McHartner was the head teller, who was probably involved with the security guard, Lyle Hanscom. He had been a security guard in ten of the banks that were robbed, dating back to 1982.

Yes, he was a small fish. But how small? Did he have valuable information or was he just a worm, bait if he ever got caught?

Sarah said the closet in the laundry room was small. How small, Q did not know. Though he was sure Lyle Hanscom was not much of a threat, he was a cautious man. Being cautious had done him well for almost forty years. No way was he going to abandon that for Hanscom.

He slowly opened the shuttered double doors of the laundry room. Then he positioned himself at an angle, where he could easily see the dryer and the closet door next to the dryer. His weapon was pulled and pointed at the door.

"Lyle! Lyle Hanscom!" Q called out. "This is Agent Morales of the FBI. Open the door slowly, put your weapon on the dryer and come out slowly."

Nothing.

"Lyle, don't have me act a fool!"

Nothing.

"Ok, asshole, let's do it this way!" Q fired his gun at the top of the closet door. Immediately, the door opened and a handgun was put on top of the dryer. Simultaneously, the front and back doors of the townhouse were knocked off their hinges by overzealous agents and policemen.

"Everyone stop!" Quentin shouted out. "Everything is ok!"

"We are coming in!" he heard someone yell.

"And I promise whoever comes in will be shot! By me!" Q did not take his eyes off the closet door. The door was slightly ajar. "Lyle, bring your ass out here. Believe me, no one crosses me. You will be safe in my hands . . . guaranteed."

Lyle Hanscom stepped out the door and slid behind the dryer. It was the only way he could close the closet door. After he closed the door, he looked at the man who was now his captor.

Before he could take another step, Q called out again. "Hold it right there. I don't play games, Lyle. I see the .38; now put the Glock on the dryer. If it takes more than three seconds, your ass is dead."

Lyle Hanscom put his right hand up and slowly reached around his back with his left hand and pulled out his security guard issued Glock 17.

"I guess you are going to shoot me now, Mr. FBI?" Lyle Hanscom asked.

"Not at all, I could have done that anytime I wanted to. Hell, I can still do that anytime I want to." Q smiled as he cuffed the man and slammed his face into one of the shuttered doors.

Chapter 25

FOR EVERY ACTUAL FACT in the National Capital Region, the name for the D.C. federal government area, they say there are at least ten rumors. For every ten rumors, at least five have some merit. For Julia Carson, she knew this was more true than false. Reviewing the videos of the bank robberies, one rumor jumped off the screen in every robbery and smacked her in the face. For every action, there is an equal and positive reaction. Her reaction was simple: to pick up the phone and call the man who verified rumors.

"Have a seat, Dale," Elliot offered the short, balding man. When they shook hands, Elliot's huge hand swallowed the small hand of Dale Lippett, the Deputy Under Secretary of Domestic Finance of the Department of Treasury. It was a great title for a complex job — he had day-to-day responsibility for the country's Federal Reserve.

"Elliot, I had the understanding it would just be you and I," Dale Lippett responded. Dale looked at Julia out of the corner of his eye. He knew why he was summoned to the office of the Deputy Director of the FBI. He often wondered why his predecessors had never been summoned to this office or the Director's office.

"You know my executive assistant and analyst, Julia Carson. She is heading the bank robbery portion of this investigation. She and I are the only two you will brief. Nothing you say will leave this room."

The trepidation held fast on Dale's face. He owed Elliot, owed him his career to be exact. He was always a fast burner. He made bank president at age 27, held CFO positions at three major corporations by age 35 and was the youngest person ever to be selected for an executive director's position. It was then when his weakness caught up with him.

An intelligent man who considered himself unattractive, his fetish of choice was ladies of the night. He didn't have the confidence to approach women on his level. Women of the night became his preference. Why go through the stress and embarrassment of always being turned down when he could simply pay for it?

He never thought he would fall for a lady of the night. But Tyla Buford was no ordinary prostitute. She was a couple of inches taller than his short five six frame, but she loved wearing her three to four inch heels. He actually picked her up near the pier in Baltimore. Who would have thought his one night would end up being a year and two months?

He loved everything about Tyla; from her beautiful bronze skin to her long legs to her nice smile and pleasant attitude. She became his savior. In his mind, she was a woman who made him feel special. And for that, he couldn't see or imagine her as a prostitute. He never understood why she did what she did. But he didn't care. He was just grateful she cared about him and decided to take him up on his offer to only serve him and not walk the streets of Baltimore.

When she came up dead in the home he bought for her, he called the Baltimore FBI Chief, Elliot Lucas. Elliot kept his name out of the investigation, thus, keeping his career in tact. He owed the man and there was nothing in the world he wouldn't do for him.

He missed Tyla. Looking at Julia Carson, she reminded him of his Tyla. Yes, he owed Elliot.

"Elliot, we never had this discussion."

The two men looked at each other and Elliot smiled.

Dale began, "Years ago in the 1940s, President Truman established a system to horde money for the war effort, if we needed it. It became known as the 'Rainy Day Fund.' It was decided that only three people would be briefed on the transaction: the Vice President, Secretary of the Treasury and the Assistant to the Executive Director of the Treasury, which is now the Under Secretary of Domestic Finance, my boss. Of course, the original plans didn't fare well because of a gentleman named J. Edgar Hoover. He became the fourth person to be briefed on the 'Rainy Day Fund.' Anyway, over the years, things changed. Only certain people were briefed on the Fund. At least ten cabinet members are briefed today, including your boss.

"But the way it worked initially was the government selected one bank in each state to deposit money. The amount of the transaction was only known to three people: the VP, Secretary of the Treasury, and the Assistant to the Executive Director. Today, those same three positions are still briefed on the amount of the deposits.

"The number of banks has increased to at least two per state, all in the capital city. Where we used to have ten former agents to make the deposits, we now have at least twenty-five agents. Most are former agents but all retired from the government. As you probably know, the deposit is made right as the bank's vault is opening and consists of packages in brown wrapping paper. Very nondescript in nature; nothing special about them. Believe it or not, many people think they are just dropping off copier paper or something like office supplies.

"All of the deposits are handled by the head teller, along with the bank president, they are the only two people per bank who know what's going on."

"Hold up, Dale," Elliot interrupted. "Why you refer to the transactions as deposits?"

"Because that's what they are, sir," Julia answered as she got a whimsical look from Dale Lippett. "Simple math. Put the money in a low to medium risk, set rate money market or certificate of deposit, sit back and watch your money grow. If the market is booming, take the risk and invest in high risk stocks or funds. Is that right, Mr. Lippett?"

Dale smiled at Julia, while nodding his head in the affirmative. "Smart lady you are, Miss Carson."

"Why make the deposits in person, Dale?" Elliot intervened. "Hell, it's a new millennium. We live in a world of technology, computers and what not. Why not make an electronic transfer to these banks?"

Elliot liked Dale Lippett. He knew the man was a talker and a whiz in the world of finances. Undoubtedly, he was a very good man but a lonely man. He lacked confidence on a social level but more than made up for it on a professional level. In a roundabout way, they were acquaintances now, both professionally and socially. Before he called Dale, he made sure he cleared his calendar to give Dale time to elaborate.

"Care to answer, Miss Carson?" Dale said in jest.

"Sure, I'll give a try," Julia replied, with a deadpan look on her face. "First, the money is not directly coming from Treasury. It's probably money from drug busts or other illegal transactions that the government confiscated. If the money did come from Treasury, it probably came from a slush fund no one knows about or from the old money that will eventually be burned. The idea is to get it and deposit it before it is officially thought of as old money."

Dale Lippett's smile grew wider. To him, this was foreplay. He knew Julia Carson was married and who she was married to. But it always thrilled him to talk to a pretty lady who knew about money, and not just spending it.

"That was excellent, Miss Carson. Thanks for relaying to Elliot what I'm sure he already knew." Dale looked at Elliot. He was enjoying the banter between he and Julia. He was relaxed. He knew why he was here. History was one thing, getting to the good stuff was another. The stuff Elliot really wanted to know. The stuff he shouldn't tell, but it was Elliot.

"Elliot, we all know what you want to know. I truly cannot tell you how much money each transaction is or how much money has been stolen. I wish I could, but truthfully, I just don't know. If you asked my boss or the Secretary of Treasury, they don't know either."

"All the banks that were hit, they had federal deposits minutes prior to getting hit?" Elliot asked.

"Yes they did," Julia answered before Dale could.

"Dating back to '82, Dale, how much you guesstimate has been stolen?"

"Between fifty and sixty million," Dale quickly blurted out.

"Why no concern at Treasury or even the White House, Mr. Lippett?" Julia asked.

"Remember, Julia, this money doesn't exist," Elliot added. "Deniable plausibility. If the money disappeared, no big deal, it never existed. The only way a lost or missing transaction was important, was if one of the transporters walked away with it. And even then, the money wasn't important, finding the transporter was."

"Like I said, Elliot, why bring me over when you probably know more than I do about this?"

Elliot smiled now. "Because Dale," he stated as he got up, walked around his desk and stood directly in front of Dale Lippett. "This is about more than killing agents. It's also about ripping off the United States of America. The two go hand in hand. These hate groups; I'm going to get them. But I want the men behind the scenes. Each and every one of them. And you are going to lead me to them. I want the name of every bank that's a part of the Rainy Day Fund, the name of every bank that has been hit thus far, plus the names of every head teller, bank president and who made the drop-off, deposit or whatever you called it."

Chapter
26

QUENTIN DIDN'T LIKE HIS predicament. He felt like he was burning the candle at both ends, but this was a short day compared to what he was used to. When he walked Lyle Hanscom to his car, he was met by rowdy Oklahoma City police and detectives including the chief of police. To make matters worst, the local and national media had also shown up. And that was the good part.

The distance from the front door of Sarah McHartner's townhouse to his sedan parked on the curve was at least twenty yards. This had to be the longest twenty yards he had ever walked. He had afforded Hanscom the same courtesy he ensured Damon Blake afforded Sarah — a coat over his head.

Q didn't respond to the heckling police force. He played it cool. When he reached the car and opened the back door, an officer in uniform roughly grabbed for Hanscom and Q did what he supposed to do. He swung a backhand and connected with the officer's face. He then pushed Hanscom into the back seat and when the officer attacked him a second time, Q grabbed him by the back of his head and smashed his head into the sedan's passenger window.

It all happened so fast. He wondered where his partner, Damon, was during the commotion. But it seemed as though time had stopped. Then he felt a hand on his shoulder and when he swung back around, he saw it was Jonah Turner, the chief of the Oklahoma City FBI office. He asked Q to take it easy, get in the car and drive off. Q knew Jonah. As he drove off with Jonah in the passenger seat, he noticed the officer getting assistance, the remainder of the police force still screaming and yelling, and unfortunately, the cameras rolling.

"Heard you have had a very interesting day." Q had to smile because he knew the man on his cell phone making the comment was smiling — his boss, Deputy Director Elliot Lucas.

"Yes, sir, one helluva day indeed. I'm sure you have seen the news footage."

"Yes, I have. Don't worry about it. We will deal with the aftermath after this case is over. Right now, I have calmed down the big dogs. Director Tellis wanted your head on a platter but he'll wait. I heard President Cabot wants you taken to the gallows but he will wait, too. Good news though. After the officer received his twenty or more stitches, I had him arrested for impeding a federal investigation. Give the media something more to talk about. It also gives us more uninterrupted time to do our investigation. Have you had a chance to talk to Mr. Hanscom, yet?"

"Yes, sir. I was waiting on Julia to call."

"Well, she's here with me. Start your report now."

"He was only able to tell me about the bank robberies. Julia was right. Linus "Demon Dog" Cummings is the leader and the person who planned all of the bank robberies. Interestingly, Hanscom only knew the man by his first name, Linus, and his nickname, Demon Dog. Though he has known the man for 25 years, he didn't know his whole name. But Demon Dog did all of the planning from start to finish. He has at least eleven guys on his payroll that skips over the country performing guard duty. He has the guys get a job with the bank at least three to six weeks before they hit it. They use a different alias every job.

"Lyle Hanscom, who real name is Potsie Lyles, is one of four guys who have been with the group for the past 23 years. Four of the other seven guys have been with them since '93, and the last three guys are new. He provided me with at least five of the guys' names. I have already sent

Julia an e-mail with the names, plus some additional information."

"Good deal," Elliot responded. "Talk to me about Miss Sarah McHartner."

"Unfortunately, sir, not sure what to tell you. I had a very good rapport with Miss McHartner, but something happened between our last conversation and Damon transporting her to the office. As soon as I approached her, she asked for an attorney and has refused to answer any questions without an attorney present. I was thinking of giving her a little time before I approach her again."

"You talk to Damon?"

The pause over the speakerphone was magnified. Immediately, both Elliot and Julia knew something was wrong.

"Damon has disappeared. He brought Sarah McHartner in probably five minutes before we arrived with Potsie Lyles; which is also not understandable. Jonah Turner told me he left a good twenty to thirty minutes before we left McHartner's townhouse. He should have been here probably thirty minutes before us."

"I know you promised Miss McHartner you would help her, but let her know all deals are off if she doesn't start talking. I want to know what Damon said to her. If she doesn't cooperate, tell her she will be tried for murder. Not accessory to murder, but first degree murder and we will be going for the death penalty."

Chapter 27

I WAS CALLED INTO a meeting with Elliot, my new associate, Bobby Small, Jr. and an old friend, Lewis Burling III. Seeing Lewis surprised me. If you saw his resume, you would probably say he couldn't keep a job. He had stints with the State Department, FBI, CIA, Senate Investigative Committee and now the Secret Service. Every job was a step up and he was personally requested from the top man in each organization. Yes, he was personally requested by President Cabot to serve on the White House's Secret Service staff.

It was a long day that was getting longer. I knew the day had been long for Elliot. He took it on himself to call every agent's family that had died that day and delivered the condolences of the Bureau, the White House and himself. Elliot was hard but a compassionate man. This case was indeed personal for him. His employees and former counterparts were dying; people he had worked side by side with, others he had hired and some he had personally groomed and trained. Additionally, they say possession is nine-tenths of the law. Elliot had claimed the Bureau as his own and his FBI was being attacked. How much more personal could it get?

"I think we all know each other, so no sense in wasting time or words. You three probably noticed you all have something in common."

Lewis, Bobby and I looked at each other. Maybe it was as obvious as the tips of our noses but evidently, we didn't have a clue. Lewis, the smart ass in the group, couldn't help himself.

"Ok, looking at the other guys, it couldn't be that we are all African-American." Everyone smiled except Elliot, which immediately translated to the rest of us cutting our laughter short.

"None of you are agents with the Bureau. No offense, KC, though you turned in your badge and I still haven't gotten around to completing your paperwork or destroying your badge, you haven't been around to say you are one of us. With that said, I need your help."

Elliot looked at us individually. He was in his signature position; right elbow on the arm of his chair and the right side of his face and chin in the palm of his big right hand. He was sitting at his desk and we were sitting in three chairs in front of his desk. He was the leader and we were his minions.

"KC, to bring you up to speed, both Bobby and Lewis have been working for the Bureau and reporting directly to me. Bobby, as you know, has been trying to get a handle on the groups and members who make up *Just Cause*. Lewis on the other hand has been trying to track down who in the Bureau is assisting *Just Cause*."

I looked at Elliot and then at both Bobby and Lewis. Being in the far right chair, I didn't have to turn my head to see the both of them. It was still hard for me to process that someone we might have known or have worked with was betraying us. Julia had planted the seed on several occasions but the phone caller had validated the nightmare. It was still hard for me to process that those I worked side by side with could possibly be involved in such betrayal.

"I want you to know this because we are about to enter an ugly world you may not be able to handle. What I need is someone who can deal with the ugliness. I need the old KC. I don't need your old baggage. And I apologize for doing this in front of Bobby and Lewis, but it is what it is, KC. Are you with me or would you like to work on another part of the case?"

I didn't hesitate to answer. "I'm with you, Elliot." No other words were required.

"Sounds good. Lewis tell us what you have."

"Rick Peoples is dead. We haven't found the body yet, but we think it is probably buried in a wooded area off I-95 South, probably not too far from Quantico or where he lived. He hasn't been heard from since the football game at your place, KC, which I did not receive an invite to this year." I smiled at Lewis's comedic comment.

"Unfortunately, my man I had on him got to his house as whoever abducted him was driving away. The garage was opened and after my man conducted a quick investigation, he tried to pick up the trail, but was unsuccessful."

"Was Rick working undercover?" I asked.

"No," Lewis answered. "Rick Peoples was probably the top source, i.e., the leader within the Bureau. I am sure he is also the one who turned off your alarms and ordered the hit on your family."

"What the hell!" I was flabbergasted. I had known Rick Peoples ever since I joined the Bureau. We had worked on several cases together. I had worked with his two sons on football. One was in senior high school and his youngest son was in middle school. Additionally, he was a member of the secretive Section H, the Hot Squad.

"How do you know and why do you think he's buried in a wooded area off I-95?" I asked.

"My man who was following Rick Peoples lost his trail several times in wooded areas down I-95 South," Lewis answered. "He had to keep his cover and only tried once to actually go in the woods, but within a couple of minutes he was lost. He was sure Rick knew he was being followed, so he backed out. Good thing he did. Within a minute or two, several other people had entered the woods."

"Why don't we have the folks at Quantico search the woods down that way?" I asked.

"I just ordered our folks at Quantico to get on it ASAP," Elliot responded. "The Marine Corp at Quantico Base will also be assisting."

"What about his partner, Damon Blake?" I asked.

"Thus far, Rick Peoples is the only confirmed member of *Just Cause*," Lewis replied. "I am sure there are others but we don't know who they are as of now."

"I think that's confirmed now," Elliot added. "Damon was investigating the bank robbery and murders in Oklahoma City when he up and disappeared in the middle of the investigation. We don't know where he disappeared to and we don't have the manpower or time to look for him. But the tapes confirmed he left of his own accord."

Damon and Rick had been partners and good friends for years. It was hard for me to imagine Rick doing something like this without Damon knowing about it. And Elliot was right; his disappearance did confirm it in my mind. Hell, my mind was going crazy. Two men I liked and worked with, whom I had also invited to my home, around my family, and now, Melvin Clayton was in a hospital. What type of madness were we dealing with? Damon was a dead man if I saw him first. No questions asked.

Elliot leaned forward in his seat and directed his eyes solely on me. I knew he was about to school me. I knew why he brought me in this briefing. This was about damage control and making sure I was down with the team. He wanted me to know this was his case and not about vengeance on my part — and that was an important point. Revenge was deep in my soul—from the death of Steve to the attack on my home to the betrayal of associates. But I knew it was about teamwork and I was a part of the team.

"Keep your friends close and your enemies closer, KC. An age old cliché but oh so true. Quentin was watching Damon. But the job still needed to be done. In case you are wondering, that's how Damon was able to get away. When the time comes, we will handle our business. Now you know the rest of the story, son. Are you still on board?"

We will handle our business. Damn. Those words said it all. I know we will. I know I will.

"You damn right, I'm on board, Elliot. I'm fully on board."

Part II

The demon haunts me day in and day out. When I think I am rid of the demon, he reappears in full force. But the day will come when my demon will be gone. The monkey will not make a home on my back.

Chapter
28

MY MIND WAS BUSY. Once again, thoughts were dancing and playing havoc in my head. It had been three days since the bank robberies in Ohio and Oklahoma. The clock was ticking. We had 24 hours to meet the demands of our anonymous automated caller. If his demands were not met, we didn't know the repercussions or what destruction he would try to bestow on the former or present agents of the Bureau.

So many dynamics were involved in this case. During our meeting with Elliot, Q called in and told us about a conversation with a Miss Sarah McHartner. Elliot had told us a little bit about what was going on in Oklahoma City before the call, but Q went into more detail at Elliot's request. Evidently, Damon Blake had threatened Sarah McHartner in the name of *Just Cause*. He told her that her mother, father and sister would be killed if she said another word. But Q guaranteed her that her family would be safe and taken care of. She told him what she could, but Julia, Patrick and Brenda already knew the information she provided. However, she did provide us something we didn't have — the list of banks yet to be hit.

It was information that would help. We still had a tough deadline to deal with. Even without saying, I think everyone knew we weren't paying. The U.S.'s policy of not negotiating with terrorists was real. But the demand made us realize that we indeed were dealing with a no-shit agent. His 96-hour demand was a realistic demand. He understood the working of the system, the working of Uncle Sam. This was not some movie of the week or TV show demanding millions of dollars in an unreasonable amount of time. This was real world. Hell, even if someone kidnapped the President's wife, he shouldn't expect to get money sooner than 96 hours.

This was like no other case I had ever worked before. Elliot was in control, more than I had ever seen him take control before. My last case involved the death of his best friend, but I was the SAC and he let me take the lead. However, he was truly the man on this case.

The tension and intensity around the Bureau were unheard of. Many of us had been around some sticky situations before, but never like this. One day a car backfired and all of us hit the ground. Another moment, someone left a satchel by an elevator on one of the floors and the bomb squad was deployed within five minutes. While the building was evacuating and the poor guy was trying to get his satchel, he was thrown against the wall and treated like he was Theodore Kaczynski, the Unabomber. Good news: it was a false alarm; bad news: the satchel belonged to SEA Jim Hudlin. But that was the combination of tension and intensity within the confines of the Bureau. *We had the monkey on our backs and his scratches were deep, penetrating and painful.*

To make matters worse, the media was having a field day and eating up everything involving the FBI. Q's outburst in Oklahoma City gave credence to the media's speculation that we were involved in a case of cat and mouse, trying to catch a group that was killing agents and robbing banks. The day after the Columbus and Oklahoma City robberies, we had egg on our faces from a two-page story in every national newspaper across the U.S., from the USA Today to the Los Angeles Times. The story detailed the current events and the past events from 1982 and 1993.

I felt uncomfortable reading about the death of Scott Rooker, Bonner McGill and his team, and the attack on my family in Virginia Beach. Whomever we were dealing with was using the media like a five-dollar hooker and sadly, the public relations division of the Bureau validated no details of the story. Following that story, several others had circulated. Instead of being portrayed as the victims, we were being portrayed as a tight-lipped organization trying to hide something. Public opinion was being manipulated and the reputation of the Bureau was taking a beating for it.

Fortunately, I was able to take a quick trip to Virginia Beach to see the family. I wanted to melt when Steve and Devin raced out of the house and ran into my arms. It was special holding my two little men. Their mouths were on super speed as they tried to tell me everything that had occurred since we had last seen each other. Both Julia and I had made it a point to call every day we were gone, but I realized there is nothing like that comfort of being physically close. In the four hours I was there, I tried to talk to everyone, and received a detailed report from Howard and our security team on everything that had happened. Fortunately, the report was all of five minutes long. In all, it was a good trip. I hated leaving, but I had to check out Dr. Melvin Clayton before I left the area.

They say you can never pick your family, but you can pick your friends. So pick them wisely. It was safe to say Clayton and Quentin were like brothers to me. We were always there for each other, regardless of the circumstances. When I needed them, they came running. I always hoped it was a mutual thing when they needed me.

When I got to the hospital to see Clay, I learned he was in and out due to the medication he was receiving. He looked okay but the doctor said it would take a while before he was his old self. He still had to undergo physical therapy to regain full operational strength in his arm.

I was happy Gloria was by his side every minute of the day. She loved him and he loved her. Gloria and I talked for a few minutes before I had to make my way back to D.C., and she spent the time telling me how blessed she was to have Clayton back in her life. She said she would be lost if she lost him. I told her what she probably wanted to hear and needed to hear—*Clayton was not a quitter and he would be back in the saddle soon.*

We had made good progress during the three days since the robberies. Agents and Marines at Quantico had found Rick Peoples and six other bodies in several wooded areas between Dale City, Virginia and Quantico. Probably the biggest progress was made by Julia and her robbery detail. They had identified eleven members of the various groups who had posed as guards during the different robberies. Four of the eleven had survived the three crime sprees — a period of 23 years. And it was easy for them to blend because of their ages. Who would consider a 40- or 50-something year old security guard as a suspect?

Bobby Small, Jr. and his Southern House of Hatred WatchGroup had identified potential locations of the hate groups we knew about. Bobby's WatchGroup had comprehensive files on hundreds of hate and potential hate groups. More information than the FBI's recently formed National Gang Intelligence Center, which had information on all gangs that posed a threat to federal, state and local law enforcement units.

Now it was about timing, hitting them when they least expected it.

The same applied to the bank security guards. A guard named Potsie Lyles had supplied us with the names of several of the false guards. Everything was coming together, slowly but surely.

Elliot had assigned agents and some of my security specialists from CarsonOne to provide protection for a list of over 20 former agents, including Jay Joiner, Steve's best friend. Jay was shot years ago in the shoot-out when they almost captured *Just Cause* in '93. He was confined to a wheelchair, paralyzed from the waist down. I usually checked on him once a month or every other month. Because of everything that had been going on in my life, I had seen him only once over the past eight months: at our wedding. Unfortunately, I only had a quick minute or two to spend with him then.

I was still working with Bobby Small, Jr. and Lewis Burling III on finding the leaks in the Bureau as well as tracking the hate groups that made up *Just Cause*. We were looking good and making some progress. All of us had people working on the case. Bobby had his WatchGroup, Lewis had the Secret Service and I had my security specialists from CarsonOne. But none were as important as Miguel Bishop, a computer expert who occasionally worked for me.

Actually, computer virtuoso was probably a better description for Miguel. He was from my old neighborhood in Memphis. He and two of his friends had started their own computer company after graduating from college and took entrepreneurship to a different level. Due to Miguel's computer prowess, they had landed a contract with the Drug Enforcement Agency. Since drug dealers were smarter and more technologically advanced, Miguel was the hacker who wrote the program and broke into the dealers' computers.

Bobby, Lewis, Miguel and I were gathered in my computer room at the home building of CarsonOne Corporation. The computer room was comparable to the FBI's media room, but the computers were more advanced and the computer stations more refined. Miguel was the architect behind the room and personally oversaw the construction. He also put together each computer station and computer himself. He and Julia had a great relationship and she used the room a lot. Today, we were using the room to track the enemy.

"Damn it, KC, if you ever want to get rid of this young man, I can surely use his talents at the WatchGroup," Bobby complimented Miguel.

"Hey, he is his own man and has his own company. I'm sure you guys can do some business together. So what you doing?" I had just walked in from checking on other business in the building, which was located in downtown D.C., actually not too far from the Hoover Building.

"From the IP and e-mail addresses as well as the home and clubhouse addresses that Colonel Small provided, I should be able to enter through the back door of each IP address and you guys can have fun spying on whomever."

When it came to computers, everything was matter-of-fact for Miguel. He loved doing his thing and I loved the magic he created.

Lewis looked at me and I smiled. "Hey kid, can you translate that into English?"

"I'm sorry, Agent Burling. Every computer has an IP address, the Internet Protocol, which is the address assigned to every computer that has access to the Internet. What I am about to do is set-up a program that will constantly ping the different IP addresses. What the computer on the other end sees is someone trying to get in like another website, and it will log it as an attempt from another site. If that computer has a firewall or spy ware, it will be logged on as just another failed attempt. But it allows me to enter the back door through a hidden node or hidden spot, if you will."

"Hold on," Bobby interrupted. "I'm like Lewis now, English please."

We all smiled as Miguel explained as well as a computer virtuoso could. Miguel didn't look the part but he was a computer geek. He worked out and to my understanding was cool with the women, but like so many current professionals, he was glued to a keyboard, CPU and monitor. He continued his typing and I was amazed at his speed and concentration. I was a decent typist, probably able to type 40-50 words per minute, but Miguel had to be twice or thrice as good as me. I think we were all in awe of his computer prowess and I had seen it so many times before. But it didn't make a difference how many times I saw him; every time thrilled and amazed me.

Miguel continued to explain that every computer was considered a network and a network administrator could access any computer on that network; his program was set up to do the same thing. The hidden node was an entrance point to access that computer. He further explained that hidden node was not something the average Internet user knew anything about. They could understand that the firewall and spy ware protected them against viruses, pop-up blockers and spammers, but didn't understand that their computers were still accessible to hackers who could come in via the hidden nodes on their network.

Of course, Uncle Sam was probably the biggest user of hacking into computers via the FBI, CIA or other government agencies. But there were many other renegade hackers who were guns for hire — peddling their talents to the highest bidder to break into someone's computer or network. The amazing thing was I thought there were hundreds of thousands of hackers out there. But Miguel explained there were really only tens of thousands of hackers in the U.S. He also let us know that there were less than a hundred true hackers in the U.S. who could hack into a computer and no one would ever know he was there.

He put us at ease by explaining the constant pinging of the IP address allowed him to easily enter the hidden portal without detection. Additionally, the receiving computer's spy ware would just log the incoming pings as websites just trying to get entry. The average Internet user will just think their pop-up blocker was working as advertised.

Miguel told us it would take him several hours to completely finish everything he was doing. He was going to set-up a network of four computers for us to peruse the various systems we were gaining access to. In the long run, it was nice what he was trying to explain, but all we wanted to know was when we would have some viable data to look at.

I excused myself for the next several hours. I had scheduled a luncheon with my niece, Janessa, and I wanted to pop in on Jay Joiner and see how he was doing with his new security crew.

Chapter 29

I PARKED DOWN THE street from the Heavenly Burger Jook Joint, the location of my luncheon date with my niece, Janessa. I wanted to scope out the security team assigned to protect her. The only way Julia and I agreed to let her stay in D.C. was if she agreed to security protection. Surprisingly to me, she agreed without objection.

The Heavenly Burger was one of several restaurants we owned. Located in downtown D.C., it had become a favorite spot for many working in and visiting the downtown area. It was centrally located not too far from the Verizon Center, home of the Washington Wizards, and the theater district of D.C. I didn't expect trouble in this area. Since it was downtown and not too far from the national capitol region, it was well manned and patrolled by the D.C. Police Department, as well as Secret Service and State Department agents.

I immediately noticed a young brotha, probably in his mid- to late-twenties, about six five, well over two hundred fifty pounds, at the newspaper stand outside the restaurant. He was pretending to read the paper through the glass door. Leonard Hackett, my best bodyguard and a great physical security expert, was standing outside the door to the restaurant. He looked like a bodyguard providing protection for someone important inside the eatery.

Leonard and I had history.

When I initially went to the NFL, I tried out with the San Francisco 49ers as a defensive back and punt returner.

Leonard was in his fifth year. He was charismatic, flamboyant and the on-field leader for the team. He was also a character whose testosterone overflowed. During training camp, I made an immediate impact on the Bay Area media. Though I was not drafted by the 49ers, they saw me making an impact with the team. It was clearly evident Leonard did not like my preseason publicity and called himself hazing me in front of the team. Back in those days, I was a hothead out to make my own reputation as a great football player.

One day at practice, from throwing my helmet at me to intentionally running over me on numerous plays, Leonard tried his best to bait me into a fight. I kept walking away and in the NFL, that's a huge no-no. I thought the 49ers cut me on principle alone for not fighting Leonard. That same night, I woke Leonard up from his sleep and asked him to meet on the practice field. Leonard was six feet three inches tall and weighed over two hundred forty pounds. But I grew up boxing and fighting in Memphis.

We threw down and went at it for about fifteen minutes. When it was over, we were both beat and tired, and neither one of us could be a cover boy for GQ or any other magazine, including Sports Illustrated. Leonard asked me why I didn't fight him earlier at practice when it meant something. I told him I did fight him, when it meant something to me and not to others. He shook my hand and we had a mutual respect and understanding for each other ever since.

I was picked up by the team across the Bay, the Oakland Raiders, two days later and had a good career. Leonard had a good career until he started overindulging in drugs. That was Leonard or Leonardo the Terrible, as he was known throughout the league. When he did indulge in something, he always overdid it. Years later, when he had lost his family, was destitute and needed help, I and others came to his rescue and paid for his rehabilitation. When I started CarsonOne, he was one of my first employees.

I walked toward the restaurant and spotted two other bodyguards sitting in a car across the street. Though they saw me, they didn't acknowledge me, which was a sign of good bodyguards. Before I could say hello to Leonard, the young bodyguard stopped me by putting his hand on my chest.

"May I help you?" he asked.

I looked at him and I was surprised. Officially, Heavenly Burger was not open yet. But I did not like anyone putting their hands on me. Out of the corner of my eye, I saw Leonard about to grab his young charge, but I put my hand up to stop him.

"First, get your hand off me. Secondly, who in the hell are you?"

"No, who in the hell are you?" He still had his hand on me and I knew then he was about to be the recipient of something I didn't do often — fire someone in my employment.

"Didn't I tell you to get your hand off me?" I stated with attitude.

Before I could make the next move, Leonard moved in. "KC, this is Alfredo Williams, a security protection specialist with the company. He is on our detail. Alfredo, Mr. Carson."

The young charge changed his disposition. I was supposed to be impressed, but there was something about young Alfredo Williams I immediately did not like.

"Alfredo and Leonardo, the black Italian protectors." I smiled but inside I was pissed. I slipped pass the two bodyguards and went inside. Leonard knew me well and he knew I was pissed. He also knew we would be talking later about the new hire. I didn't do the hiring for the company, we had human resources personnel for that, but Julia and I always had the final say with security specialists. Something slipped through the cracks and I didn't like it. Or maybe, Julia didn't tell me about young Alfredo.

As soon as I saw Janessa, my smile became genuine. She was not in her usual gothic and dreary black. She was wearing a gray pants suit with a pink blouse. She really looked professional. I was proud of her. The more I looked at her, the more I thought she looked like her Aunt Alyse.

At the age of twenty-six, Janessa had brought fresh ideas to the company. CarsonOne's primary interest was safety, security and security systems. We specialized in providing security and safety consultation and systems to the federal government and many major corporations. Some of our clientele included the Departments of Defense, Interior and Treasury as well as many other government agencies. Like Miguel, she knew computer systems and business. She brought the newer innovations federal agencies were looking for, but her business savvy and maturity made her indispensable in the boardroom. Her learning curve was high and the faster it came, the faster she picked it up. She was an integral part of a great staff and Julia's absence did not affect the operations and dealings of the company.

Additionally, we owned other interests such as the Heavenly Burger, several other restaurants, a couple of parking garages in downtown D.C. and several housing subdivisions. We were a quiet company making a difference and a profit. Janessa was a prime player in our success. Her destiny was CEO one day, and one day soon.

We hugged and I kissed my niece on the cheek and put her at arms length as I looked at her.

"You are so wrong for that," she said with a smile. I felt good seeing her like this. She reminded me of the younger Janessa before her dad's death.

We sat down and I was enjoying and capturing the moment. She looked like a ray of sunshine versus the young girl in black waiting on Death to call her home.

"Who are you and what did you do to my niece?"

"Ok, we got jokes. Keep your day job, old man. Richard Pryor you're not."

"So young lady, how goes it?"

"Stop it right there, Uncle Kenny. You didn't want to have lunch for small talk. I know what's going on and I know you are concerned about me and my safety, but I also know you want something."

She was right. She had always been perceptive, even as a child. "Before we get to that, how is the detail working out?"

She looked outside at young Alfredo Williams and I didn't like what I saw. It was a look of attraction and I did not believe in fraternization within the company. Some might look at Julia and I as fraternizing when we were dating at the Bureau, but neither one of us were in a position to help the other move up in the company. Janessa was an executive and Alfredo was an employee.

Before she could say anything, I jumped in. "No, Janessa, it's not going to happen. He is your bodyguard, your employee. You are a part of management. It's not going to happen."

"Uncle Kenny, stop overreacting," she stated while slurping on a chocolate shake. "I know he is my bodyguard but I like him. He does make me feel safe and in case you haven't noticed, I am a woman now. Remember, I'm grown and I can make my own decisions."

"Yes, you can. And as your boss, I promise you I will fire you in a heartbeat if you guys date."

We looked at each other and she knew I was serious. She was my niece and I loved her to death, but like her aunt, she was hardheaded and stubborn. She was her own person but that was too dangerous for me. I knew her family history. Steve had a quick temper and Denise used to be a hothead. Unbelievably, they were a perfect match. Janessa had traits from both sides of her family, and when I looked at her, I also saw Alyse and her stubbornness.

"You know this whole corporate scene can be a drag," she complained.

"Yeah, I know."

"I know you. Don't fire Alfredo. I will be on my best behavior. He and Leonard work great together, plus Steve's friend, Jay Joiner, highly recommended him. I think he is Jay's nephew or cousin or something."

I looked outside at young Alfredo and he had Jay's height and deep brown complexion, but so did so many other African-Americans.

"I will think about it and talk to Leonard. You know Julia and I approve all security personnel, but for now, he's good. The primary reason I wanted to see you is to get something you may have that belonged to your dad. Your dad used to keep all of his notes in a journal. I know he used to keep his papers and a lot of junk in the garage at the old house. Denise said she didn't know what happened to all of that stuff after you guys moved."

Her disposition changed and I knew something was wrong.

"Yeah, I had Steve's papers and read some of his personal journals." She stopped and looked down at her milkshake, which was completely gone. Once again, I was worried about Janessa, which was situation normal since the death of her dad. I was even more worried now because she always referred to him as Daddy, now she was calling him by his first name.

"Talk to me, 'Nessa, what's wrong?"

"I wasn't Steve's daughter. Mom had an affair and Steve questioned if I was his child. I read his thoughts, in black and white, Uncle Kenny, and his writing made me sad. But I understood. He was hurt; he was betrayed. Good ole Denise, being Denise."

Even before the death of Steve, Denise and Janessa did not see eye to eye on anything. She was truly Steve's daughter, his daddy's girl. After Steve's death, her attitude changed. She got into the whole gothic scene of wearing all black garb, lipstick and makeup. But she maintained her high grade point average and in many ways grew up and stepped up to the plate. She became the person her brothers depended on, while Denise grieved and tried to find herself.

"'Nessa, don't believe that. Your dad was hurt when he thought your mother had an affair, but it was only momentarily. He never questioned your ancestry. He knew he was your dad and that your blood flowed Carson red just like the rest of us."

She had tears in her eyes. I sat next to her and handed her some napkins to dry her eyes. I pulled out a baby picture from my wallet.

"I don't know if you have ever seen this picture."

"I thought I had seen all of my baby pictures. I don't remember this one."

"You want it?"

"You don't mind?"

"No, not at all. Now tell me about the journals and the rest of the papers. Where are they?"

"I'm sorry, Uncle Kenny. I threw them away years ago. I didn't want to think of Steve that way. I wanted to remember him the way he was with me and the twins."

I wiped her tears away and hugged her. She put her head on my shoulder, still looking at the baby picture. We just sat for a little while, saying nothing.

She broke the silence when she said, "By the way, I saw your boy, Q, on TV the other night. Darn, I thought you were bad, but it must be that whole pack you run with." We both smiled.

"Okay, young lady, let me get a move on it," I said as I got up to leave. "You know that's a picture of your Aunt Alyse and not you. And I never want to hear you call your daddy Steve again." She looked at me with tears in her eyes. I kissed her forehead and we hugged.

When I left, it was nice seeing the pleasure on her face.

Chapter
30

EN ROUTE TO JAY'S house in Roslyn, Virginia, I still had thoughts of my visit with Janessa. I felt bad for her and even worse for Denise. I remembered the difficulties she and Steve went through. He moved out of their Springfield home and moved into an apartment in D.C. The two did not talk for six months until the birth of Janessa. One look at Janessa and Steve knew she was his child.

Though we talked numerous times during that period, Steve never completely opened up to me. Most of his personal thoughts and work notes on his cases were put in his journals. It was the first time I heard about the journals. If Steve had a problem, it was released through an entry in his many journals. Every case had its own section. I wanted those books. No, I needed those books.

When Denise told me she was sure Janessa had them, I knew we would be ten steps closer to solving this case. I was surprised and a little disappointed she didn't have them. But I understood.

But something else disturbed me. When I left, I noticed young Alfredo Williams checking us out. That didn't bode well with me. I didn't know Alfredo and in no way had any trust in him. I called Miguel and told him to make a point to find everything he could on our Mr. Alfredo Williams, security protection specialist.

Jay's residence was a modern, down-to-earth, state-of-the-art house and that was being modest. Though the house was only two floors, the staircase consisted of a wheelchair rail with a wheelchair attached to take him up and down the staircase. It also consisted of an elevator and hand controls for everything. His wheelchairs, one for upstairs and another for downstairs, were like the driver's side of a car, complete with controls, aircraft-type steering wheels, telephones, small televisions and stereo equipment. He even had a remote control system that commanded the stove, microwave and computer.

Since he had been paralyzed from the waist down twelve years ago, Jay had gone through six patient care providers before his current provider, Nancy Batiste, walked into his life. Nancy was in her early forties and a decent looking woman, but I didn't like her. She had a nasty attitude and I had never seen her without a somber look on her face. Her mother was Thai and her father was White, a former Marine. She seemed to dislike the world and racial epithets were a huge part of her vernacular.

But it didn't matter what I thought. Jay was crazy about her and that was all that counted. When I asked him why he liked her so, his only reply was that she was just so damn . . . He never finished his thought, just kept saying the same thing. I shook my head but I was happy as long as he was happy. If he liked it, I loved it.

Jay was in his backyard, playing putt-putt golf by himself. "Damn, old man, what does it take to get you to sit your old butt down?"

Jay didn't stop his putt. He stayed focused on his shot, never breaking his concentration. His backyard consisted of four holes spread throughout the yard. This was his golf course. The grass was a dark, crayon green and looked just as beautiful as any golf course. Several trees and a man-made three by six waterhole were placed around the yard to give Jay a challenge on his putt-putt course. Though he was handicapped, he was still a man of pride and believed in doing as much for himself as possible.

"Damn, Youngblood," he said after his putt, "haven't you seen the replays on SportsCenter or the Golf Channel of Tiger Woods getting pissed at someone in the crowd for making noise before he swung his club?"

We laughed, shook hands and hugged. Considering how Jay ended up in a wheelchair, you would think he would hate the world. But he didn't. I had never seen him without a smile on his face or in a bad mood. He once told me he didn't have time for feeling sorry or sad for himself. He knew he had lots to be sad about, but for whatever reason, he lived when those close to him died. He often joked that his middle name was "Fortunate." I preferred "Blessed."

Still, I felt bad at times when I looked at him. At six feet five, he was relegated to a wheelchair and his world now consisted of him living at a three-foot level on a daily basis. He was a man I was proud to know and be associated with. Not only was he Steve's best friend but he was there at the warehouse in Lorton when Steve died. He tried to comfort Steve while he himself was severely injured from being shot. Steve died in his arms.

Jay always told me I didn't owe him anything. But I wanted to be there for him, like he was there for my brother.

"What's wrong? Why you look like you are carrying the weight of the world on your shoulders?" Jay asked.

Jay often knew when I had something on my mind. From his wheelchair, he taught me the intricacies and the theories of investigating a case. He believed in thoroughness and details. He talked and I listened. If I didn't or he thought my mind was elsewhere, he would quit for the day and we would pick up the next day. No explanation, he would just say, "that's it." Many thought he was moody, but I thought he was a perfectionist and someone who valued his time. Whether I or anyone else didn't think a man in a wheelchair didn't have anything but time, the man in the wheelchair didn't feel that way. I accepted that.

"You know why I joined the Bureau, Jay. I always wanted to be in a position to find Steve's killer but I didn't want it to happen this way." I gave him a condensed version of all that had been happening lately from my perspective.

I continued on, "I never thought something like this would happen again. And this time, it's different. The media is all over it, the world knows what is going on and we have to watch our backs more than ever before. On top of that, its disheartening that it may actually be someone I work with who is behind all of this carnage. And Jay, I'm not mad, just kinda disappointed. People I believe in and have worked with for years may be betraying the Bureau. I don't understand. I don't get it. Who could be that damn sick?"

"Calm down. It's a calling, son, and you have the juice. You have the Midas touch, everything you touch turns to gold. From football to business to the Bureau, success is your middle name and you wear it well. Steve would be happy to have you on the case. Remember, always stay focused, and keep your mind and your eyes on the prize. People need you. Hell, I need you; I like this whole living thing."

We both laughed but Jay was right, people were counting on me and I wanted to deliver. I loved living, too, and I had a lot to live for.

"Thanks, Jay. I plan on seeing this through and putting an end to this once and for all. By the way, what's the story with your cousin or nephew, Alfredo?"

"I called Leonard Hackett and asked him to take him in and teach him some things. He has aspirations to be a bodyguard to the stars and your company is a starting place. So I hope you don't mind. You know he's a black belt in several of the arts and a gun enthusiast, too. I really think he is a good fit for you guys."

"No problem. Leonard is the best and will take care of him. By the way, how are the guards?"

"I don't need them, but as always, your overprotective butt is overreacting. I know Elliot wouldn't have assigned any agents to me unless you and that pretty wife of yours pressured him."

"Be serious, I didn't need to pressure Elliot. You are one of us and will always be one of us. Anyway, let me get back. I will probably be back as this case progresses and pick your brain on what happened back then."

He looked at me. We had talked a little bit about the warehouse scene, but every time, one of us would find something else to talk about.

"The *Cause*," he said and just shook his head. "Next time you come by, let's do this. I want you to catch these bastards. But be careful, son. I don't usually give criminals a lot of praise, but these bastards were the best we ever encountered. They knew our every move. It didn't dawn on us that it was an inside job. And unfortunately, after all of these damn years, these bastards are still running amok killing agents."

Chapter 31

BACK IN THE SADDLE again continuously replayed in her head. Julia was excited to be back in the Hoover Building, lending a hand, providing her expertise. She felt alive — euphoric. She loved her life with Kenny, Steve and Devin, but she missed the action of the Bureau.

Her position as Elliot's executive assistant and analyst filled the void of no longer being in the field, but in her mind, she had nothing. She missed her old world; the world that brought her satisfaction and resolution, and credence to her self-importance.

Julia had taken the lead on the bank robbery portion of the case. Elliot had unconditional trust in her. He needed someone to take control and be her own person. He didn't have time to coddle Brenda Pittman, so Julia was his woman. She knew every facet of the Bureau as well as how his mind worked. After all, she was Elliot Lucas-trained.

With the information Q had received from Potsie Lyles, aka Lyle Hanscom, and Sarah McHartner, Julia was able to piece together vital information from many of the robberies. Prior to Q's assistance, she had seven leads from New York to Los Angeles that led to dead ends. But this new information helped formulate a failsafe strategy.

Elliot's strategy included a series of raids: the first was a series of phony raids to give *Just Cause* a false sense of security. Only Elliot and Julia knew about the phony raids. The agents executing the warrants were not told of the deputy director's strategy. Elliot didn't know who to completely trust and who not to trust. He knew he did not have a wholesale coup on his hands. He had a good group of agents working for the Bureau. But as with everything, there were always a few rotten apples. But this time, he had plans on catching and weeding out every rotten apple. This was only the beginning of his strategy.

The second series of raids were to capture the guards who helped pull off the numerous bank robberies. These raids were the legitimate ones.

Julia patiently waited for the raids to begin. Her portable mobile radio, referred to as a *brick,* was her best friend. She, Brenda Pittman and Patrick Conroy were on their way to the Williamsburg, Virginia area. Their immediate task was to meet up with a team of agents from the southern Virginia regional office in the Norfolk area. Julia was the only one who knew their primary mission — to capture the organizer of the bank robberies, Linus "Demon Dog" Cummings.

Elliot had informed everyone, from his teams of agents to Director John Tellis of the initial raids. His game plan was simple: conduct a series of phony raids at ten locations throughout the U.S. He knew the locations were drug houses and gang hideouts. None of the locations were connected to *Just Cause.* The initiator of the raids knew that. He also knew he had a major leak within his organization — an insider or insiders feeding information to the leader of *Just Cause.*

7 p.m. Eastern Standard Time. Deputy Director Elliot Lucas had situated himself in the Bureau's command center as the initial raids began. One by one, the reports came in. One by one, the same report: drugs and guns were confiscated but no members of *Just Cause* were found. Elliot made his notifications. For those he notified, it was a moment of disappointment. For Elliot Lucas, it was only the beginning.

An hour later, Elliot was in his office ambitiously typing on his keyboard. He was focused. This was his baby. Thus far, everything had transpired as planned. He spent the next hour beating the keys and clicking his computer mouse. He was in and out of the Bureau's intranet and web directory gleaning information. The data he needed was primarily in his head but the Bureau's resources helped clarify it all. He leaned back and he knew he was ready.

He picked up the phone and let his fingers do the dialing. Five minutes and ten phone calls later, his next series of raids were in motion. This time, he didn't make any notifications. He personally selected his team leaders for this series of raids. His confidence was high. He knew the results would be good.

Ten successful raids and over seventy arrests later, there was only one more place to raid. Elliot called Julia and said one word, "Go."

It was midnight and Julia knew the word had spread throughout *Just Cause* that the FBI had failed in their attempts to capture anyone during the first series of raids. Before any calls could be made about the second series of raids, Elliot wanted to do one more. The raid that was the icing on the cake; the only one he really cared about.

The short street was located in a desolate part of Williamsburg, Virginia. Eight houses sat on both sides of the street. The house in question was tiny and had lights on throughout the residence. A car was parked in the small unpaved driveway, another was parked in front of the house and a third broken down vehicle was parked in the front yard. The house was surrounded by a metal, wire fence.

Julia was a creature of habit and experience. Elliot had always taught her to do her homework, to concentrate on the I in FBI. She had had the house staked out for several hours. She knew there were at least two pit bull dogs on the premises roaming between the front and back yards. Around ten o'clock, she had two steaks laced with a sleeping agent for animals thrown in the yards.

She knew at least five men and one female were in the house. Looking through her high-powered night vision X-ray laser scope, she knew two guys were in the living room, doing drugs and watching TV. Another guy was in the kitchen. One was in the bathroom and the female was in the only bedroom with the last of the bad players, Linus "Demon Dog" Cummings, the leader of the pack.

On this summer night, he was prime suspect #1 on the FBI's most wanted list.

She gave the order for her force of twelve agents to move in. Four agents were stationed in back while another six went through the front door. The last two agents stayed outside to ensure no one escaped.

When both the front and back doors were knocked in, the agents rushed in to the surprise of the residents. The two suspects in the living room and one in the kitchen were dumbfounded and gave up without a fight. The suspect in the bathroom was literally caught with his pants down. But Demon Dog and his girlfriend in the bedroom had no plans of giving up without a fight.

As soon as the door was kicked in, shots were rapidly fired from the bedroom and the barrage of bullets hit two agents who had rushed the bedroom. Julia gave the order for someone to get to the side of the house just in case they tried to escape through the window. Julia and Patrick squatted on opposite sides of the wall at the entrance to the short hallway that led to the bedroom. The rest of the suspects were already handcuffed and lying on the living room floor, being guarded by agents.

"Talk to me, Demon. Tell me what you want," Julia asked.

Demon Dog had been a security guard for numerous bank robberies the past 23 years, including the robberies in Phoenix and Columbia, South Carolina. With assistance from Q and Miguel Bishop, she had pinpointed Demon Dog as the organizer of the bank robberies in '93 as well as the most recent robberies. Through the identification of members of McKale's Army, the group that tried to kill her family, Julia had Miguel hack into the computers of the dead members. What he found were numerous e-mails referring to Demon Dog as the leader of a group called the Angels of Life and Liberty, and *Just Cause's* point man for their bank robberies.

From everything she read, Linus Cummings set the assignments for the guards and hate groups. She knew his history. She had read his dossier. His first run-in with the law was when he was twelve years old. Eight dogs had been stabbed to death in his Long Island, New York neighborhood, and he was found to be the culprit. He stayed in and out of the juvenile system until age 18. At the age of 20, he spent six months in prison for a string of break-ins in Wilmington, Delaware. While he was serving time, he started his group, the Angels of Life and Liberty. Though his dossier included a series of run-ins and incidents with the cops, none of them resulted in additional jail time.

"Demon, we can work this out. This doesn't have to end in blood. Tell me what you want. Talk to me, Linus."

"Oh, you know me, huh? Or you think you know me. Bitch, I don't go for that shit. Who you think you fucking with, some kindergarten lil' kid, Bitch? I be Demon Dog. I be calling the shots in this muthafucker."

Julia looked at Patrick and made hand figures, telling him to *hold on a minute, she had a plan.* She went in the living room and whispered something to one of the agents. The agent immediately went outside. As soon as he did, the pit bull in the front yard had awakened from his brief stupor and came running towards the agent and leapt. A bullet from Julia's gun killed the dog in mid-air.

"What was that, what happened? Talk to me, got damn it. Talk to me!" Demon Dog shouted repeatedly from the bedroom.

Julia threw a piece of paper to Patrick. After he read it, he looked at Julia and nodded his head in the affirmative.

Suddenly, bullets started firing from outside. The panes of the bedroom windows shattered. Julia and Patrick ran and dived in the bedroom, blazing shots from their FBI-issued Glock semi-automatic handguns.

After the smoke had cleared, Demon Dog's girlfriend lay in her own blood. She had been shot at least three times. Demon Dog was still alive. He had been shot in both shoulders and his left thigh. Julia stood over the assailant with her gun pointing at his head.

"Bad news for you, Mister Demon Dog; the agents were wearing vests. You did give them a good scare. I take my hat off to you."

She squatted down, picked up his .44 Magnum and MP5, and gave it to one of her agents. Looking at the hate group member and bank robber, she secretly admired her work. But in the back of her head, she knew it was just the beginning of things to come.

She looked at Patrick and he informed everyone to vacate the room. Everyone, in turn, looked at Julia and awaited her word.

"No," Julia responded. Though her comments were not directed at Patrick, she continued looking at him. "Call the medics and have both of them taken to the Fort Eustis medical facility. Make sure we have a couple of agents standing guard at Cummings' door until Agent Conroy and I get there in the morning. Only one guard is needed for the girlfriend."

Patrick walked off as Julia watched him depart.

Chapter
32

WHEN I ARRIVED BACK at CarsonOne, I wasn't prepared for what came next. Evidently, Miguel ran into problems hacking into the computer systems of some of the suspects. But being the computer geek he was, he didn't give up. A job that was supposed to take several hours ended up taking all day. By the time we were able to jump on the computers, it was past the dinner hour and a late day was only getting later.

The four of us, Lewis, Bobby, Miguel and I, jumped on our respective computers, read e-mails and searched file after file on too many systems to count. Many e-mails and files were about one thing: *hate*. I didn't think I could be amazed by the amount of hatred in this world. But as I read the many files and e-mails, it was very obvious the amount of *hate* in this world was unlimited. Besides Bobby, I don't think any of us could have even imagined the kind of hate we were reading. I wondered how the Colonel could deal with so much hatred on a daily basis.

It took over six hours but we finally found something — something big. It was e-mail traffic between someone named Joke and Ranger 1, a member of a group called the FBI Rangers. The handle, Ranger 1, probably implied he was the leader of the FBI Rangers.

From: Ranger1
To: Joke
Subject: Next Assignment

Boss, we're waiting on the next assignment. This is 2 easy...lol. You told us this would b hard work but I think u over judged your boys ☺. I see why this country is n the fucked up state it is n. Waiting on your orders.
Ranger 1

From: Joke
To: Ranger1
Subject: Ref: Next Assignment

Never underestimate your enemy. Be careful, these guys are the real deal. We were selective in the groups we chose and the agents, but make no mistake; we're going against the best. As you know, I have respect for these guys. Though I want to kill as many as possible to send a message, I know who I am dealing with. A Freudian slip and a gravestone may have your name on it.

As far as the fucks we have working for us, also be careful and know what you are dealing with. They will do as told but all have dreams of grandeur. They know not who they be fucking with and in the end; it may be best to off them all. Hate doing it but they are a detriment to our future plans.

Keep watching your back and be vigilant.
Joke

From: Ranger1
To: Joke
Subject: Ref: Ref: Next Assignment

Boss man, u worry 2 much. Let me do your worrying 4 u by doing what I do. We have your back, always have, always will. Like we got rid of the assholes before, we will get rid of the

assholes again except this time, we will get them all. U still didn't tell me when the next hit is. I say we surprise them again by hitting 3 banks at the same time and taking out more agents. I still can't believe these guys r so damn disorganized. Maybe your bitch really is worth a damn. She is a lot better than that damn RP guy.
Always vigilant
Ranger1

From: Joke
To: Ranger1
Subject: Ref: Ref: Ref: Next Assignment

Hold your horses, soldier. We will make a move soon. I need to get a handle on what's happening. My bitch as you call her ☺ is having problems getting free time. I'm not sure her cover is blown or if she is busy b/c of the investigation. Hopefully, I can reach her soon. I had to have DB taken care of. But I get paid to be careful and u get paid to be equally as careful.
Joke

We were all stunned. We found our leader of *Just Cause*. The Joke, aka the Boss, was swinging the big stick. We didn't have a real name for the Joke, but at least we knew more than we did before. Additionally, we learned that the Joke had a female agent on his payroll. That hurt. With the help of our fellow agents, someone was masterminding our destruction; their game plan was to kill as many agents as they possibly could. Immediately, we got on the phone and asked Elliot to come to CarsonOne. It didn't take him long to get there since he was spending limitless hours at the Bureau. I think he was actually spending the night there.

We were still in the computer room when he arrived. The room was bug free and tempest cleared. The walls and ceilings could not be penetrated for communication leaks and was very secure for speaking freely. Additionally, we swept for bugs. Elliot knew Miguel and knew he was a man who could be trusted to keep what was said within the walls of the room.

"Shit, do we have any idea who Joke is?" Elliot asked.

"No, sir," Miguel answered. "I have been having a hard time getting a beam on Joke's location. His system is one of six I haven't been able to break thus far."

"Well, I think we all know who RP and DB are," Elliot stated in jest. "Now we need to figure out who is the female agent. But believe me they are not the only three working against us. But it will all come out in the wash. How many systems have you broken into?"

"Thirty-seven out of forty-three," Miguel replied.

"Do you think the other six are government computers and that's why you're having a tough time breaking into their systems?"

"No, sir, I have broken into government computers before for the DEA. I actually think it may be a home or standalone PC connected to a government system and routed probably through twenty to a hundred routers. And a good number of those may be federal government systems, which makes it even harder to track."

"Hold on," I intervened. "Are you saying someone is connected to a federal government system like the FBI, CIA or even the White House without anyone knowing about it?"

"Yeah, that's what I'm saying."

Chapter 33

IT WAS AFTER FOUR in the morning and we were on the move. We all had been up for almost twenty-four hours and considering what we were going through, exhaustion was not an option. This was somewhat different for me. I didn't have Patrick, Q, Beth and Clay by my side. Though it felt funny, I felt honored being with the likes of Bobby Small, Jr., Lewis Burling III and of all people, the lead man himself, Deputy Director Elliot Lucas.

We had a total of 20 agents on this mission. We were after Ranger 1, the leader of the FBI Ranger group. Miguel worked hard to find the street addresses of the systems we were hacked into. To our surprise, Ranger 1's computer system led us to an address in Gaithersburg, Maryland, a location just a hop, skip and a jump from D.C.; a place less than an hour from the Bureau, especially during the wee hours of the morning.

We hit the Beltway and took I-270 to Gaithersburg. We had downloaded the directions and had been briefed by Elliot. It was a mass briefing via video teleconference. Elliot had orchestrated a multiple raid on nine locations throughout the U.S. — all happening simultaneously. Over 20 raids had happened earlier, half of them a smoke screen orchestrated by Elliot to set up the person they thought was behind the bank robberies. The other half had resulted in 70 or more arrests.

We were out for bear and Papa Bear's handle was Ranger 1. Neither Bobby and his WatchGroup nor anyone else had ever heard of the FBI Rangers. We didn't know if it was a new group or a group from the past. The only thing we knew about the Rangers was regarding Ranger 1 and tidbits of information we found via e-mail traffic. All of the Internet search engines came back with information on the Bureau. Something told us Ranger 1 was the right hand man of the man ultimately in charge. From reading the e-mails between him and the person called Joke, as well as e-mails between Ranger1 and other addressees, it sounded like Ranger 1 was the one issuing the orders he received from the Joke.

I wanted to meet the person who went by the handle Joke. Ranger 1 had referred to him as Boss or Boss man, which meant he was the man. For many reasons, he was probably laughing at us — from his moniker to the various crimes, he was having himself a big laugh. As ironic as his name was, Joke, he had reasons to laugh and declare us as a joke. It had been three decades, a total of 23 years, and he was not serving time in any Federal prison or anyone else's prison system. He had won twice before and we did not want to make it three times.

We were surprised as we slowly rolled into the Gaithersburg Arms Estate. It was a nice subdivision that sat in a secluded wooded area several miles from the I-370 exit. I looked at Elliot and I think he was the only one not surprised. It definitely takes all kinds, but this was one of the most affluent areas in the proximity of the nation's capital. Politicians, highly paid executives and attorneys, doctors, professional athletes, entertainers and many others with money to spare lived in the Gaithersburg Arms Estate. I was sure the cheapest home probably sold for two and a half million dollars.

The two security guards reluctantly let us pass after Deputy Director Lucas assured them he could arrange for them to spend time in his jail for several days for impeding a federal investigation. But I took my hat off to the security guards. They were sharp and ready. Like many of the estates or areas like this one, they hired the best people, usually state troopers, deputy sheriffs or local cops who were dedicated to the job and wanted to make extra money on the side.

Sometimes these jobs paid two or three times more than their regular jobs.

The Gaithersburg Arms Estate was huge and spacious. The front yards alone of many of the houses could fit a small mansion. We were fortunate our targeted house was not far from the estate entrance. We parked one house down from our intended destination, at the bottom of the small incline to the house. Immaculate would be the proper word to use for what we were looking at, even at five in the morning. Globe driveway lights ran on both sides of the long sprawling horseshoe driveway. The grass was a beautiful dark green with several nice rose bushes on each side of the huge porch, which included four white pillars that stood at least twenty to thirty feet tall. I wasn't sure who we were dealing with or if Miguel had made a mistake.

"Who lives here?" Lewis asked.

I turned on the pen light, but before I could answer, Elliot volunteered the information, "Dave and Carol Ball."

I thought about it and the name sounded familiar but I couldn't place it. Additionally, it was possible for Miguel to make a mistake. He had been up longer than us, traveling from Memphis to D.C. a couple of days ago at Julia's request. Since his arrival, he had been up continuously pecking at the keyboard and looking at the monitor. I knew his eyes and his body had to be tired. I was reluctant to suggest this hypothesis to Elliot, but as his subordinate, it was my job.

"You know, sir, Miguel could have made a mistake. I know they had programmed the sites to jump all over the map and it took Miguel a while to pinpoint the actual sites. Maybe he got it wrong."

"Do you really believe Miguel Bishop made a mistake, Carson, especially a mistake of this magnitude?"

He turned his head and looked at me. I think my eyes told him his answer. Tired or not, Miguel Bishop didn't make mistakes like this. I knew it, Elliot knew it.

"Dave Ball is an international corporate attorney for many of the huge conglomerates in the world and his wife, Carol, is the attorney to the politicians, including—"

"Former FBI Director Basil Dooling and current Secretary of State, Ian Bradley," Lewis completed Elliot's statement. He was the driver, Elliot was riding shotgun and Bobby was with me in the back seat of the FBI's black SUV. We were the lead vehicle in our convoy of six SUVs. No words were spoken for at least a couple of minutes. There were 19 followers waiting on their leader to make a decision. I was sure the agents in the other SUVs weren't certain what was going on. They didn't have the information we had. But looking at the houses we had passed getting to our destination, I was also sure they had an idea of what was going to happen.

I knew it was a tough decision. Dooling and Bradley were powerful men and both carried big sticks. I knew Dooling personally, just like many who had been with the Agency for ten years or more. He was the director in 1993 when the last attack occurred. Many agents with the Bureau questioned many of the decisions made during that case. This was too ironic. From the tension in the car, I knew we were all thinking the same thing.

"Carson, I ever tell you Steve and I used to team up on cases?"

The question was out of the blue from Elliot. My first thought was, *What in the hell did that have to do with the price of tea in China or this case?*

"No, I didn't know that. I know you guys were pretty cool with each other."

"Yeah, we were cool, but more importantly, I was his friend and mentor."

I was speechless. I didn't know what to say. It was good information but I didn't know why it was necessary to talk about it at this specific moment.

"I can remember this one case we were on," Elliot continued. "We were waiting in a car on our suspects to make a move and we were just talking. It was football season and I think it was that game against Detroit where you had two interceptions and a punt return for touchdowns." He turned his head and looked at me. I just stared at him as he turned back around.

"Your brother was proud of you. I remember telling him you had great instincts and would probably make a hell of an agent. But he shook his head and said no way; he said you were too pigheaded and believed in doing things your own way. I told him it sounded like the brothers were cut from the same cloth."

Lewis and Bobby both looked at me. I still didn't know what to say. There was a message Elliot was conveying but at that moment it was escaping me. Maybe the simple fact I, along with everyone else, was sleep depraved.

Elliot looked back again and I knew he was ready. We were ready. Miguel didn't make a mistake, we all knew it.

"Time to move, people. I will deal with the consequences later."

Elliot gave the word over the radio. As we got out of our vehicles and slowly made our way up the small incline, blinding lights suddenly turned on and two gates, one on each side of the house, swiftly opened. A total of four Hummers, two on each side, sped down both sides of the driveway with bullets blazing. We dived out of the line of fire but I knew several agents were hit. We returned fire but I was sure it was to no avail.

Bobby, Lewis and I started running after the Hummers and Bobby was the first to stop, squat and aim. We followed suit and we all had the same thought in mind, *shoot for the tires of the last vehicle.* As we continued our shooting, the last vehicle flipped over. We got up and started back running. I could hear footsteps behind us and knew we had more agents following our lead. As we got closer to the vehicle, the driver and a passenger in the back seat were getting out of the Hummer still trying to play the aggressor. We all hit the ground and returned fire. Within seconds, the two men were down — and out.

Bobby and I went to the far side of the vehicle and pulled the two remaining passengers out the right side. The one in the back seat was still unconscious, while the passenger riding shotgun was barely conscious.

"Get your hands off me, Nigger," he said to Bobby.

My first thought was that was a big mistake. Even before the thought completely formulated in my head, Bobby Small, Jr. had rapidly gotten off three or four good punches to the face of our big-mouth, stupid assailant.

The lighting was decent now. It was the latter part of August, still summer and fairly warm outside. "Bobby, take a look at your hand."

He looked down at the back of his hand and saw the black chalk on his knuckles. He looked at his assailant who was on the ground, lying on the side of the overturned vehicle. As we dragged both men safely away from the Hummer, we could plainly see both men were light-skinned African-Americans in black face.

Chapter
34

ONE OF THE FIRST things you learn in law enforcement was how to control a crime scene. Though we had three wounded, we still took control, and set up a perimeter around the house and downed vehicle. Elliot had already called the Bureau and other agents were transported by helicopter from D.C. He had also called in the Federal Marshals. They collaborated with the local Gaithersburg Police Department, which was providing assistance.

We each had our duties. Bobby and I had taken the two assailants up to the house. Elliot had directed a search of the whole house. He had wasted no time in entering and securing the house. He had Dave and Carol Ball in a room with an agent until he had time to question them. Lewis had taken two agents with him to procure the security guards at the gate, who we were sure not only alerted the Ball household that we were on our way up, but also made sure the two big wrought iron gates were opened for their escape.

Unfortunately, only one guard was left behind and he was shot in the back of the head. We had had a mental glitch in not accounting for the guards. We had no reason to suspect the guards. It made me wonder about the reach of *Just Cause. Who in the hell were we dealing with?*

I knew the residents of the Gaithersburg Arms Estate had never been invaded like this before — and it was invasive. We had ambulances to pick up our wounded agents, and at least two medical examiners and crime scene units were on the scene. Helicopters were touching and going. As soon as one hit the ground and dropped off some agents, another one would do the same. There was so much going on, it was hard to keep up, but Elliot had it all under control.

Rumors used to float around the Bureau about how Special Agent in Charge Elliot Lucas would work a case. He was said to be the best. Meticulous, organized and a stickler for details were synonymous with Elliot as a field agent. He was usually handpicked by the Bureau's or CIA's Director to work a case. They knew he would get the job done. I think that's why the Bureau and the *Company* had such a great current relationship. Seeing him in action on this case had me in awe. He was a man born to lead.

Elliot had told us the other locations had resulted in the arrest of over twenty assailants. However, none of the suspects were arrested in a grand house like the Balls. We were the honored ones to have hit the big cheese.

How big?

When we saw the private helicopter land and former FBI Director Basil Dooling get out, we knew the big cheese probably called the big rat as soon as the gate guard called the house.

Dooling retired from the FBI five years ago and from the looks of his belly, retirement fit him well. He was balding up top and what hair he had was completely gray. The man moved fast and those of us in the know knew why he was here. It was protection, cover-your-ass time.

I wondered why Elliot had not questioned the Balls, but something told me he had something up his sleeve. I wondered if he decided not to speak to them because he knew they would ask for their attorney, being attorneys themselves.

"Elliot, I need to talk to you if I could, please," Dooling stated as he shook Elliot's hand. The two men moved to an isolated spot, actually about ten feet away from us. We were standing in the driveway, directly in front of the house, while Elliot and Dooling stood directly in the doorway. Bobby, Lewis and I speculated on what was being said, but we all knew it was politics at its best.

Dooling was escorted to the study on the right side of the first floor of the two-story mansion of a house. Elliot was so calm, cool and collected, and I was trying my best not to get caught up in the madness and chaos.

Elliot and I had a hot and cold relationship. Sometimes I was his favorite lead agent and he was the boss I loved working for; other times, I think he wanted to wring my neck and I wanted to stay away from him. This day was different for me, I was seeing the man do what he did best — lead.

"Lewis, get in the SUV and monitor the conversation between Dooling and the Balls. KC and Bobby, I want you two interviewing the two we pulled from the Humvee. Carson, let me talk to you first." We walked over to a quiet spot in the huge foyer, while Bobby waited by the doorway.

"KC, the reason I wanted you on this team is because I have always loved the edge you brought to every case. Be yourself and stop holding back. I know you are overwhelmed: first, learning Julia's role in the Bureau and secondly, working with the likes of Colonel Small and Lewis Burling. But you have the badge, they defer to you. You don't defer to them. They are waiting on you to take control and be yourself. Get your ass in there in take control. Steve knew I was right; you have the instincts for this job. Stand up and be counted, son."

I didn't say anything. There were no words necessary. I knew what he wanted from me. Nothing special, just be myself.

After all, the Joke and his minions invited me to this party; they wanted me on this case. My family being attacked was a thought not too distant on my mind. Elliot was right, I had to stand up.

Bobby and I entered what we thought was a study on the left side of the first floor, but it was more like a family room. We relieved the agent, who asked to stay. I told him I didn't think it was good for his career. He understood. In some ways, Elliot had given me carte blanche to act a fool. I didn't have plans of overdoing it, but I went into the room knowing what I was going to do. However, my plan changed when I saw what the room had to offer, like the pool table and pool sticks.

Something one learns when dealing with power structures is positions. If four people are riding in a vehicle, most of the times the driver is the least important person or second important person in the power struggle. The shotgun position is usually the leader of the team or the most powerful person in the vehicle. In our case, that position belonged to Elliot. In the case of the four Hummers, the last of the four vehicles was the least important. But that didn't mean these guys did not have information that could have been helpful. We had the shotgun guy from the vehicle and his partner who sat behind him.

Both men were sitting on the sofa with both hands handcuffed behind their backs and shackles on their ankles. They could see my movements, which was what I wanted. I picked up a pool stick and did a couple of practice swings. I was smiling, actually laughing inside at the two. The black chalk had been removed from their faces. We could see the men behind the chalk. Whatever they had planned, they wanted whomever to think they were Black. Why, I did not know but I would soon.

The funny thing was they actually were Black. Their features were African-American. They were both light enough to be considered Caucasian, but at first glance, one immediately knew they were Black. They both had big wide noses and though their hair was wavy, you could tell it still had some kink to it. The looked so much alike, I was sure they were brothers.

"We want a lawyer," the shotgun guy volunteered. I took a couple more practice swings and moved in closer. I could see the fear in his partner's eyes. My strategy was simple as I swung the pool stick and hit the shotgun guy hard with the small part of the stick. The stick broke and the hit knocked our assailant off the sofa. This was the same guy Bobby had hit earlier. I picked him up by the neck and started to choke him with my left hand. Out of the corner of my eye, I saw his partner inching away as far as he could on the huge sofa. When I let go, his light-skinned complexion was a dark red.

"Nooo! You can't have an attorney," I added.

"You are crazy, mutha'fucker. You tryin' scare me. It's not working, bitch. Now get me my lawyer, mutha'fucker, and now!" I stepped away and smiled. "If I had these cuffs off, I would kick your ass."

I didn't have to look at Colonel Small, he read my mind. He unlocked his ankles first.

"What you doing?" the shotgun guy asked as he jerked his ankles away and tried to steadily move them to keep Bobby from unlocking his shackles.

"We are granting your wish," Bobby replied as he was able to calm the shotgun guy down and unlock his shackles.

"No, no sense in doing it. I'm not going to give you reason to kill me."

"We're going to kill you anyway. So you might as well fight back." Bobby knew exactly what to say. Neither one of these tough guys knew the one we wanted was the one we were not paying attention to.

Bobby had picked up the assailant, turned him around and unlocked the cuffs. As soon as he did, the knucklehead charged me and tried to tackle me. I moved out of the way, grabbed him by the back of his collar and slammed his head into the pool table. Then I picked him up and punched him in the nose. On impact, I knew it was broken. I grabbed him by his neck with my left hand and he reached back with his right hand and grabbed a pool ball. When he tried to hit me with it, I let his neck go, grabbed his wrist with my left hand and punched him in his right eye. I turned my back and then swung around with my right elbow, which connected with his chin. I moved away as he collapsed on his face.

"Now it's your turn." I turned my attention to his partner. It had been a while since I had seen fear like the fear in his eyes at that moment. I wasn't quite sure if this was what Elliot wanted from me, but I felt good. I felt like an agent again. I actually felt like I was the special agent in charge again.

Hell, this really felt good.

"I . . . I . . . I will tell you whatever you want to know."

"I know you will," I smiled.

Chapter 35

BOBBY, LEWIS AND I stood nearby as Deputy Director Elliot Lucas prepared to give an interview to CNN reporter Monica Houston. I knew Monica. She had worked her way up from a beat reporter to the top reporter for CNN, covering the Washington beat. She was everyone's favorite choice and had been for the last couple of years in D.C. She was able to get interviews from politicians and Washington insiders that many other reporters could not get. Every now and then, she would pop up with a CNN special report on something big in Washington or the world of politics. Not since Bernard Shaw or Ed Bradley, had an African-American made such an impact in the television media.

"Deputy Director Lucas, can you please tell us what happened this morning here at the Gaithersburg Arms Estate? Does this have anything to do with the attack on the FBI and its agents? And the numerous raids that have been reported throughout America yesterday and today by the FBI, are those also a part of your operation?"

Monica came across as charismatic and studious. Her onslaught of questions was smart. She had interviewed Elliot on several occasions and knew he was the type who preferred the questions up front so he could make his statement.

"Miss Houston, I have a statement that should answer all of your questions. It is true the Federal Bureau of Investigation has been under attack for the past couple of weeks. We have lost almost forty agents and local law enforcement officers around the country to death and many others have been seriously injured. But I want the families of these agents and officers to know we are going to bring their attackers to justice. Over the past twelve hours, we have arrested a great number of suspects throughout the country. Our operation today was a success. And we have no plans of letting up. You attack us, expect us to hit you back."

"Do you know who is responsible?"

"Yes, we do. The name of the group is *Just Cause*. The group is made up of various hate groups. These are homegrown terrorists. American born, on the same scale as a Timothy McVeigh."

"Are high-profile attorneys, Dave and Carol Ball, a part of the group *Just Cause*?"

"We have the Balls in custody for questioning. Presently, we don't know their involvement, but I want this to be a message to everyone out there. If you want to assist in the attack on the federal government, we will treat you like what you are: criminals, terrorists and a threat to the United States of America."

The four of us were in the SUV headed back to D.C. and the J. Edgar Hoover Building. I think Bobby, Lewis and I were still in shock from Elliot's comments. We were on the offensive but I didn't think anyone expected Elliot to tell the whole world our strategy. Truthfully, I didn't think any of us knew our official strategy. Whatever thoughts we did have I'm sure were discarded after Elliot's interview. There were three hours left before the 96 hour deadline imposed by the anonymous automated caller who was probably the leader of *Just Cause*. Could he possibly be the Joke? We didn't know and under Elliot's leadership, we weren't speculating. I got the feeling this was old news for retired Lieutenant Colonel Bobby Small, Jr. and Secret Service Agent Lewis Burling III. I was the only person in the dark.

We checked out the hidden video of the conversation between Dooling and the Balls. When former FBI Director Basil Dooling entered the room, he looked around and put his finger to his lips, telling Dave and Carol Ball to be quiet.

He walked around the room looking for the bugs we might have planted. He picked up a writing pad and pencil from the desk that sat in the study. He then walked over to the couple and sat in between the two of them on the small sofa. He wrote something on the pad and the couple both nodded their heads in the affirmative. This process continued for another ten minutes. No words spoken, just yes and no answers via movements of the Balls' heads in the negative or affirmative. Lastly, Dave Ball took the pad from Dooling and wrote something.

When he finished, Dooling took the pad back from Dave Ball and went over to the desk. He picked up a big eraser and started erasing the sheets on the pad. Then he put every sheet in the shredder behind the desk.

He was the former Director of the FBI and he knew procedures — never leave evidence. Dooling left without saying a word. The Balls were immediately taken into custody as terrorists, enemies of the state. Therefore, they weren't obligated to be provided with immediate counsel.

"Did the assailants talk?" Elliot asked.

Bobby laughed. "When you have some crazy motherfucker swinging a pool stick at you, you would probably sing like a canary too." Everybody laughed, including Elliot.

"The two assailants, Emmanuel and Eric Halston, belong to the FBI Rangers," I began. "There are sixteen members of the Rangers. The group was created two years ago. Only one person has seen the leader of *Just Cause*. That person is the Rangers' leader, Carmine Ball, the son of Dave and Carol Ball. Carmine is Ranger 1. Emmanuel told us the goal of the Rangers is to wreak havoc on the Bureau, because we are the true enemy of the United States. They wanted to send us a message."

"Message sent. Now feel *my* message." I had never seen Elliot this way but I liked it. At times, I thought Elliot was suffering from a state of melancholy. Other times I thought he was just being an asshole because he could. But something told me this Elliot was the real Elliot. The man who was always two or three steps ahead of his competition.

"Additionally, the Balls knew what the group was about. Emmanuel told us sometimes one or both parents would sit in on some of their conversations. The Rangers also participated in some bank robberies and at least half of the Rangers have military experience. Lastly, he didn't know Director Dooling."

"What's the deal with Dooling anyway?" Bobby asked.

Elliot let out a half-hearted sigh and shook his head. "I think my former boss knows something but I doubt we will ever find out what. However, I do plan on putting him on the spot."

Elliot's cell phone rang and he smiled when he answered.

"I will make a bee line to your office as soon as I hit the door of the building."

Chapter
36

IN SOME ASPECTS OF her life, Julia Carson considered herself at a crossroads. There was no doubt she loved KC and the boys but something was missing. At least, she thought something was missing. Maybe it was this case. Before the case, she was fine, everything was wonderful. KC had made a commitment and they were happy as a family. Or so she thought.

Since the attack in Virginia Beach, internally she had been awakened. Her past life had been stirred within and the echoes of Special Agent Julia McEntyre were awake and ready for action. After all, women like her and Denise were Jane Bond to 007's James Bond. For Halle Berry, it was a part in a movie; for her, it was her life.

She did the prudent thing and called the bodyguards at the Virginia Beach home. She notified them that she and Patrick would be stopping by.

It was past three in the morning and she was still wired. One of the bodyguards had breakfast and coffee waiting for her and Patrick. They needed something to eat. It calmed them both down. Eating and being in a familiar place was a much-needed distraction. For Julia, it simmered her thoughts and eased her mind.

Before checking on Steve and Devin, she looked in on her father-in-law, Howard Carson, and her nephews, Jerald and Jarrod. Looking at Howard, she wondered how he felt losing his wives and children — people he probably loved. She also wondered how it felt to have his only son not love him as a father or person. Kenny could be a hard man, but it was hard for her to feel bad for Howard. She was not crazy about any man who refused to accept his responsibility as a man. But she wanted to hear his story one day; she knew there were always two sides to every story.

Her body was tired and she knew she needed at least a couple hours of sleep.

Checking in on her boys, she kissed them both as she smiled at them in their bunk beds. Devin was on the top bunk and Steve was on the bottom. She remembered when they bought the bunk beds. Just like any mother, she was afraid the top bunk might have fallen on the bottom. So she and Kenny gave it the *jump up and down* test, making love on the top bunk. When the bed held up, she felt comfortable.

Maybe that was her problem — she needed to make love to her husband. She laughed at the thought as sleep called her name.

Before sitting next to Steve's bed on the lower bunk and lying her head down on his mattress, she straightened Devin in bed and unfurled the covers he had kicked off himself. She would never understand how he started with his head on the pillow at the head of the bed and several hours later, his body was completely turned around. She smiled at the thought. She also had to pick up Steve's cover and put it back on him.

The last thought she remembered was about the sleep patterns of her kids. When she awakened several hours later, both boys' heads were lying on her thighs. She remembered Kenny once telling her, *Life is a song worth singing, a dream worth dreaming, a moment worth saving.* Stroking the heads of two of the people she loved most in the world, this was her song, dream and moment.

In a flash, she knew why she was doing what she was doing. It wasn't about saving the world and revenging fellow agents, it was about criminals attacking her family, the people she loved most in the world.

Linus "Demon Dog" Cummings was taken to the medical facility at Fort Eustis, the home of the U.S. Army

Transportation Corp. He was secured in a private room with four agents standing guard. Three of the agents were on the outside. Brenda Pittman was the only one inside the room.

As Julia and Patrick entered the hospital room, Brenda was surprised to see them. Julia wasted no time asking the obvious question. "What's going on?"

Both Demon Dog and Brenda were uncomfortable. It was obvious they had been conversing but Julia wasn't sure it was just a conversation between agent and suspect.

"Nothing," Brenda answered. "Mr. Demon Dog and I were just having a disagreement."

Patrick and Julia looked at each other. Julia whispered in Patrick's ear and stared hard at him. She asked him if he understood. He shook his head in the affirmative. She then signaled Brenda to come outside with her.

"What's going on, Brenda?" Julia asked as they stood in the hallway, away from the other guards.

"Nothing," Brenda responded. "I don't think he knows anything worthwhile. I have been trying to get him to talk for the past couple of hours. He told me a little bit but not much. He has never met the leader of *Just Cause*. However, he is the one responsible for planning the bank robberies. But he had nothing to do with the killings."

Julia continuously nodded her head. She didn't believe Brenda. Something wasn't right but she didn't know what. *Is Brenda working with Just Cause?* It was a thought that kept repeating in her mind. She wasn't ready for this. But she wasn't sure either.

"Ok, you guys are relieved," Julia stated to Brenda and the other agents.

"I think I should be in there with you and Patrick," Brenda said matter-of-factly as she walked towards Linus Cummings's room.

Julia grabbed her arm. "No! Thanks but no thanks, Brenda. You are relieved of duty."

Brenda's eyes were on Julia's hand around her arm. She raised her eyes to meet Julia. Julia did not let her arm go. One of the agents walked over to run interference.

"Back off, Walkens," Julia said. The agent backed away.

Julia let Brenda go and suddenly drew her gun and thrust it in Brenda's mouth as she forced her to the wall. "Are you a part of *Just Cause*, bitch?"

Brenda was stunned. Her mouth was bleeding and she didn't know what to say. She knew she needed to say something, but this was unexpected.

"Answer me, bitch! Are you a part of *Just Cause*?" Julia was loud but she was under control. She reached in Brenda's jacket and took her FBI-issued Glock. She handed the weapon to Walkens, who took a couple of steps back.

Brenda began to shake and weep. "I . . . I . . . I . . . don't know anything," she sobbed loudly.

"Bitch, answer my fucking question, or is God as my witness, I will blow your ass away!"

Sometimes, the world can be explosive and run at the speed of a bullet. Julia's focus was on Brenda. She saw the door swing open out of her peripheral vision, then she grabbed Brenda by the hair, swung around and the familiar sound of Glock weapons filled the hallway.

When the smoke had cleared, Agent Hank Walkens lay dead on the floor. The gun he had received from Julia was the same gun he used to try and kill her.

"Thanks, Patrick. But you know I had this, right?" she smiled as she and Patrick looked at each other. He too had a smile on his face.

"Brenda Pittman, you are under arrest for being a traitor to your country. Deadbrook, read this bitch her rights," Julia ordered one of the other agents. "Shoot her ass if she moves or says a word. If the bitch sneezes, shoot her."

Chapter 37

LINUS CUMMINGS REMEMBERED THE day like it was yesterday — the day "Demon Dog" was born. He was twelve years old and the gang that wanted him to join, the Island Warlords, challenged him. If he could walk a quarter mile through his neighborhood without being bitten by the gang's eight dogs, he would be a member. Linus did not intend to join a gang. But even at age twelve, he was ruthless and unrelenting. *A daredevil.* That was his challenge.

He took off running from his starting point, more ready than the gang members knew. Unbeknownst to them, he had two six-inch kitchen knives on his person. When he reached his final destination, to the dismay of the gang members, all of the dogs were dead. Linus was dripping in dog blood. The first six dogs attacked him and he made them pay. The last two were afraid and ran away from him. He actually caught the dogs and stabbed them to death.

One of the gang members called him a demon. From that day on, he called himself, *Demon Dog.* Though he never officially joined the Island Warlords, he was the leader of the gang. A gang who embraced him out of fear. And who wouldn't fear a demon who killed eight vicious dogs with two common kitchen knives.

"Mr. Cummings, or do you prefer Demon Dog?" Julia asked. The man did not answer but it didn't deter Julia from proceeding with her introduction and interrogation. "I am Special Agent Julia Carson and I think you know Special Agent Patrick Conroy."

Patrick had actually interviewed Linus Cummings, security guard of the Second American Bank of Arizona in Phoenix. He told Patrick he had been working for the bank for two months and the bank robbers completely surprised him. He gave Patrick no reason to suspect him. Additionally, his record checked out. Of course, it was the record of Luis Montalez.

"We have some questions for you. Unfortunately, I am pressed for time, so your cooperation will go a long way in helping us out."

Linus finally looked at Julia, then at Patrick. He was uncovered lying on the hospital bed. Both of his shoulders and his thigh were heavily bandaged. He laid flat on his back. Both wrists and ankles were cuffed to the bed side rails. Initially, the man didn't speak; just rolled his eyes as he turned his head away.

"What happened outside in the hallway?" he asked as he continued to look at the wall.

"We were just target practicing, so when we let you escape, we can hone in on you," Julia replied.

"Fuck you, bitch!"

Patrick grabbed the man by the throat. Julia walked around to the other side of the bed to look at the face of Linus Cummings. She cleared her throat and Patrick let go.

Linus coughed hard, trying to catch his breath. He continuously gagged and tried clearing his throat. Patrick picked up a glass of water and was about to throw the water in his face when Julia shook her head no.

"Mr. Cummings, it's been a long week and quite frankly, I'm tired," Julia stated. "You just don't know how tired I am. And I'm really having a huge dilemma here. On one hand, I'm assigned to question you and get answers. On the other hand, Special Agent Conroy is a dear friend and I don't know how many times he saved my husband's life, but he wants to kill you. Or at least, beat the shit out of you. And you know what; it's hard as hell for me to stop him."

The comment made Linus look up with a sneer on his face. "Bitch, first, you think I give a damn about you being tired! You shot me, ho! If I wasn't handcuffed, I would kick your black ass! Matter-of-fact, fuck you, fuck both of you! Now give me a mutha'fuckin' lawyer and get the fuck out of my room."

Julia looked at Patrick and smiled. She shook her head and took a seat. "Mr. Demon Dog, we can try this one more time or Agent Conroy can do what he does to make you talk."

"That bitch doesn't scare me!" Demon Dog responded angrily as he looked at Patrick. As soon as the words were released from his mouth, Patrick threw a straight right hand that connected flush with Linus Cummings's nose. Blood shot out of it and didn't stop.

Linus was trying to say something, but his speech was slurred and stuttering. Patrick's left hand was around his neck and he was about to hit him again, but Julia got up and grabbed his hand. But it wasn't a grab to stop him, she gave Patrick a set of brass knuckles and made sure Linus Cummings observed the transaction.

"W-W-W-What you trying to do?" Fear was in the eyes of the bedridden man, which was something he was not used to. His demeanor was no longer one of a tough bad guy, but a man in pain.

"First, he already broke your nose," Julia explained. "Now he is going to blacken both eyes. If you still decide you prefer not to talk, then we have to really get mean and break everything. Matter-of-fact, I think you said fuck you both. Patrick, break both *fuck you* fingers."

Though Linus tried to resist, Patrick grabbed his left hand, the hand closest to him and pulled his middle finger back until it broke. Linus Cummings screamed out in pain. A nurse came running in the room and Julia immediately told her to get out.

"Do you plan on talking or do we need to continue with this tough guy routine?" Linus writhed around in pain, unable to administer any type of corrective action to his ailing nose, mouth or finger. Though he was trying his best to hold back the tears, they slowly flowed down his face.

"This is illegal. I know my rights," he stuttered as the blood continued to trickle out of his nose and mouth.

"Patrick, have you ever seen a man bleed to death out of his nose?" Julia asked. Linus's head was shaking side to side and his body was still writhing from the pain. His ankles and wrists being cuffed limited his movements.

"No, Julia, I haven't."

"It's not a pretty sight. First, the blood flows out at a steady pace, and then it becomes hard to breathe. Next comes the gagging and the hurting throat. Then the head gets weak and the splitting headaches come."

Linus winced in agony. He didn't know if the agent was telling the truth, but sometimes, pain coupled with fear make bad bedfellows. "I have rights," he repeated.

Julia got up from her chair and moved closer to the man. "First, Linus, you have no rights because we are holding you on being a threat and terrorist to the United States of America. Therefore, we can hold you forever without even pressing a charge. The only decent thing about the Patriot Act is it gives some of us investigators just so much damn power. So Mr. Badass, what do you want to do? You want to bleed to death or do you want to talk?"

Linus Cummings closed his eyes and in that moment, he knew his life was over as he knew it. Years ago, he was offered an opportunity to be somebody. The man who came to visit him, didn't provide a name. He talked for twenty minutes and when it was over, he wanted a yes or no answer, no questions allowed. Linus voiced a yes and since that day, his life had changed. When he opened his eyes, he noticed both agents were sitting down.

"Okay, I'll tell you what you want to know, but I need some protection." Julia and Patrick stood and Linus Cummings looked at her, the agent giving the orders and the authoritative voice. "You guys are the big and bad FBI, but this guy is bigger and badder than the FBI. If he wasn't, you would have caught him twenty something years ago."

Chapter
38

THE DRAMATIC EFFECTS OF life can take a toll on people. Denise Carson knew this all too well. Since the death of her husband twelve years ago, she had taken her time finding herself. After all, if there were such a thing as soul mates, Steve was definitely hers. He was the one man who let her be herself. She was wild and definitely out of control in so many ways. He was her guide and her controller, but a controller out of love and not arrogance.

As much as she had tried over the years to stop thinking about him, she couldn't. For the first three years after Steve's death, she went through a state of depression. The alcohol and promiscuousness were easy; parenting was not. Janessa was fourteen and she was going through her own depression of losing her father. Their relationship was never good, but Steve was the referee and the father who made everything better for everyone. She never truly understood how he did as much as he did, especially when he was always on this case or that case. She didn't work half as much as him, but he managed to do more with the kids. He managed to be the father they needed and the father he always wanted to be.

She looked at her watch. She knew she only had ten more minutes before its rightful owner would occupy the office she was using. After the massacres in Ohio and Oklahoma, Elliot called her in his office and gave her a list of ten names. Three of the names were highlighted in yellow. Elliot told her to find out what the names on the list had been doing for the past ten years. When she referenced the three highlighted names, he looked at her and told her they had priority and he would tell her when the time was right.

Her mind continued to recall memories of the past, while she adjusted her scope on her high-powered long-range rifle.

She remembered KC telling her she was voluntarily enrolling in an alcohol rehabilitation program and that he was hiring her as a security consultant for the new company he was forming.

Her mind traveled to waking up in the middle of the night and looking at herself in the mirror. She didn't like what she saw. Once the queen of Section H, she was now relegated to putting her life back together with the help of others. Her seventeen-year-old daughter was raising her nine-year-old sons. The brother-in-law she never liked was there for her. KC would check on her every week and checked on the kids daily.

Researching and tracking the ten names were easy. She knew all of the names on the list. She had worked with many of them and was familiar with the others. The information she found was not meant for public dissemination. She learned early in her career the public truly could not handle the truth. And this truth included espionage, slander, assassinations, spying and a host of other illegal acts committed against citizens, foes and allies.

She shared the information she found with Elliot. Two days later, she received a phone call and he said *when*.

Her target walked in his office and though she had a clean shot, she wanted to wait until he sat down. This was the last of her hits today.

The other two hits were quick and dirty, a *Q and D*.

Vollentine Raymond was the former Special Executive Assistant to the FBI for the last two directors, prior to the current director, John Tellis. Raymond lived in the Mount Vernon area of Alexandria, Virginia. He was twice divorced and lived alone in his three-bedroom split-level home. She actually spent over four hours in the house before she finally made her move at the strike of midnight. She turned on the light in his bedroom and was surprised he didn't wake up. She then got a pencil and put the eraser end in his ear. When Vollentine Raymond woke up, he was startled, especially seeing a former colleague dressed in black. He reached for his glasses. Denise's actions were swift and fatal. She stabbed the pencil in his eye, took her knife and slit his throat.

The next target was Otis Adamis, the former Executive Director of Criminal Investigations under Director Basil Dooling. Adamis always liked living close to his job. That's why he lived in a penthouse in the downtown D.C. area. After leaving the Bureau five years ago, Adamis returned to his old job as the Chief Operating Officer of a Fortune 100 telecommunications company, which also resided in the downtown area.

Otis Adamis was an early riser and workaholic. He believed in being the first in the office and usually got there between five-thirty and six. Regardless of the season, he usually caught the elevator at five-fifteen and walked the four blocks to his job. This morning was no different. When the elevator doors opened, he was surprised to see his old colleague dressed in black. He didn't have time to be surprised after the bullet entered his head.

Denise controlled her breathing, took a deep breath and held it. Her M-82A1 long range sniper rifle felt good in her hands. It had always been her weapon of choice when assigned on a kill mission.

When Barry Collingshed, the former Assistant Director of Counterterrorism sat down, her scope was already pinpointed to the back of his head. She knew her time was running out, but she still displayed patience.

In a prior life, as each mission came to an end, she used to think about getting back home and making love to her man — her Steve. Her mind was still on her man. This time, she was thinking about killing those who were responsible for his death.

She gently squeezed the trigger and the bullet shattered the window and the head of Barry Collingshed.

She gathered her things quickly and walked calmly out the door as several people were walking in. Like a daylight shadow and days of old, she blended in and disappeared. That's what she did, even when she was married.

Chapter
39

HE STOOD UNDER THE cascading hot shower in his office bathroom. His mind was clear. He refused to think about the happenings of the past several hours. He had over an hour on the so-called ninety-six hour time limit the FBI was given to procure $100 million for murderers and terrorists. He felt he needed a shower to wash away the sweat and dust from his morning's activities as well as wash away the acts of indiscretion he had committed and was going to commit.

They say it's lonely at the top. Deputy Director Elliot Lucas knew that all too well. He had had many lonely days executing the responsibilities and duties of the Bureau. But he knew from his days as an FBI operative that one day he would be the one at the top of the totem pole, executing the demands of the nation's number one investigative agency. He had been groomed by others and by himself for the responsibility — not for this job, but the job as Director of the Federal Bureau of Investigation.

As the water beat down his face, he knew it was ironic to have a case like this that involved some of the most powerful people he knew to determine his worth.

He straightened his tie as he looked across his desk and stared into the face of SEA Jim Hudlin.

"Your dime, Jim, talk," Elliot demanded.

"What can I say that you don't already know? The director is not a happy man. President Cabot chewed his ass and wants to know what in the fuck were you thinking. You are the Deputy Director of the FBI and a man in your position doesn't make threats like that. Damn, Elliot, what in the fuck were you thinking?"

Elliot said nothing. He picked up the remote control to his television, took aim and pushed the mute button. The television which was already on, blasted the views of the day.

"Joe, the big story of the day is Deputy Director Elliot Lucas's comments this morning, and the pro-FBI opinions throughout the nation. Many around the U.S. consider the eye-for-an-eye approach to be the best retaliation if the FBI is indeed under attack from terrorists, hate groups or enemies against the country.

"I spoke to at least fifteen people today and all wholeheartedly, unequivocally agree with Deputy Director Lucas. In sixteen years as a reporter, I have never seen this kind of support for the FBI or CIA. I'm kind of flabbergasted at the support for the deputy director. I think his being on the scene and his willingness to arrest high price attorneys, Dave and Carol Ball, are resonating with Americans that he is a leader. He is viewed as a man leading his troops or I should say agents, in this situation, into battle."

Elliot pushed the power button and the television turned off. Throughout the broadcast, his attention was turned towards SEA Jim Hudlin. When Jim turned back around to face him, he was silent, searching for the right words.

"Elliot, I know what's going on. Shit, we all know what's going on, but just because people are behind you on this, doesn't make it right. The White House is not happy, the executive branch of this country is not happy, Elliot. Open your eyes, man. Get a grip on reality. This is more than your vendetta against those killing agents."

"How does my tie look?" Elliot asked Hudlin as he put his coat on. The expression on Hudlin's face confirmed to Elliot that he did what he intended to do — keep the man on his toes and thinking.

"Damn it, Elliot, this is serious!"

"Does that mean my tie is okay?" The two men looked at each other. For Jim Hudlin, he was confused and wondering what was his friend trying to accomplish. His friend's thoughts were ten clicks ahead of the bad guys.

"Jim, remember the line, 'We the people?' That means we the people of the United States. The people have spoken and they are not on my side, they are on the side of justice and America. That grip on reality you were talking about includes *we the people*. You see, Jim, on this hand, we have politics, all-American politics." Elliot held up his left hand to prove his point.

"This is the government which fails to hear or recognize the people. On the other hand, you have *we the people* who this country was built to protect and serve." He held up his right hand to represent *we the people*.

"We forget about the people. The same people who believe in stepping up and want a safe America. You want to know what in the fuck I was thinking? I was thinking about *we the people*. The people I was hired to defend and protect. And as sad as it is to the administration, my people, my agents, are a part of *we the people*. And once and for all, I am putting a stop to the killing of my agents. In twelve or thirteen years, this is not going to happen again. And that's a promise.

"I also guarantee you, if you are or were involved in killing agents in 1982, '93 or today, you are going down."

If Jim Hudlin could have stepped back, he would have. In some ways, he didn't understand. He didn't know if Elliot was accusing him or putting him on alert. He knew the rumors around the building that federal agents or other government officials were involved. He slowly got up while still staring at Elliot. He hated when the man went on a tirade but his facial features never changed. They were friends, had been friends for years. But for the first time during their friendship, he felt uncomfortable.

Jim walked to the door, turned around and looked at his friend one more time. No words were exchanged. His last thought — was he considered an enemy of the Bureau?

"Dooling wants your badge and President Cabot wants to know are you all right, and if you are, he wants to know did you hit your head?" Director John Tellis did not smile when he made his comment, prompting Elliot to gauge the seriousness of the pending conversation.

He walked over to Tellis's desk and stood until the director motioned for him to sit. He felt good. Regardless of the situation, he knew John wouldn't fire him. He was the best chance they had of bringing *Just Cause* down and the only thing that might come out of firing or replacing him on this investigation was starting over.

Elliot was not cocky as the deputy director of the FBI, but he knew his boss, John Tellis. He always looked at him as a righteous man, but also as a true and blue politician. Tellis was a man on the move and all of his dreams and aspirations involved the house at 1600 Pennsylvania Avenue.

"Well, hell, Elliot, talk to me, did you hit your head?" John Tellis asked as he walked over to the cabinet in his office that contained his stash of spirits and glasses. He poured two small, half glasses of bourbon. When he offered Elliot the drink, Elliot put his hand up, signifying not today.

"No, John, I didn't hit my head, just doing my job. The President knows that. As far as Dooling, he will be locked up in due time."

"Is he our man? No, let me re-state that. Do you have evidence corroborating that he is our man? Do you have evidence stating he is the leader of *Just Cause*?" The Director gulped down his glass of bourbon in two swallows, then he set the glass down and picked up the other glass that Elliot refused.

"We have less than forty minutes before these lunatics call you back or send you a message when they don't receive their hundred million," Director Tellis continued. "What do you think is going to happen? The President is worried. I think he received the word on Raymond, Collingshed and Adamis the same time I did. You know Collingshed and Adamis were two of his friends and colleagues. They have history together. And you know Raymond and I came up together, went to college together. Do you think that was the message? You think they already knew we weren't going to pay?"

Elliot sat in the chair and leaned forward. He signaled with his fingers for John Tellis to give him the drink of bourbon. He had never been a morning drinker. Actually, he was never much of a drinker. But after considering it, he realized he could stand for a couple of quick swallows. John Tellis obliged as he went back to his cabinet and refilled his glass.

The bourbon felt smooth and hot going down Elliot's throat. He knew he made a face. But it was good. He would drink the rest before he left the office.

"That may have been the message but we will see. As you know, these were three men close to Dooling as well as three of the names on your list." Elliot looked at John Tellis, who just nodded his head in the affirmative. "We made a point, we took a stand and it would be a major mistake if we stepped back now. I plan on increasing the pressure. I plan on staying vigilant, aggressive and on the offensive. I am no longer playing with the lives of the agents who serve this country well."

Tellis took a small sip of his bourbon and just looked at the glass. In the five plus years Elliot had been his deputy director, he had never questioned him. In his mind, now it was different. The stakes were bigger — or were they? He too had served side by side with some of the agents who had died over the years. He too had served his country well. How could he not trust the man who had always been there for him?

"As far as the phone call," Elliot began as Tellis looked back up at him. "Everyone will be in my office in the next fifteen to twenty minutes. We will deal with the outcome when the call occurs. I can't do anything until then. But believe me, Dooling or whoever is in charge, knows he is in a fight now."

A knock on the door interrupted the meeting. "Enter," was the reply by Tellis. He and Elliot both stood when they saw who was at the door.

"Sorry to disturb your meeting, John, but you are wanted at the Capitol Building and I need to talk to Elliot." John Tellis was stunned and speechless. He hesitated before he made the right decision of doing what his Commander-in-Chief directed.

"Sir, what can I do for you?" Elliot asked.

"Sit down and let's talk, Elliot. We have a lot to talk about," President Cabot responded.

Chapter 40

FIFTEEN MINUTES INTO THE meeting with Elliot and other members of the staff, and our anonymous automated caller had not called. Our ninety-six hour time limit had expired fifteen minutes ago. We were scheduled to discuss the progress of the case. A lot had occurred since our last meeting including the robberies and murders in Ohio and Oklahoma, but evidently, more had occurred than we realized.

When we arrived, Elliot had just gotten out of a meeting with President Cabot. Under the assumption our anonymous caller would call back at the end of the time limit, the President stuck around for ten minutes. When the call didn't happen, he decided to go back to his home at 1600 Pennsylvania Avenue.

He actually shot the breeze, waiting on our anonymous caller. When that didn't happen, Elliot decided to press on with the meeting. We didn't have as many in attendance as we had before. There were still agents in the field investigating leads.

The effects of this case were far reaching within the halls of the Bureau. Those in the meeting could feel the effects.

Brenda Pittman was working for *Just Cause*. A shocker.

There were also rumors flying around that some former Bureau executives were killed overnight, possibly in retaliation for the raids we staged.

As I looked around the table, I noticed Special Agents Denise Carson, Dr. Beth Storm and Charlie McClary were sitting next to each other. I don't know what they had been doing during the investigation. I hadn't seen Denise since the last meeting four days ago. I got a chance to talk to her for a couple of minutes to ask about Steve's journals, but she was called into a meeting with Elliot soon after. My mind was still on the journals. Why? I did not know.

Horace Schmidt from the Secret Service was at the foot of the table and Lewis Burling III was next to him. An empty seat separated Lewis from Paul McGinley, the rep from the CIA, and retired Lieutenant Colonel Bobby Small, Jr. was sitting next to Paul. I sat on the other side of Colonel Small. Elliot was standing at the front of the room and preparing to start the meeting.

"For the record, President Cabot officially gave me a good chewing out. Unofficially, he told me to catch the bastards by any means necessary. *Don't ask, don't tell.*"

We all smiled. Translated — he wouldn't ask Elliot and Elliot wouldn't tell. It was nice having the President back Elliot's play. Rumors were already flying about the President and Elliot's meeting. Supposedly, it was just Cabot and Elliot. Director Tellis was called to Capitol Hill. Something wasn't right, but who was I to question rumors. The director and Elliot were the best of friends. I think it was all about business.

"This is a progress meeting," Elliot continued, "and I'm happy to report, progress is what we have been making. Yesterday, we conducted a series of raids throughout the country in relation to finding the bank robbers. These raids accomplished what they were intended to. They gave *Just Cause* false confidence that we were following bad leads. Around midnight last night, Special Agent Julia Carson and her team captured the planner and organizer of the bank robberies, Linus Cummings, who happens to be the leader of the Angel of Life and Liberty. I am convinced we have no handle on how many groups or gangs we are dealing with. And that is no sleight towards Colonel Small and his watch group.

"Last word, Agents Carson and Conroy were **interr**ogating Mr. Cummings. I am very hopeful their interrogation will shed some light on the robberies and the murders of our colleagues. Our series of raids throughout the country, including the one in Gaithersburg, Maryland, led to the capture and arrest of over seventy assailants. And unfortunately, it also caused the deaths of at least fifteen. The raids also resulted in the gathering of invaluable information.

"As all of you know, thanks to CNN, we have attorneys Dave and Carol Ball under arrest. It was their house we raided in Gaithersburg. I will be personally conducting the interview with the Balls. Through the interception of e-mail traffic, we are convinced their son, Carmine, is a major player with *Just Cause*. He is also the leader of a group called the FBI Rangers. We are still conducting interviews with our detainees, who all are being held as terrorists and enemies of the United States."

We were an attentive audience. Much of the information we all knew. It was nice hearing everything from the top. Looking at Elliot, I knew something was not right, something was bothering him. He continued with his briefing.

"This morning, in what may be an act of retaliation on the part of *Just Cause*, three former Bureau division heads were killed. Two, Vollentine Raymond and Otis Adamis, were killed in their homes and Barry Collingshed was killed in his office. What does it mean? We don't know yet."

I was floored. Raymond, Adamis and Collingshed were former high rollers within the Bureau. In fact, they were still high rollers in the world of business and government. All three had ties to the President. Maybe that's why he went over to the FBI office versus calling Elliot to the oval office. I didn't know our next step, but I did know it was time for some research; some serious research. There were active agents dying but it seemed the central focus was on former agents.

As an agent, I knew every case had its own craziness and took on its own flavor. The *Just Cause* case was beyond crazy and the flavor was indistinguishable. I didn't know everything. But clearly, Elliot knew what was going on. I was hoping he, Lewis, Bobby and I would have an opportunity to talk after the briefing.

The remainder of the briefing was ho hum. Paul McGinley gave a short spiel on the Secret Service's take on things. Nothing worth mentioning. The President's and Vice-President's protection staffs were increased.

Elliot assigned some tasks, including researching the connections between the agents of all three decades, to Charlie McClary and Beth Storm. He told the rest of us to go get some sleep. I knew Lewis, Bobby and I needed some sleep but I wasn't sure about Denise. Elliot told us we all looked like shit and he was right. Looking at Denise, I saw that she looked like she had been up all night as well.

When I asked Elliot if Lewis, Bobby and I could bend his ear for a minute, he politely said, "No, go get some sleep."

Chapter
41

"WHAT IN THE FUCK happened last night and this morning?" the Boss asked over the phone. "You are supposed to be the eyes and ears within the walls of the Hoover and look what happened to us. What in the fuck are you doing?"

"Who in the hell you think you talking to, boy?"

"I told your ass before, Dooling, if you ever called me boy again, I would fucking kill you. You weren't worth a damn when you were the damn director and you aren't worth a damn now."

Basil Dooling took a deep breath before saying another word. He knew the Boss was right. He was supposed to be the eyes and ears in D.C. and though he had a good excuse, excuses were not what was needed.

"Boss, I apologize." The apology was hard for the former director, but he knew he needed the man called the Boss. They had worked together for over twenty years and the Boss had a way with getting the young gangbangers and hoodlums to do his dirty deeds — their dirty deeds. He really was indispensable. Indispensable until this whole ordeal was over. Then the former director wanted to put the bullet in the Boss's head himself.

"Shit. Apology accepted. Now tell me what happened. We got hit hard today. This sets us back a few days." The Boss was exasperated and it came across as clear as purified water over the phone.

"Our contacts didn't come through. Our sources within the Hoover Building may be immobilized. Our other contacts were not informed of everything going on. To my understanding, there is a lack of trust within the building. We need to stop operations for a day or two and get back on the right track. Agreed?"

"No, I don't agree," the Boss retorted. "We got hit hard today and what we need to do is send a message."

"We sent a message. I don't understand it, but we sent a message."

The Boss was confused. He didn't have any idea what Basil Dooling was talking about. "Please explain to me what message we are talking about. Columbus and Oklahoma City were four days ago. This was retaliation for the robberies. So what message are you talking about?"

"The murders of Raymond, Adamis and Collingshed. I'm only assuming you did that to send a message and to get the White House's attention."

"Dooling, I don't know what in the fuck you are talking about. This is a case of the left hand not knowing what the right hand is doing. I did not sanction the hits of Raymond, Adamis and Collingshed. Hell, we needed those guys. I thought you sanctioned the hit."

"Shit. Please tell me Elliot Lucas would not do something like that." The phone went silent. Both men were dumbfounded and lost for words.

"Dooling, Elliot would not do anything like that. He can be rambunctious and unpredictable, but Elliot has always been by the book. That's not his cup of tea. He is more straight-laced than that. And no way would Tellis authorize a hit on three executives so close to the President. And why would they? Do you really think they knew about our connection to Raymond, Adamis and Collingshed?"

"Boss, I am so fucking lost right now. Who else could have authorized a hit on them, if not us or Elliot? He is so fucking out of control now; he is subject to do anything. If not him, it had to be your FBI Rangers."

"I haven't talked to the Rangers since the raid on Carmine's house, but no way, I didn't authorize it, so it wouldn't happen. By the way, what's going on with Dave and Carol? Did you get a chance to talk to them?"

"Yes and I told them to shut up. Carol is afraid, but they both know not to answer any questions. I explained the procedures to them and they know after 72 hours, they will be able to call an attorney and they know to call Holton Buford."

"Damn it Dooling, you are the damn former Director for the fucking Bureau and you don't know the procedures. If they are holding them on suspected terrorists' charges, they can hold them indefinitely. Damn it, man, pull your head out your ass."

"That type of language is not called for," Dooling meekly replied.

"Anyway, how were they able to get the lowdown on our operations?" the Boss asked. "They knew where my guys were held up and everything. I don't get it."

"I don't know, Boss. I really don't think Blake and Pittman sold us out. I know they have Colonel Bobby Small working with them. You know the asshole that was running around killing hate groups. His ass should be locked up; instead, he's working with the Bureau. Damn fools."

"Both Blake and Pittman are ok. I've talked to them both. Blake is holed up in the D.C. area, while Pittman is relaying me information on Demon Dog. Also, she's staying with Demon Dog and acting as a relay between me and Mr. Dog."

The Boss never predicted things would move so fast. He had to ponder his next move. He wanted badly to strike now, but how could he? His folks were distraught and disorganized. He didn't want to take the risk of giving the advantage to Elliot Lucas and his agents.

"Boss, you still there?"

"Yes, and I know what we need to do. Sometimes the threat of doing something is better than the actual act. I plan on calling Elliot later and threatening to rob a bank or kill his agents or whatever. I will think of something by the time I call. We need to keep them on the defensive, keep them guessing."

"Sounds good, but don't bring up Raymond, Adamis or Collingshed. If they didn't do it, I don't want them thinking we have renegades or mavericks within our group. They need to continue to think we are a united front. Plus, I'll see if I can find out what happened to Raymond, Collingshed and Adamis."

"Good enough."

The Boss had lounged around for the past several hours thinking of his strategy. He didn't want anyone around him or anyone to disturb him. He had mixed himself a couple of drinks and had several beers. He hadn't received any e-mails from Ranger 1 since the raid this morning and that bothered him. Additionally, Demon Dog was out of commission and now he had to think of another strategy for their bank robberies. He knew Demon Dog. He was a tough one. He doubted Demon Dog would spill anything about their operation or future plans. But could he take that chance?

His head had been hurting the whole day and he was tired of being in the house. But first things first. He needed a strategy. He needed to keep bringing the fight to the Bureau.

He rubbed his face and wondered why he ever agreed to do this some twenty-four years ago. He remembered the day well.

It was cloudy outside. He and Bradford Norton were on day five of their stakeout. He liked Brad. He was always professional and treated him well. They had been partners for three years and he could always depend on Brad.

Their friendship went a step above and beyond when Brad asked him to spend the night and sleep with his wife. Liza was average looking, petite, with brunette hair. Brad often talked about how freaky and kinky she was in bed. Whenever the Boss saw her, it was hard for him to concentrate on anything else.

She had a pleasant smile, a deceptive smile. He had never been with a white woman before. Brad told him Liza wanted him. The Boss thought he was talking about both of them at the same time, but when he spent the night, he found out she wanted him only. And he gave her what she wanted. He fulfilled her Mandingo fantasy that night and five days and nights after that night. It brought him and Brad closer.

Three weeks into their stakeout, Brad opened up and told him about the group called *Just Cause*. He outlined their purpose and game plan, and told him the role he could play within the group. Then he popped the question, "Will you be the one who gathers the hate groups together and make them a united team?"

That night he pondered the question and took in everything Special Agent Bradford Norton had shared with him. He knew the other agents Brad had mentioned. They were all cool with him. As bad as race relations had been in the Bureau, he was one of the few Black agents who got along with the majority White agents in the Bureau.

He drank and hung out with them and now, had shared one of their wives. But the turning point was their purpose, what they were trying to prove. He was down for that. He was one of them. As simple as the reason was, he liked it. It made sense to him. It made even more sense for him to lead the field troops. After all, he was the most qualified and best agent they had.

He thanked Bradford Norton for the opportunity on several occasions, including the day twelve years ago when he put a bullet in Brad's head.

Chapter
42

CARSONONE CORPORATION OCCUPIED THE first ten floors of a twelve-story building. The two top floors were used as pseudo hotel rooms. Both floors consisted of four separate suites with a huge living area, kitchenette and bedroom. At the east end of the eleventh floor was a four bedroom, penthouse-style, two-level apartment — the residence of my niece, Janessa.

It was around noon when Bobby, Lewis, Denise and I arrived to get some shuteye. I called Janessa and let her know we would be crashing on the eleventh floor. She ordered us some food and we ate before calling it a day. It was obvious we were all tired and needed some sleep.

We didn't get a chance to see Janessa. She was busy handling business in her office. I thought it would be nice for her and Denise to at least say hello to each other. They talked sparingly and that worried me. It wasn't anything new, but talking to Janessa briefly at the Heavenly Burger made me realized how much they needed each other.

More importantly, Janessa needed to forgive her mom for the mistakes she had made in her life. Additionally, Denise needed to accept she was not the only one who lost someone when Steve died. Two sons and a daughter lost a father, but Janessa also lost a part of her — the man and person she loved and admired most in the world. There was no doubt in my mind that Steve and Janessa would have become more than father and daughter; they would have been best friends.

Denise awakened us all around six that evening. We had been summoned to the Hoover Building by Elliot; he wanted us in his conference room by seven. We agreed to meet downstairs in the lobby in thirty minutes.

The hot shower did me good. I felt refreshed and invigorated. But I still couldn't get my mind off Steve and his journals. I felt bad because the outlet he used to express his thoughts and feelings was hurting the person who loved him most in the world. I didn't have a daughter, but most of the men I knew who did, lived and died by their daughters.

My father, Howard Carson, loved his daughter, my sister, Alyse. To my understanding, when my older half-sister, Beverly, was younger, she was also the apple of his eye. Though Elliot was Julia's uncle, he raised her and I knew the bond they had. He replaced her father and their relationship was very much like a father and daughter.

Janessa loved her father and his expression of his feelings in one of his journals had inadvertently hurt her. I understood. I could have kicked myself in the ass because even if she really thought he was not the man who fathered her, she still shouldn't throw away the memories of the dad she knew. There was no doubt Steve was her father, but she was young and emotional. She was worried about me or someone else reading about how Steve thought someone else could be her father. I wanted to be diplomatic about approaching Janessa, but time was not on our side. I knew when I got time, I had to meet up with her and get those journals.

She was upset and disappointed with her dad, but I know she still loved her dad and she would never throw away his journals.

I also needed to sit down with her and tell her how her dad used to ramble on for hours about his little girl. I smiled because I knew if Steve were still alive, she would still have been his little girl and they would probably be bumping heads at her independence. Janessa and I did not have the type of relationship Elliot and Julia had. I was her uncle and we truly had an uncle-niece relationship. But she became my little girl after my brother's death. I was the one there. I was the one she brought her problems to and I was the one responsible for her.

When we arrived at the Hoover Building, the place was abuzz with activity. Evidently, our anonymous caller had phoned again and had a lot to say. Folks were running around like chickens with their heads cut off. When we stepped into the conference room, my world brightened as I saw Julia. She smiled and all was right with the world. We had a full crew. Julia and Patrick had returned as well as Q and the others.

I was fortunate enough to sit next to her and we were able to at least hold hands for a brief minute under the table. When Elliot walked in, he immediately hit the remote control and a voice feed came over the computer-generated system. The voice was the same automated voice we heard four days ago.

"Elliot, you are truly a fucking nigger," the automated voice blasted. "You think because you capture some of my guys and raid some houses and try to intimidate people, that that gives you the upper hand. I am the HNIC, Elliot, not you! They call me the Boss for good reason, boy!"

Automated or not, it wasn't hard to tell our caller was extremely angry. So angry he may have given us a clue to his nationality. Or maybe it was a ploy to deflect us.

"You want to play hardball, we can play hardball. You don't give a damn about your agents. If you did, we would be discussing how I would be receiving my money. Instead, I am telling you now to expect an agent to die everyday until I receive my money. And yes, Mr. HNIC, this is about money. Regardless of what you may think, this is simply about money.

"Elliot, you are not smart enough to capture me or destroy *Just Cause*. You are a good office boy, always have been, always will be. From day one, you have always been Tellis's or someone else's boy. Yeah, they taught you well. Showed you how to solve a crime or two. But when it comes down to it, Elliot, you are just another fucking nigger trying to live in the white man's world and play the white man's game."

The caller started laughing. I didn't know if he was laughing at his perceived humor or the irony of his words. Elliot was wearing his trademark stoic expression on his face. He was also the center of attention in the room. *Just Cause* never came across as having a personal grudge against one person in the Bureau. Their cause seemed to be one against the Bureau as a whole. But everything coming out of the caller's mouth was personal.

The last two attacks were against the Bureau. *Was this attack about Elliot?*

"Before I hang up," Elliot's voice came over the computer. "Do you want to tell me what you want or why you called?"

"Interesting," the automated voice responded. "Elliot, you don't want to know why we are doing what we are doing or why we have kicked the dog-shit out of the FB fucking I the past couple of decades."

"I don't give a damn. I care about one thing — stopping you and your band of mercenaries."

The recording on the computer was silent for at least a half-minute. "Elliot, do you think you know who this is? Do you think you know me?"

You could feel the sense of anticipation in the conference room. The question was a surprise, but considering the personal attack, it was probably warranted.

The next thing that came out of the computer recording surprised me, and I think everyone in the room, except the man himself. We heard the sound of Elliot laughing on the recording.

"Listen, Mr. *Just Cause,* Boss or whatever you call yourself, and listen good," Elliot shot back. "Yes, I know you and your Board of Directors. As God as my witness, before this whole charade is over, you may kill me but I guarantee – *Just Cause* will be no more."

"Don't hang up!" the automated caller screamed. It was a scream that sounded like a demand. The next thing we heard was the sound of a gunshot. Shocking. "That was a gunshot to the head of Damon Blake. I know you have Brenda Pittman. No way was I going to let the likes of Damon Blake bring me down. You have Brenda but she knows nothing.

"No, Elliot, it's not going to be easy. And by the way, I know you don't know me. If you did, I would be in prison now. You will definitely die before this is over with, Elliot. And that's not a threat, it's a promise."

The call ended with a hard click. Elliot rose from his seat, clicked the remote and looked around the room. Several folks had shocked looks on their faces. I felt privileged to be in the know. I couldn't feel bad for Damon or Brenda. They were the enemies. Though Damon was dead, I knew there was a bullet with Brenda's name on it.

"Unfortunately," Elliot began. "Special Agent Blake is dead. We received a picture and location, and it was him. He had made his way back to Virginia. He was found shot in the head in his garage. I feel bad because he was an agent. However, I feel worse because he had information we needed."

The room was silent. I thought many in the conference room needed to digest all that had just happened. I was sure Elliot thought the same thing and gave us all a few minutes to take it in.

"Ok, let's go around the room," Elliot brought us out of our brief stupor. It was time for business. Often times, Elliot would go around the room and everyone was expected to give their status on the portion of the case being worked.

Considering everything that had transpired over the past couple of days, I thought we all just wanted a moment of serenity and maybe, a moment of levity.

Chapter 43

WAKE UP AND SMELL the roses. That's what his lover used to tell him. Damn, he hated her. But she was right. For everything he did, they never recognized his accomplishments. Wasn't he the one who made everyone look good? From regional chiefs to division chiefs, hell, even the directors and deputy directors, and what did he receive in return? Nothing. Not a damned thing.

He recalled when he was asked the ridiculous question. "Can you organize several hate groups of different nationalities into one cohesive group?"

He laughed at the questioner. He wanted to tell him he was insulted. But the questioner was the big man himself. He laid out the whole plan that night, a night that included women, beer and cash — his three favorite indulgences.

The big man informed him that he needed him, wanted him. Guaranteed him he would be the number two man in the organization. An organization called *Just Cause*.

The big man wanted him to make *Just Cause* his cause. In the big man's organization, he would be the Director of Operations. He ran the show.

That was the day he was truly born — the day the *Boss* was born.

That next day, *he* devised his three-phase plan. Phase One consisted of bank robberies — good ole fashioned bank robberies with one exception. *Organization.*

It was his job to organize and plan to the smallest detail the bank robberies of certain banks. The chosen banks were the ones where money was guaranteed and wouldn't be missed. It didn't make much sense to him at the time, but the Boss was willing to go along.

The plan — rob one bank in the capital city of every state in the continental United States.

The time — hit the bank within five to ten minutes after a person dropped off several nondescript packages.

The drop-off person was an employee for the Federal Reserve Bank and these packages were delivered on a monthly basis to five or six banks throughout the United States. Everyone knew about the money the Federal Reserve burned every year, but no one knew about the "Piggy Bank Fund," which was money put aside for a rainy day. It was money that made Operation Desert Storm, the Iraqi War and so many other operations possible.

The first three robberies would be his tests. He knew it. He knew the big man. He knew his minions. He knew he wasn't the second in command. But he had his own plans.

He wanted the big man's job, but it wasn't happening. He was the wrong color. Plus, he needed the big man. The big man could run interference, open doors and get the right people on their side. No. He would be the second in command as long as he ensured everything was flawless, down to the minutest of details. He would outlast the big man's minions or kill them. Either way, it would be his organization.

He had finally found his niche, doing what he was good at doing.

He recruited a wannabe tough guy named Linus Cummings. *Demon Dog* was his handle. He liked Demon Dog. He had used him on several occasions as his C.I., confidential informant. He was a hard man. Smart, sensible and ruthless. The Boss liked that about the young hoodlum.

He sat Linus down and told him about his plan. Of course, Demon Dog didn't believe a federal agent would be so bold and stupid as to rob banks and commit the kind of carnage the Boss was outlining. Hell, forget agent, what person in general in their right mind would even consider doing the type of shit he wanted to do?

But the Boss drew up the plans to the exact detail. He had everything outlined. Linus was to recruit eight reliable men and the nine of them would get employment as security guards at three banks: the Third Federal New York State Bank in Albany; the First Maryland National Bank in Annapolis; and the Fifth Bank of Georgia in Atlanta.

Phase Two was to find guys who answered only to the Boss. He needed guys he could train and trust. These guys would be his bank robbers. He didn't want everyday criminals. He wanted guys who didn't have criminal records, could follow orders and were hungry for money.

Over a month's period, he recruited fifteen college-age men of different nationalities and backgrounds, and from different regions of the country. He and Demon Dog spent a month training the young recruits. He loved their willingness to learn and their aggressiveness. Their progress was amazing. These were the type of young men who should have been serving in Uncle Sam's military; instead, they were serving him — the Boss.

Before Phase Three took place, the Boss wanted to execute his plan. How could he forget the day? It was March 1982 and still winter in the northeastern states, including New York. At least three inches or more of snow covered the ground, but the sun was out and the snow was slowly melting.

Some would say it was a bad day for robbing a bank. But the northeast was used to snow. More importantly, they were used to clearing the roads and sidewalks, allowing for good driving and walking conditions.

The big man had given the Boss the dates and times of the Federal drop-offs. Though the Boss was skeptical, he had faith in the big man's information. After all, they both had a lot to lose.

The Boss was taking even a bigger chance. He was still an agent with the FBI and he had decided to participate in the first several robberies. He wanted to lay the groundwork and set the standard for robbing banks the Boss's way.

Demon Dog and one of the eight recruits, using assumed names, would be pulling security guard duties at the Third

Federal New York State Bank in Albany that day. A half-block outside the bank, the Boss and five members of his bank robbery crew patiently waited for the delivery by the Federal Reserve employee.

Unbeknownst to all except the Boss, the big man was also in attendance at the bank. He was located in a building across the street, providing the Boss all of the information he needed.

As soon as the drop-off man departed the bank, the big man informed the Boss to take a five-minute time hack. Five minutes later, the Boss and his crew pulled up in front of the building, jumped out of their van and rushed into the bank.

Immediately, the Boss began giving orders to the bank's employees. As a one-time member of the Bank Robbery Section of the Bureau, he knew the alarm procedures. He notified the tellers and other bank employees that if they hit their silent alarms or pulled the famous last bill from the cash drawer, everyone was dead.

He asked who the bank president was and once the short, balding man identified himself, the Boss shot him. It was purely instinct on his part, but he knew he had gotten his point across.

Within three minutes, they had pulled off the unbelievable. When the Boss opened the nondescript packages in regular brown wrapping paper, he was surprised. They had stolen over $1.4 million of disposable cash.

He waited a week to see what would appear in the local or national newspapers. The only mention was in the local Albany paper and it was stated the robbers got away with $55,000. The Boss was impressed with the big man's information.

The next two bank robberies were just as flawless and brought in similar takes. *Just Cause* was on its way. And everyone was making a profit — from the big man down to the lowest subordinates.

The Boss was proud of himself. He had the juice, always had. Now he had someone who truly recognized that fact.

Now came the hard part — recruiting the hate groups.

He had been thinking about how he would approach the leaders of the groups. After all, that's who he needed, the leaders, plus three of their closest comrades. He had two important motivators: wreaking havoc on the FBI and money. But was that enough. He was a black man trying to do the impossible — get hate groups of different nationalities to work together for one common goal; groups that hated each other primarily because of the color of their skin.

The first leader he approached was called Spike, aka Timothy Roberts. Spike was the leader of the Neo-Nazi group, the Pure Angels. The Pure Angels had been around for ten years. Spike's leadership spanned the entire ten years. It was a long tenure for a leader of a gang or hate group.

It took the Boss a lot to get Spike to a sit down meeting. He was a wanted man for crimes against humanity, including shooting a black man in the face in Montana. The Pure Angels were on the run. Running from city to city, state to state. Spike was surprised the Boss had found him. Still, he did not trust the man. He turned down the previous six meetings the Boss had requested.

Then one day, out of nowhere, the Boss appeared at his doorstep. Actually, he appeared at the doorstep of Spike's girlfriend. Before he could make it to the back door, the Boss said one thing that stopped him in his tracks.

Spike asked him to repeat what he said.

"Ten thousand in cash if you give me ten minutes of your time," the Boss repeated.

The Boss explained the mission and plans of *Just Cause* and shared with him the success of the bank robberies. Within ten minutes, the criminal hate leader was convinced he could do business and make some money with *Just Cause*. Though he wasn't crazy about working with or taking orders from a black man, he was willing to give it a try. Plus, besides the money, he got the chance to kill FBI agents.

Within two weeks, the Boss had met with and convinced the leaders of the Black Mavericks, the Deadly Skinheads, and the Asian group, the Red Death of Mercy, about the good of *Just Cause.*

The Boss and *Just Cause* were well on their way.

He never questioned if he needed the big man. The big man had served him and the group well over the years. But the Boss had reaped the benefits; he was the second in command. He didn't mind being the second. He was wealthy beyond his belief as a black man who grew up in the worst parts of America's ghettos. He lived well and though he was the true mastermind of *Just Cause's* operations, he was happy to have the big man.

The big man had made all his dreams come true.

Chapter
44

SOMETIMES, REST CAN BE the most overrated thing in the world. In my case, it wasn't overrated. It was something I needed and needed immediately. There was something pressing I had to take care of, like going through the files I had procured from the Bureau's archive section.

Steve was on my mind. I knew the best thing I could do was find his killers and put an end to this whole world of madness. We were in a war with Iraq and Afghanistan, and dealing with so many other things in the world, and the last thing anyone wanted to deal with was an attack on America soil by her own citizens.

Without Steve's journals, I had no choice but to hit the archives. I hated going through the tons of files. It truly was a necessary job.

We didn't know what to expect next from *Just Cause*. However, it was a waste of time to anticipate what might happen. Instead, we were actively trying to find out who made up *Just Cause*. We had already made major leaps and bounds. But how close were we? Hell, no one knew except the head man, Elliot Lucas.

Did Elliot really know the so-called Boss and the group's Board of Directors? If so, what was the hold up on us putting the group on ice? It was a stupid question on my part. I knew what it took to make a case. If we had the evidence, they would be arrested by now.

It made me wonder about Elliot's wants. I knew what I wanted. I wanted *Just Cause* dead. Though I had only killed three people in my life and even that was recently, I could do it. I could kill those who killed my brother. The way Elliot felt about his fellow agents, something told me he could probably kill the members of *Just Cause* just as easily as I could.

I had brought a box of files home. It was late. For Julia and I, this was different. We were actually in the same house together. We were not used to that since this craziness had began. She had thrown something together for us to eat and it was nice to be eating and sleeping at home.

I was halfway through the box when Julia started massaging my neck. Her hands felt good as they slid down to my shoulders. I stopped working and tried relaxing. Fortunately, the touch of Julia's fingers made relaxing easy.

I was sitting at my old oak desk and it was the best I had ever felt sitting there. Julia had pulled my shirt off and was letting her fingers do the work. Magic fingers, indeed.

I laid my head on the desk and Julia pulled me back upright. She kissed the top of my head and began massaging my chest. Considering everything that had happened, this felt like heaven.

I reached my hands around and rubbed her legs and slowly made my way up her thighs. The higher I inched up, the more I realized that my wife did not have any bottoms on. I was initially fighting myself getting aroused. Then, I decided to let myself go. The more my hands traveled upward, the more aroused I got. When my hands reached Julia's bare ass, I couldn't help myself, I wanted more.

She began kissing my neck and upper body. I felt her breasts touch my face and spun my head around. Her beautiful breasts were within licking and kissing range. I stuck my tongue out and the tip touched her breast. Her body shivered as I concentrated on her nipple.

Julia put her hand on the back of my head and I knew what that meant. She slid around the chair and I steadily alternated between breasts. At times, I was sucking her nipples, other times I just flickered my tongue and lastly, put as much of her breast in my mouth as I possibly could.

Julia finally pulled away, got on her knees and pulled my sweatpants and underwear off. She then kissed and licked my stomach and thighs. My member had grown. I was ready for action. When Julia put it in her mouth, my head went back and her attempt at relaxing me was in overdrive.

The warmth and wetness of her mouth sent sensations throughout my body. I was glad I was sitting down. If not, my knees would have buckled. My wife was very good at what she did. From licking up and down on the shaft to taking the whole thing in her mouth, she had me going crazy with excitement. At times, I tried to rub her head; other times, I could hear my profanity-laced tirades of pleasure.

Julia was sucking and licking like she was possessed and I was her victim. I liked being her victim.

I couldn't take it anymore. I pulled her up — against her will, actually. She was relentless doing her bidding. She finally gave in to my persistent tugs to get her up.

She straddled me while I sat on the desk chair. My shaft slid into her wetness. Immediately she lurched forward and began kissing my face and neck and sticking her tongue in my ear.

Julia was frantically excited and I was bucking like a wrangler trying to break in a new bronco.

"Hell, yeah! Do it, baby! Do it! Work that shit, Kenny! Work it!"

I can never recall a bad lovemaking or sexual moment with my wife. Usually, I was the one who needed some tension relief. And the current case was very intense. However, we both needed to release tension. I think the love of my life needed release more than me.

Earlier, Patrick had told me about the events at Fort Eustis's hospital. He was surprised by her aggressiveness and take-charge attitude. He had never seen that side of her. Patrick surprised me. He liked that Julia versus Julia the executive assistant to the deputy director.

I loved every side of my wife. At this moment, I loved her sitting on me, riding my member and screaming in my ear to "Work that shit!" And that was what I was doing, *working that shit!*

Chapter 45

THERE IS NO MESSAGE stronger than the power of love. Our appetite for each other had never been stronger. We loved making love just as much as we loved each other. But something was wrong with Julia. It seemed as though she had a lot on her mind.

Our sexual escapade lasted almost two hours. We eventually left our computer room after breaking the desk chair and surviving carpet burns, and moved our act to the bedroom. It was August and still hot outside. Though our air conditioning system was working overtime, the amount of sweat and secretion we released were extraordinary.

Our sheets were drenched with our body fluids. We decided to sleep in a spare bedroom.

I was worried about Julia. When we slept together, we always woke up the way we went to sleep. If her head was on my chest when we fell asleep, it was the same way when we awakened. Sleeping together, our sleep was peaceful. When she was not next to me, I was restless.

I could count the number of restless nights Julia had had over the number of years we had been together. Last night, she was restless and then some. It worried me.

Throughout the night, she steadily tossed and turned. At five in the morning, she kissed me on the cheek.

"I love you," she said.

I smiled and kissed her back. "I love you more."

She hugged me tighter. "I'm sorry."

"Sorry for what?" I asked.

"For not sleeping so well. I don't know what's going on with me. It's been hard."

Hard. That was not what I was expecting to hear from her. She had always been the strong one in our relationship. She was the never cracking rock, the glue that kept us together. I wasn't used to chinks in her armor. She was on my highest pedestal. I knew it was dangerous to put anyone on such a high pedestal, but for the boys and me, she was our Queen.

"What's been hard, baby?" I asked. "What's going on?"

"Being back in the mix. I love being back, but I feel guilty. The boys, they need me. I feel like I am letting them down by being happy to be back . . . to be an agent again. I love you so much, Kenny," she stated as tears rolled down her face. "I just feel so guilty."

I kissed her lips, followed by soft pecks on her eyes and cheeks. I wanted to kiss the pain away. And she was in pain. Unfortunately, I knew how she felt. I had been there. Too many times.

I was there when I decided to walk away after my last case. I chose family over job.

But I was in the wrong for convincing Julia to do the same — to walk away from the job she loved. After all, she had given up being an undercover agent several years ago to take care of my son, Steve. Now I had to find the right words to say.

"Hey, you," I began as I continued to lay kisses on her face. "You have nothing to feel guilty about. We are a family. I'm the damn fool for forcing you to give up what you love. I'm the one who is sorry, baby. It's all on me."

Our gazes met. She smiled and I, in turn, did the same. She rubbed my face. "You are the best thing that has ever happened to me. You, Steve and Devin are my life. I—"

I put my finger to her lips, interrupting her. "You don't have to explain. Remember, we are a family. If you feel you need to be an agent or Elliot's executive assistant again, we will support that."

We continued looking into each other's eyes without saying a word. Sometimes words are overrated. Sometimes words are unnecessary. Sometimes love really did conquer all.

We didn't need words.

We had love.

The song by Johnny Kemp, *Feeling Without Touching,* was one of my favorites. In the song, he talked about *feeling without touching, speaking without talking.* That was our relationship.

No. Words wasn't necessary, not required.

Love conquered all.

"Damn, Kenny Carson, you are a keeper," she broke our moment of silence.

I saw that gleam in her eye. I was actually revitalized from last night's session. Damn, I loved her smile and the way she made me feel.

Damn. I'm married. That's the woman I married. That's the woman I love. That's the woman who stole my heart a long time ago. The woman who gets me . . . who makes me the man I am.

"No, you are the one," I stated as I kissed her, kissed her hard. We were already naked. Before I knew it, we were on our way to another round of lovemaking.

Chapter
46

THE UNITED STATES PENITENTIARY Marion located nine miles south of Marion, Illinois, and 120 miles east of St. Louis, was opened in 1963 when the infamous Alcatraz was closing. It was supposed to be the replacement for Alcatraz — the home for most of the worst offenders of the law. At 42 years old, it had become one of the oldest and largest federal prisons in America — still the home of the bad guy, but not so bad. The pen in Florence, Colorado, was considered the home of the most dangerous criminals in America, the lair of the super bad. Marion was just a step down, a baby step. Many would disagree with adding a high-profile international corporate attorney to the list of inmates.

Dave Ball had been isolated from the other prisoners since his incarceration. That isolation included a couple of days in solitary confinement. Elliot wanted to give him a taste of prison life without exposing him to the other prisoners. Dave Ball was a tall, slim man. His hair was chopped short and usually better groomed than its present look. In prison, it had become frizzy and wildly stuck out all over his head.

His body looked frail and beaten. His hands were cuffed in front of him and his ankles were shackled, causing his walk to be slow and awkward. Actually, he had to walk very awkwardly for a man used to walking very fast and deliberate. It had been less than a week and already, he was feeling the effects of life without caviar and vintage wine.

Elliot Lucas sat patiently as the man stopped at the door of the visiting room. His hesitation may have been partially because of the deputy director. The other reason may have been the six foot seven, 300-pound plus visitor sitting across from Elliot.

"Come on in, Mr. Ball," Elliot said in a facetious tone. "I want you to meet someone."

Dave Ball continued to stand at the door. His eyes were red and threatened to release tears. He didn't know why he was afraid, but fear had gripped him. Maybe it was the reputation of Elliot Lucas. The rumors he had heard about Lucas being a force to reckon with and never adhering to the normal rules of the average Washington politician were probably true. Hell, even the leaders in *Just Cause* really didn't want to deal with the man. He had to be trouble.

"No thank you, Elliot. I prefer to stand," the man nervously replied.

Elliot leaned forward, looking at the big man sitting across from him. "Mr. Ball, I'm disappointed. You don't know me. We have never met, formally or informally. Yes, I have met and know your wife, but I don't know you. Our only time meeting was at your house, when we arrested you. But you insist on disrespecting me by calling me by my first name."

Elliot slowly turned his head towards Dave Ball. The big man did the same thing.

Ball couldn't move. It was awkward for him. He wasn't intentionally trying to disrespect Elliot. Right now, he was isolated in Marion. As bad as that seemed, he liked it. But he knew if he stayed there, he would become a part of the general population. And that was not good. So no, the last thing he wanted to do was disrespect the man who had him by the short hairs.

Elliot suddenly slammed his fist on the small table and Dave Ball jumped. "First, you disrespect me by trying to kill me, and then you call me by my first name like you fucking know me."

Elliot rose from his sitting position. "Mr. Ball, this is Albert Walton. You might know him by his nickname, Justice."

Dave Ball stepped back when the big man, Albert "Justice" Walton, stood up. Though Ball was only several inches shorter than Justice, he was outweighed by over a hundred pounds. He knew of Justice's reputation. Who didn't? The man was legendary. Seven years ago, he killed over twenty attorneys from California to Maryland.

Ball felt weak in the knees. He was afraid and his fear meter increased when Elliot asked Justice to shake his hand. Ball's hand completely disappeared inside of Justice's. Everything about Justice scared him. To add to his fears, unlike him, Justice did not have handcuffs or shackles on.

"Mr. Ball, I should have told you. Albert and I have bonded since his incarceration. In case you didn't know, I am the one who brought Albert to justice. Amazingly, he didn't give me any shit. He did what he felt he had to do and when I tracked him down after his last killing, he gave himself up. Very noble. Very noble indeed."

Ball was stunned and confused. He didn't know how to take the look of admiration from Elliot to Justice.

"The reason I wanted you two to meet, Mr. Ball, is I have convinced the warden to make you guys cellmates if you end up spending your time here at Marion. It will make it easier on me, since I visit Justice once a quarter. But we need to make something clear. I probably should have elaborated more on the reason Albert is here. Most times, Justice's reputation precedes him," Elliot smiled at the big man who returned the smile.

"But I like telling his story to other attorneys. He killed attorneys because all of the strife in his life was at the hands of attorneys."

Dave Ball backed up again but couldn't go anywhere. His back was against the door. The previous nondescript look on Justice's face had suddenly changed. For Ball, his fear meter had pegged out. He didn't know what to do. He felt faint. He was an attorney. Justice was an attorney killer. And the Deputy Director of the FBI was an accessory and instigator. *Would he actually let this man kill me?* In a way, Dave Ball knew the answer to his thought.

"Albert, put Mr. Ball in his chair and you can go back to your cell. I will make sure I call your kids and let them know I visited you, and expect those DVDs in a couple of weeks."

Justice just nodded his head in the affirmative as he grabbed Dave Ball by his shirt, lifted him up, placed him in the chair and glared at the man.

Ball's face was beet red. The glower from Justice had him shaking. He was still holding back the tears of fear. He breathed an air of relief when the man turned and walked out the room.

"This is your future, starting immediately, if I do not get the information I want." The two men looked at each other. Elliot could see and smell the fear of Dave Ball.

"I . . . I . . . I don't know if I can do that," Ball stammered.

"Yes, you can. Trust me, Dave," Elliot put emphasis on his name. "Justice will make your life miserable in ways you couldn't imagine. But what is worse, I guarantee Carol will never be the same. I know. I just left her not so long ago. Didn't ask her any questions or for any information; just wanted to introduce her to her new cellmate. She kept saying, 'I will tell you whatever you want.' I felt bad when I left her. I wouldn't be surprised if she went crazy being isolated by herself."

"Elliot . . . I mean . . . Director Lucas, h – h – how can you do this? You are the deputy director." His voice and tone was weak. The tears he was trying to prevent were flowing down his face. His mind was going crazy. He couldn't stop thinking about his wife, Carol. He had no idea where she was or how she was doing. He didn't even know if he believed Lucas. Of course he did. It sounded like Carol. That's why she was the attorney to the politicians — she didn't like visiting jails or prisons.

"You and your group have been killing my agents for over twenty damn years. It stops here, Dave. Here and now. I want to know everything you know. Every damn thing!

When I walk out this door, I'm looking at either a witness or a dead man. Make your choice!"

Chapter 47

SOMEONE ONCE SAID POLITICAL clout was more a state of mind than a state of being. For the big man, his state of mind *was* his state of being. For over twenty years, his planning and execution had been flawless. Now, his world was coming apart. He didn't like that. What he didn't like, he fixed or made go away.

"What in the hell is going on?" the big man said in his calmest, yet, most heated voice.

"You are the one whose supposed to have all the inside connections with the Bureau, White House and the whole national capital region. So why in the fuck are you asking me what happened?" the Boss replied.

"What are your plans? What and when are we striking back?"

"Do you think that is the prudent thing to do, to strike back like we are as mad as a banshee?" the Boss questioned. "Do I want to strike back and strike back hard, you're damned right I do. Hell, you know I do. But we need to be very smart about how we strike back. We need to catch the Bureau unprepared and hit them in areas they're not expecting."

The big man continued to look out his study window. His home was isolated in a wooded area outside of Fort Meade, Maryland. He liked the area. In the growth that had occurred over the past several years, this sparse area was still his haven, protected against the advances of corporate America.

"Boss, you remember years ago when we started this undertaking?"

"Of course I do."

"You remember us agreeing that one day we may have to hang up our guns and walk away with a full belly and a smile on our faces? That day may be upon us."

The Boss didn't immediately reply. He knew the problem. He also knew how the big man wanted to end his undertaking, as he called it. His codes were frustrating to the Boss. The big man talked a good talk. But he had issues. Acute paranoia was at the top of the list.

"We cannot kill the head of the Federal Bureau of Investigation. One, it's not what we signed up for. Two, we both have history with the Bureau and Elliot Lucas. Three, I have always been your staunchest supporter, but what you want to do is wrong."

"Is this a black thing, Boss?"

"No, it's a do the right thing, thing," the Boss responded quickly. "We cannot kill the head of the Bureau!"

"John Tellis is the head of the Bureau, damn it! Not Elliot Lucas! We are talking about getting rid of the deputy director of the Bureau, Boss. Get it right, goddamn you!"

"What's the problem? Why so high strung?"

"It's the same fucking problem you always have, Boss! For too long, Elliot Lucas has been reaping unjust, undue credit. I am tired of his black, chicken eating ass receiving the credit for the hard work of others. He is expendable!"

"Yes. We are all expendable," the Boss suggested. "You have hate for one man, a man who has served his country well. Served the Bureau and the White House well. A man who has sacrificed a lot for the sake of this country. And you want him dead. Why?"

"Because he is the problem!"

Chapter 48

THE BOSS NEVER MUCH liked grunt work. He loved being in command, being the leader. The kids today called it "a shot caller." And that was him, a *shot caller*. But the tasks at hand, he didn't like. Elliot Lucas and his crew had put him in this position. He smiled at how great an adversary Elliot was. How funny, he thought, two Black men fighting for a cause they believed in.

"Unfortunately, Elliot, only one of us will come out victorious," he said to himself. "How sad is that!"

The Boss was still distraught at the thoughts of the *big man*. How could he even imagine taking out Elliot. Hell, he knew why. With Tellis moving up to take Ian Bradley's position as Secretary of State, who else would be the most logical and qualified choice for Director of the Bureau than Elliot?

The Boss smiled at the irony. Every dead agent pre-1980 would probably be turning over in their grave and every minority agent would probably sit up and salute President Cabot for making the right choice, the bold choice. Hell, every damn living minority agent would probably kiss Cabot's butt from here to eternity. Not only was it the right thing to do, it was the right political move.

The Boss knew his thought process wasn't too far from the truth. Though the next election was several years away, even as a Republican, President Cabot's selection would probably go a long way in securing a good majority of minority voters.

The Boss knew politics. He knew how to play the games. He had a political science degree from Georgetown and a law degree from Columbia University. Additionally, he spent over fifteen years as an agent before he left the Bureau. He was a studious man, one who loved mind games. He wanted to know how the brain functioned in certain situations.

The Boss knew his limitations, which in his mind were not many. Why he joined *Just Cause* was never too far from his mind. It was about proving he was the best.

Some would call that reason the reason of a crazy man. But the Boss knew he was far from crazy. After all, on two separate occasions, he had brought the most powerful investigative bureau in the world to the brink of self-destruction. He was the one who instilled the self-doubt and fear in his fellow agents. No. No crazy man could do that.

He even participated in what he called the *minion* work. He had robbed his share of banks and killed his share of agents. But his biggest claim to fame was the planning and organization of everything. The big man got the credit, as most big men do. But even the big man knew, he, the Boss, was *indispensable*.

He made *Just Cause*. Hell, he was *Just Cause*.

But it didn't matter after this undertaking, did it? This was the last time around. Once he took care of Elliot, he had to kill the big man. Elliot was truly the winner. At least the Boss would let him live and possibly become the next director of the world's most powerful investigative bureau.

Imagine that, a black man at the reins of the Hoover.

He smiled at the thought. He remembered the days of being called a boy, nigger, coon or other degrading names he preferred to not even think about during his initial years with the bureau. Hell, he would take his hat off to Elliot Lucas till the day he died for putting up with the junk he and others endured during their time with the Bureau.

In his heart, he knew Elliot and others paved the way for him and others to become agents. Elliot and others he knew who wore the title of FBI Operative were the Bureau's equivalent of the Tuskegee Airmen or the Golden Thirteen.

Hell, he wished they recognized the name of the first black agent like they recognized Jackie Robinson.

But in actuality, it was still J. Edgar Hoover's FBI.

Once again, a smile graced his face. He hoped J. Edgar's and Clyde Tolson's gay asses were turning over in their graves at the thought of a black man taking over the Bureau. The Boss couldn't help but release a hearty laugh. How fitting, he thought. A black man who learned from the dictator himself and who J. Edgar could not stand, taking over his organization and possibly being just as powerful as the former dictator. Hell, this was possible movie material.

The Boss put his thoughts away and went back to his grunt work. Since Linus "Demon Dog" Cummings was in captivity and Ranger 1, Carmine Ball, had not resurfaced since the raid, he was the man, once again, responsible for doing the detail planning for the bank robberies and killing of agents.

With the help of the big man, he knew what operations and banks he wanted to hit. If this was the end of their fun, he was going out with a bang. He wanted everyone with the Bureau past, present and future to know one thing; the Boss was the best agent who ever graced the halls of the Federal Bureau of Investigation.

Chapter
49

I WAS CONVINCED THIS was the calm before the storm. It had been three days since the $100 million deadline had come and gone as well as the last phone call from the automated caller. In spite of the caller's threats, nothing had happened over the past three days. Absolutely nothing.

I had spent countless hours doing research. I needed to connect the dots and there were enough dots to connect. I had one thing on my side — an archive with many detailed files. I was able to access the names of every agent who had perished or been injured at the hands of *Just Cause.* In my mind, something told me there had to be a connection amongst the agents. I had to look at every operation. I was ninety-five percent sure Bonner McGill was the target of the attack in Houston. Unfortunately, the other two agents, Corners and Kirkman, were victims of circumstances.

I had no clue what variables were applicable. For each agent who was attacked or perished, Elliot made all of the personnel records available to me. This was only phase one of my elaborate research and I didn't know my variables. I had never felt overwhelmed as an agent. From day one, I adapted to the strenuous lifestyle of a field agent. The hardships, long days and hard work never bothered me. But this was different.

Initially, my mind was on overload. Actually, I felt the fear set in. My first five years, I combed every nook and cranny of these files. I tried my best to find Steve's murderer. Back then, I thought it was my destiny. Looking at the files now, I was reluctant. So many thoughts came rushing to me. *Did I really want to look at the files? Was this still my fight?*

Elliot wanted the old KC back. I knew deep inside, he was there. He had always been there. That dark, edgy part of me would never die. I was sure of that.

During my days in the NFL, we had a saying deep in the game: *find your legs.* If someone were tired or overwhelmed, he found a way to press on, to overcome and to shift to another gear. Hell yeah, I was overwhelmed. At times, I felt as though I was over my head. I wasn't sure if I belonged in the company of Colonel Small, Lewis Burling, Elliot or even my wife, Julia. I needed to find my legs. Whatever shortcomings I felt, it was time to put them behind me.

This was my destiny. I had to put all else behind me. It was time for me to find that next gear. As soon as I did, my mind became a whirlwind and a steel trap.

Every agent who died was an award recipient: from regional and Bureau agents of the year to honors of achievement and commendation to Daedalian award recipients, the highest award an agent can receive. In a two or more person operation like the one with Bonner McGill and the other two agents, one of the agents killed in the operation had received an award.

Steve was a recipient of numerous awards during his time, including several regional agent of the year awards, honors of achievement and commendation, and the prestigious Daedalian award.

It wasn't hard to figure out what was going on. This was about more than just killing agents. It was about killing the best agents of the Bureau. I didn't understand it but I accepted it. This was personal with the leader of *Just Cause* — the Boss. He was out to prove a point, that he was the better agent. It made sense if Elliot and I were on his list. Elliot was probably the most decorated agent in FBI history and I had a couple awards myself.

The more I researched, the more things made sense to me. The bank robberies were about money, financing the cause. The killings were to prove a point. The phone calls probably signified that this was the end of the road. He didn't have anything else to prove, plus whoever the leader was, he had to be up in age. Something told me as a former agent, he got snubbed in some capacity with the Bureau. Maybe he was passed over for a regional chief or division chief position, or possibly a deputy director or director position.

This might have been true or it might have been my active imagination. What role had former Director Dooling played in this? Was he the leader of *Just Cause*? Or did he know the leader? Or was this a business venture for the former director?

My mind was in overdrive. As each minute passed, I felt better. My confidence was back. The two days were long and grueling, but it was worth it. The two days of waiting for something to happen helped me to get my edge back.

I was a kid in a candy store. I called Elliot with my exciting news. He told me to go with it. He recommended I get with Miguel Bishop and the Bureau's Information Systems Section and run a list of former and present agents who were major award recipients.

I gave Miguel a call and he told me he would jump on it right away.

Be careful what you ask for, you just may get it.

The cliché kept replaying in my head. I kept smiling as I made my way to pick up Janessa.

We had an appointment to keep.

Chapter
50

BLACK'S HOUSE OF CATFISH was Steve's favorite restaurant. Whenever I came to visit, it was a required stop for him, Alyse and his three kids: Janessa, Jarrod and Jerald. Located in Woodbridge, Virginia, it was a trek down I-95 South or Route 1.

I picked up Janessa from the CarsonOne building and we drove in silence to the restaurant. She wasn't in a talkative mood, especially after I told her new bodyguard, Alfredo Williams, I did not need him or Leonard to accompany us to the House of Catfish. Something was going on between the two. What, I didn't know, but I had a good idea.

When we arrived, Denise was already inside, talking to the owner, Black. I liked Black. He had had the restaurant for almost thirty years now. His name was in contrast to his light-skinned complexion. People were often surprised when they found out he was the owner. Barely over sixty, the man still looked all of forty. His jet-black wavy hair, thin mustache and goatee had no trace of gray setting in. He was also the person I went to when I wanted to open up my restaurants in the D.C. area.

"Excuse me, sir, could you please tell the owner I would like to see him?" I jokingly bantered.

Black spun around and replied, "I'm sorry, my father doesn't give smartasses the time of day."

We shook hands and hugged. Then he saw Janessa.

"Girl, bring your butt over here and give me a hug," he said as he held his arms wide. Seeing the two of them hugging brought back memories of when Steve and I used to bring the whole family here. Black would hug all of the kids and then spoil them rotten.

"Didn't I just see you here a week or so ago?" he asked. "You were with that . . ." He scratched his head as if he was searching for a name. ". . . that bodyguard guy."

Janessa looked at me out of the corner of her eye. "Yes, sir, Angelo," she deliberately lied.

"Yeah, that's his name," Black said in his jovial voice. That's one of the many things I loved about Black, he was always jovial. "He was a decent young man, but he wasn't for you, baby gurl."

"You mean Alfredo," I corrected as I looked cockeyed at Janessa.

Black was right. He wasn't for her and their relationship was inappropriate. I'm sure Denise saw my expression and rushed Black off. She told him to bring us the usual, which was the all-you-can-eat catfish for me and all-you-can-eat catfish and shrimp for the women, as well as the hush puppies, French fries, cole slaw and dinner rolls that came along with the meal.

"I'm a grown woman, Uncle Kenny," Janessa volunteered as soon as we sat down in our usual booth. I was sitting in the middle of the horseshoe style booth as each woman sat on opposite ends, facing each other.

"Too damn grown sometimes," I replied as we stared at each other. "Business is business, young lady, and he is your damn employee. Or did you forget about that?"

I was livid. I didn't care that he was Jay Joiner's nephew, I didn't like the young hothead bodyguard.

"Hell, even Mr. Black can see you two don't belong together."

"Uncle Kenny—"

Before Janessa could complete her thought, Denise started laughing and laughing hard. We looked at her. She finally settled down after a couple of minutes.

"Ooohhh boy, damn, I needed that," she said with tears in her eyes. By this time, I was smiling and Janessa had a confused look on her face.

"Excuse me, but you two remind me so much of Steve and Janessa, and how they used to go at it. A lot of times in this same old booth," she was still laughing between words.

"Oh, man. Kenny, did Steve ever tell you about the time Janessa came home from school with a hickey on her neck? We came here to Black's and it was a nice day outside. Well, Miss Janessa had on a turtleneck and we were all wondering why. Then her dad pulled the collar down and he went ballistic."

Denise started laughing again and this time, Black, who had made it back with our drinks and bread, had joined in, along with Janessa. Steve had told me about the story, but it wasn't funny when he told it. Not like now.

"He literally ran around the restaurant trying to catch Lil' Nessa," Black picked up the story. We were still howling. "One of the other customers said, 'Leave that little gurl alone or I will call the cops,' and Steve stopped, pulled his badge out and told the customer, 'call 'em, asshole, and tell 'em the FBI is in pursuit of a suspect.'"

I burst out laughing. "You have to be joking," I stated. Everyone was still in stitches.

"No, it was so damn crazy that night," Denise said. "Boy, I really miss those days."

Black left and we just chilled, telling stories about Steve and some of the crazy things he did or said at times.

Denise was the best storyteller. I saw something in her and it made me feel good. She missed her husband; probably more than me missing him as my brother or Janessa missing her father. We all lost something when he died, but Denise lost a husband — someone who was definitely her cornerstone.

After we ate as much as we could, it was time to get down to business. The real reason why we met at Black's.

"Your dad and I were both sluts when we first met," Denise jumped in. I was completely shocked by her comment.

"Mom, I don't wanna hear that!" Janessa spoke up.

"You need to hear it," Denise expressed. She was relaxed and comfortable. There was a glow on her face . . .

not a sexual glow, but the glow of contentment. Her life had taken a turn for the better.

"This is life, baby. Our life." She took a swallow of her drink. "We fell in love with each other, got married and unbelievably, I don't think either of us was expecting our lives to change. We were both on the fast track and Steve was still playing big brother and daddy to Kenny and Alyse. I'm not even sure we loved each other in the beginning.

"But things changed. We steadily fell in love and when you were conceived, I think that was the clincher for us. Then another agent told your dad we had been sleeping together."

Denise paused. Mother and daughter had eye contact — strong glances that could have awakened the dead. I was surprised by Denise's candor. She wasn't holding anything back. Maybe she realized it was time to be upfront with her daughter and make everything right.

"This agent, I had slept with once since your dad and I had been married. He wanted me. I didn't want him. He told me about the sexcapades of your dad, but I didn't care about that. But your dad could not say the same thing. He believed the agent, and I moved out. It took four months before we were able to reconcile.

"Steve and I made a deal. He raised the kids and I moved up the corporate ladder," she half-heartedly smiled and leaned forward. I saw a tear in her eye. "What your Uncle Elliot is doing, that's what your dad should be doing. But Steve didn't care. He wanted to be a dad, a good dad. He wanted me to stay on the fast track."

Denise grabbed Janessa's hands and I saw the tears in both of their eyes. "Your dad sacrificed for me. I will always love him. I have always loved you and your brothers, 'Nessa. But your dad was my life. You and I never really got along, but it was because I didn't know anything about being a mother. And truthfully, I didn't try to learn anything about being a mom. Your father was the parent in the family. He made our world great — all our worlds.

"I know you guys lost a great father. But I lost the love of my life. I lost the man who treated me like a queen, baby.

And yes, your dad was your dad. I only made one mistake after that, baby, and it was a matter of life or death while I was on a mission. Your father knew about it. He forgave me.

"In so many ways, 'Nessa, I failed you guys as a mother. Your aunt and uncle did a better job of being there for you. Your dad taught you well. At age fourteen or fifteen, you were better for the twins than me."

I didn't know what to think. Damn. Denise laid it on the line. I thought this was her regaining her daughter's trust and love, which truthfully, I didn't know if she ever lost in the first place. But Janessa was strange sometimes. I loved her to death, but she had to be the moodiest damn person I ever met. And she was my niece. And next to Julia, she was the only other woman I loved unconditionally.

"I love you, mom," Janessa said.

Both women got up and hugged each other. I saw Black and his wife out of the corner of my eye. They were smiling. I was smiling.

I looked at Denise. Tears were still rolling down her face. "I love you, too, baby," she told Janessa. "And when I kill the fools who killed your dad, then mommy will have her closure."

Chapter
51

THIS WAS THE PLACE. Where one life ended and another life began. Denise and Janessa decided to spend time together. That was a good thing. On my way back to the city, I somehow ended up there — the Lorton Warehouse District.

The warehouse district was five miles off Route 1 in the Lorton, Virginia area, actually not too far from the Virginia State Penitentiary. The first three miles off Route 1 was paved road, followed by a mile of dirt and gravel road, before the final mile of paved road.

This was the site where Steve died. The place was abandoned now. Twenty-three buildings of empty warehouses. I took my time driving down the empty road. It was a good drive for someone trying to get away from the hustle and bustle of everyday life. The greenery of the trees and bushes for the five miles was breathtaking.

I slowed my pace. I was fixated on the scenery. Unknowingly, I had pulled over to the side of the road. I had actually gotten out of the car and just chilled. There was a slight breeze that day. It had been threatening rain for the past week, but not a drop had fallen. However, it did make for a good breeze.

I was kind of melancholy after the lunch with Denise and Janessa. We had a good conversation during lunch and afterwards, we talked in the parking lot. Denise was in a talkative mood. She told Janessa things I never knew about Steve. It was good for Janessa to hear both positive and negative things about her father.

At one point, she mentioned Steve wanted a woman like his mother. That surprised me. Then she explained the relationship between Steve and Miss Kathy, my mother. I soon realized that Steve looked at Miss Kathy as his mother. That made me feel good, but I also felt a little despondent.

I didn't get it. I guess in my mind, I didn't see a comparison between Denise and my mother. I loved Denise. She was still my sister-in-law and we had a better relationship now than when Steve was alive.

Truthfully, I never realized how much she loved Steve, until he died. She was a wreck for several years before she got her life together. Her once young-looking face had aged. When Steve was alive, she looked ten years younger than her actual age. Now, she looked five years older than her true age. But that was good. A couple of years ago, she looked ten years older.

She explained to both Janessa and me that my mother was a strong-willed woman who didn't take stuff off anyone. She had two sides to her: the mild-mannered mom and the take-no-shit wife. She told me things I never knew. Things Steve knew. But he was the protector . . . and they had a great relationship.

Many psychologists say most children want to date someone like their mothers or fathers. Denise probably had a point. If Miss Kathy did have those two sides to her, my Julia was probably the splitting image of my mother. That was freaky to me. Did I marry someone like Miss Kathy? Maybe I did.

I knew Denise had only seen one side of Miss Kathy and Steve loved that. I knew some of the women he dated or slept with, and they all came from the same mold. But Denise was his soul mate.

He died happy.

He died in this warehouse district.

Sitting on my car, enjoying the day, I hit "Beach Home" on my cell. I was surprised at the voice on the other end of the line.

"I'll be damned. It's alive. Stop the presses and hide the criminals, Homicide Detective Melvin Clayton lives," I joked.

"Is this Special Agent Kenny "KC" Carson or is this Mr. Kenneth Carson, private citizen?" Clay bantered.

"Damn, boy, how in the hell are you?"

"I'm cool, bro. Question is, how are you? How you holding up?"

That was a good question. *How was I holding up?* It was a relevant question. Of course, I had a vague answer. "Doing good, doing good. Just rolling with the punches," I lied. At times, I didn't know if I was coming or going. Every time I thought I was good, I had to take a step back.

"KC, you talking to me, don't do that. If you need to talk, talk. But don't give me that lame ass shit."

I didn't know what to say. I actually felt bad. Clay and I had so much history over the years. We grew up in the same neighborhood in Memphis. We hooked up every now and then when I was in the NFL and used to visit Steve. He taught me how to investigate a case. We were boys and I was acting ill, like I couldn't talk to my friend.

"I'm surviving, bro. Trust me, I'm surviving."

"Ok. Well, all's well here. We're holding down the fort. This is actually good. I needed some time off. Gloria is taking care of me and driving everybody crazy."

We laughed. I knew how Gloria could be at times. When she wanted to take over, the best thing you could do was just do what she said.

"Hey, man, I really called to talk to my dad. Is he around?" My voice cracked and I knew Clay probably picked it up. After all, he was probably the best detective on the D.C. force. He was also the leading forensics expert on the East Coast.

"Dad? Big step, my brotha. I think a step in the right direction."

There was a pause. The twins jumped on the phone and wanted to know when they could come home and live a normal life. Lil' Steve was happy to talk to dad and Devin missed Julia. Everyone was well.

"Hey, son, what can I do you for?" Howard Carson, my father, asked.

I didn't know how to respond. He was my dad. To have Denise tell it, he loved my mom just as much as she loved my brother. I was the hard son. The unforgiving son. I couldn't let go of my mother's death. I always blamed Howard. I became what I was in spite of Howard. But I loved my dad, because he was my dad.

Everyone saw something different in Howard. What they saw was something good — from my mom to Alyse and Steve to Denise and Julia. Why didn't I see what they saw?

"Yeah. I was just wondering," I said, then paused. I had to muster up the words. "Yeah . . . ah, could you tell me about my mom?"

Part III

Closure is something foreign to me. People talk about closure after the death of a loved one, a divorce or breakup, or even losing a job. It's supposed to be the end of a dire road and the bridge to a new beginning. Maybe closure is a good thing and a needed necessity. But I don't need closure — I just need to kick some ass.

- Kenny "KC" Carson

Chapter 52

I'M BACK AMONGST THE living, was all the caller said. He didn't need to elaborate. The Boss knew what he meant. Ranger 1, Carmine Ball, was free to operate. That was good news to the Boss. His plans were simple, but with Carmine's availability, he was assured success.

He was determined to make a point with his last attacks. They had been playing this game for twenty-three years now. At some point, it was time to say enough was enough.

Game — set — match.

This was the last shot at the end of the game to win the NBA Championship. The winning field goal at the Super Bowl.

The Boss liked Carmine. He was the best protégé he ever had. He had mentioned to Carmine on several occasions that one day he would be the Boss.

Carmine was a fast learner and good listener. They made a good team. The young man had brought something to the team that they needed: technology. The internet opened up a new world for the group. It became easier to communicate with everyone. As a result, location really didn't make a difference.

From: Joke
To: Ranger1
Subject: A New Day

Glad u survived the onslaught by the boys in dark blue jackets...lol. They have made life difficult, but I'm actually glad they have fight in them. So they have altered our plans, but such is life. Are you ready to kick some more governmental ass?...rofl...

Your vigilance is rewarding
Joke

From: Ranger1
To: Joke
Subject: Ref: A New Day

Bring it on. We are definitely ready to kick more ass. These fucks do not have a clue who they are fucking with. But we do need some leverage. They have my dad and mom both locked up. I want them released. We need to kidnap someone high in their hierarchy or high in the Cabinet. My folks were not a part of the plan.

Talk to me. What are we going to do about that? You know I would follow you to hell and back. But this is different. My folks will not be casualties of war. Understand?

Still vigilant
Ranger Man

From: Joke
To: Ranger1
Subject: Ref: Ref: A New Day

Don't worry about your parents, I already have a plan to have them released. Never count me short, u know that. Your parents are strong and know their rights. Though they are being held as terrorists, they still have certain rights.

These next attacks will render the Bureau helpless. They will know who they are screwing with. We have handled everything they have

thrown our way, but the games are over. I take
my hat off to the deputy director. But now it's
time to take off the kids' gloves.

Wherever u r, go out and have fun tonight.
Tomorrow is a new day…we will begin again. A
new day for Just Cause!

Have enough fun for me tonight
Joke

From: Ranger1
To: Joke
Subject: Ref: Ref: Ref: A New Day

We r n the city. We have plans tonight. If we r
striking tomorrow, when r we going to get the
info? Remember, planning and organization
have been our cornerstones to success. I like
the new day, the new beginning. But I want
Lucas to hurt and hurt bad. We need to be ready
and readiness means planning.
Ranger1

The Boss knew Carmine was right. He needed to get the
ball rolling, and as much as it pained him, he had to come up
with something viable to appease young Carmine. After all,
he was the future of *Just Cause*, if *Just Cause* lasted another
decade or two.

But the Boss felt strange. Maybe it was the simple fact
he had not heard from Carmine. *Where was he? Where had
he been? Why hadn't he communicated until that e-mail?*

Maybe he was too paranoid. But didn't he have reason to
be paranoid? His paranoia had paid huge dividends for *Just
Cause.* Maybe he needed to stay paranoid.

From: Ranger1
To: Joke
Subject: Ref: Ref: Ref: Ref: A New Day

What's the deal, Big Joker? What u want me
to do, besides having a good time? Talk to
me!
Ranger1

From: Joke
To: Ranger1
Subject: Ref: Ref: Ref: Ref: Ref: A New Day

Get to a secure phone and call me...
Joke

The Boss knew he had to trust someone. Trust was not a
word near and dear to his heart. He was a man who knew his
weaknesses and strengths. He was a superficial man. From
his charm to his trust, even to his love . . . it was all
superficial.

This was about the big payday. He had a plan and he
knew it would work. After all, he was the Boss. He was the
best. He proved it as an agent and again, as the leader of *Just
Cause* in '82, '93 and the present day.

When the phone rang, he knew he had to give Carmine
Ball his amount of superficial trust.

Chapter
53

THE POWER OF THE mind was usually the *limiting factor* in every case. We called it *limfac*. Criminals screwed up either by being too dumb or even being too damn smart. Amazing to think that criminals could be too good for their own good, but that was life. Everyone had a *limfac*.

My limfac at the moment was my back. It wasn't completely a mental thing. In my case, it was muscle spasms in my lower left back. The pain had kicked in several days ago and knocked me on my butt. It was so excruciating, it took me twenty minutes to walk twenty feet from my bed to the bedroom door.

Many people wouldn't understand how a lower back pain could render a person completely helpless. But I knew how, from personal experience.

In my second year in the NFL, I intercepted a pass and was headed to the end zone when I jumped over a would-be tackler. Another potential tackler reached out, grabbed and twisted my facemask. It wasn't my neck that hurt, but my back. I lay on the field for a good ten minutes.

That was the first time I had muscle spasms. It was the same day my doctor informed me I would have recurring back/muscle spasms the rest of my life. I wasn't ready for that; I needed a second opinion. The second doctor told me someone my age and in my profession had a fifty-fifty chance of reoccurrence. In other words, he didn't tell me a damn thing.

My first doctor was right. I had recurring back pains at least twice a year for about ten years. I had been more fortunate recently. I hadn't had a back spasm for the past several years.

I guess I had stressed or worried myself to a spasm this time. It made my talk with Howard stressful. He told me about my mom, but I was the one who had asked him not to hold back. What I got in return was a man who loved his wife and really missed her. I could hear the tears falling through the phone, as in, I could hear his voice cracking and the mixed emotions of smiles and sadness. He really did love my mom, Miss Kathy.

Listening to Denise and my dad, I realized I had been holding a grudge for too many years for nothing. How could I be mad at a man who loved my mother and who, in turn, loved him? Yeah, I had stressed myself into back spasms.

The timing was bad, but isn't that when something like this usually happens. When things were progressing with my research, boom, the bottom dropped out. Or so I thought. It had been over a week since we had heard anything from *Just Cause.* I felt like they were waiting on me to heal.

Julia was there when she could be. She initially thought she was the one responsible for my condition from the sex and various positions we tried. Typical female reaction.

I laughed at the thought, even though I gave her her just due. She definitely knew how to work it in the lovemaking department. But I was sure my back pain was from worrying and stressing.

Then, I felt the best I had in several days. The timing was right. The phone call I received was unexpected.

"How's it going, Mr. Back Pain?" I heard the joking voice of Dr. Beth Storm.

"I'm doing much better, thank you very much," I replied, smiling from the comment.

"Well, I have some news for you. Guess who has been spending time at Big Dick Peter's?"

It was a name from the past. I smiled at the question from Beth. "You do know everyone in the real world calls it by the name on the outside of the building, *BDP's?*" I bantered.

"You still didn't answer my question . . . guess who has been spending time there?" Beth repeated herself.

"Ok, I give, who has been spending time at BDP's?"

"Well, Pete has a regular who likes to think of himself as a big man in the making. He's been spending time there for the past three to four months. He has a crew of five to eight guys of various nationalities who hangs out with him."

"Does this young man have a name?"

"Yeah. His name is Carmine Ball. Sounds like a winner!"

I could hear the excitement in Beth's voice. She had done well. I knew where she had received her information. She and Peter Brown had met several years ago when we were looking for a child molester and murderer.

They were complete opposites in so many ways. Beth was a psychologist, conservative, very professional and sometimes uptight. Pete, on the other hand, was a comedian, outgoing and funny. Additionally, Beth was white. I sometimes joked that she was too white and petite, compared to the six five, two hundred seventy pound Pete.

Their first meeting was somewhat dubious. Somebody who matched Pete's description was raping and killing young white girls, between the ages of twelve through fifteen. We received an anonymous phone call that the owner of BDP's Comedy House was the rapist and murderer. The caller also informed us that he had his next victim at the club.

I was the lead agent and Beth was on my team. We rushed over to the comedy club in downtown D.C., not far from the White House. It was broad daylight as we broke down the front door and searched the club. Beth and I made our way to the upper floor and the back of the club before we came upon a room blasting music through a thick door.

When we burst through the door, Big Dick Pete was banging a white girl, but she was not a girl. She was a young woman, blonde with huge breasts. Undoubtedly, Pete was surprised when we burst in. He stood and wanted to know what was going on.

After we explained and checked the young twenty-three year old blonde's identification, we apologized to Big Dick Pete. Before we left, Beth told the club owner that he should leave the young girls alone and find him a real woman. Before departing, she flipped her business card to him.

We later learned the anonymous caller was the young lady's boyfriend.

For Pete and Beth, that was the first meeting of many to come. They had an on again, off again relationship.

"Definitely, Beth," I responded. "A winner and then some. Question is, when is the next time he will be there?"

"Not sure, but over the past week, he has patronized the club three times."

"Damn, we are looking every damn where for this man and he is right here in our backyard."

"Where's the best place to hide, KC, when people are looking for you? How about the place you know they won't be looking for you? Right in your own backyard."

Beth was right. What better place to hide than within walking distance to the White House. These guys were probably smarter than we gave them credit for. My back spasms had ceased, but my determination to capture the bad guys had increased.

I told Beth I was on my way in. We had a breakthrough.

Chapter
54

AS I DROVE TO the Hoover Building, my mind was in overdrive. I remembered this was always my time of the year, getting ready for another season of football. It didn't make a difference . . . junior high, high school, college and the NFL, I was always preparing for the upcoming season. Then came Steve's death and I dropped everything.

The past year was the most relaxing year I had ever experienced. I didn't have to worry about getting ready for the season or what case I was trying to solve. The only time I had to wake up early was to get the boys ready for school and drop them off. Before and after our marriage, my life was complete.

But I was back in the world I ran from. Amazingly, I liked being back. Talking to Julia, I was aware that we both had the same problem. We both liked being agents. I didn't know if I should feel guilty or happy. I was an agent again. Did I want to be an agent full time?

They always say to weigh the pros and cons when trying to make a tough decision. I too was a novice at the pros and cons. If the pros outweighed the cons that was a good thing, right? However, if the cons outweighed the pros, then you still went with the pros. Did the cons ever win?

I guess it depended on the situation.

My goal while I was driving was to figure out the angles as much as I could. I knew the Boss was a former agent who disliked his fellow agents, especially those who received major awards. The thing I didn't know was what scared me.

Was the Boss still an agent or somewhere in the government food line? Did he still receive a regular paycheck or monthly stipend from Uncle Sam?

The questions and thoughts were beating me up, and I needed answers. Could the answers be with Carmine Ball, aka Ranger 1, at BDP's Comedy House later that night? I hoped so. He had been there three times in the past week. We hoped that night would be the fourth.

Beth had presented a new profile on the Boss based on the information we had. The phone calls and attacks had provided Beth with enough data. He was African-American, a classic control freak who was hell bent on being the best. Money was a secondary priority to him, next to being number one. Beth was sure he was a former agent who probably left the Bureau just before or after the first murders in '82, but she wouldn't have been surprised if he left the Bureau just before or after the '93 murder spree. It was too wide a window to work with.

I didn't know if her profile was on the money, but I was sure it had some merit. The good thing was the nationality of the Boss. Trying to find that one person, that needle in a haystack, had become much easier. Over the years, especially in the early '80s and '90s, the number of black needles in the Bureau's haystack was small.

As I entered the Hoover Building, I was convinced that the Boss had my name written all over him. He was my kill. I couldn't imagine the locality of our gunfight, but I knew it was going to be a gunfight. Just like the old days of the cowboy, the black and white westerns. I was holding on to that thought.

Another thought not far from my mind was the intimidation factor. As I walked into the conference room in the presence of Elliot Lucas's dream team, the intimidation factor kicked me in the face. Intimidation was a fact of life.

Up until then, it hadn't been a fact or factor in my life. I grew up an athlete and never backed down from a battle on the basketball court, football field or running track. But I had never walked away from something and come back — until then. I left the Bureau after my last case and a year later, I was donning my badge and FBI-issued Glock again.

I didn't expect we would be walking into a meeting when I arrived at the building. Everyone was sitting and waiting. There was a little chit-chat here and there, but for the most part, the room was quiet.

I found a seat just as Elliot was walking in the room with a long-time partner in tow. The slender, light caramel complexioned man was Darrell Adams, Special Agent with Alcohol, Tobacco, Firearms and Explosives.

"We received another phone call from the Boss yesterday," Elliot's booming voice echoed throughout the room. "Hit the control button, Julia."

Julia hit the remote and the familiar sound of the computer-generated voice jumped out.

"Elliot, my boy. I really hope all is well with you and the family. That would be the FBI family. Where do I begin? First, let me congratulate you on a job well done. You really put me in a bind. You killed some of my team members, arrested others and have the remaining ones running around like chickens with their heads cut off."

The Boss started laughing. I knew Beth was honing in on his every word and anything else she could glean from the computer voice. Even though I wasn't a psych person myself, I think we all knew it was a nervous laughter.

"Why are you calling, Boss?" Elliot interrupted the brief silence. "To give yourself up, I hope."

It was a little strange hearing Elliot on the computer and looking right at him in the flesh.

"Come on, Elliot. You know how this game is played. The only difference this time is the bad guys are going to win. You are a formidable opponent, Elliot. I will give you that. The previous occasions, the Bureau didn't have anyone who could match wits with me. Now they do. And sadly, it's another black man. How ironic is that?"

"Yeah, I'm laughing my black ass off," Elliot responded. We could hear the sarcasm in his voice. He was pushing the Boss's buttons.

"Fuck you, Elliot!" the excited but flat voice blasted back. "You are the reason your agents will be dying in droves! You, you pompous ass! You were successful at one thing — pissing me the fuck off. You altered my plans and you know the crazy thing? I take my hat off to you and I salute you. But you are only the second best nigger, Elliot. I am and will always be the top nigger!"

"Boss, you can have the title. If you know me and I know you do, you know I don't believe in the N-word. Call me what you must. This is not about you versus me, but *Just Cause* versus the FBI. You won the first two battles. But know this, Boss; this is another day, a new day!"

"Poor Elliot," the computer-generated voice was calmer than before. Maybe he recognized that he was losing it. "You cannot and you will not stop me or *Just Cause*. And this is about us, you and me, probably more than you realize.

"But Mr. Deputy Director, this is what I want from you. In two days, I plan on robbing four banks and attacking four Bureau operations. Additionally, within a day, expect a top official in the U.S. government to be kidnapped. And yes, we want money. We want a ransom for the golden boy we plan on kidnapping."

Before Elliot could respond, the phone went click.

Chapter 55

"AS OF THIS MORNING, Secretary of State Ian Bradley was abducted," Elliot dropped the bomb on us. "His three bodyguards were gunned down and he was kidnapped outside his home in Sterling, Virginia. The following note was left on the Secretary's car." We all looked up at the computer screen at the front of the room:

> Elliot,
> This is for you. You can have the Secretary back. My demands are simple: Secretary Bradley for Dave and Carol Ball.
> Additionally, we want $40 million. If both stipulations are met, then Bradley will be returned intact. I will get back with you on the time and location for the exchange.
> Terms are not negotiable.
>
> Just Cause

"Obviously, *Just Cause* is back," Elliot continued. "This was definitely a surprise. Two of the bodyguards were shot by a long-range rifle and the third was shot close range. We have a crime scene unit on site. This occurred a couple of hours ago. Nothing has been leaked to the media yet, but I'm sure it will be soon. Director Tellis has been summoned to the White House. I'm sure we will hear something soon.

"In front of you is a psych profile put together by Dr. Storm as well as a list of sixteen viable former and present

African-American agents who meet the physical similarities
of the Boss. Our information on the Boss has been sketchy,
to say the least. For the most part, he has been described as
being six feet four, two hundred fifty pounds or more, short
afro, dark complexion and no distinguishing marks. Our list
actually consists of 14 agents six feet two inches and taller.

"Before I get to the last item on my agenda, I'm going to
turn you over to ATF Special Agent Darrell Adams."

"Good morning," Darrell began. "We have been tracking
a shipment of military-issued arms that were stolen a month
ago, prior to reaching their destination — Fort Bragg, North
Carolina. The info we have has led us to the D.C.
metropolitan area and possibly to the group the FBI is trying
to catch, *Just Cause.* Unfortunately, we do not have an agent
on the inside, but one of the guys on the team who stole the
weapons has been working with us. His brother is in jail, and
we are willing to make a deal if we can procure the weapons.

"Our informant gave us six locations within the Beltway
for the possible drop-off. We have a team at each site
providing surveillance for the time being. As far as weapons
are concerned, we know from the manifest that we are
looking at hand grenades, various types of Glocks, M-15
rifles, MP5 submachine guns, long range sniper rifles and
the XM8 lightweight assault rifle. Those are just some of the
weapons. In other words, there are enough weapons in this
shipment to start a healthy war against America."

Special Agent Adams thanked everyone and took a seat.
The room was quiet. We all were shocked by the briefing.
Elliot didn't waste time moving on.

"ATF has a team at every possible location," Elliot
added. "Two is in the District, two in Virginia and three in
Maryland. I am assigning a two-man team to all sites to
augment ATF. The ATF team chief will be the lead at each
site. If activity at those sites pick up, it will be both the ATF
and FBI on scene.

"Lastly, we would love to wrap this case up within the
next several days. I'm sure some of you have heard about the
hurricane headed towards the gulf coast. As of now, they are
predicting the hurricane will hit anywhere from Florida to

Texas, but in all likelihood it looks like this hurricane, Hurricane Katrina, may definitely hit New Orleans.

"So let's wrap this case up. I don't want anyone rushing, but if the Boss sticks by his prediction, we may be all over the place tomorrow. The kidnapping means they are desperate. I believe the threat of a major criminal wave tomorrow is more than just a threat. I think it is real and will probably be bloody. *Just Cause* is desperate. We made them desperate. It's time we put an end to them. Then our fellow agents who have died at the hands of *Just Cause* and their families will be able to rest in peace."

Chapter 56

ALL MEN ARE EQUAL, but some are just more a pain in the ass than others. That's how his mother explained racism to him. He couldn't help but smile at the thought. She was a strong one, his mother. Elliot just hoped that both his mother and father approved of the man he had become.

He often wondered about the characteristics and roots of men. He even wondered about the trendy word of today — equality, and if he would ever truly see it. He knew what traits and characteristics he received from his mother: compassion for his fellow man, love, honor and respect. All those good things that made a man attractive to a woman.

Then there was his father, the prime example of a strong black man. He worked for the railroad, repairing rails and trains, and doing whatever dirty work he had to do to feed his family. If he made it home twice a month and spent a whole week home, that was a good month. He was a strong man from head to toe. Elliot remembered doing chin-ups on one of his father's powerful arms, like it was a monkey bar.

His father taught him what it meant to be a man. And he was respected — by all. He remembered Old Man Fisher, the white sharecropper, who often bullied the black folks into working for him at wages so low that a man couldn't put food on his family's table after working seventy hours per week.

Old Man Fisher came looking for him when he was eleven years old to work the fields. At age eleven, he looked like he was seventeen or eighteen.

Old Man Fisher didn't know Elliot's father was home. When the sharecropper grabbed young Elliot by the arm, Yancy Lucas walked out on his porch. What happened after that stayed with Elliot forever. His father walked up to the man and grabbed him by his throat.

"If'n ya 'ver touch mine agin, Mista' Fisher, I promise ya, I be burying ya 'afore they can git ta me, ya 'ear?"

And Old Man Fisher did hear. Elliot knew they would be moving that night before the posse came and lynched his daddy and probably lynch him too. But no one ever came. It was rumored that Old Man Fisher went to the railroad folks to get Yancy Lucas fired. Who in their right mind would fire someone who did the job of four men?

His father gave him strength to endure anything and everything that came his way. He was the one who told Elliot he was going to college and make something out of himself, to do what he was never privileged enough to do.

Yeah, he had his father's strength.

As he walked through the doors of the White House, he knew why President Cabot had summoned him. He had the strength of character and knowledge that served Cabot well. And he did like Cabot. The President didn't see black and white, and Elliot knew that that *should be* a good thing; but it wasn't.

In a world and country that thrived on black and white, the man in charge needed to be more realistic. Elliot knew what a world *should be* was still a hope and a dream in 2005 for people of color. And the day might come when he did see a colorless world. But he was not willing to put money on it. Not today, probably not ever.

"Mr. President, Donny, John," Elliot greeted the men in the Oval Office.

"Glad you could make it," President Cabot jokingly bantered.

"For you, sir, anything," Elliot quickly retorted.

He looked at the face of John Tellis, his boss, and wondered what was going on. Tellis's face was beet red, like he had just gotten spanked for stealing candy, while Don

Caughman, the Director of the CIA, was looking cool as a cucumber.

"Elliot, I was just telling John and Donny about our conversation a little while ago," President Cabot began. "We are talking about the best course of action on the Ian Bradley situation. I want to hear your thoughts."

Instantly, Elliot knew where this was going and why his boss was beet red. Ian Bradley and John Tellis had been friends since their days at Harvard. When the President came to the Hoover Building to talk to Elliot, he disclosed that he thought Bradley was the true leader of *Just Cause*. First, he knew Tellis was mad at him for not disclosing this type information to him. Secondly, John Tellis was what his mother used to call a "prideful man." He didn't like stank sticking to him. The stank of Ian Bradley might actually discourage the President from nominating him as the Secretary of State.

"Sir, I think you should make Secretary Bradley a martyr," Elliot offered.

The room was quiet. The four men were congregated in the sitting area of the Oval Office. Elliot chose to sit in a chair facing the President, while Donny Caughman and John Tellis shared a sofa.

"Damn it, Elliot, you sound just like Donny," the President said. He smiled and walked to his desk to retrieve some papers.

"Gentlemen, as I stated earlier, I went to Elliot and asked him to provide surveillance on that son-of-a-bitch. Elliot had his assistant, Julia, hand-carry this to me this morning." The President passed out a folder to Caughman and Tellis. "By the way, Elliot, is Julia your damn executive assistant again or an agent?"

Elliot liked the President's sense of humor and how he could break the tension in a room. But as he scanned the face of John Tellis, he wondered if his boss could handle the pressure of his best friend betraying him and his country.

"Are we sure about this?" Tellis asked. His question was not aimed at anyone in particular, but Elliot decided he was the one who needed to answer the question.

"Yes, it's accurate. There are photographs in the back to validate the report."

Both Tellis and Caughman thumbed through the documents to reach the photographs in the back of the folder. What they saw left both men flabbergasted.

"This is terrible," Tellis barely murmured.

"Terrible is not the word for it, John," President Cabot chided in. "This is the asshole you recommended to me . . ."

Tellis looked up and Elliot couldn't believe he could get any redder than he already was when he walked in the room. But he was.

". . . and no, I don't blame you, John. But do not sit here and tell me we need to rescue this asshole when he set up two agents to be killed by a sniper and he shot the last agent his own damned self." He paused as he took a swallow of his bottled water. "Now, do you want to be the one who goes to the families of these three agents and tell them your *best friend* set up your agents?

"No, John, we are not playing this straight down the middle. The U.S.'s stand is we do not negotiate with terrorists. If he is the leader of this fucking *Just Cause,* no sweat on his brow. However, if he is not the leader, they can kill his ass and make him a fucking martyr. And if and when that day comes, I will sing his praises and lie about how great he was to this country and how he always put country before self until he got sick.

"But if I see the son-of-a-bitch first, I will probably shoot his ass my own damn self."

Once again, the room was cloaked with silence. Elliot knew why the President had come to him. He was the disinterested party. He had no ties with Ian Bradley. His ties were with the man he called Commander-in-Chief. But Ian Bradley moved to number one on his *shit list* when he had his agents killed and worse, killed one himself.

"I guess my question should be to you, Elliot," Tellis began. "Why didn't our agent who took these pictures do anything to stop it?"

Elliot had known John Tellis for a long time, longer than anyone else in this room. To him, this was the real John

Tellis. He didn't like the pressure, so he passed the buck elsewhere. But Elliot was used to it. He knew that was why Tellis wanted him as a Deputy Director — he could handle the pressure.

"Our man was there for surveillance only," Elliot responded. "As much as he wanted to help, there was nothing he could do, it happened so fast. Additionally, it was not in our best interest to confront Bradley or the sniper."

"How do we play this, sir?" Donny Caughman asked. "Do you want us to get in the game or leave it to the Bureau?"

"Donny, the CIA and FBI are enjoying the best relationship the two have ever had. I take my hat off to both you and John. But Elliot is running this show. He is not to blame for what happened with Ian. Ian is my mistake. Elliot knows what I want and he will deliver."

The President leaned forward in his seat, looking directly at Elliot Lucas. He smiled. "Donny, Elliot is my man. He knows what I want. He's good at catching and eliminating the bad guys."

Chapter
57

CARMINE BALL FREQUENTLY BRAGGED about being overly blessed. No, he was not a religious man. His religion was money, women, a good time, adventure and money. And yes, in that order. Money was first and last with him. His money. Not the money of Dave and Carol Ball.

But he did thank God everyday, thanked Him for bringing the crazy motherfucker named the Boss into his life. Man, did he love that man or what?

The Boss was more of a father to him than his own wimp of a father. After he had known the Boss for several months, he was happy his mother had snuck out and had an affair with the tall, studly Boss. He just wished he had happened sooner. Then maybe he would have been born to a real man. Not like his father.

Sure, his father was a provider and gave him everything he wanted. But he never received the thing he wanted most — time. The Boss gave him that. Damn, he loved the man. He would go to hell and back for his mentor.

He noticed when his mother introduced him how they looked at each other and talked back and forth. He had never seen that look on his mother's face before that day. She was actually glowing. At first, he was mad. *How can she look at a black man that way? Doesn't she still loves my father?*

As time passed, he understood. The Boss was something special. He could screw another man's woman and the man would thank him for doing it. Hasn't his father thanked him?

His mother knew what young Carmine needed — a real man in his life. The man who had made her a real woman.

Carmine never believed he would do what he did. Before and after his training sessions with the Boss, he would do his exercises outside in front of the house, while his mother and her Mandingo did their business in the bedroom. And he was happy for his mother. She had everything a woman wanted or needed, except a good man. The Boss was her good man.

It was 1992 when he met the Boss. The man had been his mother's real man for ten years before that. Damn, how come he wasn't around to be his father?

Alexandria, Virginia

From the first sentence out of his mouth, Carmine, aka Ranger 1, liked the plan the Boss had devised. Like the commercial, it was *genius*. What made it more beautiful was the carnage would be in the backyard of the nation's capital, the FBI's stomping ground.

He wished he could be in on everything that was happening today, but he was only one man. What the Boss had planned required at least forty to fifty men. He deployed sixty — guaranteeing success. *Simultaneous combustion.*

Yep, that's what the Boss called it. At the bottom of the thirteenth hour, all hell would be breaking loose in the nation's capital and three surrounding cities. After that day, only one day would be more devastating to America; and that was September 11, 2001.

The sweet part of the plan was they were not expecting anything until the following day. Of course, they were taking the Boss at his word. *Damn, I love that man*, kept echoing in the mind of Ranger 1.

He smiled to himself as he checked his watch. Ten minutes from chaos time. He and his team of five were actually parked across the street from their target — the First American Federal Bank of Virginia on Route 1, only a couple of miles from Fort Belvoir.

There were three Alexandria Police Department cars in the parking lot of the bank. Ranger 1 loved it. He hoped they would still be there in ten minutes.

He wished he was there from day one back in 1982 when the original chaos began. But he was still happy when his mother introduced him to the Boss. Damn, he loved that woman. He laughed at himself. Hell, he loved everyone at this particular moment.

He recalled his first time robbing a bank. It was the same damn bank, First American Federal. It was a practice run. He and the Boss. They killed four people that day: the bank president, two security guards and a customer who tried to play hero. It was a high he had never felt before. The money wasn't important, but who couldn't use $120,000?

He laughed to himself again. The year was 1992. He was only seventeen years old, not yet legal drinking age. And the clincher — the Boss gave him $90,000.

His team knew him. They knew he internalized everything, and then when he laughed, he was ready. They believed in him just as much as he believed in the Boss. To his team, the Boss was a ghost. He was the only one who had ever met the mystical leader. However, they didn't give a damn. Each of them had seen more money than they ever dreamed possible.

Ranger 1 was still in his own world when they drove from the shopping center to the bank.

"Lock and load!" Ranger 1 shouted. "We take out the cops first, and then I will take out the bank president. It's about the money, baby! All about the money!"

They pulled up in front of the bank's front door in an all-black SUV, blocking in two of the police cars. All six men rushed in the bank, guns blazing.

Chapter
58

"BABY, GO OUT THERE and build your foundation." I can remember when my mama, Miss Kathy, said that to me. I was only twelve and an inch shorter than her at the time. My mom stood five six and had a small frame, but stout shoulders. She carried the weigh of the world on those shoulders.

She died four years later. I always thought that was the end of my world. But I still had Alyse to raise and Steve, my big brother, who actually completed raising both of us.

I was still trying to absorb and resolve everything Denise and my dad had told me about my mom. I never saw that spirited, high strung side of my mom. Maybe I didn't want to see it. To me, she never reached her potential. I knew she would have been a great teacher at any level. She had so much to offer. But she settled. Why? I would never know.

For years after she died, I talked to my mom. In my mind, she talked back to me. We used to have some lively conversations. If anyone ever saw me during these conversations, I was sure they would have tried to have me committed. But our conversations stopped the day I said, "I do" to Julia. I thought she let me go. I was sure Alyse let her know Julia was a great woman and we would probably be together forever. Hell, we were two peas in the same pod, Julia and I.

"Thank you. I love you both," I said to Miss Kathy and Alyse as I got out of my car.

I was at the Hoover Building and didn't have a clue what was going on, but I was told to go to the armory, and then report to the Deputy Director at the first floor conference room. Everyone was running around like they were getting ready for battle. Agents were putting on flak vests and arming themselves to the max.

After I put on my vest and FBI jacket, I checked out another Glock to go with the Glock I already had. I also picked up several extra clips. I turned down the MP-5 the agent issuing weapons tried to give me.

When I made it to the conference room, Special Agent Charlie McClary swept me up along with eight other agents. He told me he would brief me on the way. I was at a lost for words. I saw Julia walking towards the lobby. She saw me and said she loved me in her silent voice. It put a quick smile on my face as we headed towards the parking garage.

Whatever we were about to get into, Charlie was the right man to have as the leader. Charlie didn't take shit off anyone. He was the man in Section H. He had been trying to recruit me for Section H for years. We were pretty cool, Charlie and I. He especially liked me since Steve was the one who trained him.

Charlie loved driving. We shot out of the building, made several quick turns and stopped. We were actually within walking distance of the Hoover.

Charlie told me two black SUVs were parked a block away from the Hoover Building and Elliot was convinced it was *Just Cause.* Five teams had been deployed. There were three teams to control the traffic, i.e., block off the traffic in all directions as well as stop any pedestrians from walking into the danger zone.

One team consisted of five snipers, with two on top of the Hoover Building and the other three on top of buildings in our area, providing us sniper support.

Our team was the attack team. Our assignment was simple: stop them before they attempted to do anything.

Additionally, an urgent message via phone, e-mail and fax had gone out to every FBI office in America. This was

Just Cause's big moment. Only one day earlier than the Boss had stated.

I didn't know who the Boss was. He had to be a damn good agent. Maybe he was overlooked when he was with the Bureau. But he was a mental case, this I was sure of. He took everything to the extreme, but he was one hell of a planner. Everything he did was Strategy 500. One had to think on a grand scale to keep up with the Boss.

I had to take my hat off to him for organizing hate groups as a cohesive team. He had found diversity in the most extreme cases as early as twenty something years ago. Black and white was still a problem in America today, even after 9/11, let alone twenty years ago. Somehow, the Boss had created unity amongst America's extremists.

Additionally, the bank robberies and death operations against the Bureau were stellar and perfectly planned. On a small scale, I admired the man's organization. *He was smart.*

That was fortunate for him.

But we had the grand master in Elliot — he was Mister Strategy 1000. I was convinced he was the best. It was a great game of chess, but in the end, I was sure Elliot and the FBI would be the victor.

We had stationed two Bureau heavyweight SUVs at each end of the street.

The two black SUVs were parked on the curb, one behind the other. All of the windows were up and just as black as the truck itself. The vehicles looked identical to our SUVs.

We had them blocked in. Initially, I didn't know if that was good or bad.

Our team of ten was split into two five-man teams. Charlie and his team had the first SUV. I was the leader for the second team.

We slowly approached the vehicles from the back. They were parked probably three to four feet from each other. I didn't know what time it was, but it was a Friday afternoon in the nation's capital. The last time I looked at my watch it was slowly approaching one-thirty.

It was a beautiful day. The sun was out. The breeze was low. We weren't sure anyone was in the SUVs. To my understanding, there had been surveillance on the vehicles for the past thirty minutes or so.

Charlie called out, "This is the FBI. Slowly open your doors, throw out your weapons and slowly, get out of the vehicle, one at a time, starting with the first vehicle."

Time stood still. The world was moving at a snail's pace. I remember how quiet it was. This was downtown D.C. The nation's capital had never been this quiet at one in the afternoon. *Time stood still.*

Charlie called out again.

Still, no movement.

Charlie and I, along with two other agents, were standing in the street on the drivers' side of the vehicles. There were another four agents on the sidewalk on the passengers' side. We had two directly in the back of the second vehicles.

We were actually at a standstill.

"What you think?" Charlie said to me. He was on my left. He was asking my opinion, but he was the lead man for Section H. This was a courtesy and I was honored.

I didn't hesitate. "Have a sniper shoot the tires out."

Before he could give the order, the blaring hovering sound of helicopters disturbed the still. Charlie and Price Bakken, the agent next to me, on my right, did the unforgivable — they looked up and took their eyes off the prize.

The helicopters drowned the noise of the SUVs' engines starting. I yelled into my headpiece for a sniper to take the tires out. Suddenly, the back doors of both vehicles swung open, as well as the back hatch of the second vehicle.

Assailants dressed in black with black and green face chalk and black bandanas jumped out of the vehicles, Uzis blazing. We returned fire.

Our snipers were lifesavers and they were doing the same thing I was doing — shooting any part of the body except the chest area. We knew they had on flak vests as well.

This was crazy. We were actually having a close range firefight in the middle of downtown D.C., around the corner from the FBI's Hoover Building. We had agents running our way to provide more firepower.

I saw when Charlie and Price went down. We were holding our own, when the driver and front passenger doors of both vehicles flew open. What I was looking at was outrageous. A damn medium sized machine gun.

God grants prayers. He granted mine.

Our snipers took out both of the drivers before they got off one shot.

When everything quieted down, time was still once again, except it didn't last long.

The call came over the radio. Two black pickup trucks had broken through the barrier blocking traffic and were headed towards the Hoover Building. We heard the sound of gunshots. I saw the trucks whiz by the intersection.

I kept a couple of agents for assistance while everyone else ran back to the Hoover Building. Only one assailant was left alive. The passenger in the first vehicle was still standing.

I hoped all was well. The last thing I heard was a loud bang.

Chapter 59

SOMETIMES LIFE COMES AT you a mile a second. That day, I thought it was a mile a millisecond. We had received the call over our headsets that all was well. That was a good thing. I wished I could say the same. I wished time was still.

We had four agents down. Two were dead: Price Bakken and Kincaid Long. I knew both men. Both men had families. Charlie McClary and Dave Higgins were critically shot. Charlie was shot on the left side of his neck. Dave sustained three hits: two in the groin area and one that seemed to take his right ear off.

It was hard to believe the rest of us walked away unscathed. I looked at the machine gun and just shook my head; still thanking the Good Lord. It was a Marine-issued M240G medium machine gun. I had seen several in action. If the driver had gotten a chance to squeeze the trigger, I would have been shot to shreds.

We still had everything blocked off. Several ambulances were allowed through to tend to our fallen warriors.

I felt a hand on my shoulder and quickly spun around.

"Hold your horses, Big Guy," said Julia, whose sweet voice instantly calmed me. She was indeed a sight for sore eyes.

I grabbed her chin and pulled her closer to me. Her lips were sensual and soothing, magic to my soul.

"Tell me something good," I said. "Please."

"From looking around, you should tell *me* something good," I heard the voice of Elliot behind me. I turned around, somewhat startled.

"Hey, sir, didn't know you were back there," I stammered.

"Yeah, I know. Too busy burying your tongue down another agent's mouth," he said matter-of-factly.

"I couldn't help myself," I bantered.

"Where is the one asshole still living?" Elliot asked. He had a look of determination in his eyes. The three of us looked at the sky as the helicopters were hovering overhead way closer than they should have been.

"They got Price and Charlie shot," I muttered. Surprisingly, both Julia and Elliot heard me. The look on his face meant I needed to explain my statement.

"When they started hovering, Charlie and Price got distracted and that's when all hell broke loose. Charlie was hit with the first shot fired."

I was pissed and somewhat emotional. I hated being emotional. I also hated death. I was in the wrong profession and I had no plans on retiring soon.

No words were spoken. Elliot and Julia walked around the vehicles and surveyed the damage. Julia had a pad and pen out. She was worried about me. She kept looking back as I followed them, making sure I was all right.

And I was all right. Never been better. I was ridding the world of the bad guys or so I thought.

Elliot was on his cell and his expression said it all. He was slowly walking to the FBI sedan to the only perpetrator to survive.

"The Boss shot his best shot," Elliot said. Julia and I listened intently. "He tried to hit four Bureau offices, all on the East Coast. The Richmond, Norfolk and Philly offices and of course, here. They were all unsuccessful. Unfortunately, they were successful with robbing four banks today: two in the Maryland area, Oxen Hill and Fort Meade; and two in Virginia, Springfield and near the Fort Belvoir area on Route 1."

We knew Elliot. This was just the tip of the iceberg. It was growing and getting nastier.

"Our location is the only Bureau location that sustained any casualties or injuries," he said in a downhearted tone. "Unfortunately, the bank president at every bank died today. Additionally, at the Route 1 location, they killed seven other people: two security guards and five Alexandria police officers."

Elliot gestured to have the assailant pulled out of the car. Someone had taken his face paint off. He was a young white guy, medium height and build.

When he was pulled out of the car, I heard Julia say, "Oh shit."

"What?" I asked.

"That's Tory, the nephew Basil Dooling is raising," she replied.

We were speechless.

Time stood still. Again.

Chapter
60

IN MY DREAM, JULIA and I were walking in a field, hand in hand. We were older. The field was a nice dark green with trees sparsely situated. The smell was nice and springy. We were near a lake and mountains were in the distance. Lil' Steve was no longer little. He was a grown man with a family. Devin was also grown with a family.

My dream was a Carson family reunion. Julia and I were celebrating an anniversary. Everyone we loved was there. Gloria and Clay were married; Q was still kicking it; Jay Joiner was being pushed by his mean nanny, Nancy Batiste; Elliot and his wife, Portia, were the elder statesmen; and Janessa was running the show, the top CEO in the country.

It was a dream — hopefully of things to come.

Coming back to reality, I saw the two pickups that were completely demolished in front of the Hoover Building. Both were turned upside down, with numerous bullet holes. The bang I heard earlier was one of the pickups blowing up.

The Boss might have been the man, but Basil Dooling was the damn leader. We had his nephew in custody, the same nephew he had raised since he was seven years old. He was being detained at the Hoover.

Counting the pilot, we had a six-man detail taking a short helicopter ride to Alexandria, Route 1 South, a couple of miles North of Fort Belvoir Army Post — the scene of a repulsive and grisly crime.

The pilot didn't have much room to land. There was a big parking lot in the back of the bank. On the lot was a TV helicopter. First come, first served. It didn't last long. The pilot called over the radio for the TV chopper to move.

When we landed, Elliot had already given me instructions to stay on his coattails, though he didn't have a coat on. We all had on Bureau-issued dark blue windbreakers with gold F-B-I lettering on the back.

The scene was wild and out of control. People were everywhere and Alexandria's finest was trying to control the crowd. Once the media types saw Elliot, they immediately tried to make their way to him. Luckily, the officers on duty, as well as our agents, kept them at bay.

We walked in through a side door and the scene was unbelievable, like something out of a 1950s' black and white gangster movie. Bodies were everywhere. *Innocent bodies.* Someone had lied to us. The initial report was eight had died. I quickly counted thirteen bodies.

The beast within needed to be controlled.

I felt a rage brewing inside of me. How could anyone be this damn cold and callous? This was heartbreaking to say the least.

"Deputy Director, how you doing?" the Alexandria Police Chief, Tom Beamon greeted Elliot. I knew Chief Beamon. He was a good man; fair and patient, and he absolutely loved people. And the people of Alexandria loved him. He and Elliot went back a good twenty years, when Chief Beamon was an agent for the Secret Service.

"Tom, I'm sorry," Elliot stated. He was sad and hurt. I saw it on his face. He had it together. That was his nature. But you had to be inhumane not to feel something with this kind of devastation.

Four of the thirteen killed were women: a cop, a customer and two tellers. The bank president was a young guy who we learned was also an associate pastor at one of the local churches. The two security guards had been working together for four years. The five cops combined had over sixty years on the force. The female customer who died was recently married to an Army infantryman and was two months pregnant — though she didn't know it.

All of this was information we found out later. Everyday people, living everyday lives.

Elliot and I walked around, making sure we did not disturb the crime scene. It was the Alexandria Police Department's crime scene and us being there was a courtesy. Chief Beamon was hesitant to give up the crime scene, and that was understandable. Elliot just wanted to know what happened. The Chief did let two of our guys from the Bank Robbery Section case the crime scene as well. Maybe they would find something that his guys missed. Somehow, I doubted it.

Though there were thirteen dead, there were six left alive. How nice of *Just Cause* to spare their lives. One woman in particular was waiting to talk to us, the FBI.

Her name was Linda Moser. She was probably in her mid-thirties, brunette with several streaks of gray, medium build. The first thing I noticed about her was her sparkling eyes. Her demeanor at the moment was excitable. She was a woman dying to escape the tragedy of men.

We walked into her office. She was the vice president of the loan department. She was also a mother of three and happily married. The six or seven pictures that adorned her office space attested to that.

She sat in a chair in the corner of her office as if she were in someone else's office. She was terribly distraught and the glass of water in her shaking hands was spilling on her dress. Elliot bent down and squatted in front of the loan officer. He gently covered her hands on the glass with his two huge hands.

"Linda, it's going to be all right," he said in a mellow voice. I personally had never heard Elliot speak so softly and gently to anyone. I was somewhat shocked. I looked at Chief Beamon, but his eyes were glued on Elliot and Linda Moser.

"Most times, Linda, in situations like these, people don't know what to say," Elliot continued in the same voice. "And I'm no one special. I'm like everyone else. But believe me, Linda, when I say this. The devil was extremely busy today, but God is going to get you through this. And he is going to empower the good in the world to smite the evil that caused this wickedness."

Something happened to me at that moment. I looked at Linda Moser and she was calm. It was as if a heavy weight had been lifted off her shoulders. She was no longer burdened with the tragedy at hand.

"Linda, you will never forget this day, but don't let this event define your life. You have three kids and I know they are wonderful kids who probably work your nerves sometimes."

She smiled at his comment.

"But stay strong and stay in God. Because in the end, He will be there." Elliot took the glass out of her hand and was about to rise, when she threw her arms around his neck. He reciprocated and hugged the woman back.

"Damn, he's good," Chief Beamon whispered to me. And he was right. Deputy Director Elliot Lucas was a born leader.

I looked around the room and spotted a bible on her bookcase and on her desk. She also had two inspirational paintings on the walls with biblical passages. Somehow, it took Elliot all of several seconds to absorb that information and come up with the right words to calm Linda.

"He wanted me to tell you," Linda said through tears and sobs, as she let go of Elliot's neck, but her hands somehow found his hands. "That this was payback and your day was coming."

Suddenly, an Army major in his battle dress uniform came rushing through the bank and made a beeline to Linda's office.

"Baby, baby, you ok, darling?" the major asked as Elliot gave way to Major Moser, Linda's husband.

"Yeah, Jerry, I'm fine now," she replied in a weak, but calm voice.

As we were leaving the office, she called out to Elliot. We stopped.

"Thank you, sir. For the kind words." They looked at each other for several seconds. Elliot smiled and nodded his head in the affirmative once. "And when you find those motherfuckers, kill them for me."

Chapter
61

DEATH IS A NATURAL thing, so why did I hate it so? The brain could be a tricky organ. I heard people talking about the left brain and the right brain. Hell, I even knew psychologists and psychiatrists who wanted to know why killers killed or criminals committed crimes.

I didn't give a damn. I cared about one thing at that moment in time: catching and killing the bad guys. In the case of *Just Cause,* they were ruthless, heartless and morbid killers who had killed for no apparent reason other than to send a message.

We looked at the videotape before departing the bank. Four men and two women in all black attire from head to toe walked in the bank with Uzis blazing. The apparent leader did the talking, what little talking there was and also did the majority of the killing. I didn't need him to take his mask off or call out his name; both Elliot and I knew it was Carmine Ball, Ranger 1 himself.

The whole robbery/murder act took three minutes and twenty-five seconds. Everyone was so much in shock, no one had a clue how much money was taken. And quite frankly, I doubted if anyone really gave a damn. I didn't.

Thirteen dead. Three minutes and forty-five seconds.

Elliot and I were the only two going back to the Hoover Building. The remaining three guys were staying to help out and do some investigating. As we walked out of the bank, the media frenzy started again. Elliot had me lag behind so I wouldn't be on camera.

I think the only reason he decided to do an interview was because our favorite CNN reporter, Monica Houston was there.

"Director Lucas, can you tell us what happened today?" Monica shouted over the other screaming and yelling reporters. "Not only here, but at the J. Edgar Hoover Building in Washington, the attack at three other FBI offices and the other bank robberies today, and is the hate group, *Just Cause,* responsible for this?"

Before Elliot could say a word, Monica asked her last question. "And what about the kidnapping of Secretary of State Ian Bradley?"

Monica was not dumb. She threw it all out there — the attacks, the robberies, this gruesome nightmare and Secretary Bradley. She hit him with all she had and she might have gotten fifty percent of what she wanted. But that was still a great amount for a terrific story. There was only one reporter better than Monica; and she was tending to her man in Virginia Beach — Gloria Kingsbury.

"I will make a statement, but I am not fielding any questions," Elliot said. The reporters shut up, but shoved numerous mikes in his face. "Today, unfortunately, was another tragic day for America. I cannot tell you who is responsible until we investigate. I also cannot tell you if the bank robberies were in fact associated with the attacks on the offices of the FBI.

"I can tell you this. It's a sad day when Americans are terrorizing Americans. We are at war in the Middle East and a possible hurricane is heading towards the Gulf Coast, and those are the things we should be spending our energy on. Not Americans terrorizing and killing other innocent Americans for the hell of it.

"Like our brothers in blue across America, our job is to protect and serve, and to deter terrorism. It's my job to put those who terrorize America behind bars; I take my job very seriously and because I believe in America. I intend to do my job."

I was stunned. Elliot walked away and many of the reporters, including Monica Houston, were quiet. I caught up with him as he was walking to the FBI helicopter. Our pilot was just starting the engine.

"The Boss didn't sanction those killings," Elliot blurted out.

"Why you say that?" I asked, shouting over the winding blades.

"It's not his style. If he was going to do something like that, he would have done it himself."

I stopped and looked at Elliot as he was getting in the helicopter. He looked back at me.

I was speechless and dumbfounded. *I'll be damned,* I thought. *He really does know who the Boss is.*

Getting on the chopper, he patted the area next to him, signifying that was where he wanted me to sit. My curiosity was at an all time high.

"How long have you known?" I asked, speaking loudly as the helicopter lifted off.

"Since day one. But it's time to end this, Carson. It's time I ended this."

I didn't say anything. I didn't know what to think. Damn, *since day one.*

"These deaths are on me, Carson," Elliot volunteered. "The Boss, Basil Dooling, Ian Bradley, the Balls, several others and their leader, they all want me."

I will never forget how I felt. It was as if we were in a canyon and big, huge boulders started falling from the mountaintops. The more we moved and dodged, the more the boulders fell. Then, when we stopped moving, the boulders stopped. When we moved again, the boulders started falling again, except the next time they were bigger and faster.

Someone was throwing bigger and faster boulders at us with one target in mind — Elliot Lucas.

"Why, sir? Why you?"

"Life is different today, Carson," Elliot stated as loudly as he could. "Things I thought I would never see in my lifetime, I am seeing and you don't know how that makes me feel."

He turned and looked at me. For some reason, I thought I was seeing him for the first time.

"Today, Carson, we have Black CEOs running major corporations, Black quarterbacks playing in the Super Bowl, Black head coaches in the three major sports, even Black politicians qualified to sit in the White House one day. And all of that is great.

"But you know the one thing no one wants to see?"

We were still looking at each other, and though the answer should have been on the tip of my tongue, it wasn't.

"A Black man running the Federal Bureau of Investigation, the house that J. Edgar built."

Damn, was the only thing I thought.

Elliot went on to tell me that *Just Cause* had stolen over $150 million and wreaked all kinds of havoc on the Bureau. There was two primary purposes: to get rich, or in some cases, richer, and to prove they were smarter than the best agents recognized by the Bureau.

The most amazing thing he told me was *Just Cause's* true membership consisted of fourteen corporate types who all used to be in the Bureau. Only two were minorities: the Boss and a Japanese-American.

Amazing.

The ruins of men can be catastrophic. The lives of the unholy and unforgiving can be abysmal. And in the end, a powerful force will cleanse the wicked.

I was looking at the powerful force, his name was Elliot Lucas.

Three minutes, forty-five seconds. Thirteen deaths.

Chapter 62

"WHAT THE FUCK WERE you thinking? the Boss blared over the cell phone. His plan was perfect, built with a certain degree of failure. He was hoping for two of the four attacks on the FBI offices to be successful. That failure did not upset him. He knew the bank robberies would be a success, but he never expected his proud pupil to run amok.

"I'm sorry, Boss. I just lost it," Carmine Ball said to justify his actions. "I wanted to send a message. I wanted them to hurt just as much as I am hurting. Shit, they still have my mom and dad. What do you expect from me?"

"I expect you be the staunch professional I raised you to be! They needed to see the long arm of *Just Cause* today. That we can strike whenever we want to. We don't need the whole federal and state governments coming down on us."

Silence filled the phone line. Carmine knew the Boss was right. He was always right. He had never told him anything wrong. He loved the Boss. He had never led him astray before.

Dave Ball loved money and business. That translated to corporate power for a weasel of a man. He hated thinking of his father that way, but it was true. He never liked his father. He only loved him because his blood flowed through his body. His parents' marriage was a sham; his father slept around. He knew it. His mother knew it. But she was happy. She loved the man he truly considered to be his father — the Boss.

"Carmine, don't worry, we will get through this. Understand?"

"Yeah, Boss. I'm sorry. I feel like shit now."

"They have Tory Dooling. They will be after Basil Dooling next. Hopefully, Tory doesn't break. We still need to plan for the worst. I want you to take out Dooling. I need a day to set something up. We need to lure him away from his bodyguard detail. I think I have a way to do that."

"What about my mom and dad?" Carmine asked.

"Carmine, I don't give a shit about your dad. I'm sorry for putting it that way, but I don't. I love your mom. Always have, always will. We will probably never see or talk to each other again. But when you do see her, tell her I love her.

"As far as what I plan to do, I'm exchanging Ian Bradley for your mom. Even if Elliot Lucas or the White House knows he is a part of *Just Cause,* they will still be willing to exchange your mom for Ian. However, your dad, they won't do it. I'm sure your dad has opened his mouth. Your mom," the Boss paused on his delivery. "She is a good woman, a warrior. She would never sell us out."

Carmine Ball understood. Those few words made him happy. The Boss was a lot of things to a lot of people.

To his mom, he was her king, her knight in shining armor. She would never betray him, because he would never let her down.

To him — he was his father.

"Boss?"

"Yeah, Carmine."

"Thank you."

"For what?"

"For being there for mom and me. You literally taught me everything I know. And you love mom. She needed someone to love her for her. My dad couldn't do that. Hell, he wouldn't do that. You have always been there when she needed you. And for me too. I know if anyone else would have done what I did today, you would put a bullet in their head. Thanks for giving me life and letting me live."

As he hung up, the Boss knew how this would end. Prior to today, he knew how he wanted it to end. But things changed today. Carmine changed it. He had served the hungry dog porterhouse steak and pulled it away just before he took a bite. That hungry dog was Elliot Lucas and the Boss knew he didn't like to be teased or ridiculed.

That's what Carmine did today — ridiculed a man who symbolized power and success, a man who knew all too well about keeping his eyes on the prize.

Some dogs shouldn't be unleashed and unfortunately, the biggest dog in government had been given unneeded incentive.

He was expecting the phone call. "Yeah, what you got?" the Boss asked.

"What I got? What I got? You have always been in control of your troops, what happened today?

It was the *man*. Unfortunately, for the man, the Boss didn't see the need for the man anymore. He had taken orders for twenty-three years now. That day, it stopped.

"One, *Just Cause* is soon a distant memory. Carmine lost control today, but that's not important. What we have to do now is damage control and Operation Elimination."

"Stop! I think you have bumped your head, Boss. You don't give orders, you take orders."

"No!" the Boss retorted. "You haven't done shit since we started this operation years ago. Yes, you had the connections, but being in the position you are in, you can't help us. If you can, you need to speak now or forever hold your peace."

The man didn't speak. His mind was working but everything was coming up blank. He knew this day would come. He just didn't figure it would be so soon. The Boss had him. He knew the Boss had been waiting on this moment and he hated it. The Boss was right. Hell, the black son-of-a-bitch was always right.

"Okay, how you want to do this?" the man asked. He was exasperated. He loved being in control, to be able to just sit back and see his plans come together. In actuality, he knew he had never made plans. It was always the Boss. Truthfully, he was surprised he was able to go so many years and decades without the man complaining.

"We need Dooling dead. I will have a plan available—"

"It's too late," the man interrupted.

"What? Speak up damn it, I didn't hear you!" the Boss interjected.

"It's too late. The Bureau took Basil in a couple of hours ago."

"Shit! We can still get away with this. Let me take care of it. If you can have someone take out Dooling, that would be great. If not, just keep a low profile. If we don't talk anymore, I will get with you in a month, like we planned."

Chapter
63

UPON RETURNING TO THE Hoover, it seemed like we were in another world. The press had been hounding agents all day. The circus was still outside and Elliot didn't give the order to clear them out. Usually, we could call D.C.'s finest to clear the press out, but not that day. Elliot was proving a point. But what? None of us had the slightest idea.

The good news: Tory Dooling only lasted thirty minutes before he gave up everything he knew. I think it had a lot to do with Q doing the interview.

Q said it was strange. Tory had never spoken a word about *Just Cause.* He had been a man of his word. However, he had never been in a small room with someone like Quentin Morales before.

I had seen Q in action. He told me later he used the same technique he always used. He walked in the room and whispered in Tory's ear, "I have thirty minutes to get the information I need." Then he walked around to the other side of the table and sat down. Next, he was quiet for ten to fifteen minutes before he would even open his mouth. The first ten to fifteen minutes would consist of him just staring at the suspect. Then he would lean forward and say, "There is no one in the other room. You know I could kill you now and no one would ever know."

By the time he leaned back and asked his first question, the perp would be ready to give up the farm.

In Tory Dooling's case, that's exactly what he did. He gave up the farm. The first to fall? His uncle, Basil Dooling, the former Director of the Federal Bureau of Investigation. Before it was all over, we knew every damn hate group in *Just Cause,* what former and present agents of the Bureau were a part of the *Cause,* the Balls' involvement, and the possible location of a major weapons buy.

Tory Dooling also gave up something we didn't know. Every remaining member of *Just Cause* was in the metropolitan D.C. area.

In the end, Tory asked Q what kind of deal he would get for being cooperative. Q told him, "You get to breathe another day."

Basil Dooling was arrested as an enemy of the state. He was a homegrown terrorist; American born, U.S. made, FBI and CIA trained. A graduate from the school of bastards.

The day started off bad and shitty. In the midst of hell, the silver lining was looking good.

Elliot had called an emergency meeting. He laid out his elaborate game plan. He planned for operations over the whole metropolitan area. He had called in agents from Norfolk, Baltimore and New York.

Tonight was the night of the F-B-I.

Chapter 64

"I WANT TO TRADE, Elliot," the automated computer voice stated. The voice had a different tone than his previous calls. It was more relaxed and caring. It was a voice with feelings.

"What do you have to trade that I want?" Elliot asked.

"Ian Bradley, the Secretary of State," the automated voice replied.

"He is one of you."

"But no one knows that but your people and my people. Imagine the embarrassment to the White House if it becomes national news. I know Cabot is a President with strong shoulders and a Teflon shield, but do you really think this is something that won't stick to him? Come on, Elliot, you and I have been around a long time. As loyal as you are, you are not dumb. No President can survive a traitor in his Cabinet."

"What do you want in return?"

"Carol."

"Why the automated voice? It's over. It was over in '93. Why couldn't you let bygones be bygones?"

"Elliot, you know me. You haven't talked to me in twelve years, but you know me. I love the challenge. Yeah, the money was good, but there is nothing like the challenge. You couldn't touch me in '93 and you can't touch me now."

"Yeah, I can touch you. Your luck has run out. Those you trusted are weak. They have always been weak; from Dooling to Dave Ball to Ian Bradley, weak men."

"You speak the truth, Elliot, but I have the juice and the money. They wanted me to do their bidding for them and I did. But guess what, I am the better for it. I can sit back and live a life of luxury."

"No, you lost that chance when you murdered Steve. KC is not going to let you live."

"I like the kid, Elliot. But if he gets in my way, I have to drill him. You know that. I beg of you to keep him away from me."

"Sorry, I can't do that. Remember, I don't owe you anything. Never have, never will. You signed your own death warrant. Funny, unknowingly, you selected your own assassin."

"He's a kid to me, Elliot. You know I'm way too smart for him. Don't make me the killer of both brothers."

"Like I said, you signed your own death warrant."

"No, Elliot. You know me, but you are getting old. I have insurance. We make the trade in the morning: Bradley for Carol Ball."

"I have to run it by the President."

"I'm not worried about that. That's a done deal."

"What is this insurance you refer to?"

"It's to keep both KC and Denise off my ass. I have *my daughter,* Janessa."

Chapter
65

MADNESS . . . MAYBE CYNICAL WAS the right word. The more I thought about it, the more it made sense to me. How could I not be a cynic when it came to this case and the betrayal of those I worked with and trusted? Basil Dooling, Ian Bradley, the Balls . . . none of it made sense. I wasn't sure if it was power and money or really about Elliot becoming the first African-American director of the Bureau.

It was stupid to me. It was 2005 and we were still putting up with shit like this. I still smiled inside. That Elliot was some kind of uncanny. His plan was by no means ordinary. First, he had a mass meeting. Then he had numerous smaller meetings. I even saw Lieutenant Colonel Bobby Small, Jr., Darrell Adams from ATF, Lewis Burling and of course, Denise.

I didn't know everything that was going on, but I truly didn't think anyone else had the whole picture either, with the exception of Elliot and his trusted sidekick, the child he raised, Julia Carson, my wife.

We all went in our separate directions. Julia called me over and gave me one helluva kiss before I left. "In case you don't come back," she told me, and then laughed. I laughed too. I knew her ass would go crazy and kill every member of *Just Cause* and their relatives. For some reason, that turned me on. I loved her just as much as she loved me. Actually, I loved her more.

I had a team of fourteen to bring in a team of eight. My boss, Deputy Director Elliot Lucas, told me shoot to kill if I had to. I didn't want to do that. Somebody needed to serve time. Maybe it was my sixth sense, but I knew this was not over.

Unfortunately, Tory Dooling did not know the Boss and Basil Dooling refused to give him up. I think the former director was sincere and genuine when he said the Boss would kill his whole family if he gave him up. I didn't understand. We had him by the small hairs and he was still afraid of someone who could no longer get to him. I didn't think we could have convinced Basil Dooling of that in a hundred years.

Dr. Beth Storm, Q and I along with eleven other agents were at BDP's Comedy House on the D.C. downtown pier, off Main Street. I liked the pier. I used to go down there every now and then, and just walk around the area. It was my serenity.

I loved BDP's and its owner, Peter Brown, Mr. Big Dick Peter himself. The club was housed in a two-story elegant, red-brick building. I was amazed at Pete. He didn't allow smoking in his club. Whoever patron the club, played by his rules.

The stage area was huge for stages in a comedy club. It was the type of stage that belonged in an auditorium. The first floor was split level with at least ten round tables on the bottom level closest to the stage; and the upper level probably had another ten to fifteen smaller round tables. The second floor sat back and only covered half of the first floor, but the view was good.

Six team members, including me, Beth and Q occupied two of the second floor tables. Four of the other agents worked the bottom floor, and the remaining four agents were outside, waiting on my signal to cover the back door.

I was still somewhat amazed that we were there. I had thought big time criminals would be smarter. I guessed that was why some things never surprised me. People were people and some people were as dumb as bricks. I expected better from Carmine Ball, aka Ranger 1. Unfortunately, he was the average criminal. All testosterone and no damn smarts.

It proved that he had no regard for us. From reading some of his e-mails, he really thought we were the idiots of the world. I was happy to prove him wrong that night.

It was eleven-fifteen on a Friday night and the place was packed, with the exception of two tables on the lower level — two tables reserved for a regular.

Everyone knew that on a Friday and Saturday night, Big Pete always opened the show. He was the main attraction. It didn't make a difference what comedian came to town, Big Pete was the man with the juice. Plus, one never knew when a famous comedian might be in the audience and just wanted to do an improvisation. BDP's was the place to test new material.

As a comedian, one could only hope Big Pete wasn't on his game that night. If he was, he would rip you a new one, just because.

The thing about Pete was he was a great comedian but he was equally a great philosopher. You never knew how he would open the show. Many people came just to hear his philosophical rants and understandably so. His rants and raves were something that were talked about at churches the next day.

"People, people, people," Pete chanted. "Welcome to BDP's! I am your host, Mr. BDP himself, Peter "I will fuck your wife and girlfriend in a heartbeat" Brown."

The crowd was already eating it up. The stage made the big man look bigger. He loved to have his small glass of coke with him. Most people thought he had a mixed drink like cognac and coke, or bourbon and coke. But Pete was a coke only man. He liked the illusion the drink brought.

"Naw, naw, I'm just joking," his husky voice rang out. "I don't do wives . . . only girlfriends. Ask some of these hoes, they will tell you. I didn't fuck them anymore after they got married." The crowd laughed. Pete was probably right. I'm sure he had his share of groupies.

He was flowing right along when the two empty tables, which held six people each, filled up. Bingo. Game on.

"But on a serious tip, we need to stop the violence, man." Pete took a sip of his coke.

"That shit today was just stupid. Killing all of those damn people at that bank on Route 1." We slowly got up, careful not to divert any attention our way.

"Man, I don't condone that shit. If the FBI or Alexandria Police Department catches those motherfuckers, I hope they give them the fucking needle."

I had called my agents on the outside and told them to come through the back door. When they were in position, they would call me.

"Crazy motherfuckers in this world, people. I think we are really fucking up." Pete hesitated and let the crowd soak in what he was preaching.

"And what's wrong with these damn folks attacking the damn Feds? Are they stupid?" Some folks clapped at the Bureau being attacked. Interestingly, none of the folks at the two tables clapped.

My agents were in the building and only eight feet away from Carmine Ball and company.

"Okay, I'm sure you folks are tired of listening to me. But let me say this: we have some special guests in the house tonight. Before I introduce them, let me tell you how we met." Pete took another swallow of his drink and I knew what was coming.

"These motherfuckers broke in on me. Yeah, the damn Feds broke in on me, trying to arrest me for fucking this sweet, badass white babe. When they realized she was over eighteen, the lead FB fucking I agent, also a white chick, told me I needed to leave little girls alone. Gave me her card and told me when I wanted a woman, to call her." He took another sip of his drink. *"Yeah, boy, the legend of BDP."* The crowd ate it up.

I had heard the story several times before and every time Beth would blush. But not that night. I noticed Carmine and his crew getting fidgety. The six of us were already in position. We were only waiting on one thing.

"Let me introduce you to our first guest — the F-B fucking I!"

The lights came on and occupants at both tables jumped up.

"FBI, no one moves!" I voiced loud enough for the whole place to hear it. The agents at the two tables next to Carmine and his group jumped up and held their weapons, while simultaneously, the agents from the back did the same thing.

In every group, there is always one fool. The one that night grabbed for his weapon and at least five of us shot him, including me. No one else made a stupid move. We cuffed the eleven other assailants and led them out in an orderly fashion. I personally cuffed Carmine Ball.

I was surprised it was so easy. In a way, I think it only worked because of Big Dick Peter's endorsement.

I didn't worry about Pete. He could take care of himself. In a matter of days, hopefully *Just Cause* would be a distant memory.

I knew Beth smiled at Pete and he winked. As I was walking out, he called out, "Hey, Agent Carson, G-man, are they the ones responsible for killing those innocent folks today?"

I looked at Pete and he took a sip of his drink. "What did you call me?" I asked.

"Kenny Carson, G-man!"

I just shook my head as I walked out the door. *Kenny Carson, G-man.* I liked that.

Chapter
66

BOBBY SMALL, JR. RECALLED his first solo mission. He had graduated from Hampton University and was in the Supply M.O.S., military occupational specialty. He met the famous Colonel Jimmie "Hackeye" Sheppard during his visit to the 101st Airborne Division. He wasn't a member of the 101st, but he gave the Colonel and the base leadership a briefing on the state of the 101st supply woes. Woes he turned into minor challenges.

Colonel Sheppard was so impressed with him; he requested a meeting with the young Captain. Two months later, Captain Small was reporting for Special Forces training.

Three years after the completion of his training, he was standing in a classified conference room in the Pentagon with the then recently promoted Brigadier General Sheppard and two black special agents from the FBI. They were briefed on their mission — the assassination of El Salvadoran drug lord, El Caponi.

El Caponi was the biggest drug dealer in North, Central and South America. He supplied 75 percent of the illegal drugs in Mexico, Canada and the United States, and 90 percent of the illegal drugs in Central and South America. As a man who loved money, El Caponi was probably more ruthless than his legendary namesake, Al Capone, the 1920s and '30s gangster. It was reported that El Caponi had killed off any serious competitors to his business. Additionally, he was not above lacing his products with poison to send a message.

Unfortunately, several of those poison shipments had hit the streets of America. In one fell swoop, El Caponi had killed over 300 innocent souls, from the average dope fiend to college students to professionals, and everyone in between. The group of everyone included the offspring of a couple of powerful politicians.

El Caponi had signed his own death warrant and it was up to Captain Bobby Small, Jr. and two Bureau agents to execute his sentence.

Through intelligence reports, it was learned El Caponi would be relaxing for several days at his villa outside of a small city called Corozal, Belize. Corozal was located in the northern part of Belize, off the Caribbean Sea.

Captain Small's mission was to infiltrate the villa and touch El Caponi up close and personal. He heard the man was good with any type of weaponry, from gunplay to knife play. That didn't faze the Special Forces officer.

This was considered his first solo op. His operations in the past were leading his entire unit or at least five to ten members of his unit. Also, there were two agents there for sniper support. They would be located 500 meters away with long-range rifles, picking up the slack. It was Captain Small's job to handle the close up groundwork.

As expected, he was uncomfortable when told he would be working with two snipers besides his normal crew. However, General Sheppard assured him he was working with the best.

When he got into position, the general's reassurance was proven correct when within a minute's time, the two agents took out ten bodyguards.

As he penetrated the three-story house, he maneuvered his way up the two flights of spiraling stairs to the third floor. When he reached the third floor, he blended in with the shadows and took out the security team in the room next to the master bedroom, where El Caponi was getting comfortable with three of the local women.

Captain Small made his way outside to the adjoining balcony and quietly observed the room from the balcony door. The three women, who looked like young girls, were fast asleep. The drug lord was not around. But he did see the light on in the master bathroom.

He silently made his way to the space outside the bathroom door. He knew he was in trouble when he heard the squelch of the radio from the bathroom. When the drug lord did not receive an answer to his frequent calls, he heard the click of an automatic weapon. He knew the sound, a .45 automatic colt pistol.

"Girls, wake the hell up!" El Caponi screamed from the bathroom.

No reply.

He raised his voice and called several more times, before one of the girls finally stirred from her nap.

Captain Small did not fret. He blended in well with the shadows.

"You bitches wake up," the drug lord screamed.

"Si," the young girl responded, rubbing her eyes.

"Is anyone out there?" he asked.

"No, no one," she replied as the other girls started to stir.

Captain Small was not worried as he eased his way closer to the door. When El Caponi opened the door, he saw the barrel of the automatic first. As soon as he walked through the door, Captain Small grabbed him and stuck his Army-issued Ka-Bar knife in the side of his neck, and twisted it for good measure.

The captain knew he was not out of the water. As he made a quick exit, that was when the fun began. El Caponi's men started appearing out of nowhere. He knew he was in trouble. As he ran down the hallway to the staircase, he felt his chances of surviving the mission were slim; that was, until he saw the bodies falling around him.

When he thought he was completely free of the bad men, one assailant tripped him as he was making his way to the seashore. He fell hard, and was disoriented and helpless. When the assailant grabbed his forehead and positioned his neck in a cutting position, Captain Small was extremely happy when he looked around and half the bad man's brains were on the ground.

He thanked the two agents. He really underestimated their skills. When he departed, he thanked Special Agents Elliot Lucas and Denise Carson for saving his life. Elliot was sure they would work together again. Bobby Small, Jr. was looking forward to it.

Chapter 67

ELLIOT USHERED BOBBY TO his office and showed him a list of ten names. He immediately recognized over half the names. Three names were already lined out in red ink. The three names were of dead people: Raymond, Adamis and Collingshed. Three other names were highlighted in florescent yellow. The first two names didn't ring a bell. The third, he knew well. Too well.

"One night," Elliot stated. It was an order.

Bobby shook his head in the affirmative. Then he asked one question, "Why him?" as he pointed to a name.

"You always wanted to know who financed the group that killed your family, right?"

The shadows were his friend. He could remember being a kid and always hiding in the shadows. He was always able to surprise his parents and brothers by jumping out of the shadows. He never understood why he was automatically assigned to the Supply M.O.S. But faith has a way of placing people at the right place, at the right time. Accomplishing his supply briefing while then-Colonel Sheppard was visiting was the right time. He was in the right place.

Name one on the list was Casey Browning, former Special Assistant to the Executive Director of Counterintelligence. Browning's misgivings were providing *Just Cause* with the names and assignments of agents in the field during the '82 and '93 killings.

Bobby didn't need to know anything else.

He caught up with Browning at his Stafford, Virginia condominium. The garage door went up and the man, who was used to blending in with the shadows, didn't worry about the shadows. He rolled on the floor, underneath the garage door sensors. When the car door opened and Browning got out of the car, he grabbed the man by his throat and stuck the Ka-Bar in the side of his neck.

He looked at the man, twisted the Ka-Bar and Browning's eyes rolled back. He let the man's throat go as he slumped over the car door. Bobby Small, Jr. disappeared.

Donner Hartsbright believed in Donner Hartsbright. He was a charismatic man. Throughout his lifetime, he had always received everything he ever wanted. He wanted to be a millionaire — the easy way. The Boss and *Just Cause* made his dream come true.

As the one-time Finance Operations Director for the Federal Reserve Bank, he provided the Boss the drop-off schedule to the state banks. It was an easy task for him. The only person who would be hurt was the bank president. Bank presidents could be replaced.

He was having a late dinner at his favorite bistro, the Americana Grille, in Georgetown. As was his tradition, he had his Wall Street Journal in hand.

Bobby Small, Jr. was hungry. Killing did that to him. He could eat a small cow but settled on a Caesar salad and half-pound hamburger. No fattening fries. He laughed at the irony — half-pound hamburger and a Caesar salad, how healthy!

Elliot told him Donner's routine, which included reading the paper both before and after dinner. The last thing he did was hit the latrine before he left.

When the man entered the clean, spotless restroom, he halfway smiled at the black man who looked up from washing his hands. He did his business at the urinal and laughed inside at how anal the man was washing his face and hands. He was just as anal.

When he turned around, the black man surprised him. The big gun with the silencer barrel popped three times: two times to the heart from four feet away and the last one in the gut at close range.

"This is for Elliot Lucas," he whispered in Donner Hartsbright's ear.

Bobby Small, Jr. left the latrine and exited stage left through a side door in the restaurant.

He didn't mind waiting. In so many ways, he had been waiting for something all of his life. His beautiful wife, Shirley, made him wait for two years before she accepted his invitation for a date. Then she made him wait another four years before she said yes to his wedding invitation. That just set the stage for him always waiting for something good in his life.

This was no different. It wasn't as sweet as marrying the woman of his dreams or having the kids he always wanted. But at last, he would be able to put to rest the death of his family.

He sat in the living room and read Tom Clancy's *The Sum of All Fears*. In his mind, he knew it was the type of book he would read. But he knew it wasn't a book for entertainment. He knew his former subordinate was trying to glean information on making a nuclear bomb. Why not? That was, after all, his nature.

"I see you like my reading selection?" the tall, slim, pasty white man asked.

"Yes indeed," Bobby replied.

"You want to talk first or just do this?" Watson Redd asked. He was an impatient man. Those who knew him well nicknamed him "Once." Everything in his professional life, he did once and moved on. He spent eight years in the U.S. Army and received his Special Forces training from the man sitting in his living room. From there, he did stints with the CIA, FBI and State Department, before hooking up with an organization called *Just Cause*.

They paid better was his justification for joining *Just Cause. Why not get paid over a half million dollars for training dumbasses?*

"We had our differences, but I never thought you would kill my family. I pushed you when I could, always went to bat for you and that was my payback, I guess."

Bobby Small, Jr. was different. Yes, he was focused, but his calmness was somewhat devastating. He was a thin line away from dangerous. But dangerous for whom?

"I never had my own unit. I wanted my own." The slim man smiled. He was trying to provoke his former commanding officer. Thus far, it wasn't working. He actually thought he wouldn't have to motivate him. In his heart, Watson Redd was afraid.

"Once again, Colonel, how do you want to do this?"

Suddenly, Bobby reached over his shoulders to his back and in one motion, he threw a Ka-Bar with his left hand. Watson dodged the knife aimed for his groin area, but he failed to see the second Ka-Bar thrown with the Colonel's right hand.

Bulls eye.

The retired lieutenant colonel stood over the man with the knife in the side of his neck. Watson Redd was still alive — just barely.

"Sergeant Redd, Agent Redd, Leader of the New Knights of Anger or Watson. I don't know what title you prefer, but you asked me, *how I want to do this*? I want to do it my way."

He reached around his back with his right hand and pulled out a .22 automatic, pointed the gun at the fallen man and squeezed the trigger — repeatedly.

Every shot was aimed at the former soldier's head.

Chapter
68

IT'S THE NIGHTMARES THAT had haunted him for the past twelve years. Nightmares he had never been able to shake. He wished he could count or even remember the troubling nights he had had over the years. But they all led back to one night — or maybe it was a combination of nights that really led to that one night.

Some nights, he just lay in bed, hoping sleep would call his name and whisper sweet lullabies to his mind, lullabies he wished would lull him to sleep for a week. Other nights, he would just get up and do some work. He had to laugh at his use of that word, *work*. Hell, he had the greatest job in the world. He didn't work. He traveled, made pick-ups and deliveries.

No, it wasn't work. It was an income — a good income.

No, he got up and played on the internet. See what perversions were going on in the world. Yeah, that was his job, surfing the 'net.

Then, there were the nights like these, where he was restless and his mind floated to places known and unknown. Floated to a time when life was life and he enjoyed being a part of it.

Did he miss those days? Of course he did. Who wouldn't? It was a hard lesson, but he never figured he would be as lonely as he was this very day, this very moment.

He didn't know how long he had been in the bathroom. *Ironic*, he thought to himself. He loved the bathroom. The amount of hours he had spent in this room since his days with the Bureau was also countless. This was where he did his reading and his meditating. This was where his memory replayed year after year of his life. Where he could escape.

He was disappointed he had read the more than ten books and magazines he kept on his handcrafted two-shelf bathroom bookcase. That bookcase was his creation, born out of another one of his pastimes over the years — building things. He had learned well from his father, a true craftsman if there ever was one. His father taught him the trade as his father before him had done the same; their family tradition — building things. But he was the one who broke the family tradition of craftsmen.

No, he was a Bureau man. One of their best. He smiled at the thought. *All a part of the plan.* After all, he remembered every story his grandfather ever told him about being in the concentration camps in California during World War II. They were the same concentration camps his father, mother, uncles, aunts and grandparents lived in. And it was all because the country they loved, trusted and accepted, didn't love, trust and accept them during times of strife.

Before the tears could dislodge from his eyes, he washed his face. Yes, he was indeed human. He missed his father and grandfather.

This was what it took some times — thinking sad thoughts of family and years past to get him to that point of sleep.

He smiled at the memory of those perished and gone; those who always made him smile, even when times were bad. He opened the door and before he could hit the light switch on the bathroom wall, his eyes focused on the bed. In contrast to his training, his body could not move. The sight of his wife, Yoshima, with his recent purchase, a Japanese Katana Sword, sticking in her body was a grisly and bloody sight.

He had options — guns and knives throughout the room. Yoshima often questioned him why he needed so many weapons in the room. Now, unfortunately, she knew.

He had a subcompact Glock 29 on the back of his handcrafted armoire seven feet away. And on the back of the chair next to the armoire were a .22 automatic and a knife, and the chair was only five feet away.

How long have I been standing here? He was rusty. This was not his world anymore. He told the Boss he would help with drop-off dates for the bank payrolls. Even that led to too many deaths.

He had known it was only a matter of time. The time had come.

He knew his assassin and he knew this was his day to die.

He made his move and before he could reach the chair, the knife was in his right shoulder blade. He fell back against the wall. He was momentarily immobilized. She was still quick as ever.

"How you doing, Gerry?" the voice of Denise Carson greeted her old friend and partner, former FBI Special Agent Gerry Ho.

"Mi Cheri," he replied. The two stared at each other. It was obvious Gerry Ho was in pain. He settled against the wall, only inches from the small bamboo chair with the .22 automatic gun in a holster on the back leg.

"Time to pay the piper, Gerry." Denise was dressed in black. She looked the part of a sleek Ninja in the eyes of Gerry Ho. He had always admired her. And he fell in love with her after they had sex while on a mission. It wasn't a planned thing, but it happened. From that day on, he was smitten.

"I wish I was happy to see you," he struggled to say. He raised his left hand slowly to pull the knife out of his shoulder blade.

"You don't want to do that, Gerry. You do, I have to kill you sooner than later."

He looked at Denise, the woman he called Cheri. He actually got the name from his favorite artist, Steve Wonder, and his favorite song, *Mi Cherie Amour.* "Yeah, we don't want that, do we?" He tried to smile but even that hurt.

"*Just Cause.* Tell me what I want to know, Gerry."

"If you are here, Cheri, you know I don't know anything." The man was sweating now. The agony and pain of the knife in his shoulder blade was starting to really bother him.

Denise saw his grimaces and paid them no attention.

"Still as mean and ornery as ever, I see," Gerry added. Denise did not reply. For Gerry Ho, this was sweet and indifferent irony. He loved seeing his Cheri, but he knew why she was here. Hell, he knew she would be coming one day. It was their destiny.

"How we going to play this, Cheri?"

"No play, Gerry. I just want my information. Names, Gerry, that's all I want from you." Denise knew how Gerry felt about her. Any other time, this would probably be her toughest mission. She didn't care that Gerry turned bad. She cared that Gerry turned bad on the biggest case concerning the Bureau — *Just Cause* killing agents. She knew he probably didn't squeeze the trigger that killed Steve, but he was a part of the group. And that in itself was reason enough to kill him ten times over.

"Cheri, we have so much to talk about," he said as his face contorted in pain. He shifted his body to get more comfortable. "You know I have put money in your account every month for the past twelve years."

"I know. $2500 every month, religiously on the first of the month. Restitution for my husband's death."

"No, Cheri. Nooo, not restitution. Respect, honor and love, Cheri. I have always felt bad about Steve's death, but it wasn't me, Cheri. You know that. I would never hurt you like that. I know you don't believe me. I guess if you did, Yoshima would still be alive."

"I did that for Sandi. You disappointed her, disappointed me."

Gerry Ho's eyes got bigger. A sudden sadness fell over him. Sandi was his first wife. She died five years ago. Five years before that, Gerry divorced her and left her destitute. When Denise found out about Sandi, she gave her the monthly stipend Gerry was putting in her account. In turn, Sandi told Denise everything.

She knew one day she would strike back, but the timing had to be right.

Yes, Gerry Ho disappointed her.

In her own way, she lost two people on that dreaded day in 1993 — her husband, Steve, and her best friend and partner, Gerry. It had never dawned on her that Gerry was a member of *Just Cause.* Though he didn't pull the trigger, he was also responsible for Steve's death, just as he was responsible for Sandi's death.

Though she died from lung cancer, in the mind of Denise, the prime cause of death was heartbreak. How could a woman not be heartbroken when the love of her life marries her niece?

"I'm waiting, Gerry. Tell me what I want to know." Denise's patience was growing thin. The reunion was over. She didn't want to think of Sandi and how she died alone — lonely and heartbroken, which she knew might be her own destiny one day. Besides, Steve was always on her mind when she performed her assassin's duties. The thought of him and the love he had for her, always soothed her mind and kept her focused. The scene at hand was not a time to lose focus.

"Shit, Cheri, I can't tell you anything you don't already know. You know who the Boss and the leader are. Hell, you and Elliot both know who is running the show. Both of you have always known."

"It's not about what we might think we know. We need to hear it from a member of *Just Cause,* someone in the know. Someone like you, Gerry."

The man pulled the knife out of his shoulder and breathed a sigh of relief. He didn't know what to expect from Denise. If he was to die tonight, he at least wanted to die comfortably.

"I missed our friendship over the years, Cheri. You are the only one who truly understood me. You were the only one I could have an intelligent conversation with on any subject. Damn, Cheri, you just don't know how much I missed that."

"Yeah, Gerry, I missed you, too. I could have used you these past twelve years. And not the money you put into my account every month, but you, the person. It would have been nice to talk to a true friend. But what I went through made me whole again, Gerry. Plus, it brought both me and Kenny closer. Now, he is helping me with my relationship with Janessa."

"Yes, Janessa." There was a lot of cynicism in Gerry Ho's voice when he said Janessa's name.

Immediately, Denise knew something was wrong. But she didn't panic. She couldn't panic. She knew Gerry was not the Gerry Ho of old, but he was still cunning and uncanny. He was a master of mind games with everyone back in the day. Even with her.

"What Gerry? What about Janessa?"

"The only thing I have left to give you Cheri, is your daughter's life." The comment was made matter-of-factly. So much so, Denise didn't know what to make of it.

"Don't fuck with me, Gerry. Tell me what you are talking about."

The man repositioned himself, still wincing in pain. Pulling the knife out of his shoulder made it bleed more, but it was pain he could deal with.

"The Boss's big move was made tonight. Simple but brilliant plan — grab Janessa and get Special Agent Kenny Carson to fork over $25 million in ransom." Gerry saw the incensed look that took over Denise's face.

"No need to panic or try to do anything now, Cheri. If I am right, while you were out doing your deeds tonight, your daughter was being snatched. Now, as we speak, I'm sure she is sound asleep or crying her eyes out with fear."

"Where is she being held?" Denise asked in a very calm voice. Gerry knew that was the time to fear her most.

"Cheri, you know I don't know that." As soon as the words came out of his mouth, Gerry Ho grabbed for the .22 automatic on the back of the bamboo chair.

Three shots were fired. Gerry Ho had bullets in his forehead, between his eyes and in his neck. All perfectly aligned.

As she walked out the bedroom door, she pulled her cell phone out and turned it on. She had two messages from KC.

Chapter 69

I LIKED TO THINK of myself as a reasonable man, but that was probably far from the truth. We as people all had rules. Some simple, some complex. Hell, some of us never even realized we had rules. But we did and many of us had the same ones, like don't fuck with my family.

Up until that moment, I honestly did not know what I was planning to do when I found the person who killed my brother. I was sure my mind was leaning towards letting him spend a lifetime in prison. And I wasn't stupid. The Boss killed Steve. I knew with every fiber of my body, the Boss was the killer of my brother, as in, he pulled the trigger.

We were in Elliot's office. It was only five-thirty in the morning. I was on pins and needles, pacing throughout the room. Elliot was actually brewing both tea and coffee. Denise was laying down on his sofa, while Q and Bobby Small, Jr. were sitting.

"Fuck, sit down Kenny, you driving everyone crazy," Denise said. "And if you're not, you are certainly driving me crazy."

I stopped my pacing and looked at Denise. Her eyes were closed and though she knew my eyes were on her, she kept her eyes closed.

Q rose up and slid his chair to me. "Sit your ass down," he stated matter-of-factly. "Denise is right, chill the fuck out."

I wasn't in the mood for this. I sat down but my mind was all over the place. When Julia walked in, followed by Patrick and Beth, I didn't know what to think.

"What's going on?" I asked.

Denise sat up, walked over to Elliot's desk and sat down. "You wanted your old team, Kenny, you have them. Now what?" she asked.

"What you mean?" I responded, ten degrees past distressed.

"Everyone get some coffee or tea, and let's get this party started," Denise ordered.

I was lost. The only thing I could think of was I was in a bad dream and I couldn't wake up. Denise was sitting in Elliot's seat like she was the deputy director and he was serving coffee. *What the fuck?*

I was the last to get coffee, which was a joke to me. My idea of coffee was to have coffee with my cream and sugar, because I probably had more cream and sugar than the average coffee drinker could endure. My idea of coffee was disgusting to every true coffee drinker I knew.

"Okay," Elliot began. "We need to decide what time we are going to do this."

Something was wrong with me. Maybe my equilibrium was off. I wasn't understanding. *What time we are going to do this?* This was my niece Elliot was talking about. I had to pinch myself to make sure I wasn't in a lost episode of the *Twilight Zone.*

"Kenny, your call," Denise said.

I was exhausted both physically and mentally. I really didn't know what I was feeling. I put my face in my hands and I felt the tears. Then I heard myself sob and I repeatedly said shit. I was in another world and that world spelled breakdown — *nervous breakdown.*

I heard Elliot tell Julia and Q to stand down. I was lost. What was happening to me?

I felt a hand on my knee. "You know, I can remember one night Steve and I were lying in bed," I heard Denise say in a low voice. "Probably a week before he died. I told him I didn't know what I would do without him. He smiled like he always did and told me not to worry about it, KC would take care of me. I told him Kenny didn't like me."

She smiled and I felt myself calm down. She grabbed my hand and wrapped it in both of her hands.

"He told me that may be so but he loved the kids and 'Nessa had his heart, and he would always be there. He later told me that it didn't make a difference how you felt about me, that you would honor the fact that he loved me so. And I loved him, Kenny. This is your op. You tell us what we are going to do."

I was calm, but I felt like shit.

I was embarrassed.

I didn't want to move.

"Go wash your face, Petey, and let's get this show on the road," Elliot said.

Denise kissed me on the cheek and I walked to the bathroom with my head down. Julia grabbed me by the waist and I didn't know what to think. She came in the bathroom with me. Just her presence calmed me.

While I washed my face, my mind was traveling a mile a second. How could anyone follow me after that display? Damn, how could Julia want a man who was weeping like a baby?

At that point, Julia said, "I love you," as if she had read my mind. She grabbed a hand towel, dried my face, then pulled my head toward hers. We kissed. Man, did we kiss. I don't know how long we kissed, but each second that passed increased my confidence level.

Man, I had embarrassed my whole family, hadn't I? Now it was time to undo the damage and restore the family name. With Julia standing by and having faith and confidence in me, I knew I could conquer the world.

Nervous breakdown or anxiety attack — whatever it was, I made up my mind I would deal with the aftermath later.

I thought about what Elliot called me, "Petey." When we initially met years ago at a barbeque at Steve and Denise's place, that's what he called me. We talked sports and every time we saw each other, he would greet me the same way, "What's shaking, Petey?"

What's shaking was my renewed thirst for vengeful. I just hope I was still accepted by my peers.

When I walked back in the room, I could see the anticipation and support on everyone's face. With the exception of Bobby Small, Jr., I instantly knew my folks had my back.

"First, I apologize," I began. "Secondly, I understand, sir, if you don't want to follow my lead," I said to Colonel Small.

"I'm in, but you owe me a steak dinner, home cooked," Bobby stated.

"No shit, me too," Q added as everyone joined in.

I got us back on track. "Ok, what do I need to know?" I asked Elliot.

"We have three possible warehouse locations to choose from. They all are *Just Cause* locations. But we need to pick the right one. We are looking at Northwest D.C., Temple Hill and Silver Springs in Maryland. All three are busy areas, even for a Saturday. We have satellite coverage, but the same amount of personnel at each site. All calls are via cell phones. However, they do have wireless internet service."

We were looking at a computerized map on Elliot's big screen TV. Something wasn't jiving with me. The same amount of personnel. Too staged. Too programmed. Something was missing. I knew what it was.

"What time is the drop-off?" Elliot asked.

"The computerized voice said noon," I answered.

Denise and Elliot looked at each other. I played it off. I was concentrating.

"Check out the map," I said.

No one said anything. They didn't know what I knew or could see what I saw.

"What's going on, Kenny?" Julia asked.

"Escape route," I said matter-of-factly. "If you wanted to get out of town, which site would you choose?" I thought it was a valid question.

Elliot smiled. "All three locations would be a bitch to get to an interstate or highway. What makes you think they are at that location, Carson?"

"One, you can jump on Route 1 and within a couple of minutes you're on I-95. Two, if you had helicopter support, it would be much easier to maneuver a helicopter in that area."

"What damn area are we talking about?" Bobby asked.

"The same area that was used in '93," Denise said. "The same location my husband died. The scene of the crime — the Lorton warehouse district."

Nodding at Denise, I continued, "Three, I was there reflecting not too long ago. I noticed fresh tire tracks. I thought it was probably folks using it as a good spot to have a booty call. One thing I did see was red laser beams on the side of the road. It could be alarm detectors. Plus, when I got out of the car and used the phone; a car and a truck turned on the road and turned around when they saw me. I didn't think anything of it."

"Sounds good," Elliot said. "Lock and load, you ready to ride?"

"Yeah, I think we should send teams to the other three sites first to divert their attention. From all indications, I think the Boss would probably be monitoring the sites from his headquarters. What you think?"

"I think it's a good plan," Elliot stated. "We can have the teams rolling in the next five minutes. For your team, we have allocated four helicopters and five or six Suburbans will be headed your way within the next five minutes. Good to go?"

"What you think?" I asked Denise.

"Yeah, that sounds like Jay," Denise replied.

"Jay?" I asked. "Jay who?" My curiosity was up. I knew it wasn't who I was thinking it was.

"Jay Joiner," Julia responded. "Jay is the Boss, baby."

Chapter
70

EVERYBODY PLAYS THE FOOL. No exception to the rule. Yep, that's what the song says. How appropriate . . . how appropriate indeed. Jay Joiner killed Steve. I was in the helicopter with Julia, Bobby Small, Jr., ATF Special Agent Darrell Adams and Patrick. We had four helicopters with a total of 17 agents.

Darrell Adams was protecting ATF's interests. No problem. I had a lot of respect for Darrell and he knew my agenda. It wasn't a secret: get my niece back and kill Jay Joiner. That simple.

But I understood Darrell's mission. No way was he going to miss his crates of stolen weapons. He also had another 14 agents en route via the interstate. I didn't give a damn. I had death on my mind, either mine or Jay Joiner, aka, the Boss.

Q and Denise were in the lead helicopter. *Reconnaissance and sniper duty.*

Their first time around it was about recon. We were on a special channel. There was no chance for interception by *Just Cause.* They had three guards pulling roof duty and three pulling ground duty.

The original plan was for Denise and Q to take out the sentries. However, they didn't figure on the sentries on the rooftops. All was well as long as they didn't make another pass by.

Jay wasn't stupid, he had everything covered.

Denise changed the plan. She wanted us to land first. Julia and Bobby were assigned the job of taking out the ground sentries. Once accomplished, Denise and Q would do another pass by and take out the sentries on the rooftops.

Once we landed, Julia and Bobby were on the move. I had never seen Julia move that fast. *Damn,* was the only thing I could come up with. She and Bobby had disappeared within ten seconds of us landing.

We slowly moved out at a snail's pace. Within two minutes, we were cleared to move in.

We moved and moved fast. Julia and Bobby already had the gate open. I saw two bodies. One sentry was gutted with an additional wound through his heart. The other sentry's throat was slit.

My life is what it is. That was my thought as we prepared to enter the warehouse in the Lorton district — the same warehouse where my brother died. The location where his daughter was now being held hostage.

My life is what it is.

I could accept it or say the hell with it. But Janessa was going to have a life. There was never a doubt in my mind. Jay or I was dying today — not Janessa.

Jay Joiner was about being the best. His handle, the Boss, was about wielding power and being in control — control of any and every facet of his life and the lives of others. He pulled the strings for 23 plus years and dangled his minions like they were puppets.

But now, it was time to surprise the puppet-master.

Elliot did what Jay wanted him to do, what Jay expected. We had teams en route to the three locations he had given us. The element of surprise was all mine.

This was my play. I was the lead agent.

The old Lorton district consisted of at least 23 huge dilapidated warehouses. Our destination was Warehouse #8.

"Q, you got me?" I asked into the blue-tooth type earpiece.

"No, I have you, Kenny," Denise responded. "When the guys get in position in the back of the warehouse, just go in through the big front door. Trust me, though there are 20 –

25 people inside, they don't have a clue. Jay is convinced he has outsmarted us."

When I received word from Patrick that his team was in place in the back of the warehouse, I had two agents pull the huge aircraft-type hangar door open.

We walked in cool, calm and casual, completely unnoticed by everyone. The area was open with the exception of the numerous crates of all sizes near the back entrance of the warehouse. Everyone was attending to the various crates. Patrick was waiting to receive word from me before he came in.

The only person who saw us was Janessa, who was sitting in a chair in the middle of the warehouse floor, with sticks of dynamite and C4 strapped to her person. Her eyes got big but there was tape over her mouth. I noticed dried up tears on her face.

I made it a point not to call out, "FBI." I wanted it to be a surprise and it was. Shouting out FBI, DEA, police or anything else was overrated and an invitation to a shooting fest. The quiet approach was always the best approach.

Sitting behind a metal table pecking on a laptop computer was the focus of my new rage within. Jay Joiner, aka, the Boss. He looked up and we glared at each other, the Boss and I. He was shocked.

I could hear his mind ticking. "What the hell? They weren't supposed to come here."

Yeah, he was the smartest — the smartest nemesis I ever faced.

But it was a new day.

I signaled Patrick and his team to come in through the back door.

It was wild. Looking around the warehouse and thinking of my own team, the diversity was creepy. Of course, Jay had assembled hate mongers of several nationalities as well as agents and others from different nationalities. The *creepy* part was his team was just as diverse as or more so than my team.

"That's far enough, Special Agent Carson," Jay said as he got up from his seated position, behind a small Formica table with a laptop computer on it. In his right hand, he had a Glock 37. It had been so long since I had seen Jay stand on his own and completely upright, I forgot how big and tall he was.

"I guess we meet after all, son."

We were about twenty feet from each other. Janessa was between us. He took a couple of steps toward her and I raised my weapon.

"Not another step, Jay." He froze.

"Now, is that a friendly way to greet family, KC?"

"Sure it is, Uncle Asshole," Julia replied, who was standing to my left.

"Fuck them, Boss!" an excited Alfredo Williams appeared from behind Jay. He was trying to make his way to Janessa, before Jay grabbed him by the arm.

"Hold your horses, partner," Jay stated with a smile on his face. "Trust me, these people will kill you. It's not a time to be a hothead. You see that woman," he pointed toward Julia. "She will blow your ass to Kingdom Come." He paused. "And trust me, partner, that's the truth."

"Let him go, Jay," I countered. "He's a dead man anyway. Doesn't make a difference how you paint it, young Alfredo Joiner is dead. You can give yourselves up, but he is dying today, right here, right now."

Jay continued to smile. "Damn, maybe I did outdo myself. So you know Brotha Alfredo is really my son?"

Alfredo smiled and I almost shot him then. Time was on my side. I was sure as dumb as he was he still knew his father was his way out of there. I was equally as sure he saw the seriousness in my eyes.

"KC, we are walking out of here and you can have your niece. After all, she didn't believe I was her daddy anyway." He smiled and I could see the fear in his eyes.

"Why should I let you go?" I asked.

"Because we don't need anymore bloodshed. Because I am walking out of here come hook or crook. Because a true leader always have a backup plan. Take your pick."

"Jay, you are it," I stated. "This is the last of *Just Cause* or should I say, the *Cause,* as you like to call it. We have

Dooling, Bradley, Dave Ball and Carmine Ball, and the rest of your so-called leadership is dead, including Gerry Ho. Denise wanted me to tell you that. And all of your hate groups and other gangs are under lock and key." I was smiling now.

"By the way, Bradley was killed this morning when the exchange took place," I threw that in for GP, *general purpose.*

"You are eating this up, aren't you, youngblood?"

"Yes, I am," I answered the Boss.

Suddenly, we all heard the shots outside. No one moved. I knew what it was. Even if I didn't, Denise told me. Q had picked off three of Jay's men outside and Bobby Small, Jr. had killed another four.

I smiled. "I guess there goes your backup plan." I smiled some more.

I saw the desperation on the face of Alfredo. Behind him, trying to keep a low profile was Leonard. Even if they gave up, in my mind, I saw three people dying today.

"This little reunion is good but I need those weapons. Special Agent Darrell Adams, ATF, put down your weapons and put your hands up."

I almost laughed at Darrell. I heard Denise say, "Darrell, are you serious?" I actually think we all almost laughed.

We were at a standoff. I started thinking about the various Wyatt Earp movies I had seen. I never realized it, but I actually liked Wyatt Earp. Or maybe I was like a lot of guys who loved western movies. I loved James Garner and Burt Lancaster's old time portrayal of Earp, and Kevin Costner and Kurt Russell's updated versions.

The thing I liked best about the movies was the gunfight at the OK Corral. Good versus evil. The Earps versus the Clantons.

And now, the *FBI* versus *Just Cause.*

Chapter
71

I NOTICED THE SWEAT forming on Jay Joiner's forehead, when Alfredo pulled out his cell phone. I was thinking he wasn't much of a boss now. One thing was for sure, his son had no heart.

"The bomb attached to Janessa is controlled by remote control," Alfredo volunteered. "All I have to do is dial a number and we all blow up."

"Q, on two," I heard Denise say. Then she counted, 1 – 2. The shots rang out. The first shot broke Alfredo's cell phone. The second hit him in the center of the neck, silencing him and his vocal chords forever.

Jay saw that and lost it. I wasn't stupid, I knew both Jay and Alfredo had cell phones and something told me there was a third.

Jay was confident we had fallen for his plan. He didn't expect us. The element of surprise caught the master planner without a flak vest on.

When all hell broke loose, my full clip was emptied into the chest of Jay Joiner, the Boss. Denise and Q were responsible for Leonard.

Julia, Darrell and I had surrounded Janessa. The bullets were flying. I remember praying that we walk out of there alive. I saw people falling from both sides. Even if any of the bad guys wanted to turn themselves in, they couldn't for fear of being shot.

The military called it a firefight. Many others referred to it as an old-fashioned shootout. It was good versus bad. A close combat firefight. Bullets were flying and bodies were falling.

Through it all, I only thought about Janessa and her having a life. I hated my niece being caught up in the madness. And worst, being in the middle of a firefight with a bomb strapped to her person. I prayed to God this ordeal would not have a lasting affect on her.

When it was said and done, we had six men down. Initially, I wasn't sure of their status. We all had flak vests on. The final report recorded three of the six dead.

My mind thought about the thirteen dead in three minutes and forty-five seconds. Before I left the Bureau, the last thing Elliot said to me was exactly that, "Thirteen dead. Three minutes, forty-five seconds."

I didn't know if this was some kind of payback, but I hoped all of the agents, law enforcement officers and innocent lives lost would find some solace in Warehouse #8.

"Rest in peace," I voiced to myself.

Something told me Steve Carson heard me as I looked at mother and daughter hugging each other. Darrell Adams had defused the bomb attached to Janessa's torso. I had her look at me while Special Agent Adams handled his business. She didn't blink, she even smiled. Julia and Denise stood behind me. If Darrell made one wrong move, all of us would have been blown away. But we were family. If one died, we all died.

In the clean-up effort, I took one last look at the man called the Boss — Jay Joiner.

I once had respect and love for the man. It was easy to call him demented. Was he? I truly didn't think so. He was his ego. The people who gave him power were all white. He took that power and became bigger than the people who empowered him. Like a cartoon character whose head grew bigger and bigger, Jay's head did the same as his ego grew.

In some ways, I probably put him out of his misery.

Just Cause was no more. The Boss was dead — he was *Just Cause*. And as I looked at him, I resisted the urge to shoot him one more time to make sure he was dead. I didn't want him to come back alive like the bad guy in many horror movies.

We had five prisoners. But they were insignificant. They weren't Jay Joiner.

As our helicopter lifted off, I took one last look at Warehouse #8. In six months, the building would burn to the ground.

Chapter
72

WHAT CAN WE LEARN from history? How to defeat the past, deal with our demons, clean up our mistakes and much more. Elliot Lucas and the Bureau had learned a lot from the past. We were victorious and the monkey was off our backs.

When we returned to the Hoover, President Cabot was leaving the building. He congratulated us on a job well done. I was surprised to see Miguel Bishop in the building. It was about cleanup now.

Carol Ball was a free woman. However, Basil Dooling and his nephew, Tory, were behind bars. Dave and Carmine Ball had a lifetime to look back at their mistakes. The Secretary of State Ian Bradley was dead; a death contributed to *Just Cause.*

Several months later, they would find Dave Ball hanging from his cell door. His cellmate, Albert "Justice" Walton, reportedly slept through the incident.

Former Special Agent Jefferson "Jay" Joiner was branded as a former disgruntled agent, who was a traitor to his country. To my understanding, Carol Ball was the only person who attended his burial.

My head was spinning from the madness.

I didn't know how much President Cabot knew or wanted to know. I did know he had to approve certain acts. However, I also knew and understood that if he was ever asked certain questions, his denial in his mind would be genuine.

Just Cause was more than a formidable enemy or challenge. They were an organization that hit the government from the inside out and almost won. When I looked back on it, Jay Joiner really did wreak some havoc — he exposed our vulnerabilities, our weaknesses. One day, we might have to pay for those exposures.

Miguel was summoned to the Hoover by Elliot. Evidently, Elliot had tasked him with what I thought would be an impossible task — tracing and tracking down the monies of the members of *Just Cause.* All of the accounts were located at offshore banks. Many have said where there is a will, there is a way — except when it came to offshore accounts.

Miguel found a way. Over a hundred million dollars was transferred to a new offshore account. Elliot was going to use the money to pay *unknown* insurance claims to the survivors of agents, bank presidents and others who had died at the hands of *Just Cause* the past 23 years. They would be unknown because there were no such insurance policies. It was Elliot's way of saying, "Sorry for your losses; please accept this at the condolences of the FBI."

The remainder of the day was filled with accomplishing paperwork and damage control. Elliot and his staff, in coordination with the White House press secretary, handled the media attention. Elliot finally told all of us to get out of the building and go home. After all, it was a Saturday evening. People were departing the New Orleans area due to a possible Category Five hurricane. Katrina was its name. We didn't know the expected damage, but we might be tasked with some post-hurricane actions.

Sleep called my name. Actually, sleep called *our* names. Both Julia and I went home and knocked out. I think we slept for eleven or twelve hours straight when we finally got some sleep. I was completely spent. I felt like a lifelong burden had been removed from my shoulders.

I remembered standing over Jay. I just looked at the man who had killed my brother and betrayed both Steve's and my friendships. In one sense, I felt bad for the man. He had a brilliant mind. He had to — only a brilliant mind could create the chaos and carnage, and wreak the havoc that Jay had on three separate occasions. Something told me he had committed numerous crimes over the years. Crimes we probably didn't have a clue about and never would.

I also realized Jay was a sick and lonely man. That was the only way I could explain someone pretending to be handicapped for twelve years. When we checked his house, his home care provider, Nancy Batiste, was dead. Shot in the back of the head. His FBI-provided security team had been pulled off three days earlier. Elliot knew if he didn't pull the team, Jay would have killed them.

I didn't understand why he killed Nancy, but Julia was sure it was Alfredo. Angelo Alfredo Williams had a criminal record a mile long. From petty thefts to sexual and criminal assaults, he had accomplished his share of crimes. Interestingly, from interviewing one of the five remaining assailants of *Just Cause,* we learned Alfredo and Carmine Ball were the major players during the bank robberies in '93. Simply amazing. They had to be all of eighteen or nineteen at the time.

Julia and I woke up sometime in the middle of the night, or actually in the wee hours of the morning. We had decided to fix breakfast. When we walked in the kitchen, there were four medium sized boxes on the island counter in the middle of the kitchen. I read the note on the first box.

KC, here are the journals you have been pressing 'Nessa about.
Elliot

I looked at Julia and she was just as lost as I. She reminded me I was the one who wanted everyone and their ancestors to have a key to our place.

Additionally, there was an envelope on top of the box addressed to Elliot. I knew the handwriting. It was Steve's. I hesitated before I opened the letter. I stared at the letter and Julia stared at me. She stepped forward and kissed me. That gave me the confidence I needed.

E,

If you reading this, it means we lost the battle and probably the war. Elliot, you have always been like a brother to me. Your friendship has meant the world to me. I love you and Portia like family. And that's why I need to write you this letter.

You know how much I love Denise. We have had our ups and downs and you have always been there for both of us. Now what I am about to ask is huge, E. My brother, Kenny, and Denise are like cats and dogs. I know Kenny. He will always do what's best for the family. Alyse will always keep him in line. I know he will never disrespect Denise, but get to know him if you could E. He really is a good man.

And more importantly, talk to him about me. Let him know I was human with human flaws. Let him know Denise was not the only one who screwed up in our marriage. Yeah, he is a grown man, NFL star and you would think being over thirty, no longer looking up to his big brother, but he does. And I love him for it.

But he can be emotional and sensitive at times, actually too damn much. But let him know I love him and Alyse, and that he is more man than I ever was. Let him know he deserves to be happy, and have a family, a wife and kids. And tell him not to shotgun over Alyse and my baby girl, 'Nessa. Since our mother died, Kenny tends to be very overprotective when it comes to Alyse and 'Nessa. I know him and Alyse, and I wouldn't be surprised if she shoots him one day. Funny, but that's my family, E. You know that, all that I have shared with you.

E, you are a good man, always have been and the best damned friend I ever had. You took care of me, always been there for me. I know I am asking a lot, but I know you will come through. Take care of my Denise for me and continue to be an uncle to my kids.

Thanks for everything, E. I love both you and Portia. And keep Julia on the right track. Besides you, she is probably the best agent I have ever worked with. Keep her focused. Like I always joked with you, if I was ten years younger, she would be a Carson. She is a special girl. Dangerous girl, but outstanding people. Keep telling you, you have your hands full with that one. Remember what I told you; never put her and Denise on the same team. They would probably kill everyone.

I know E, I don't have any sense. But you just don't know how afraid I am. Too many forces are against us this time, my brother. You and I, our band of agents, we have always been able to rule the world. But not this time. Not this damn time.

No sense putting off the inevitable. Elliot, I hope you are around the next time Just Cause comes back. You have to be around, E. You are the smartest, most courageous person I have ever known. I know the planner, you do too. It's Jay. Yeah, that SOB. He is the reason I am dead.

I know this is strange, E. Me talking from the dead. But if I am dead, Jay Joiner killed me. And as much as you might want to kill him, Elliot, you can't. Jay is a small fish. Yes, he is the planner, the man carrying out the missions, but he is not the big fish. The only ones I can tell you for sure are Dooling, Adamis, Bradley, Raymond and Collingshed. And no, E, none of those guys is the big tuna.

In the end, E, I tried. I needed you on the case. We could have done this together. Now I know why Dooling and Adamis would not put you on the case. You know about my journals. I have shared with Denise that if anything ever happened to me, to please give you my journals.

I know I have put a lot on your mind, Elliot. I wish you luck and Godspeed. And thanks again for always being there and being my brother.

Love you,
Steve

P.S. It won't be easy with Kenny, but I think you guys will have a good relationship. Please, never tell him about Jay. Believe me, what you see on the football field really is him. Agent one day? As you suggested. No, I don't think so. You crazy as hell, Elliot, he is too much of a hothead.
Take care of my family!
Steve

I felt tears falling down my face. I didn't know what to say. I gave Julia the letter and she read it. We hugged. I don't know how long we stood in that very spot, just hugging each other.

She finally made breakfast. Sausage, eggs and toast. I sat at the kitchen table, because I was afraid of being alone. We ate and went back to sleep, because we were expecting the kids sometime during the day. We hoped later rather than sooner.

Before we fell off to sleep, Julia explained Elliot and Steve's relationship to me. They were the best of friends, as close as brothers. Enough said.

I also didn't know her and Steve were friends. Evidently, what Elliot was to me, Steve was to Julia. I always thought Elliot was the one who taught Julia how to be an agent. I was wrong. It was Steve and Denise.

Epilogue For The Future

PROBABLY AROUND NOON, I heard some noise in the house. I asked Julia and she said, yeah, go check it out. Of course, I went back to sleep too.

I didn't know if minutes or hours passed by before Devin and Lil' Steve came jumping on the bed. All I remember was Steve saying, "Mommy, Daddy, get up, we barbecuing today." And Devin jumped on my back, saying, "Uncle Kenny, get up, Uncle Clay said get your big butt up."

I looked at Julia and she had one eye open. "I love you," she lip-synched.

"I love you more," I lip-synched back. "I'm not taking a shower first, you go for it," I voiced aloud.

"Why don't y'all take a shower together," Lil Steve shouted.

"Yeah, take a shower 'gether," Devin repeated, jumping up and down on my back.

I finally sat up, grabbed Devin off my back and started to tickle him. I felt a pillow smack me upside the head. Then I heard Julia say, "Pillow fight." Before I knew it, Steve and Julia were smacking me with pillows. All four of us were rolling around on the bed trying to hit each other with pillows when Gloria popped her head in.

"Excuse me, ghetto black people!" Gloria tried to interrupt us. She raised her voice, "Black people!" she shouted. We all looked at her with that *what do you want* look on our faces.

"Get over yourselves, put some clothes on and come mingle with your guests."

"Girl, who said we were having a party?" Julia asked.

"Your uncle."

We all shut up. When I thought about it later, it was a funny sight to see. Julia told Gloria we would be there after we showered and put some clothes on. Gloria was laughing when she left. I knew she was laughing at the fact we jumped when she mentioned Elliot, without even saying his name.

A few minutes later, Julia and I were leaning on a counter in the kitchen, talking to people here and there as they passed through. We were two tired warriors. We didn't pretend. We could only shake our heads at the situation. We actually had twenty or thirty people in the house, and another twenty or so in the backyard mingling as Q was throwing meat on the grill.

It was funny. Julia and I had our spots and we were comfortable. We weren't trying to mingle with anyone in particular and no one was sweating us to do this or that. It felt nice that our house was their house. At one point, I was sure everyone who was at the house came in the kitchen and we talked for a minute or two, and in some cases, longer.

I remember Clay coming in with a sling on his arm and he hugged me with the other arm. Then he hugged Julia. We could tell he had been drinking, but he wasn't drunk, just emotional. He relayed how afraid he was. Then he told us how in love he was with Gloria, because she didn't give up on him and stayed by his side. He was proud of her. And we equally were proud of her. Gloria had proven over the years she could be the most selfish and self-absorbed person on the planet Earth. This was a big step for her; actually, for both of them.

Howard came by with kids in hand. He was the grandfather who loved his grandchildren, and in turn, they loved him. I was finally all right with my father. It only took forty something years.

Miguel thanked us for the opportunity. I asked him how much I owed him for the time and work. He told me Janessa had already paid him. It was over six figures. I didn't say anything. I would later learn the money came from the offshore account, courtesy of Deputy Director Elliot Lucas.

Later, the two people we had been missing came waltzing in the kitchen: Denise and Janessa. Denise hugged and gave me a peck on the cheek. Then Janessa unexpectedly fell in my arms and laid her head on my chest.

"I'm sorry. I know I should have listened to you," she said between sobs. "I know I'm hardheaded and don't listen. I know you were worried about me."

I kissed the top of her head and told her to stop crying, that everything was fine as long as she was okay and fine. And I was okay and fine. The first of Steve's three legacies was still walking and living. If it took my last breath, she was going to live.

It really was that simple.

The more I thought about it, it wasn't a breakdown or anxiety attack I had in Elliot's office. It was the fear of another Carson dying — the fear that I might be letting down another one of my family members.

That fear had subsided. We all lived to see another day.

Janessa was my niece, and she was going to have a life as well as her brothers and two cousins, Lil' Steve and Devin. They were the Carson legacies and Janessa was the first. I kissed her head again and held her tighter.

She was still hugging me with her head still on my chest when Elliot walked in. I didn't know what to say. He stuck his hand out and we shook.

"Thank you," I said.

"No, thank you," he returned.

"When did you get the journals?" I asked.

"I got them from 'Nessa a couple of years ago. Told her her Uncle Elliot needed them."

I slowly nodded my head in the affirmative. Elliot and I looked at each other. I didn't know what to say. He took a swallow of the beer he had gotten out of a cooler when he walked in the kitchen.

"I needed something to read at night and during my free time," he volunteered.

Miss Portia had pulled Julia and Denise out of the kitchen. I didn't think she could have pulled Janessa away if she wanted to.

"Why didn't you tell me?" I asked.

"This was bigger than you, me or Steve, KC. Steve knew that. He wanted me to have them, because he knew I would know what to do with them when the time came."

I kissed Janessa on the head again and she turned, hugged and kissed Elliot on the cheek. "I'll leave you men to talk," she said. She closed the kitchen door behind her.

I hugged Elliot. He returned the gesture. We sat at the kitchen table and he told me about my brother, his brother — Steve Carson.

Epilogue For The Past

True leadership is both lacking and underrated in a world that is in need of real leadership. The days of men standing up for something meaningful and everlasting are over. Geronimo was described as a fearless leader, Patton spoke his mind, MLK, Jr. died for righteousness and Rosa refused to give up her seat, thus the beginning of a nation changing. Where have our true leaders gone?

THE LOVE OF FAMILY can never be understated. Elliot was family before I even knew he was family. Julia was destined to be my wife just like I was destined to be an agent. My brother was my hero and so was Elliot.

He had eliminated the so-called leadership of *Just Cause.* The great thing was that he arranged for the blame to be placed on *Just Cause.* The deaths of Adamis, Raymond, Collingshed, Browning, Bradley and Hartsbright were his handiwork, credited to *Just Cause.* How cunning, how brilliant was that?

The party finally dispersed around ten. We all had to work the next day. Elliot told me that he had always planned on having a party after this case. It was twelve years in the making and we had a great time. He told me to keep the letter.

Julia and I made passionate love that night. I think we both had a longing to just hold each other. The kids were staying with Miss Portia. We had business the next day.

We picked Elliot up at five thirty, Monday morning, August 29, 2005. We had an unannounced appointment to meet a man.

His family was still enjoying their family vacation in the Hamptons. The door was open as if he were expecting us. Something deep within told me he was.

Elliot walked in the study of the big house. That day, he had his FBI jacket and hat on. It was not a leisure visit. It was strictly business.

That day, it ended.

I felt bad for Elliot. I knew he didn't need my pity. This was a bad thing for a good man. But something also told me he had been planning this day for years, just like he had been planning that after party.

The man he once admired and had called boss and Director for the past five years continued to play his putt-putt golf. The tall slender man didn't acknowledge the presence of his deputy director or two of his agents. But he knew we were there.

"How long have you known, Elliot?" John Tellis, Director of the FBI, asked the question.

"In the back of my mind, I probably have known for at least twelve years, since '93. But Steve Carson's journals gave me the definitive information I needed. So to answer your question, I have known two years and just couldn't prove it."

Tellis still played his putt-putt. I wanted to snatch that putter out of his hands and wrap it around his scrawny ass neck. Elliot was Elliot — the same cool cucumber he always was. Julia was on edge. I could feel her tension.

"Did you really need your sidekick and her husband?" Tellis asked facetiously. I didn't like his tone. Even without looking at us, Elliot threw his hand up for us to shut up.

"Yeah, I had to bring them," Elliot said as he took a step forward. "You didn't like his brother and you don't like him. But Carson has made your worthless ass shine over the past five years. Now, he is here to put the shackles on the man responsible for his brother's death."

I saw the fear in Tellis's face. He had turned a shade of red. He was nervous, fidgety. He had stopped putting. All of our jackets were open.

John A. Wooden

The man looked bad. His five o'clock shadow was at least three days old or older. His clothes were unkempt. He looked like what he was — a broken man.

"Steve connected Jay Joiner to the case," Elliot stated. His tone had changed. I knew he was upset. Suddenly, I was more worried about him. "If Jay was involved, so were you, you son-of-a-bitch. Unbeknownst to you, I have always known Jay did your dirty work for you. He was the field boy, trying to manipulate himself into the big house by using and destroying his own kind."

Tellis walked over to his bar area and poured himself a small glass of bourbon. He gulped the eight-ounce glass in a matter of seconds before pouring another.

"Who else knows?" he asked.

"President Cabot, members of his Cabinet, the Attorney General and Lieutenant Colonel Bobby Small, Jr."

"Was that his mission, to spy on me?"

"Yep, his one and only mission. To keep my enemy close."

Damn, I was flabbergasted. Colonel Small. The man was too much. I would later learn that he had been doing surveillance on Tellis for two years, including taps on his phones.

"Elliot, this was never about you. I have always liked you, always been fond of you."

"John, fuck yourself!" Elliot shot back. "People are fond of dogs. I'm not a fucking dog! I know this is not about *me*. This is about *you*. You are a sick and disturbed man. You are what the ghost of J. Edgar Hoover wanted you to be — that asshole who kept the Hoover legacy alive and well. Cabot spooked you when he told you he wanted me to take over as director of the Bureau. You didn't want a Black man holding J. Edgar's position, sitting in his seat. Imagine that, a Black man running the Federal Bureau of Investigation. But that day has come, John. The day you, Clyde Tolson and J. Edgar Hoover thought would never be, is here. The day a Black man assumes the position of Director of the FBI."

"I never thought you would be the one to gloat, Elliot," Tellis retorted as he continued to drink. The bottle that was full was nearly empty. They say liquid courage can make a man do anything. It strengthens the weak, adds gumption to the meek and creates a spine for the spineless. In some cases, it allows us to deal with our greatest fear.

"No, John, I am not gloating, just being realistic."

Hell, I didn't know this Elliot Lucas. But after reading Steve's letter to him, I knew how close he and Steve were.

Elliot walked within a foot of the perp, John Tellis, Director of the FBI. Inside, I wanted to rip the man's guts out. I could only imagine what Elliot wanted to do. But sometimes it's about the fear. I could tell Elliot wanted Tellis to know the fear . . . up close and personal.

"I want you to know this day and every day you are behind bars that a Black man sits in that proverbial chair of goodness and power. I want you to know a Black man put your sorry ass behind bars. And lastly, John, I want you to know that those agents in the Bureau now, who are white, are not following me because I am a man of color, but because I have demonstrated to each and every one of them that I can do the job."

"I guess I should be proud, Elliot," Tellis said with a smug look on his face. "After all, you were my protégé."

"No, John, I was never your protégé," Elliot had calmed down and spoke with the confidence of the Elliot Lucas we knew and loved. "You never taught me a damn thing. I learned from the school of hard knocks. I learned from the school of no opportunities, not missed opportunities. I knew I had to be a hundred times better than you or anyone else to get where I am today. So no, John, when you are in that cell, don't think you had anything to do with me sitting in that position. Because one thing I will always know is this, you kept me close because you have always looked at me as being your enemy."

John Tellis was speechless. He had always been a man of poise and control. Many looked at him as being the man needed in a state of crisis. That day, his crisis was upon him.

"So what now, Elliot? You plan on marching me out of here in handcuffs?"

"That's up to you, John. I don't owe you shit, but I am willing to just walk out the door with you in front. I will be behind you."

John Tellis smiled, "Is that a symbol or something?"

"No, not at all. It's a sign of good policemanship. You are the suspect, I am the crime fighter. Why would I risk you being behind me and doing something stupid?"

"May I use the bathroom before we walk out?" The two men looked at each other. It was a look of respect. They had known each other for almost four decades and for the first time, Elliot Lucas could say he had respect for John Tellis. They studied each other and Director John Tellis finally knew he underestimated his deputy director.

"Be my guest," was the reply from Elliot.

Elliot walked to the door of the study and grabbed the handle. We looked at each other. Maybe no words were needed. Mere seconds later, a shot was heard throughout the Maryland countryside. Elliot opened the study door and slammed it closed.

A moment later, John Tellis came out of the bathroom. The shock on his face was priceless. He had a gun in his hand. A shot rang out. I looked. Only Elliot had a weapon out.

Tellis dropped hard from the chest wound.

"How did you know?" I asked.

"The man was a coward, KC. He was always a coward. I did his legal bidding. Jay Joiner did his illegal bidding. The only move of a coward is to run."

"What about the aftermath?" Julia asked.

"What aftermath, sweetie? The byline has already been written. Gloria Kingsbury wrote it last night. It will hit the afternoon edition. *FBI Director Killed — Last Desperate Act of Vigilante Group.*"

We were speechless.

"Besides, neither the White House nor the Bureau could afford this type of scandal. He had to die. I prefer to make him a martyr than take down the Cabinet or the FBI. We all deserve better."

I looked at Julia and I loved the look on her face. I smiled and she just shook her head. Unfortunately for Tellis, he wouldn't even be one day news. The devastation of Hurricane Katrina and its sad aftermath would steal the headlines and make him back page news. How fitting, I would think later.

Elliot had already walked out the door of the study and was near the front door. We caught our leader. The next Director of the Federal Bureau of Investigation.

He was looking skyward. Something told me Steve, Bonner McGill, Scott Rooker and every other agent and bank president who died at the hands of *Just Cause* were approvingly smiling down at the *big man*.

As we descended the stairs of the huge house, several Bureau Suburbans were pulling up; led by Patrick Conroy.

Someone once told me the true leader is the one the bullet is intended for and the one you would take a bullet for. Unfortunately, there are not many of those around anymore.

Elliot was our leader.

He took a deep breath and something told me he was taking in the fresh taste of *closure*.

He put his sunglasses on as agents filed past us without a word spoken.

Julia put her sunglasses on and I followed suit.

As we walked toward the car, I imagined we were walking in slow motion as the sun rose.

The End

John A. Wooden is a retired Major from the U.S. Air Force, a feature writer/columnist for *The Perspective* magazine in Albuquerque, New Mexico, and a freelance editor and ghostwriter whose clients have appeared on the Essence Bestseller's List. His first novel, *A Collection of Thoughts,* was an expression of his thoughts on life and love. His second novel, *A Moment of Justice, A Lifetime of Vengeance,* was a murder/suspense thriller that spanned thirty years and brought his unique writing style to the forefront of the literary industry. It was also the novel that made many stand and take notice of his storytelling skills. He is the proud father of a young adult son and a beautiful teenage daughter.

Q & A with Author John A. Wooden on the significance of an African-American FBI Deputy Director

Q: Why was it important to select an African-American as Deputy Director of the FBI?
JW: I think too often in fiction, we automatically write-in white characters in powerful positions. It's a stretch of the imagination or huge paradigm change if the character is another nationality. But in the world we live in, Alexis Herman, Ron Brown, Colin Powell and Condoleezza Rice have broken through the color barrier and proverbial glass ceiling and held prestigious Cabinet positions. I think its time, we as authors, do the same thing and show people of color in powerful positions.

Q: I understand, but even today, an African-American director or deputy director really is a stretch of the imagination, don't you think?
JW: I was asked this question by several book clubs after my last book, *A Moment of Justice,* and my answer then, as it remains, is the same, no. I have often said true change will occur when we have a Black FBI Director more so than when a Black President is elected, but I'm sure I'm being naïve when I say that. I hope one day we will see a Black man as Director of the FBI and CIA. And when it happens, I'm sure there will be individuals who are more than qualified to be in those positions.

Q: I heard the character, Elliot Lucas, was actually named after a former mentor who recently died. What made you name the character after him?
JW: I wanted to write a character who was calm and collected, had an even tone and temperament and didn't know the meaning of panic when the world was falling apart around him. I could have made up a name, but the person I patterned the character after, the real Elliot Lucas, was all of

those things. He was a retired Chief Master Sergeant in the Air Force. I know many people think its strange that an enlisted man would be a mentor for an officer, but Elliot believed in brotherhood and the *each one, teach one* concept. He believed in those around him being the best and if he could lend a helping hand to achieve that goal, he would. I thought it would be a great gesture and a sign of my admiration for him.

Q: How did he feel about you naming a character after him?
JW: When I asked him, he did the Elliot thing (smiling). He said I didn't have to, but he appreciated the gesture. But the more we talked about it; I could tell he liked the idea.

Q: Do you plan to continue with the character or will fiction imitate life?
JW: Presently, my game plan is to continue with the character, but I will respect the wishes of Elliot's family. I love writing the character, love what he brings to my stories and readers equally love the character, so hopefully he will be a mainstay, for a little while anyway.

Q: That sounds as if you plan on killing off Deputy Director Elliot Lucas?
JW: Well, that day may come (smiling). As an author, I will never say any character is completely protected, including my main character, Kenny Carson. I just hope all my characters and novels continue to resonate with readers.

Printed in the United States
107759LV00003B/91-348/P